PRAISE FOR

The Last Nude

"[An] amazing book . . . A wholly original and engrossing story, set in a fascinating time and place . . . Scenes that might fall flat or offend, written by a lesser talent, singe the page, and the hand that holds it. . . . Writing this novel was an act of courage and a display of exceptional talent."
—*The Boston Globe*

"A compulsively readable novel."
—*The Washington Post*

"The plot heats and heats until it boils over with dramatic intrigue, finely woven twists, and the kind of revelations that keep a reader up too late at night, greedily turning pages . . . reminiscent of Sarah Waters's historical novels . . . *The Last Nude* breaks important ground for literature, and does so with exuberance, skill, and grace."
—*San Francisco Chronicle*

"A taut, elegant novel . . . [Avery's] prose sings." —*MORE* magazine

"The left bank in the twenties, famous artists, lots of (bi)sexuality, and betrayal—what's not to love about Ellis Avery's romantic novel, *The Last Nude?*"
—Oprah.com

"Seductive and compelling, the novel is painted with as much drama and precision as one of Lempicka's canvases." —*The Daily Beast*

"[A] sumptuous second novel." —*Lambda Literary*

"Ripe and real and vital . . . a gorgeous Parisian love story."

—*SF Weekly*

"A fascinating story . . . *The Last Nude* left me hungry for more, eager to explore further the art of both Tamara de Lempicka and Ellis Avery." —*The Washington Independent Review of Books*

"A remarkable portrait of 1920s Paris and one thrilling love story . . . engrossing." —*Matchbook* magazine

"Avery is an economic, unfussy prose stylist whose rendering of 1927 Paris makes for a fun and transporting travelogue. The author's effusive enthusiasm for era and place is palpable. . . . Avery astutely captures a heady piece of history with an appropriately wide-eyed excitement." —*Time Out New York*

"Playing throughout her story with the contrast between beautiful and ugly, good and venal, amusing and pitiful, Avery seduces just as effectively as her beguiling subjects. We are, as they say, putty in her hands." —*B&N Review*

"A book so human it practically sweats with longing . . . The story is a compelling and vivid romance, but even more exhilarating is Avery's prose. . . . [*The Last Nude*] makes the heart ache with joy and the fingers grope for a paintbrush." —*NewCity Lit*

"Heartbreak transcends the page in a beautiful novel of love and regret between painter and muse." —*Shelf Awareness*

"Avery weaves historical fact with electrically charged narrative. . . . Filled with fabulous literary anecdotes and characters that seem to leap off the page, *The Last Nude* is a novel perfect for lovers of the 1920s, of Paris, or simply of love stories." —*BookPage*

"A riveting lesbian love story of heart-stopping passion, rapture, and stunning duplicity . . . Avery's breathtaking shimmer of first love and its aftermath will turn heads." —*Booklist* (starred review)

"Avery does a lot for us here, creating two stunning characters—the earthy, heartfelt Rafaela and the conniving de Lempicka—then shows us both the heat of their relationship and the very act of creating art. In the bargain, we get Paris itself, particularly demimonde and artistic, boiling over with possibility. Absorbing, affecting . . . highly recommended." —*Library Journal* (starred review)

"The strength of Avery's novel lies in her depiction of a driven and accomplished artist and an impressionable waif who finds that her beauty no longer belongs to her." —*Publishers Weekly*

"A dark, sexy romp." —*Kirkus Reviews*

"As erotic and powerful as the paintings that inspired it, Avery's artist-muse love story is moreover a tale of money, class, and betrayal." —Emma Donoghue, author of *Room*

"*The Last Nude* is a remarkable novel: at once a seductive evocation of Lost Generation Paris, a faithful literary rendering of Tamara de Lempicka's idiosyncratic and groundbreaking art, and a vibrant, intelligent, affecting story in its own right. It's also smoking hot." —Emily Barton, author of *Brookland*

The
Last Nude

ELLIS AVERY

RIVERHEAD BOOKS

New York

RIVERHEAD BOOKS
Published by the Penguin Group
Penguin Group (USA) Inc.
375 Hudson Street, New York, New York 10014, USA

Penguin Group (Canada), 90 Eglinton Avenue East, Suite 700, Toronto, Ontario M4P 2Y3, Canada
(a division of Pearson Penguin Canada Inc.) • Penguin Books Ltd., 80 Strand, London WC2R 0RL,
England • Penguin Group Ireland, 25 St. Stephen's Green, Dublin 2, Ireland (a division of Penguin
Books Ltd.) • Penguin Group (Australia), 250 Camberwell Road, Camberwell, Victoria 3124, Australia
(a division of Pearson Australia Group Pty. Ltd.) • Penguin Books India Pvt. Ltd., 11 Community
Centre, Panchsheel Park, New Delhi—110 017, India • Penguin Group (NZ), 67 Apollo Drive,
Rosedale, Auckland 0632, New Zealand (a division of Pearson New Zealand Ltd.) • Penguin Books
(South Africa) (Pty.) Ltd., 24 Sturdee Avenue, Rosebank, Johannesburg 2196, South Africa

Penguin Books Ltd., Registered Offices: 80 Strand, London WC2R 0RL, England

This is a work of fiction. Names, characters, places, and incidents either are the product of the author's
imagination or are used fictitiously, and any resemblance to actual persons, living or dead, business
establishments, events, or locales is entirely coincidental. The publisher does not have any control over
and does not assume any responsibility for author or third-party websites or their content.

Copyright © 2012 by Ellis Avery
Cover design by Alex Merto
Cover art © 2011 TAH, Licensed by Museum Masters International NYC
Book design by Michelle McMillian

First Riverhead hardcover edition: January 2012
First Riverhead trade paperback edition: January 2013
Riverhead trade paperback ISBN: 978-1-59448-647-0

The Library of Congress has catalogued the Riverhead hardcover edition as follows:

Avery, Ellis.
The last nude / Ellis Avery.
p.   cm.
ISBN 978-1-59448-813-9
1. Lempicka, Tamara de, 1898–1980—Fiction.   2. Women painters—Fiction.   3. Young
women—Fiction.   4. Americans—France—Paris—Fiction.   5. Artists' models—Fiction.
6. Paris (France)—Fiction.   I. Title.
PS3601.V466L37   2012   2011027708
813'.6—dc22

PRINTED IN THE UNITED STATES OF AMERICA

10   9   8   7   6   5   4   3   2   1

For Katrin Burlin

and Elaine Solari Kobbe

in memory

and for Sharon, with love

Part One

1

I ONLY MET TAMARA DE LEMPICKA because I needed a hundred francs. This was sixteen years ago. I had just learned that if I had a black dress with a white collar, I could take over my flatmate's department store job. In 1927, you could get a bed or a bicycle for three hundred francs; one hundred was a fair price to pay for a ready-made dress, but I didn't have it.

I would try my friend Maggey first: I had given her money once when she needed to see a doctor. After my interview at the department store, I looked for her in the Bois de Boulogne.

Maggey went by the name of her place of employment, a magnolia tree on the southernmost lip of the bigger lake, close to the road. I could see a man turn as I walked by, and as I approached the magnolia tree (where was Maggey?) I could see another, a man in a *fiacre*, pointing me out to his driver.

For my part, I couldn't help noticing the jewel-green motorcar parked on the grass up ahead, out of which emerged a woman with a dog. They formed a triangle at the edge of the trees: greyhound, green Bugatti, slim stylish woman. Her bobbed hair gleamed pale beneath an exquisitely useless aviator's hood done in putty-colored kid. Her dog's whole body strained toward the trees, yet he stood as still as a hound in a medieval tapestry, quivering patiently until the woman unclipped his leash. He looked up at her, waiting. *"Vas-y!"* she cried, and the dog vanished into the green, a long-bodied blur.

I reached the neck of land between the two lakes, and saw neither Maggey nor the overdressed boyfriend she sometimes brought along. I would walk as far as the Chinese pavilion on the island, I decided, and if I didn't see Maggey when I came back, I'd give up and ask my flatmate, Gin, for the money. Unfortunately, I couldn't ask for her uniform: Gin had the boyish, birdlike looks that were in vogue then, while next to her I felt heavily, irredeemably, New York Italian. But if she could give me both of her uniforms, I thought, maybe I could use fabric from one to work gores into the other. That would take time, though, and I needed the dress first thing the next morning. The sunlight broke the lake into a thousand hard-edged mirrors, but the pines were cool overhead, their needles fragrant on the ground. One of the men on the path said something to me and I looked away. But then I heard footsteps behind me, and a woman's voice. "Where did you get your dress, Mademoiselle?"

I had chosen my lucky blue dress for the interview at Belle Jardinière precisely because it often drew comment. I looked back: it was the woman with the green car. She didn't speak French like a French person, but she spoke it better than I did. "I made it," I said, struck shy by her beauty and her obvious wealth.

In her twenties, the woman stood as tautly slender as her greyhound, yet her Eastern European features suggested a fleshy, languid ease. *"Comme c'est joli,"* she said.

I pointed at the Bugatti. "I was just admiring—" I said, or hoped I said.

"It's not mine—should I speak Italian to you? English?"

"English, I guess," I said in English, embarrassed. But I switched back to French, explaining, "I try to practice—"

"—but I am thinking I might buy myself a car like this one," she said. Her English was like sandpaper, Slavic and pained. *That's* why her French sounded strange, I thought. Was she Russian? "Would you like to help me try it out?"

I laughed uncomfortably, and looked over at Maggey's tree. No Maggey, so I lingered with the woman as she called her dog. "Seffa!"

"Seffa?" I had to repeat the woman's explanation out loud to understand it. "Zee Vest Vind? Oh!" I said, catching on.

More gale than zephyr, Seffa suddenly burst out of the trees, carrying a bloodied rabbit. He tossed his prey to the ground and rolled around on the torn body, legs in the air. "No, Seffa! That's enough," the woman said in French, and the dog stood, trembling. He was slow to let her open his jaws and pry something out. When she leashed him, he stood close by her side near the car, but looked back, openmouthed.

The top of the car was down. The woman reached inside for a copy of *Le Temps* and opened a sheet of newsprint across her dog's back. She wiped the blood off him, and he whined when the corners of the paper nipped at his legs. "In," she said, and in two leaps the greyhound was helming the backseat, eyes and nose trained on his relinquished prize. "See?" she said to me. "Now we can go any-where you like."

"You're kidding," I said, laughing again.

The woman laughed, too, but her gloved hands wound together. Her red mouth moved before she spoke. She seemed afraid she might offend me. She looked down at my sad old shoes, and sud-denly I knew we were thinking the same thing: she had money and I needed it. It was the Bois de Boulogne, after all. What was *she* doing here? "I ask because you are beautiful," she said, "and I am a painter. I paint nudes. Please, may I give you my card? May I paint you sometime?"

Was that all, then? I looked at her carefully. Whatever she had in mind, I figured, I could get out of it if I needed to.

The woman was named Tamara, she said. Her studio was in the Seventh, a quick ride. Her car shone bottle-green, a praying man-tis, a cunning toy. As I stared at it, a man in a fedora addressed me in flat Chicago English: "Well, can I paint you too?"

I glanced over at him: a nattily dressed midwestern boy, stand-ing too close, but smiling so hopefully I felt a spike of pity for him. I relished it. "Sorry, Charlie," I singsonged, and then someone called out to him in French.

I watched the American and his friend spar in greeting like box-ers, glancing over at me from time to time. It felt good to harden my face against them the way Tamara did, to turn away. And toward a car that wasn't a taxicab, at that. I looked up at her. "Would you think about it?" she said.

"For a hundred francs, I would do it," I said. "I would do it right now."

"A hundred francs for five hours, yes?"

I could have Gin's job and owe her nothing. I looked back again toward Maggey's tree: still no Maggey. "Let's go," I said.

It was a warm day, but between the cool Bois and the open car, my summer dress was what seemed impractical, not Tamara's thin cape and aviator's hood, not even her long driving gloves. I felt a little breathless in my gray leather seat: I'd never gone so fast before. At one stoplight, Tamara asked my name and wrote herself a note. "Rafaela," she repeated, drawing out the middle two syllables. She had a stainless-steel mechanical pencil and a creamy little notebook, exquisitely plain. I wanted both. At another stoplight, she reapplied her lipstick. I had never seen a mouth so red. Her bloodied gloves were the pale yellow of her hair, her cape and hood the gray of her heavy-lidded eyes.

The trees flashed by. As my skin puckered into gooseflesh, I was glad for the heat that seeped into my thighs, glad again when we burst into an open field and, briefly, heat poured into me through the windscreen. I leaned back for a moment, basking in the hot light, the speeding car, Tamara's beauty: this was why I had come to Paris, I thought. Back home, a year ago, one glimpse of a Chanel dress had made me crave glamour, and now I had found it. Tamara's eyes flicked toward me, the color of chrome. It was too loud to hear what she said, but I smiled in reply. She reached over and touched me under the chin with a gloved finger, tipping my face toward her. Her eyes moved from my face to the road and back. She gave me a last, approving look and took the wheel in both hands again. I had seen that look before, on Hervé's face. On Guillaume's, too. I would ask for the money first thing.

We burst out of the green silent bubble of the Bois into a hot bright day crowded with scrambling taxis and squawking claxons. People flooded the little streets. Pushcarts crammed with vegetables, flowers, and books inched through the crowds. When we stalled behind an orange-and-brown horse-drawn sewage truck, Tamara grimaced at the smell, then pitched her car into a pedestrian square and passed the horses, frightening two nuns up onto the plinth of a statue. Tamara looked back at them and laughed, and I nervously followed her lead. We sped along the river and crossed the Pont de la Concorde. The Seine glowed like a sheet of lead foil.

Tamara parked in front of an apartment house in the aristocratic Seventh. I followed her—led by Seffa, clawed feet clacking—up two flights of stairs to an apartment much grander than any I'd ever lived in. "My daughter's room," she said, pointing to a door off to the side. I caught a glimpse of a kitchen, too, before we reached the apartment proper: three wide handsome rooms, each one leading to the next through French doors, all hung in the same gray velvet as the low couch where Tamara seated me. Both sets of French doors stood open: from the middle room I could see both the dining table at one end of the apartment and the starkly elegant bed by the far wall of the other.

On a low marble table before me sat a glass jar containing the remains of what might have once been a hair ribbon, burned to a stiff charcoal curl. Beside the jar sat a bottle of mineral water and a glass, a bunch of grapes, and the skull of a small animal. When the dog sighted the skull, Tamara moved it to a sideboard behind us and poured me a glass of water. "We can eat this still life. It was no good," she said, glancing down by way of explanation at the one hint of disorder in her cool, bright flat: a torn sketchbook page on the floor.

As I nibbled at a proffered grape, Tamara moved quickly through the three rooms, wiping down her dog and gloves with a wet cloth, hanging her cape and hood, shaking out her bobbed blond hair. Something about Tamara's apartment made me think of the street where I lived, which was home to a series of art dealers, but it wasn't the paintings on the walls: the art dealers, as if trying to outdo each other in drabness, hid away their wares like gold bricks. It was the smell, a resinous vapor that spindled the room. "What's that?" I asked, sniffing.

"*Huile de lin,*" she said, gesturing toward a table full of brushes and glass jars. "Is that *linen-seed oil* in English? And *térébenthine.* I do not know the word."

I nodded. "The grapes are delicious," I said. Even mixed with the sharp oil smell, I liked them: tart skin and sweet pulp, but full of seeds.

"Once, when I was very poor, I brought home some pastries to draw. I set them on the table here, and then I am sitting down with my tablet, here, and I look and I look, and all the time my stomach is saying, 'Eat them, eat them.'"

"You ate them?"

Tamara pulled off her driving gloves while she spoke, revealing long wrists, long fingers, red-painted nails, and a wealth of rings, one with a square topaz as big as a walnut. It flashed as she nodded, repeating my words, Slavic and vehement. "I ate them."

"Are you very poor now?" I asked, pretending to joke as Tamara vanished behind her bedroom doors. "Should I worry about the hundred francs?"

"No, no, no, no, no, no, no. No!" Tamara called from the next room, as she exchanged her mauve crepe afternoon frock for a black cotton housedress and a white chef's apron. Reëmerging, Tamara looked at me. "You understand the job? You do not move. I will paint you for forty-five minutes. Then you will rest for fifteen. Then forty-five again, and so on for five hours. It is noon now. We will stop at five." Belle Jardinière would close at six. I needed to show up in uniform at nine the next morning, before the store opened. I nodded.

"The WC is down the hall, or you may go behind the screen," she said, pointing at the dining room. "You change there."

I knew I had agreed to model, but here it was: I would have to take off my clothes. "How many people come in and out of this apartment?" I asked warily.

"No one all day," Tamara said, spreading both hands in a gesture of fiat. "And then at five, the housekeeper will come by and make dinner for my mother and daughter."

"Your mother lives here too?"

"Oh, no. We are just myself and Kizette. My mother lives close by, and she looks after Kizette when I go out at night."

"And your husband?" I asked, before I could stop myself.

"Is in Warsaw," she replied curtly. And then, as if to forestall further questions, she crossed the room again. "This is for you," she said, unlocking a drawer. She drew a banknote from a gray satin envelope-style purse and set it on the table by the grapes. One hundred francs: a black dress with a white collar.

"Thank you," I said. I was relieved to see she was serious about paying me, but even so, I took a long drink of water. I wanted to make it last, the moment she owed me, before I picked up the money

and owed her. I proudly set down my glass. "I'll take it when I go,"
I said.

Behind the screen in the dining room, I discovered a bathtub,
a chamber pot, and a hook on the wall with a single empty hanger.
I guess that's for you, I thought, addressing my lucky blue dress.
Here we go.

Just one look at a dress had been enough to lure me to Paris. The
summer before I met Tamara, I was living in the Bronx with my
stepfather's mother, my Nonna Gioia. The farthest she let me out of
her flat on Grand Concourse Boulevard—a cell of furniture polish,
porcelain figurines, and Italian prayer cards—was onto her tiny
balcony, to water the plants. I didn't miss looking after my brothers, four boys between the ages of nine and three, but I was so
bored without them, I watered those plants twice a day. Nonna
Gioia disapproved of her next-door neighbor, a pretty, young
widow named Theresa, but I liked peeking into Theresa's apartment from the balcony. She went out often. From five on, Theresa
sat near the window with her hat on the table beside her, until a
black motorcar pulled up outside. Then she pulled her cloche so
low it covered her eyes, tripped outside in her long light coat, and
got into the back of the car without talking to the driver. Sometimes she didn't come home until morning.

Every afternoon, Theresa went out to the balcony to drink a cup
of coffee and dry her shining bobbed hair. One day, after sweating
at the stove for Nonna Gioia all morning, I stepped out onto the
balcony, panting, to find myself face-to-face with my neighbor,

dressed radiantly in rose, black hair wet from the bath. "Oh!" she said. "I didn't know Mrs. Russo lived with anyone."

"She's my grandmother. My stepfather's mama. I'm just here for the summer." I looked behind me, into the apartment: Nonna Gioia was at church and could come back any moment.

"You in trouble?"

"Sorry?" Did I look as unhappy as I felt?

"You in trouble?" she repeated.

"Well, my parents are sending me back to Italy to get married," I said.

"Oh, after the baby comes," she said. "That's convenient for everybody, huh?"

I stared at her. What baby?

She reached over the railing and touched my shoulder. "You'll have another one someday," she consoled.

"I—"

"And meanwhile"—she shrugged, giving me a smile like a secret handshake—"you only lose your reputation once, right?"

"You think I'm pregnant," I protested awkwardly. "But I'm not."

Theresa's smile, startling in its sudden warmth, vanished. "Oh," she said. "Sorry, sweetheart. A girl goes away to live with her grandmother for a few months, and . . ." She gestured in a way that made me self-conscious about my all-too-female body. ". . . Sorry."

"I see," I said. "I understand. Don't worry."

"And I never see you outside," she added in her defense.

"It's really all right," I assured her. "She keeps me pretty busy in here."

"Well, come outside sometime. The nice weather won't last."

"I like your dress."

"You do?"

I nodded. Theresa was wearing a solid pink drop-waist sheath with an extra pleat in front, knit out of light wool that clung without bulging and made her long legs look all the stemmier. Four ribs knitted into the fabric gave the dress the sleek, metallic look of a motorcar, while a row of soft loops at the neckline doubled as buttonholes where the vee of the dress closed, showcasing a ridge of pink buttons that plunged almost all the way to Theresa's navel. I stared at the wink in the fabric: I had never seen a girl's navel through her clothes before. I had never seen a dress so simple, yet so stylish, so seductive, yet so classy.

"It's from Paris, sweetheart," she said, both relieved that the awkward moment had passed and genuinely proud of her dress. "Coco Chanel."

Theresa and I did not speak again after that fumbling exchange. More than once I've thought about that smile she gave me, a smile quickly offered and as quickly retracted, a smile that intimated we were two of a kind, that we two alone had somehow bested all the others. When I first met my flatmate in the barroom of the Vaudeville restaurant in December of '26—the men we were seeing then made us climb up on chairs with them and sing "La Marseillaise"—Gin's slender, nervy poise had made me think of Theresa in her little ribbed dress. Since then, I'd seen Gin go off in a taxi just as effortlessly as Theresa had. I'd seen her reappear a day later, just as coolly buoyant. Until Gin had met her current banker, Daniel, she and I had often exchanged Theresa's conspiratorial smile.

࿆

My lucky dress, inspired by Theresa's Chanel confection, was cut from a sky-blue blend of raw silk and linen that caught the light like sequins when I went outside. It fit like a coat of paint. If I wanted a change from baguette and cheese at home, I could wear that dress to a café and, every time, someone—though rarely anyone I liked—would take me to a restaurant. As I stepped out of that dress behind the screen in Tamara's apartment, the painter's high heels crossed the room toward me. She passed me a handful of fabric. "Wear this," she said.

The dress Tamara handed me was a far cry from mine: a dull brown cotton sack-like affair with wide straps for sleeves. Though the garment looked finished enough on the outside, I was surprised when I pulled it over my head to discover raw fabric against my skin. I felt a little superior as I smoothed down the selvage that lumped under the bodice: I knew how to finish a *seam*. Had Tamara made the dress herself? Had she been looking for a girl whom she thought this odd costume would fit? Walking back into the salon, I felt like a sausage in my sack.

"Sit," she said, pointing to a café-style table and chair. "Good. Lay the right hand here, on the left wrist. Good. Stay there. First I will draw you for ten minutes."

Sitting opposite me on the gray couch, a tablet braced against her knees, Tamara held a slender twig of charcoal and looked at me. Her eyes were like mercury. They moved over me with a flat, empty look that made me uncomfortable. When her gaze flicked down and her hand moved over the page, I looked away, relieved.

〜◎〜

More stylish even than Theresa, more coolly poised even than Gin, Tamara reminded me of a third woman, someone I had met just three months after seeing my neighbor's pink dress, the day I first entered Chanel myself, on the well-upholstered arm of my boyfriend, Guillaume. After whisking me up a mirrored staircase, he had me fitted for a tight satin ruby-colored cocktail gown by the most sophisticated, the most *competent* woman I had ever encountered. The way Tamara spoke to me, without hesitation, without doubting herself, made me think of that tailor at Chanel, as uncowed by Guillaume's age, bulk, and money as she was by the shining, buttery fabric in her hands. As the seamstress draped and pinned the satin on me, I could not speak, awed. When we left, Guillaume took me across rue Cambon into the Ritz, where we cut through the city block using a plush corridor that ushered us into the octagonal, moneyed hush of Place Vendôme. *"C'est beau, n'est-ce pas?"* he said. It *was* beautiful: the silent column, the airy beveled square bounded by arches. I nodded, still dumbfounded.

I never did wear the red satin dress. While we were together, Guillaume kept me in a flat with a doorman, a lift, steam heat. He had a beautician pluck my single brow into two arches and a coiffeur bob my hair. He dressed me in new clothes, from Perugia pumps to a Lanvin cloche, from silk stockings to a fox-collared coat. He sent me to the Alliance Française and paid for classes. However, the day I graduated from *Is this a salad?* to *Why do you like me?* he stopped. *"Ça commence à bien faire!"* he said, meaning he was fed up. I stared at him, baffled. *It begins to do well?*

Within a week, Guillaume had moved a mutely bewildered
Swedish girl into the apartment next door to mine. When I met her,
I thought, *You found another duckling to swan, is that it?* I didn't wait
around to see if we'd go back and collect my dress. Instead, I slept
with one of his employees, a man too young to have even fought in
the war, named Hervé. By the time I made it back to rue Cambon
with Hervé's money, the red dress was gone.

I smiled wryly to myself in Tamara's apartment: I couldn't just nod
and simper at my rich boyfriend, not even for a gown from Chanel,
so now here I was, posing by the hour to pay for a dress off the rack.
A uniform. "You must not move," Tamara said.

"Sorry."

Tamara switched from black charcoal twigs to yellow-brown
bars of pigment, using a heel of bread to erase her stray lines.
I glanced outside. Tamara's parlor window cleared a low carriage
house across the street, so the wide room shone in the hard north
light. The most magnetic thing in the apartment, short of Tamara
herself, was her couch. Low and wide and covered, like the walls,
in gray velvet, it glowed with a pearly sheen, as sleekly featureless
as a doctor's examination table. I wanted to lie down on that couch
like a child and push my cheek against the nap of the velvet. I
wanted to fall asleep on that couch for hours. Tamara's eyes met
mine and she smiled. "It's pretty," I said, stupefied, pointing.

"We will talk later," she said. Embarrassed, I looked away again,
this time at the canvases that surrounded me. Tamara's dining room,
lit green by the ivy framing her window, contained no artwork, but
her bedroom and parlor shimmered with paintings: they hung on

the walls; they perched on easels; they leaned edgewise in stacks in
the corners of the rooms. The largest of them hung over Tamara's
bed in the next room: a portrait of a woman dressed as a man.

"You may rest a moment," Tamara said, massaging her shoulders.

"You painted that?" I asked. Tamara gave me a patient, sarcastic
smile. I crossed the room for a closer look. The painting was taller
than I was. Its width enclosed my width. The woman in the painting
wore a long black coat, a white collared shirt, riding trousers, and
tall shiny black boots. She looked like a dandy or a dictator, posed in
front of a city as if she owned it, half her body standing and victori-
ous, half slouched against a table hidden in drapery.

"The Duchesse de la Salle," Tamara said. "The mother of a
friend of mine. But I painted her as Violette Morris, the athlete."

Violette Morris was often in the papers. A professional soccer
player, she had also become the French national champion boxer in
1923, after defeating a series of male opponents. Her hobbies, I had
read, included motorcycle racing, auto racing, and airplane racing.
Her lovers, it was rumored, included women as well as men. I had
seen her picture quite a few times. More than any physical or sarto-
rial similarity, Morris and the duchess shared the same smug look,
the same arrogant *froideur*.

I stepped back from the painting. *What does Tamara's husband
think of waking up to that every morning?* I thought, looking down at
her big gray velvet bed, decked out in pillows of darker gray satin.
That's when I noticed the headboard: carved into the gray lacquered
wood was a line drawing of two ladies in a dreamy, stylized land-
scape, their naked bodies interlaced. And what did he think of *this*?
"How long has your husband been in Warsaw?" I asked.

"He is not coming back," Tamara said coolly.

I should have guessed, but I had never met a woman of her type. *Donna uomo* was how your mother warned you'd turn out if you were too lazy to bleach your moustache. Two women in bed was something your boyfriend wanted to watch. I looked over at Tamara, nervous. Well, I thought, it seemed like she did only mean to paint me. And I could leave anytime, I reminded myself. I felt less afraid than uneasy as I stepped back into the middle room, where Tamara's most prominently displayed works rested on four wheeled stands. "There he is," she said, pointing to a line drawing of a man charcoaled onto a panel of canvas. Her husband's coat was not so different from the Duchesse de la Salle's. His hard, hollow expression made me turn away.

"Who's that?" I asked instead, pointing to a second canvas, on which a half-painted young woman sat by a window, wearing a schoolgirl's shoes and socks and a rather adult expression. Pinned to the stand I saw a photograph of the same girl, age eleven or so, also sitting by a window, looking guardedly up at me.

"My daughter. I use the photograph during the day, and then Kizette sits for me after school."

"But it's summer. She's in school?"

"She has had a difficult year," Tamara said sharply, her face closing.

Backing off, I turned to the third painting on a stand: two ladies with bobbed hair stood close together, one dreamy, looking upward, one alert, watching for something just past me. "*Die Dame* asked me to do some cover paintings for them," she said, naming a glossy German fashion magazine. "This is the first. I just varnished it."

"Beg pardon?" I couldn't understand her accent for a moment.

"The clear coat on the painting. *Gomme dammar* dissolved in *térébenthine*." I could see the shiny finish on the painting then. I could even see ripples in the sheen toward the top edge, as if the image lay just below a thin skin of water. I had not seen many paintings, and had never looked at any so carefully. For a moment, I could suddenly see three layers at once: the varnish, the paint, and the weave of the canvas beneath it. And then, just as suddenly, the painting ceased to be a thing and became a picture again. "Who are those people?" I asked.

"My friends Ira and Romana. Romana is the Duchesse de la Salle's daughter," she said, gesturing absentmindedly toward the Amazon in the bedroom. "But ptff! *That* one was the real model." She pointed to a frothy orange scarf around the watchful girl's neck that took up almost a third of the canvas. "Temperamental," she said, as if pleased with herself for knowing the English word. "Demanding. Never stayed in one place. Drapery has no memory, so you have to get it all down at once. The *painting* has to remember. Charcoal cloth is fun for practice," she said, pointing toward the burnt curl of ribbon in the jar. "But you can get spoiled." Now that I looked at the painted and charcoalized fabric side by side, I could see how she had learned from copying the hard edges of the latter.

"What's the scarf made of?" I asked, pointing. "Chiffon?"

"Why chiffon?" Tamara asked eagerly.

I pointed again. "It's light. It's soft, but just a little stiff. You can see through it a little, but not loads. And look, rolled hems," I added.

Tamara's face lit with pleasure. "Well done," she declared, and went into her bedroom to dig something out of a drawer: the very same scarf, a thin peach-colored silk that lit the gray room gold. "What a good eye you have," she said. "Here, take."

"I couldn't," I protested, though I couldn't take my eyes off it.

"Just wear it someday. For me," she insisted, pressing the soft film into my hands. Embarrassed, I thanked her, and turned to the painting on the last stand. Only the head was finished: I saw a sad woman with a small, nervous face. Below it, the large seated body was just a few charcoal lines on the canvas: arms, a pair of crossed hands, a crude sleeveless dress—oh!—like mine.

"This is the wife of a Polish friend, an art critic. He has been so good to me in the newspapers," she explained. "This is a gift for them." She saw me glance from painting to dress and back again. "The woman goes back to Poland before I finish, and I think, what can I do? But then I meet you and your body is just like hers: beautiful!" The gesture she made in the air was almost obscene. "So now I can finish. Last time you sat five, ten minutes. This time you will sit thirty."

I took the chair again and crossed my hands like the Polish wife. My eyes climbed the walls. Nude or clothed, everyone Tamara painted looked majestic. Even the mannish duchess seemed princely. The Polish wife, however, looked pinched and squalid. In the mirror behind the screen when I changed, I had seen that the straps didn't trace my back: they sagged away from it. Whoever made this dress was impatient, I thought. She cut the straps straight across instead of angling them and testing them on the model. Perhaps Tamara would correct the straps in the painting.

As the minutes passed, I realized I no longer felt uneasy. I felt jealous. Why did I get the ugly dress, the ugly painting? And why didn't Tamara paint my face? The painting next to the mannish woman showed a nude—sleek, modern, Olympian—with her arm across her face. Was this Tamara's kink? She didn't paint faces? No, I saw plenty of faces in the room, some, to be honest, not as nice as mine. It was as if, by putting me in the ugly dress, she had made herself blind to me. *Beautiful*, she'd said. Did she really think so? I wanted to take off my dress and lie down on that velvet couch for her: I wanted her to *see* me in the grand way she saw the others.

So this was what artists did: Tamara looked up, looked down, moved her hand, looked up again. Choosing among the many slender, long-handled brushes she kept in a green glass bowl, Tamara dabbed a sheet of white wood with a dozen different shades of an earthy yellow she called ochre. When she hit on a set of shades she liked, she used a different brush for each color, holding as many as four brushes at a time in her free hand, cleaning each frequently with a wet rag. When she swirled a brush in a jar of clear liquid, I realized *térébenthine* was French for "turpentine." As I watched her move small amounts of paint from palette to canvas, I noticed she didn't have a single stain on her clothes: not only were her paintings precise, she worked precisely, too.

My attention began to drift. Thinking about the *donna uomo* on the wall and the naked women tangled on Tamara's headboard, I remembered the one time my flatmate and I ever monkeyed around. It was Yann's idea: he was Gin's boyfriend before Daniel. One night he brought over a leather cock, and after we all got high the two of them begged me to give it a whirl. I did my best to look sultry while Gin got it up in me, but really, we both kept laughing. I mean, it was *Gin*. "You know, if you give me a bladder infection, I'll kill you," I told her.

"At least you don't have to wear this thing!"

"*Parlez français!*" Yann protested.

"Inky dinky *parlez vous!*"

After Yann left the next morning, I told Gin over breakfast that the only good part had been how much more fun it was to put on a show for her boyfriend than for mine, because the thing wasn't *his*, you know? "Of course!" She laughed. "He wasn't attached to it!"

I snorted, spraying a mouthful of coffee on the table. "That was pretty bad," I said.

"Wasn't it?"

I was glad we could laugh together about it, but all the same, that night spooked me out of taking any more cocaine. I didn't mind that we'd fooled around, but I minded how easy the high had made it. If Gin hadn't had a sense of humor, I could have lost a friend. She broke up with Yann a couple of weeks later, after he took her to an exclusive club that turned out to be a dirt-floored shack by the Seine where half-dressed lowlifes, college students, and society slummers groped each other in the dark. "He wanted us to take turns with some dirty sailor," she said. "Ew."

During my fifteen-minute breaks, Tamara and I ate a little: over the course of the day we polished off a baguette and half a cobble of creamy, acrid Maroilles. Twice she took her dog for a walk, and once she brushed a stretched canvas with a mixture of plaster and glue. "This is to give the painting a hard, clear finish," she explained when I asked why. Time skipped and pooled while I posed. Eventually, I felt neither nervous that she might touch me nor jealous that she hadn't. Long slow hours passed, and all she did was look, move her hand, look again. I felt like glass: looked at and looked through. My arm ached, then froze. I got so bored I itched all over. At one point I made Tamara stop a dozen times in as many minutes so I could scratch. During one break, I ate all the grapes on the table, and during another, I fell dead asleep. During the last hour, my mind slowed, emptied out. I no longer felt compromised by the money: I felt paid. By quarter of five, when she offered me a glass of wine, I just wanted to go buy my dress.

"You will come tomorrow morning?" Tamara asked, taking my two hands in hers after I had changed back into my own clothes. "Come at ten?"

"I have plans."

"No. Do not say that."

"I have a job."

"Work for me."

"This isn't really for me," I said. "You saw, I got itchy."

"I do not care."

"Well, we'll see," I said.

Her reply came, formal and dolorous: "I will wait for you at ten, whether you come or not."

I reached Belle Jardinière just before six and bought my dress. I took it home to find a note tacked to the door. Gin had penciled it on a flattened pâtisserie box:

Darling—Daniel is HERE. Already! Please be a lamb and go sleep at the Ritz or something? He's going to ASK I think and

*I want everything to be perfect—I don't want him getting cold
feet if you come in all of a sudden. Pretty please?*

I stood quietly at the door, hating her. I picked up the bag I'd set
down. And then, in case Gin had heard me at the door, I took the
stairs loudly to reassure her I was really leaving. I was so angry it
felt good to run, my high heels ringing in the stairwell like shots.

When she asked me to stay at the Ritz in her note, Gin wasn't
proposing that I check in to a room. We had friends among the
hatcheck girls, and on a couple of drunken occasions they'd rigged
up a pair of cots for us in the deserted coatroom, shooing us out the
next day when the lunch shift started. A girl could splash a little
water on her face in the powder room, but it wasn't cozy. To hell
with Gin: no one we knew at the Ritz even *started* work until ten at
night, and it was only half past six. I had enough money for a coffee
and a magazine: I decided to take the Métro to Montparnasse and
sit at a café with both.

Was Gin's banker really about to ASK, as she put it? Nose-to-
armpit with a stranger in the Métro sweatbox, I clung to the pole
beside me, thinking she *had* seemed awfully eager that morning
when she insisted I go interview for her job. "Daniel found a place
for us," she'd said, perching at the foot of my bed in the little nightgown I'd made her. "So I gave notice!"

"You're leaving?" Gin had been making noises about helping
me find another girl to share the flat for weeks, but I hadn't realized
just how serious she—or her banker—was until that morning.
Blinking awake, I watched Gin rub a towel over her wet cropped
head. "Really?"

"Madame Florin was so disappointed. I had to buck her up *somehow*." Although she would admit, in confidence, to being from Colma, California, Gin's let-the-servants-do-it British coo suited her so well, I didn't even mind the affectation. "So I said you'd go interview today."

"Me?"

"Rafaela, please. It's good luck. It's how I met Daniel."

I rolled my eyes and put on a Mayfair accent of my own. "Why, you've never told me how you met Don Yell."

"Come *on*. You know Madame Florin loves you."

I had no great desire to sell gloves to my fellow English speakers, but as I sat facing Gin's elegant, brown-lipsticked supervisor later that morning, the challenge had piqued me as much as scared me: Could I speak French well enough to get hired?

"You're aware of our uniform?" asked Mme. Florin.

"Yours looks different from the others," I noted. Although most women's clothing in Paris at that time was made-to-order *couture*, a few pieces—coats, uniforms, shirtwaists, some foundation garments—were ready-to-wear *confection*. While the youngest employees' uniforms were clearly the latter, Mme. Florin's dress looked like it had been made for her alone: the cotton sateen draped better on her, seemed thicker. Her skirt, fuller than the others', worked to her advantage. Her collar, whiter, set off her olive skin. If I worked here, I thought, I'd make myself a dress like hers. *En français?* "Nicer," I explained.

Mme. Florin acknowledged my compliment with a nod. "Some of us do wear our own. You know how much we'll miss Veer Zhee Nee when she's married," she said. Was Gin really getting *married*? "But you'll catch on quickly here, no? Just make the Americans feel at home, *et voilà*," she explained. (*Et voilà:* hired!) After the war, Americans had more money to throw around in department stores than locals, and Belle Jardinière welcomed them by hiring girls like Gin. (And me!) Mme. Florin was *désolée* about the hundred francs, but we both knew jobs were scarce, and for non-French, even scarcer.

Where was I going to find a hundred francs? A recently sold strand of pearls—Hervé's last gift—had paid my rent through the end of the month, and beyond that I had a little money left over: not a hundred francs, but a few days' grace. *A few days' grace?* As the escalator eased me down to street level that morning, it struck me: for the wage Mme. Florin offered, I could make the dress back in a handful of days. I could even save up, go back to Chanel, order something *I* chose this time. For some people, time meant money made, not money spent. What if I could be one of them, for as little as a black dress with a white collar?

I was starting to look forward to this job, I reflected, still on the Métro. Tomorrow I'd be fitting gloves onto the slender hands of wives and daughters and mistresses as their wealthy men looked on. I'd have a shining glass case to keep clean, and soon, a perfect black dress like Mme. Florin's. The part of me that had gotten old and sad at sixteen was girlishly happy that Gin's supervisor trusted me to handle money and nice things, to speak English and French to the customers, to look good for the shop. I'd go home with my own money at the end of each week whether I met my own Daniel or not. Proud of myself, I tightened my grip on my Belle Jardinière bag. I could feel the ghost weight of the pearls I'd sold lift a little from my neck.

There was the small matter of what to do next; I had planned on a quiet, cheap evening at home. A bath, a *tartine*. I'd been thinking I would hang my new dress up, so the wrinkles wouldn't hold, maybe let the hips out a little. Gin, however, had spoiled all that. Climbing up from the Métro to Boulevard du Montparnasse, I figured the chance of running into someone from my Alliance Française days—someone who might lend me money for dinner—was highest at La Rotonde: while not the most stylish of the cafés at the intersection of Montparnasse and Raspail, it was the hardest to miss. Le Sélect, La Rotonde, Le Dingo, La Coupole, Café du Dôme: Paris was compact already, but we English speakers made it just two blocks long by always drinking at the same five places near the Luxembourg Gardens. So it was only half a coincidence that the American slickster who had asked if he could paint me that morning walked by, together with his bear cub of a French friend. Painter Slick spotted me at my table and grinned like a kid at the circus. Though stocky, he was not tall: I could hurt him enough to get away, if I needed to, I thought. I might not tell him my real last name, if he asked, but I could give him a crumb of eye contact for now, just enough to let him know I remembered him. And who should reappear ten minutes later, sans friend?

Even if it was all a game, I liked that he took the table next to mine rather than ask if he could sit with me, that he met my eyes with a smile and settled in with his newspaper instead of chatting me up, that when he shook out a cigarette for himself, he offered me one, then returned to his paper. I smoked it and read my magazine, marking the French I didn't know with my lip pencil: why didn't I have a stainless-steel pencil like Tamara's? The man was older than I but not yet thirty, and more down-at-the-heels than he first appeared. His clothes, though clean and sharp, were old; his army-style haircut, though fresh, looked cheap. Sideburns would have given his boyish potato face some cheekbones, but he seemed like—I let his flat midwestern accent color my judgment here—the kind of American who'd beat up any barber who tried to make him look fussy. More's the pity. But what he lacked in looks he made up for in quiet charm: when the point broke off my lip pencil, he handed me his penknife to sharpen it. "Another cigarette?" he asked later.

"Thanks," I said. "Sometimes you need it."

"You need it?"

"My flatmate locked me out, and I have no money until my new job starts tomorrow. I'm killing time until I can stay overnight at a friend's."

"That's a bum deal," he said. "How about a movie? There's a German theater playing *Metropolis*."

I didn't mean to sigh, but my sigh came out the way my coughs and sneezes did, like a much older woman's, like my mother's. "Can I borrow some money?" I said.

"My treat."

I was ready to bolt, but the American didn't try anything funny at his boring movie, nor at the quick bistro dinner that followed, nor in the taxi we took to the Ritz. His name was Anson Hall, Anson for a Union army grandfather, recently deceased. He was, in fact, from Chicago: he freelanced for the *Tribune* as a sportswriter.

"You can live on that?" I asked.

"My old man helps me out sometimes," he said, shrugging.

"Lucky you."

Anson looked uncomfortable, and when an older couple he knew walked into the Ritz just then, he smiled extra-wide and trotted over to greet them. Either he was richer than he let on, or poorer. Or just ashamed of asking his parents for money. What did *he* know about shame? But even so, something about his discomfort—and about the way he tried to curry favor with the husband and wife who'd walked into the Ritz—made me want to protect him.

The woman glanced at me. "Where's Mrs. Hall?" she asked.

"Honey," said the man.

The woman looked at him, confused.

"Mrs. Hall and I have separated," Anson said stiffly.

The woman's hand rose to her mouth as Anson turned to order us a round of *marcs*. "He's the one you told me about," the woman half whispered to her husband. "With that Piggott girl."

Anson had heard her. His smile, already strained, popped a stitch.

"Honey," said the man again.

"Pardon me," said the woman to Anson, giving me another look.

I had troubles of my own, so I went looking for my friends. I found Laure, a thickset girl who lived with her family in the squalid Nineteenth. *"Pas de problème,"* she assured me. "We just have to wait until all these people clear out." That wouldn't be until three or four in the morning, but I knew better than to complain: she *was* doing me a favor.

As I walked back to Anson's end of the room, the bartender—a chilly young man who affected a monocle—intercepted me. "That gentleman asked me to bring you this." He pointed to a frail, gray-ing, but very well-dressed specimen alone at a table, and handed me a tightly folded sheet of Ritz hotel stationery.

I did not meet the old man's eye until after I looked inside—I found a key stamped with a room number, and a note: *50F?*—and that was to give him a look of disgust. Fifty francs wouldn't even get me a subscription to the magazine I was reading. Before Anson could come back, I took out my lip pencil, added a zero to the old man's figure, and folded the key back into the note for the bar-tender. In the bar mirror I saw the old man's eyes widen when he opened the note. I turned to give him a superior look, and he met my eyes. And nodded.

Just at that moment, Anson reappeared, minus Honey and her husband, much drunker than I'd last seen him. "Wanna dance?" he asked.

Now I see that I didn't need the old man's five hundred francs. I had a place to sleep. I'd just been hired at Belle Jardinière. But I wasn't in the habit of making money at a job in those days, and it was so *much* money, it made me laugh out loud. "Wait, Anson, one more sip," I insisted, pouring some of my drink down the front of my dress. "Oh, heavens, no, darling, I have *got* to go to the powder room right now." And I did go to the powder room first, but not without a numbing glug of *marc*. I took my Belle Jardinière bag with me.

I arrived at the old man's floor to find a boy from room service standing at his door with a bottle of champagne, so I could see before I walked in that there wasn't a gang of thugs waiting to rape and murder me. The awkward way the man tipped the boy made me conclude, in fact, that the thing I had to fear most was my own pity. The old man came from Seville, he told me in labored French. I looked like a girl he'd once known. I looked like his granddaughter, too, he said. I'd really rather not have known that. His odor was a smothering blend of cologne, cognac, and brilliantine, with fainter notes of urine, bleach, and loneliness. When he told me what he wanted, I made him pay me and braced myself against one of the bedsteads. At least I didn't have to look at him. I was glad it didn't hurt. I looked around the hotel room I couldn't afford, and tried to think about nothing, but instead found myself imagining the old man imagining me as his granddaughter. She had the face of the one Spanish girl at my school, sweet Beronica from Balenthia. *Stop thinking*, I thought. I wished I'd drunk more. To distract myself, I worried about the chilly bartender. Would he try to get me thrown out of the Ritz? A girl like me didn't raise the tone of a place. I worried more that he'd want me to buy his silence. Would he want money, or something else? And how hard would he try to get it? At the end of each of the old man's labored breaths came a faint whining sound, like the whistle of a radiator. What did they need me for, really? Why not just use some Vaseline? You won't be any less lonely when this is over, *Señor*, I thought, and then his grip tightened on my waist, and he released a steeper whine. When he finished, I tucked away the money and locked myself in the bathroom, availing myself of a long and thorough scrub.

The worst of my period had ended a couple of days before.

Soaking in the bath, I cupped a handful of water containing a last lazy drop of blood and tipped it onto the floor. *Thank God I can't get pregnant this week,* I thought. Guillaume had taught me to pay strict attention to my period and mid-month cramps, and how to look after him when there was a chance I could get pregnant: if I never take it up the ass again, it'll be too soon. I had learned, under his tutelage, how to laugh at jokes I didn't understand. I had learned to drink. I had learned how to move backward on a dance floor without incident: himself a workmanlike dancer, Guillaume enjoyed showing me off at the glittering nightclubs where his coworkers gathered. I had learned that if I acted like I was having fun, he had fun, and sometimes I even did, too. It might be tedious, until the fun caught up, but it wasn't difficult. Though I felt little for him but revulsion, compared with raising four little brothers, he was a vacation. And yet, though I learned how to make him want me like clockwork, I never stopped wondering why he wanted me in the first place. What did he see when he saw me? It was as if my body were a sign pinned to my own back, a sign I myself couldn't read.

I pictured the cot that awaited me in the coatroom once the dancing couples claimed their hats and stumbled home. It would be stiflingly hot in that windowless closet. Laure wouldn't even be able to get me in there for another few hours, and that was assuming the chilly bartender didn't rat me out. There was no way I was wasting good money on a hotel, so if I had to sit up at an all-night café somewhere, I would. *I wouldn't mind a nap first.* The Spanish grandfather had two beds, a window, moving air. *If he's still asleep when I come out, I'm just going to lie down on that other bed for an hour,* I decided as I dressed. *He'll never know.*

When I opened the door, I found him in bed with my new

uniform draped across his furred legs. Thick yellow toenails beclawed his veiny feet. Sheets of dead skin seemed to have formed on his real skin, beneath which varicose jellyfish floated, bluish. He was wheezing again. Though his fist worked the wattled misery in his lap, only his face was taut, a mask: when he met my eyes, a smile dribbled out to greet me. "Excuse me? That's *my* dress," I said, but it was suddenly too late. The resources available to me in the Ritz powder room wouldn't make any difference, no matter how hard I worked the polished cotton. I didn't want to touch it, anyway. I'd just have to buy another one. Angry, I picked up one of his wingtips—I've always been a good shot—and thought better of it. I didn't want to make trouble for myself, or for Laure. "Aw, for crap's sake," I said. I said some other things, too, and then I stepped into my shoes and left.

In the lift down to the coatroom, I crossed my arms over my handbag, upset. What kind of a person would *do* that? Behind the silent lift-boy's back, I exchanged a hollow look with myself in the mirror. I was glad for the money, and making so much at one go took the edge off. Hell, it even gave me a kick. I could go back up there and break the guy's nose, if I wanted to. Rip out what was left of his hair. But really—I gave in, suddenly, to a silent, weepy gust of envy—I just wanted what Anson Hall had: rich parents to send me a little something every month. I could eat in. I could mend my own stockings. Even more than a dress from Chanel, I just wanted enough money to be left alone, to sit and think and study French and watch people and make things. I blotted my eyes as the lift-boy slid open the doors.

The chilly bartender's back was turned. Good. But there, positioned at the bar where he could watch the lift, sat Anson, drinking alone. I felt him watching me emerge an hour after I'd disappeared—with no makeup and wrinkles in my lucky dress—and I smiled weakly. I walked past the bar without going in, and he followed me.

"Come back and let me get you one more drink, to say good night?" he asked.

I turned. Fine, let the bartender think he'd have to fight this guy if he wanted any of my money, I decided. I steered Anson toward the farthest, darkest booth, and then we looked each other full in the face. I wanted to hurt him for what he knew. I wanted to make him go away. I wanted him to like me anyway. "I'm buying," I said, putting five hundred francs on the table before Anson could take out his wallet. "Two *marcs*," I said to the waiter, and then counted out the money from the change. "The movie. Dinner. Taxi. Drinks," I said nastily, daring Anson to take it, daring him not to.

Anson slowly looked up from the money. I don't know what the look on my face was, but when he saw it, his own expression melted from affront to apology. "Even Steven, huh?" he said. "Wait." He passed me back a few francs.

"What?"

"You got the last round, but I'm getting this one."

I smiled back at him, my eyes suddenly wet again. "Thanks."

I could tell Anson wanted to ask how I'd spent the evening—and the afternoon, for that matter—and I had some questions for him, too, but we kept our mouths shut, as if to see who would crack first. The next drink made me feel sick and sad, though, and when I started crying in earnest, it was about Gin. "I don't think that guy's going to marry her, really. Do you?"

"Unlikely."

"I wish I could prove it to *her*, though. I wish I could just show her the rest of his life and say, See, you think you have all of Daniel, but you only have half. A third. Ten percent!"

"Well, some people need to get hurt to be happy," he said.

"I don't know if she's one of those," I said. "I've never seen her lose her head like this before."

"But if you really think she'd drop him if she knew the whole story——"

"Yes?" I prompted.

"Well, I might know somebody who could find out."

"You do?"

He was drunk, too. As he leaned in to tell me, his eyes were glossy with excitement. "It's complicated. And it's kind of a secret."

"*Who?*" I insisted, grinning back at him.

Anson took out a long narrow notepad from his jacket pocket.

"You really are a journalist."

"Tell me the man's name and the bank where he works, and I'll talk to my friend."

"Well, his name is Daniel Gordin," I said. "Um."

"Your roommate never told you where he works? Or"——at this, his voice colored with more judgment than it had when I'd walked out of the lift——"did you never pay attention?"

"Maybe a little of both?"

"C'mon, at least out of self-interest. He might have a coworker, somebody who could set you up sweet. It's dangerous, running around hotels," he said.

"Thanks, Mother."

"I guess I deserved that. How did she meet this banker, any-way?"

"At her job," I said, and told him their story.

"Belle Jardinière?" he said. "Jeez, that place is notorious."

"What do you mean?"

"Well, I used to work in a newspaper office, and let's just say everybody knew when there was a new girl working there, espe-cially a pretty one. The boys liked to send over this kid named André. He'd snoop around and come back with a full report."

"Who was André?"

"Just a clerk. But he was good-looking, and he had a special talent for sniffing out the girls who would from the girls who wouldn't."

We both looked away, embarrassed. I could see it all over again, my ruined black dress. It occurred to me that Daniel was not at that moment proposing to Gin. Showcased behind her glove counter, Gin may have believed she was getting her pick, but perhaps, fore-warned by his own office's version of André, Daniel thought he was getting his turn.

"Well," Anson said, breaking the unhappy silence. "All the more reason to do some research. Maybe this Daniel's a good guy."

"Maybe he is," I said. I looked down. Anson's trousers were an inch or so too short, I noted. He had a foot propped on a neighbor-ing chair, revealing a quarter-moon of badly scarred ankle above his sock. "What happened to you?"

"I got shelled on the Italian front."

"That sounds awful."

"I'm luckier than most," he said mildly. "Listen." He passed me a business card. "This is an office where I pick up messages most mornings. If you're serious about this—if you really want me to talk to my friend—call between ten and noon sometime this week, and ask to speak to me. Don't talk to anyone else."

" 'Yves Boulind et Compagnie,' " I read.

"*Oui*. He's a friend of the family. I call him Monsieur Bland," he said, barely altering the French name while giving me a look so blank, I laughed.

"You would really do this for me?"

"I don't know if my friend can help, but I can ask."

"Thank you," I said. We were the last two people in the bar, and the restaurant had cleared out as well. "Well, I'll go find my *copine*," I said.

"You don't want to come over for a nightcap?"

"And then where would I go?"

He smiled.

"Aren't you cute. *Where's Mrs. Hall? Where's the Piggott girl?*" I said, mocking Honey's accent.

"The old man had a ring on."

"The old man had five hundred francs."

"Sure, but I'm better looking."

"Don't push your luck."

He gave a good-natured shrug. "Well, I tried."

What little I knew of Anson's cluttered love life put me off, and his looks, whatever he thought of them, did little for me. However, the grace with which he gave in made me like him. "You're all right, Anson," I said.

⚬

The money was still in my bandeau the next morning when I woke up on the coatroom cot. I could buy another uniform, if I wanted it, but my vision of a clean shining glove counter was bleared over with milky spume, with old men and Andrés and *girls who would*. I opened the door a crack for some light to dress by and saw the clock in the lobby: nine-thirty. Late to work, on top of everything else.

I could go to Belle Jardinière, late, and beg Mme. Florin to let me spend another hundred francs, and then I could spend eight hours on my feet, fending off the Andrés of this world. Or I could go home. Five hundred francs was two months' rent: I could stay home for weeks before I had to look for anyone else. Sixty days to myself. Sixty days of not making nice, not to anybody. Of course, first I'd have to apologize to Gin for not taking her job. If she let me in at all. If she wasn't too busy with Daniel. Five hundred francs was only one month's rent if Gin was really leaving. And besides, in the quiet weeks ahead, did I really want that wheezy grandfather to be the last person I'd gone to bed with?

I shook Tamara's tightly wadded scarf out of my handbag: in the morning light, it was the color of apricots, light as breath. I held it to my face and inhaled tuberose, turpentine, sweat. I remembered that gloved finger under my chin, that velvet couch in the sun.

I knew you would come back," she said when I knocked.

2

WHEN I WENT BEHIND THE SCREEN to change for Tamara, I didn't put on the sausage-sack dress. I waited until her back was turned and then I draped myself on her couch wearing nothing but her silk chiffon scarf. "You were sitting at the table, remember?" she said in her careful, Slavic English, and then turned to me. She gasped. "You are perfect," she said.

I looked at her pointedly, and smiled.

"Oh," she said, her voice wavering, "I need to finish that other painting..."

"Finish it later," I said. "Paint me like this."

She nodded, her eyes dilating, and took out her charcoals and tablet. Using a timer, she made a series of five-minute sketches of me with and without the scarf: sitting, standing, lounging on her couch, head facing toward her, then away. She looked from sketch to sketch and up to me again, giddy with indecision. "I will just have to paint all of them," she said. At that, she stood, ran her knuckles lightly over the chiffon that covered me. "Now lie just the way you were when I turned. What is this?" she said, picking up my magazine. She placed it, open, in front of me. "Now, your eyes half open: you are bored and you want to go home."

But I don't, I almost said. But I lay on the couch as she asked, with my *Les Modes* in front of me.

"Do not pretend to read. Really read," she said. The French words lay on the page, inert: I was so conscious of her eyes on me that I couldn't make sense of the type. I looked up at her doubtfully. "Do not read, then, if you like." She moved the magazine just past me, re-draped the silk across my waist, and tied a black velvet ribbon around my wrist. As she came close to tie it, a pale tendril of hair curled up from her bob to brush my face. "Your eyelids are purple, no? Red. As if you never sleep. And your lips are swollen with kisses," she teased.

"I didn't kiss anybody," I said. It was the truth.

Tamara laughed. "Not ever?"

"Not not *ever*," I protested. "But not last night."

"If you say so." Looking at my mouth, Tamara bit the side of her thumb. Drew the wet thumb across my lower lip. "There. Good."

She took her drawing board and charcoal and moved her chair closer to the couch where I lay. My lower lip pulsed as she drew. I watched her glance from her page to my mouth and back. And then I felt the room change as she disappeared into drawing: it became fuller, because all her attention was in one place, and emptier, too, because *she* wasn't there for a little while. Only drawing was there. I felt that way, sometimes, when I was making things. Could I feel that way without making anything? I looked at her clothes, the white canvas chef's apron over her simple black dress. Could an

apron be a dress? For Tamara—a woman flatter-chested than I—
why not? I'd want the bib a little wider, with darts, small ones,
tucked into the sides to make it cling to her, and to play up what
little she had. The trick, like wrapping an orange in a sheet of paper,
would be getting the rectangular fabric to follow both the small of
her back and the swell of her ass. (It would be the palest, palest
gold, like her hair, my lower lip told me. Like the pale gold inner
flesh of a brioche.) But if I used the idea I had yesterday to alter
Gin's dress with gores, and I could cut up a second apron—

My lower lip, throbbing as it dried in the warm air, was having
none of it. Tamara was sitting so close I could almost feel the vibration of the charcoal on her tablet jarring me in soft waves. Uncon-
sciously, I closed my mouth and let it fall open again, just to repeat
the pleasure of Tamara's finger—my own tongue—across my lip.
Suddenly I felt the air thicken. "What did you do?" she asked.

"Nothing."

"Do it again."

"What?"

Tamara set down her drawing board, and leaned forward.
When I felt her hair wisping against my face again, I inhaled
sharply. When she kissed me, I sighed. Her tongue across my lip
made me clench at the fold of silk between my thighs. "I can tell
you are going to be a difficult model," she said, coming up briefly
for air before dipping back into my mouth. I had never kissed lips
so soft. She stood and lifted the scarf off me. Her eyes were like
silver. "Oh?" she said, holding the scarf in the air, the pale chiffon
with its darker wet bull's-eye. I closed my eyes, abashed. I couldn't
open them. I heard Tamara set her rings deliberately on the table
before she said, "What is going on here?"

"I don't know," I said, stalling. It was hard to speak with her thumbs on my knees. The world fell apart behind my eyelids in sheets of apricot light and pale gold hair. My knees slid away from each other. I shook: her breath brushed against the coiled hairs between my thighs the way her finger had brushed against my lip.

"You do not know?"

I shrugged.

"That is not good enough," she said, straightening.

Oh, no, I thought. Please don't make me look like a fool. Please don't bring me this far just to drop me. "Please," I breathed.

"Good girl," she said, and I felt her tongue flick hot across me. My body clenched again and I knew she saw. "Very good," she said. And then I watched her slide two fingers into her mouth slowly, saw how slick they got in the light. I felt them wet between my legs where she held me: the very pressure spread my lips. The nails on those two fingers are so much shorter than the others, I remember thinking, before they curved inside me, reaching what must have been the back, the spongy rootbed, of my *grilletto,* once, again, again. It had a back? I'd never known. Nobody had ever touched me there, not even me, I thought—*oh, God, I'm flying*—and then I couldn't think at all.

For a while I lay stunned on Tamara's couch, and when the little dots behind my eyelids turned into a world again, I saw that she had taken off her clothes. She lay beside me on the couch, just as golden as I'd imagined her, her pubic hair a leonine brown. "Do you know what to do with me?" she asked.

I had never put my fingers inside a woman before. "Is there a trick to it?" I asked.

"No."

I tried one finger and it sank in all the way. I tried another—nervous about hurting her with my nails—and she felt like hot liquid inside. I tried a third and she grabbed me with muscles I hadn't even known were there. She slammed against me in a hard tattoo that slowed to an easy canter, and when she came with a fast harsh sigh, her eyes rolled back in her head. When she woke, I was startled by the contrast between her body—queenly, lavish, spent—and her gaze, shiny and vulnerable. As she looked up at me, a sense of accomplishment snapped through me so triumphantly, so violently, something happened I had never experienced with anyone: I needed her all over again. "How can I ever thank you?" she whispered.

"Like this," I said. That was the moment I crossed over from letting things happen to making them happen: I took her hand and pushed her fingers back inside my body.

On my sixteenth birthday, sixteen months before that day in Paris, I had walked out of my room in the brownstone on West Tenth Street my stepfather had bought for my mother, and into a practical joke staged by the eldest of their sons: a pail of water perched atop a half-open door. "Carlo!" I screamed, drenched. If I had known the future, I might have stood at the top of those stairs a moment longer, dressed in my best for church. I might have fingered the oiled banister, savoring my last moment as a child. I did not: I stomped down to breakfast. "Where is he?"

My stepfather had always treated me like a bill it was rather good of him to pay on time, but that morning he looked at me. He set down his *Progresso*. "Sal," my mother said.

Time slowed when my stepfather set down his newspaper, his eyes widening. I think anyone eye to chest with a nippling girl in a wet dress would have stared, but that was no consolation: I watched my mother's face harden against us, and I felt afraid. I think my stepfather did too, because his voice turned forced and jolly, and what he said was more effective than any protestation of innocence. "I think it's time we found that daughter of yours a husband, don't you?"

My mother's face relaxed. "You think?" she said. I ran out of the room.

Although Cat O'Reilly, Maura Kelly, and I had plotted every detail of our wedding nights (with Fairbanks, Barrymore, and Valentino) in pornographic detail, I had given no thought to my actual future. As I changed my dress, appalled, I wondered, were they serious? When I finally slapped my little brother, my heart wasn't in it.

They *were* serious. My stepfather found a husband for me as far away as possible: his brother back in Alia had a twenty-year-old son who liked my photograph. Done.

"But I—" I mustered at dinner when they told me, "I don't speak so much Italian."

"You should," my stepfather said. My mother, buttering a roll for my youngest brother, did not look up. As with many New York immigrants, the two of them spoke to their children in Italian, and we answered them in English.

"What about school?" I tried again.

"Haven't some girls in your class already left school to get married?"

"Sure," I said. "But—" But not girls I ever talked to. Those girls—the ones Cat and Maura and I whispered about between classes—got bad grades, or got pregnant, or both.

"See?" he said. "The pretty ones always do."

My mother stopped moving the knife in her hand. "Sal."

Arranging my passport took a good deal of letter-writing to Italy, because, born at sea, I had never become an American citizen. In the meantime, my mother and stepfather sent me to live with Nonna Gioia on Grand Concourse Boulevard.

What wouldn't my stepfather do for my mother? He had moved his own mother to the Bronx for the same reason he had bought the brownstone on West Tenth Street. After his wife's death, Sal Russo's remarriage to my beautiful young mother (*that stuck-up Genovese, that slut, that Jew's widow*) had angered the women at the Church of the Most Precious Blood as much as it had stirred the men. "How do you expect me to live with all this talk?" Sal's mother would ask him. His import business had done so well he could afford to take a step back from his insular neighborhood: in response to his mother's complaints, he had set her up in a spacious flat in a brand-new building, far from the crowded tenements she'd always hated. It was only after she'd lorded her marble foyer and indoor plumbing over all the villagers she'd immigrated with that Nonna Gioia realized her son had moved her away both from the people she'd known all her life and from her burgeoning new crop of grandchildren.

I'm sure if she could have had my mother under her roof, Nonna Gioia would have exacted her lonely revenge drop by drop. But she didn't have my mother. Instead, she had a younger, darker copy of the hotsy-totsy who had stolen away her son and ruined her life: me.

Nonna Gioia kept the key to her flat on a ribbon around her neck and glared at me each time she came home and locked us in together. To prepare me for life in Alia with Sal's nephew, she taught me not only Sicilian dialect, but Sicilian cooking, and in doing so instilled in me a hatred of the kitchen that persists to this day. I can still hear her now: "That blonde *battona* never taught you how to pluck a chicken?" In the evenings, she'd look up from her *caffè corretto* and tug at her moustached top lip with two fingers, eyeing me with the same distaste she reserved for Theresa, the neighbor with the Chanel dress. Although I never learned the reason my stepfather handed her for why I needed to marry her grandson so fast, it was clear that Nonna Gioia, like my mother, thought I should be kept as far away from Sal as possible. "Just look at you," she'd say, shaking her head.

I had a plan. Once my passport was straightened out, Nonna Gioia would chaperone me to Naples, and thence to Alia. So if I could contrive to leave her behind just before the ship left New York Harbor, she would be stuck on board, unable to get a message to anyone for weeks. I could go live on the Lower East Side with the Fanos, my real father's family, and no one would be the wiser.

When we found our room on the boat, I looked desperately up and down the hall. How would I find my way out? "I don't want you opening the door to anyone this trip, do you understand?" said Nonna Gioia.

"I *understand*," I replied in English, impatient.

At that, Nonna Gioia tried to exchange a weary, eye-rolling glance with our next-door neighbor, a balding, red-nosed man. Too polite to reply, he gave a small bow and entered his own room.

"*Out* of the doorway, Rafaela," said Nonna Gioia, giving my arm a yank. I leaned out again, into the empty corridor, trying to get my bearings. "Stop displaying yourself like a *battona*."

I sat down with my unopened valise in the small, windowless room, and I stared at the door. "I'm going to go watch us pull off," Nonna Gioia said. I grinned as she shut the door behind her. And then, as my hand closed around the grip of my valise, I heard her lock me in.

I ran silently to the door: I silently turned the knob back and forth. That was when I found out I couldn't unlock the door from the inside, not without the key that hung—on a ribbon, of course—around Nonna Gioia's neck. "Wait! Wait!" I called through the keyhole. I heard her pause in the hall. "Nonna Gioia!" I cried aloud, banging on the door. I tried calling to her in Italian, with even some Sicilian thrown in. "Come back! You forgot something! Come back! Please? Please!" I listened to her walk away. Can a tread gloat? I think it can.

I knocked on the door, hoping someone from the crew would hear me. I knocked louder when the engines began to fire. "Help!" I called, making a chant of it. When the ship began to pull away, I screamed it, weeping. I pounded and pounded on the locked door.

I spent a week in the ship's small cabin. Nonna Gioia brought me meals, which I would not touch in her presence, as well as tracts from the ship's Catholic chaplain. I did not speak to her. I lay in bed, barely moving. Whenever she left the room, I ate and cried. I hoped, bitterly, that my mother and stepfather had been forced to hire a girl to cook and clean in my stead, and I hoped my brothers hated her. Why had I ever washed a single dish for those people? I mourned my last two years of high school, my friends Maura and Cat. I mourned my uncle, Elio Fano, and the terrible puns with which he teased out my shy Italian. I mourned his wife, my Zia Rina, and her almond cookie balls—buttery, evanescent, dredged in powdered sugar—that imploded in my mouth. I mourned my Fano cousins. I mourned the arch and fountain of Washington Square, the pear trees that snowed white over the Manhattan streets in spring, the weedy trees of heaven that yellowed every fall. Though in the weeks at Nonna Gioia's I hadn't missed cleaning up after them one bit, I mourned my little brothers, too.

I even mourned my mother as she'd been when I was small, her magnificent hair spreading across both our backs when she embraced me. And I cried because I felt sorry for myself: I'd really have to live in Alia, a foreigner amid local gossips. I'd really have to speak Sicilian. I could see the future: the children I didn't want, not now, maybe never. The diapers and dishes and cooking and pressing. The dirt floor. The well. God help me, the outhouse. And before all that, when I got off the boat I'd really have to marry that boy. What was his name?

On the night we docked in Marseille, as she sat gnawing on a chicken wing saved from dinner, Nonna Gioia hacked abruptly and stopped breathing. I slapped her on the back the way my mother did for my brothers. She gave a weak cough, spat blood, then crumpled onto her bunk. I opened her mouth, swabbed around, and found a wet hard morsel. She was breathing again, but didn't answer when I called her name.

If Nonna Gioia was right—if I was such a danger to myself that I had to be kept hidden away for my own good—then to change my life all I'd have to do was leave the room once. Her breathing was weak but even. I lifted off the ribbon with the room key from around her neck, and I let myself out of the room just as our neighbor—the red-nosed bald old man—was letting himself into his.

"Oh, it's the American *belle* with the Italian grandmother, I see," said the ugly man. He had a French accent, which—after eight days with only Nonna Gioia for company—made me almost laugh. "I thought she kept you locked up in your room."

"She *does* keep me locked up in my room," I told him. "But she's choked on a bone. I'm trying to find her a doctor."

"Please, let me help."

"I got it out," I said, brandishing the hard gristly wad in my handkerchief before I put it in my pocket. "But she's not doing so well."

"Let me show you the way." I was wearing my school uniform, the navy blue pinafore I'd made. As we walked down the corridor, the man touched my arm with a wedding-ringed hand. He introduced himself, and the oily pleasure in his voice made me decide not to tell him my real last name when I replied. I had never lied like that before. "They say we won't sail for days in this rain," he said, following behind me up the narrow stairway. "I was going to spend a week in Rome with friends, but at this rate, I might just take the train home tonight."

Even with the funny accent, I was so glad to hear a voice other than Nonna Gioia's that I didn't want him to stop. I could feel him watching me climb the stairs. "Where's home?" I asked.

"Paris."

At that word, I thought so violently of Theresa and her pink Chanel dress that my stomach lurched. I could hear her voice right there, ringing in the tight stairwell: *It's from Paris, sweetheart.* I wanted her to offer me that smile again, that quickly extended, quickly retracted smile that had made us, briefly, kin. I wanted to be as beautiful as she was. I wanted to live alone and ride around in a town car. I wanted a different cloche for every day of the week. With both hands clamped on the stair railing, I turned back to get another look at the man, to search his face for some sign that he and Theresa had been stamped by the same city. His yellow teeth smiled up at me, and I turned away: I wanted that dress so much I was afraid I'd reduce him to a cinder if I looked at him too hard. "Lucky you," I said.

The ugly man stood to the side as the Boston doctor and his aide looked over Nonna Gioia. "She's a little confused and weak," the doctor pronounced. "But she should be herself in no time. You did the right thing, to clear the obstruction," he said, nodding to the packet of bone and handkerchief on the bedside table.

"Brave girl," agreed the young aide. His sticky grin irked the ugly man, who stepped a little closer to me.

However much I disliked Nonna Gioia, I felt proud of myself: I'd never saved a life before. In that moment when I realized I'd saved her, I felt uncannily certain that the person whose eyes I met next would feel bound to me. Nonna Gioia might have won all of

Alia over to my side. The doctor might have paid for me to go to nursing school. The doctor's aide might have married me. I smiled at the ugly man.

As the doctor and his aide took their notes, the ugly man stole even closer and murmured, "Would you like to see Paris?"

I thought of Theresa, and I did not say to him, *I would trade anything to spend one day in Paris, looking at women in Chanel dresses. What can I give you?* No. I turned, as if away, but really so that he and no one else could hear me, and I said, "What would you give me?"

I had traded sex for a train ticket, for an apartment, for a coat and hat and shoes, and most recently—some half-dozen times since my mother's letter in March—just for money. I'd had sex out of spite, the time I took up with Hervé to get back at Guillaume. I'd had sex because it was easier than explaining myself in French. I'd had sex to get my way, to make peace, to be a good sport. All told, I had never simply gone to bed with anyone just because I wanted to. On Tamara's couch that morning, I remembered the stairs in my stepfather's brownstone on Tenth Street again, the glossy banister my mother buffed weekly with olive oil. And suddenly I remembered a day when I was very small, before my brothers came along. When my mother went out for groceries, I slopped more oil on the banister and slid down. I climbed those stairs again and again, to get that feeling: how slick my knickers got, how distinctly I could feel the spreading wings of my little *figa*, how the shock of bliss pleated up through me like lightning. I had forgotten this kind of eagerness until now, as my body sobbed into Tamara's hand. *Again, again!* I wanted to crow.

I was a giddy witch on a broomstick. I was a leaping dog. I was liquor; I was laughter; I was a sliding girl on a shining rail: something I'd forgotten how to be.

Tamara and I woke to a knock at the door and a child's voice calling, *"Chérie!"*

"Kizette," Tamara whispered. She was across the room in moments, tossing me the red silk robe that hung on the folding screen, stepping into her dress and apron. Mother and daughter embraced in the hallway: the girl looked ten or eleven, in a school uniform and white socks. Her hair, fairer and straighter than Tamara's, was cropped in the same stylish bob. Tamara's dog had clattered up the stairs with Kizette—I'd been too distracted to notice his absence before—and now the greyhound circled mother and daughter, shaking with enthusiasm, arching up in the attempt to rest his forepaws on Tamara's shoulders until a stern word sent him to his cushion. "I kept coughing, so they sent me home," the girl said in French.

Seeing Tamara test her daughter's forehead with the back of her hand made something twist inside me. "You're burning up," she said. "I want you to stay home the rest of the day, and if you're still this hot tomorrow, I'm calling the doctor."

"Can Solange come over when school lets out?"

"They sent you home so you wouldn't get the other girls sick, Kizette."

"Can we spend the afternoon on the telephone?"

"You can spend fifteen minutes on the telephone. I don't want your throat getting worse. I'm going to fix you some hot tea with lemon and jam," Tamara said.

"I want hot chocolate."

"Milk coats your throat." I had never heard the French for *coat* before, but my mother had admonished me in just the same vein years before. "I'll give you two squares of chocolate with your tea. Why didn't you have them telephone me to come get you?"

"You were staying in all morning not to miss the new model, remember?"

I saw Tamara, then Kizette, look down the hall toward the salon where I sat in the red robe. "Of course I would come to get you if you were sick, Kizette. Or your grandmother would."

Kizette shrugged, and unselfconsciously scratched her chin by rubbing it against her shoulder. "Will you stay in my room and read to me?"

"You have to read to yourself today, *chérie*. If you're quiet, you can come out and draw the model with me."

Kizette looked down the hall again, this time meeting my gaze. Her eyes were as gray as her mother's, with a frank, flat regard that seemed to drink me down in moments. She shrugged again and drifted into her room.

Tamara set the kettle on and reëmerged with an apologetic smile. "Well, we have a chaperone."

"Do you want me to dress for that other painting?"

"Thank you," she said crisply. "Tea?"

I marveled as I pulled the brown dress over my head. Sleek fashion plate, focused artist, resplendent lover, competent mother: I had seen four Tamaras in two days. She gave me tea in a glass: black and sweet, with a swirl of raspberry seeds at the bottom. "Is this the way the Russians drink it?"

"How would I know?" she asked, her voice hardening. "I am Polish, not Russian."

I felt uncertain as I sat again in the ugly brown dress, not sure if she was going to pretend the morning had never happened. "Do you ever go to Le Sentier? The Polish neighborhood?" I chattered nervously. "It's a Russian neighborhood too."

"No," she said, before I could put my foot any deeper into my mouth.

At least she'd stopped me before I could tell her about the prissy French wholesaler I'd once met who couldn't tell the difference between Russians and Poles. "Do you ever go to rue Laffitte? The street with all the art dealers?"

"All the *Impressionist* art dealers?" Tamara corrected, acid with contempt. "No." As I posed, Tamara's *no* and *no* sat in my belly, lumpish, making me regret my words. Was she through with me already, just like that? Just when I thought I might pass out from embarrassment, Tamara looked up from her easel and gave me an open, wet smile. "You beauty."

In near silence, she painted all afternoon. I felt myself dissolving into the table and chair, into the still hours, into my upraised arm. Once Kizette wandered in, stared at me with her silvery flat fish-eyes, drew a few lines, and left. At four, Tamara stretched with her whole long body, like an ermine or a snake. "We need to stop," she said. As I changed, I saw her standing at her money drawer, glancing down the hall toward Kizette's room. "Come tomorrow?" she murmured, when I stepped out from behind the screen.

"If you want," I said.

"*If?*" She laughed. "Do not lower yourself like that. You are too beautiful to fish for compliments."

"Then I don't know what to say."

"Come tomorrow," she repeated.

I felt so wobbly I reached for the wall, too dizzy to count out the money she handed me. "Yes."

The smile she gave me in reply was not a French smile: it was buttercream frosting, spread with a trowel. "What we did today?" she said. "I cannot do it again."

My face fell. Had I completely misread her? "I see."

"I have to work. I have to paint. I have to control myself."

My jaw dropped in anger. *I* was the big seductress? Blamed for my looks again, I thought. Jeez.

"You made me break my rule," she said.

"What's your rule?" I sneered. "You don't sleep with your models?"

"Not until the painting day is over."

I blinked at her.

"We work for six hours tomorrow," she said. "And then we play. No?"

Oh, I thought, thrown again. *Oh, that's all.* "All right," I said simply, glad I'd kept my mouth shut. And then I gave her half a grin. "We'll see."

I wafted home on a gust of warm July air, into an evening that lasted and lasted. I remembered my first glimpse of Paris by daylight, on a short walk with the ugly man from the ship. We had just eaten lunch in our room in the Grand Hotel, and we were heading out for a matinee: I hadn't known the opera house would be just across the street, or that the opera boxes were designed to function like private rooms in restaurants. I was just glad to be free of that hotel room for a while. The *terrasse* of the hotel was itself a miniature opera, with its jewel-colored drinks and its coffees, its wrapped squares of chocolate and cubes of sugar, its speakers of many languages, each one smoking expressively.

Leaving behind the leafy arch of rue de la Paix, I had never seen anything so magnificent: the great buildings opening onto the wide bright plaza (*place*, in French, the ugly man told me) with its spare, elegant Métro entrance, the crowds streaming both across the *place* and up out of the ground, too. I felt humbled by the massive scale and stirred by the beauty of the architecture, by the white-golden apartment buildings ranged around the traffic star in ordered harmony, rising as solemn as cliffs. "It's so beautiful," I murmured.

"What are you looking at?" the ugly man asked. "The Opéra's over there." That's when I looked left and saw the opera house itself, so grand I'd missed it, shimmering like wet fondant, like a great domed cake.

I remembered it now, my first sight of Paris: then as now, the city buffeted me with beauty from all sides. Then as now, the warm light beguiled. Then as now, I had just gone to bed with a near-stranger, but this time it hadn't sickened me. I hadn't done it to work off a debt; I'd done it for pleasure. I felt as if I were seeing Paris for the first time, a city of bridges and shining water—I detoured south, along the Seine—a city of lindens and sycamores, of cobbled islands, of bird markets and flower markets, of buttresses and gargoyles, a rose-windowed river city wheeling with pigeons. I kept walking. The cathedral bells tumbled and sang.

I crossed another bridge and bought a purple *glace aux myrtilles* at an ice cream shop with a magnificent view of the back of Notre-Dame. I ate it slowly on the Pont Saint-Louis. *This*, I thought to myself, watching the moving water, remembering the sound of Tamara setting her rings on the table. *This always. Just this.* What would I do with myself until I saw her again?

I felt like a gardenia blossom as I drifted home, fragrant and bruisable. All the familiar things in my neighborhood seemed new again: the glass-domed arcades. The odor of honey cakes stealing toward me from Pâtisserie Fouquet. The sharp chemical scent prickling out of Galerie Vollard: *huile de lin*, Tamara had said. *Térébenthine.* I noticed as if for the first time the way the white dome of Sacré-Coeur rose behind the heavy columns of Notre-Dame-de-Lorette at the end of my street, as if they were a single mismatched edifice. When I reached the fifth floor, I found another note on the door.

> *Rafaela—Could Daniel and I have the apartment to ourselves for just one more night? Pretty, pretty please?*

I paused, angry. Then I took out my key and let myself in. The chain lock wasn't on the door. Gin wasn't even there. While I ran a deep bath, I tacked up a note of my own:

I live here too.

I lay on my back in the tub, arms and legs in the air, until the water level reached my ears. I looked up at Gin's and my cosmetics lining the walls of the small bathroom. I savored the tranquil sight, and I dreaded my flatmate's return.

Virginia Wilbur was two years older than I, and had arrived in Paris only a little after I had. When a small inheritance from an uncle coincided with the arrival of Josephine Baker's first records in the States, it was no surprise that the kind of Episcopal minister's daughter who drank bootleg liquor and owned every record ever made by Mamie Smith and Her Jazz Hounds would take a steamer to Paris faster than you could say Bam Bam Bama. The first of Gin's many boyfriends was one of the owners of Belle Jardinière, so she came by the glove counter job with no effort. She kept it, however, by dint of charm, polish, and four years of private-school French, even after she exchanged her department-store boyfriend for a banker who could get her a spot in the chorus of Le Casino Revue. From there, she prevailed on the director to let her sing a solo now and then. And she was *good*. Like, in fact, Josephine Baker, she could switch, within the same line, from a staccato purr to a clear high note like a wet finger circling a wineglass. She could dance, too, like an electric eel, but I never saw her happier than when she sang.

Gin was living in the dressing room of Le Casino the night she and I first met at the Vaudeville, when our boyfriends made us sing "La Marseillaise" up on those chairs. I was living with Hervé while his wife and small children wintered on the Côte d'Azur with his in-laws. Hervé's family was due back in Paris any time, and Gin and Jacques's affair was just heating up. So Hervé and Jacques, in thrifty imitation of their superiors, decided to go in together on a room for their mistresses not far from the bank where they worked, an overwrought Delphic temple of money on rue Bergère. They installed us in a newly constructed apartment building on the site of a medieval pile that had collapsed from the constant vibration of traffic going down nearby Boulevard Haussmann. No good draught-fearing French family would live in a brand-new building while the plaster dried, so our boyfriends got the first year's lease for half-price. That's how Gin and I—strangers, but closer than most for having sung together on those chairs—became flatmates on rue Laffitte, camping with her gramophone and the steamer trunks we used as armoires, in a much nicer apartment than we could ever have found on our own. Though damp, it was cheap enough that we were even able to stay after Hervé and Jacques found other playmates, and when Gin found Daniel, he coaxed the landlord into switching the lease to Gin's and my names at the same *sèche-plâtre* rent. The postwar economy affected even landlords, especially ours, who had lost both his sons in Flanders trenches. When Daniel dangled the promise of an easy bank loan before his eyes, the landlord gave in.

As I sat up, suds coating me like meringue, I saw something had fallen under the sink: a doll's plate? An oversize white coin? With a dripping arm, I reached for it: flat on top, with a threaded edge underneath, it was the ivory cap of a man's shaving-brush tube. Daniel's. Just as I set it on the window ledge with a sigh, I heard the door bang open. "Rafaela?"

"You can come in, I'm wearing bubble bath."

Gin clicked straight into the bathroom without even taking off her hat. *"Cara mia,"* she began. She had learned the show business trick of presuming intimacy, which I often found cozy, but the Italian tidbits—especially because she only used them around me—were a bit much.

Particularly when I was already annoyed at her. "I just got in this tub. I'm not coming out until I've had a good soak."

"Soon enough you'll have the whole place to yourself, so I don't see why you can't just help me out for one more evening."

"So he asked? He really asked?"

"I'm leaving the first of August."

"Just like that?"

"I keep telling you and you don't listen. Daniel's gone to a lot of trouble to find a little place in Meaux for the two of us until we're married."

"Meaux!" Daniel regularly commuted into Paris for bank meetings, but he lived and worked an hour outside the city, in a town known largely for its mustard and Brie.

"So he really was getting that divorce all along?"

Gin gave me an opaque, pitying smile. "Yes, dear."

"And it came through?"

"In all but name."

"Ginny!" My chest flooded with giddy heat, delighted that one good story could wash away the past night's grimy cynicism. I reached for her arm and shook it with glee.

"Stop it, soapy!"

"Did he get down on one knee?"

Gin's smile tightened. She nodded.

"Ohhh! Congratulations! Can I see your ring?"

"It was his grandmother's. She was tiny. He's having it stretched."

"One big diamond? Or lots of little ones?"

"Rafaela!" she said impatiently.

"What?" I demanded. I pointed at her earrings, a gift from Daniel. "We talked about *those* for a whole hour when you two came back from Capri."

"You're being a pain."

"You're being *something*. Did you *see* this ring, or did he only tell you about it?"

"You just don't like Daniel. You don't see how he's actually being awfully fair. It'd be easier if you left, after all. Then Daniel could just come over whenever he's in Paris."

"It sounds like it would be easiest for *him* if you lived in Meaux."

"Come on. He *lives* in Meaux. His children are in Meaux. You can't expect him to never see them again."

"Gin, you're a Parisian. People who live in Meaux are called *meldois*." I made a face. "The men, I mean. It's even worse for the ladies. The *meldoises*."

"Rafaela."

"I'm just saying, are you sure you want to leave the city?"

"When two people are in love, they make sacrifices for each other."

"Yes, Miss Wilbur."

"Oh, I do sound awfully schoolmarmish, don't I?" Gin said, a little too brightly.

"Madame Daniel Gordin," I said, testing the name aloud the way young girls do. I saw her flinch. "So what I want to know is why you need the place to yourself, now that he's asked."

"He said he'd come again tonight, Rafaela. I just want to make things comfortable for him. I don't understand. Why can't you do this one little thing for me?"

"I did one little thing for you last night, and I probably have syphilis now."

"You *didn't*."

"I didn't have money for dinner. I spent every *sou* I had on the uniform for *your* stupid job, and you know what the pervert did?" Then I told her.

"Oh, *bella*. No!"

"Thank you."

"So, wait. What did you wear to work?"

"I didn't go."

Gin lowered her eyelids in long-suffering anger. "I was count-ing on you. Madame Florin was counting on you. You know, there's only one way to win at this game, and you don't even try. If you had to get an old man to pay for your dinner, couldn't you at least get him to buy you a new uniform?"

"Gin, I'll eat out. I'll piss in a pot in my room. I'll stay in there all night until I hear Daniel leave. But I'm not spending another night out like that."

"Fine," Gin said, exasperated. "Now, will you get out of the tub?"

Just before I hunkered down in my room that evening, I caught a glimpse of Gin tripping past the kitchen in her underwear, setting out candles for Daniel's visit. She was wearing the chemise I had made for her, a scanty thing we called a tunic in those days: rose colored, a heavy, drapey *peau de soie*—the kind of fabric you could just sink your hands into. Later, when I heard Gin and Daniel through the walls, I knew she was still wearing it. As I lay awake, listening to them, I wanted it back.

The sound of Daniel pulling the front door shut behind him woke me the next morning. I could feel it like a thumb pressing into the soft notch at my collarbone: the need to do something. Thanks to the wheezy grandfather, the need wasn't about money; it was about

Gin's pained lying smile, the sound of Daniel's leather shoes flap-flap-flapping down the stairs as he left. When Gin and I ate our morning *tartines* together, she thanked me for making myself scarce the night before. "It wasn't too terribly cramped in there, darling?"

I shrugged. "It sure beats the pox. Or getting chopped into little pieces. Or arrested. Or pregnant."

"All right! Shut up!" Gin said, laughing.

"So where exactly does Daniel work, anyway?"

The phone booth at Café Lorette was as snug as a confessional. "So you aren't calling to elope with me, are you?" asked Anson.

"Your dance card's a little full for that."

"Your loss."

"Listen, we were at the bar for a long time before you brought this up, but you mentioned that you had a friend who might be able to help me out."

"You're the soul of tact, Rafaela. But I wasn't as drunk as all that. Your roommate has a rotten boyfriend. Shoot."

I settled onto the shabby velvet bench in the phone booth and told him everything. "So now I have two weeks to save her from Meaux," I concluded.

"Mustardville."

"She doesn't know a soul there. She can't get work. I can't imagine he'll want her singing and dancing in his tiny town. What's she supposed to do all day, just sit in their little flat? The town's probably full of his wife's friends, who will snub her." I felt self-conscious for talking so long, but he listened quietly, letting me wear myself out. "Maybe he isn't lying," I concluded, "but an almost-divorce isn't a divorce."

"Very true," he said.

"I *see.*"

"Leave me out of this. Let's stick with your roommate."

"I just think if she knew," I insisted.

"Knew what?"

"I don't *know.* Whatever this lie is, about his divorce. I even think she knows he's lying to her, but she doesn't want to admit it."

"Sounds like. But you truly think if she knew, for example, that he hadn't actually filed for divorce, it would change her mind?"

"Of course. She loves Paris more than anything."

"More than she loves him?"

"Oh, come *on.*"

"I just wanted to make sure, before I bother my friend."

"I'm certain."

"All right. There's not much time. I'll see what I can do. Let's make a plan to meet in a week and I'll tell you what I find out."

"*Meet* you? Is *this* how you get dates?"

"So you *are* going to elope with me! Actually," he said primly, "I was going to propose we meet in a bookshop. You know Sylvia's?" He gave me the address, not far from the Luxembourg Gardens, of an English-language lending library called Shakespeare and Company, owned by an American girl named Sylvia Beach. "She published *Ulysses.* She lives with Adrienne Monnier, who owns a French bookshop up the street."

"*Lives with* lives with?"

"As in sin, my child." I laughed, my body flickering with the memory of Tamara's hands. "But you never met a more married couple, really," he added.

My curiosity made me feel exposed, and I was aware of trying hard to sound blasé. "I guess there's a lot of that sort of thing in Paris?"

"I used to run errands for a woman who called her friend her wife," he said. "They kept house together on rue de Fleurus. Americans, both. I'll bet you, ask any pair of American women in the Luxembourg Gardens, and fifty-fifty, they'll say they're married." I didn't want him to know how much I wanted him to go on. "They're not a bad lot," he concluded, "especially when you think about the messes most girls get into. Look at your friend Gin."

"True," I said, but I was only half listening. Right there in the phone booth, in that little trap of stale smoke and old sweat, a wave of desire for Tamara was passing over me so thickly I could barely hear Anson's voice as it turned serious. "Remember, my friend's not a miracle worker," he said. "He can't access court records, just bank records. But I'll see what he can do."

3

THE MÉTRO FROM NOTRE-DAME-DE-LORETTE to rue du Bac was foul-smelling but direct. On Tamara's street, I noticed *hôtels* standing apart from the usual apartment houses. *Hôtels*, I'd learned, were not hotels: single families, and titled ones at that, lived in them, set back from the street behind low walls, wide gates, and carriage houses. They didn't come cheap, these runs of sunny sidewalk. I could hear birds. Could Tamara hear them, too? The sole glint of commerce on her street came from Bistrot Varenne, an Alsatian restaurant at the corner where Varenne met Vaneau. Even in the morning, with the restaurant shutters down, I could smell old beer as I crossed onto Tamara's block. Just two buildings from the corner, outside 63, rue de Varenne, I could smell only the lemon wax on her polished wood door. The soft morning air was lush as cream. My heart in my mouth, I waited a long time after I rang the bell, until the door opened, and it was Tamara. I tipped my face up to greet her with a kiss on the cheek, but her very stillness in the doorway stopped me. "You came back," she said, and she let me in.

Because I was eager for Tamara's workday to end, the long poses she asked of me felt all the longer: sitting at the table in the brown dress, or lying naked on my side with a book. Tamara's dog, gloomy as an exiled monarch, nosed at me once or twice before settling onto his cushion to doze. Seffa dreamed what looked like complicated dreams, which required the lifting of one eyebrow, then the other. Three times the telephone rang, and three times both painter and dog alike ignored it, so I let the sound pass over me like the birdsong I'd heard in the street. "What is your last name, Rafaela?" Tamara asked during our first break.

Had she asked me two days before, in the Bois de Boulogne, I would have used a fake name, for the same reasons my friend Maggey did. But I gave her my real name instead. "Fano. Fano," Tamara mused. "Is that Spanish?"

No, it's Italian was the short answer, but I gave her the long one. "It's the village in Spain that my father's ancestors left during the Inquisition," I said. "But we're Genovese. No one in my family has spoken Spanish for centuries."

"You are Jewish, then?" Tamara asked.

"No. My father was, but he died when I was little. My mother and my stepfather are Catholic, so that's how I was raised. You're only Jewish if your mother is, officially," I added.

It was a familiar conversation. Because of the scandal my mother and stepfather's marriage had caused on Baxter Street, the explanation my mother had drilled into me never washed with the other girls at Most Precious Blood. I was the only Jew in a Catholic school, as far as they were concerned: I had no friends there. When I changed schools a year later, my Irish classmates at Saint Joseph's didn't know enough to ask about my last name.

Adult Parisians knew enough. Usually, they listened to my explanation and gave my face a measuring look. It was I, however, who measured them, based on what they said next. Responses varied from the benign (*Interesting,* or *Ah, so you're Catholic, then?*) to the slightly annoying (*You don't look Jewish,* or *Italians and Jews look similar, don't they?*) with a few distasteful ones here and there. One man had said to me, "Once a daughter of Israel, always a daughter of Israel, *n'est-ce pas?*" Another had asked, "Is it true what they say about *les Juives?*" Was what true? I didn't wait around to find out.

So I watched Tamara carefully when I explained. "I see," she said, nodding. As she ran her fingers through her hair, her topaz darted a fleck of light across the walls. "Your grandparents were ahead of their time, no? To let your parents marry?"

I relaxed. "They eloped," I said.

"They must have loved each other very much."

I smiled. No one had ever said that to me. "They did."

"It shows," she said. "Look at how beautiful you are. And how old are you?"

"Seventeen," I said, trying not to grin like a fool.

She watched me shake out my stiff limbs, and sighed. "You can hold any pose at seventeen."

"How old are *you?*"

"Twenty-seven. Just like the century."

"Not so old as all that, then."

"Not so old as I feel."

I laughed wryly: I knew what she meant. "Your English is so much better than my French," I said apologetically.

"I learned it as a child," she said, shrugging.

"You lived in England?"

"I had a British nanny," she explained, using an extra-British accent. "But you? How old were you when you came to Paris?"

"Sixteen. I've just been here a year. How old were you?"

"I came here in '18. Kizette was born just after we arrived." Kizette was younger than she looked, I realized: eight or nine, not ten or eleven.

"Why did you move when you were pregnant?" I asked. "That sounds hard."

"The decision was not up to me."

"Your husband's job?"

"Ah, to be an American. Nineteen seventeen is just a number to you?"

"I'm sorry. I don't know what happened in Poland in 1917."

"We lived in Saint Petersburg."

Oh, the Russian Revolution, I thought, feeling stupid. "Were the Poles on the White Russians' side?"

Tamara's expression—the same icy look she gave me when I asked about the jam in my tea—made me feel no less stupid. "We are always on our own side," she said. "The point is, I am a Pole, but I am also a countess. So you can understand why we had to leave Russia."

"Because of the Communists?"

"Rafaela," she said wearily. "*Belle, belle* Rafaela."

"I'm sorry," I insisted. "In 1917, I was seven."

"I will show you one thing, because it is absurd how little you Americans know, and then, no more politics. All right?"

I nodded. She turned and flipped quickly through the paintings propped against the wall. She moved a stack aside to reveal a portrait, clearly hers, of a man in an elaborate military uniform. "Prince Gabriel. Cousin to the Czar. People say he is one of the men who killed Rasputin."

I nodded, knowing better than to let on that while Rasputin's name gave me a shudder, I wasn't quite sure what he had done to earn it.

"And now he is nothing, here in Paris. He lives off his wife in a wretched little flat. He had to borrow this uniform for his portrait."

So the uniform was a costume, as much as my brown sack was. Over the prince's shoulder I saw a familiar gray velvet drape: though at first glance, the background had a majestic vigor, Tamara hadn't actually painted the man in a palace. "Did you paint him here, in this apartment?" I asked. Tamara nodded. I could see the weariness in his hollowed-out handsome face, together with a puzzled, paralyzed expression. "It's as if he can't believe he isn't still royalty," I said.

"That is the face of dispossession," Tamara said. The look of injured dignity that I found endearingly grave on her dog struck me as repellent on a person. But before I could say I was sure the serfs hadn't had a rum time of it either, she added, "My husband still has that look to him." I had no idea what she had endured, I realized. I bit my tongue.

Not being able to touch Tamara until the end of the day made me want to know every little thing about her. I knew we had run over our first break already, so I waited until the next one to ask more. "Why did you move to Saint Petersburg in the first place?"

"I went to live there with a rich aunt and uncle when I was

fifteen," she said. "They invited me. Petersburg was like a fairy-land compared to Warsaw, and I knew they would spoil me rotten."

"And did they?"

"Oh, they did. What a life. We lived at one of the best addresses in town. A three-story flat full of servants and champagne. We had a box at the ballet. My aunt Stefa lent me her diamonds so I could wear them to the theater when I invited Thade Lempicki to tea. He had all these beautiful women with him that night. But he said yes."

"Lempitzky?"

"I use the French version of my name," she explained. "Lempicka."

"But Todd——?"

"*Thade,*" she repeated. "Tadeusz. Kizette's father." She looked like she might cry.

"Could you go back to Warsaw now?" I asked, treading carefully.

"He is there and I am here," she snapped. Then her face softened. "And my mother is here. I can make a life here, as a painter. Support my daughter."

"Are you in love with someone else here?"

"I am in love with *la vie parisienne,*" Tamara replied. She followed my involuntary glance over to the next room, where it fell upon her bed. I looked away, but not fast enough. "No no," she said, with a stern wag of the finger. "We paint first."

"I know. I wasn't trying——" I spluttered. "I just—I mean, did you buy that carved headboard with someone special in mind?"

"I did not 'buy' it. I had it made. I designed it myself. *For* myself," Tamara said, flourishing her cigarette holder.

Embarrassed, I changed tack. "So, do you think in French now, or in Polish? Or Russian?"

"French," she said. "I was raised to speak French to my parents and Polish to the servants."

"Your parents were French?" I asked, confused.

"No," she said impatiently. "It is what one did then."

Although Tamara claimed it was politics she shunned, it seemed she might be averse to personal questions entirely. I could understand. When I was taking classes at the Alliance Française, I heard *So, Rafaela, are you a student? Are you an artist?* a few too many times myself. During the next breaks, I discovered the less I asked, the more she spoke, though much of it was about me. "How can something as delicious as you even exist? Look at this curve," she said, tracing my hip with a clean brush. "Just decadent." During our last hour of work, she did another series of five-minute sketches, murmuring between poses, "Which one? Which one?"

"Which one what?"

"Which one to paint first? Rafaela, *you* are going to get me into the Salon exhibition this fall. I know it. But which pose?"

Was she really asking me? "I don't know."

"Do not worry." She chuckled. Oh, I realized, she hadn't really been asking. "This is just the kind of problem an artist dreams of."

Moments later, the doorbell rang. Before, I had only heard it from the outside, dull and distant. From the inside, however, it came as a hard clang. Seffa stirred in his sleep. Tamara, working, did not look up.

Then a man's voice called up from the sidewalk, using the same Slavic French. "I know you're up there."

Seffa woke, ears perked. Tamara's eyes met mine. After long seconds, the man in the street broke the silence a third time. "I'll just let myself in with my key, then."

Tamara's hands tightened around her charcoal and tablet. Seffa ran to the front hall. I heard the building door open, a tread on the stairs. Tamara did not look at me as I sat up and pulled on the red silk robe. The apartment door opened and Seffa leapt up to lick the face of the man who burst in: I recognized him from Tamara's portrait of her husband.

Tadeusz Lempicki wore his clothes with an air of being too good for them. "I telephoned—" he said, entering the salon. He broke off to take me in with a look at once appraising, predatory, and dismissive. "But I see you were busy."

Tamara stood, set down her board, and crossed her arms. "I *was* busy, thank you."

"I brought the papers we discussed."

"I'm sure Irene's happy you did."

Tadeusz saw me listening and switched to a swishing, liquid language that could only have been Polish: *Swish wish lish wish. Wish lishya. Swish lish.* He extended a large white envelope which Tamara made no motion to accept.

Neither the man nor the woman looked down at the dog that circled them hopefully. They faced each other without a word. I could see why Kizette was so discomfitingly pretty: they must have once made a striking couple, so contemporary they could have graced an advertisement for soap or motorcars, so timeless they could have ruled a long-ago tribe on horseback. His taut, beautifully regular features threw her extravagant ones into monstrous relief; his lifting, alert look of canine sensitivity made her seem all the more like a beaky, fleshy-lidded bird of prey. I could see, too, that they brought out the worst in each other: I saw a flash of cruelty in her hooded, down-tipped eyes, while his looked like two holes punched out of tin. "Is that all?" she said in French.

With sudden violence, Tadeusz tossed the envelope onto the desk. "Let's hope you can keep *this* promise," he said. As he turned to go, the dog shot down the hall in pursuit, his eager gait mocking the man's slow one.

Tadeusz caught the dog by the collar as he opened the door, but Tamara stopped him. "You have abandoned your daughter," she threw at him. "Don't take her dog away, too." Tadeusz did not reply, but neither did he take the dog.

When the door slammed, Tamara left the room and collapsed onto her bed. Seffa retreated to his cushion, whining. I went to Tamara, uncertainly, and found her curled up on her side, staring straight ahead. Her pupils were dilated, her face expressionless. "I still love that man," she said.

I felt uncomfortable, standing beside her bed. It was such a private thing to witness. I raised my hand and realized I had never touched her to give comfort before. I wanted to, but I didn't know how. "I should go," I said. She said nothing.

I changed quickly, feeling ashamed of myself for not staying, yet at a loss. When I emerged from behind the screen, however, she was standing in her bedroom doorway, her dress pooled on the floor behind her. "You should stay," she said.

"It seemed like you just—needed to—*rest*, I guess, after seeing—"

"—My husband?" she asked. "No."

She walked toward me, fresh and crisp in her slip, as if the exchange with Tadeusz had never happened. "I know you want to try out my bed."

I was surprised, given how rattled she'd seemed just moments before, by the ferocity with which Tamara demanded I touch her, by the blinding vigor with which she came. I had never met anyone like her before: heartbreak made her want sex as much as pleasure did. We fell asleep, and when I woke up she offered me her compact mirror. *"De la poudre?"*

"No, thanks." After my night with Gin and Yann, I had promised myself I'd never take cocaine again, but I didn't want Tamara to think I was no fun, so I gave her my second-best reason. "I'm a cheapskate. I can't afford to want it," I said.

"I know what you mean, that's why I only use it on my gums," she said, thumbing her teeth.

"You scared me a little there," I said.

"What?"

"Oh, come on."

"What?"

I don't know what possessed me to imitate Tamara at that moment, instead of just tell her. But I did: I tensed my prone body like a cat, like a flamenco dancer, head thrown back, one hand behind my neck, the other reaching to caress my own breast. The moment I did it, Tamara's behavior made sense to me: demanding sex felt so much better than feeling sorry for myself. "You should *stay*, Rafaela," I vamped. Tamara was silent.

I opened my eyes. Had I gone too far, making fun of her accent? "Sorry, it wasn't funny. Sorry."

"No, very funny," Tamara said. Seeing her smile, I realized I had never made fun of a boyfriend like this before, nor had any man ever pretended to be me. I liked it. "Do it again," she said.

It felt good, to fling myself back into bed, to be the Tamara who had stood before me: an extravagant monster, a gilded grotesque, a creature who lived for lust alone. "Come to bed viss me."

"Rafaela," Tamara said. I sat up, surprised by the reverence in her face. I saw there, too, the mixture of triumph and delight that comes with solving a problem. She kissed me. "How long do you think you can hold that pose?"

4

ONE WEEK TO THE DAY after I first encountered Tamara in the Bois, Anson met me in front of his friend Sylvia's bookshop, ushering me back to a nook in its depths to tell me what he'd learned about Gin's boyfriend. As I listened, dismayed for my flatmate's sake but grimly pleased I'd been right, I began to take in my surroundings a little. The shelves crammed with gilt and leather—and the walls crowded with portrait photographs—lent Anson's potato face a distinguished look. The air smelt pleasantly of pulp and acid, apples and mold. An earnest little wirehaired terrier announced each new customer. A black cat slept on a stack of books, beneath a framed drawing of the same black cat: a caption warned female customers that Lucky was an eater of gloves. On the mantel sat a bust of Shakespeare, and on the front counter stood fat copies of *Ulysses*, bound in blue: you could read the title from across the room. The room hummed with the leafy stir of patrons reading or scratching in notebooks, talking quietly, the occasional rattle of an open newspaper, the burr—only once since our arrival—of the cash till.

Presiding over this many-celled hive was the curlytopped American girl who had greeted Anson with *bisous* when we walked in. Anson had told her my name, but another favorite customer had popped in before I could catch hers. I could see her bustling on the other side of the room, constantly in motion but not nervous, now standing with one customer, recommending Joyce's *Pomes Pen-yeach*, "just published by yours truly," now telling another, "I'll set you up with a bunny," punning on *abonné*, a library subscription.

I turned to Anson. "That's Sylvia?"

Who else would it be? his expression said. "This is her store," he explained.

"But she's so young."

"She's forty," he whispered.

"No!"

"And you're actually seeing her at half-mast. Her mother just died in June."

"I'm sorry," I said. I wanted to concentrate on what Anson was saying: her mother had died. She was sad. But I found myself distracted by the physical fact of her crossing the room. Sylvia Beach had a woman lover. Anson had said so. And not just Anson: when I had mentioned my afternoon plans to Tamara, she'd told me that she often shopped at the French bookshop across the street owned by Sylvia's friend. Not *a friend of Sylvia's*. Sylvia's *friend*. The whole world knew. Sylvia Beach was evidence to me that Tamara and I weren't the only two women in history to go to bed together just because they wanted to. Dazzled, I watched her chatting with a customer, pert features scrunching with merriment. She wore a boyish jacket over a slim dress. I had to stop staring; it was rude. "Who are all these photographs?" I asked, to calm myself down.

"Authors," Anson said, as if showing off his own living room. He reeled off a few names, some of which I'd heard in school. "And what's that?" I pointed at the list of names and signatures that hung beside us. Spread over several framed sheets of typescript, the whole display extended almost from floor to ceiling.

"An American publisher pirated *Ulysses* and Sylvia organized a protest. Look, that's Albert Einstein's signature."

"Nifty," I said. "Look, W. B. Yeats. Somerset Maugham."

"That's Yates and Mom, darling, not Yeets and Moggum."

"Oh," I said, embarrassed. I glanced around, hoping Sylvia hadn't heard me, but then something caught my eye. "Wait, look, that's *your* name. Are you an author?"

"Lord, I should've blocked it with my hat. Sylvia just had me sign this because I was in the store."

"But why don't sportswriters count? Einstein should be proud to be on a list with you."

Anson rolled his eyes at my flattery. "I did write a book, once," he said. "But it wasn't very good."

"Really? I never met anyone who wrote a book before."

"Just some poems and stories. You don't have to look at me like that. My friend Bobby paid a printer to run off a few copies, that's all."

"Is it here? Can I see it?"

"Not anymore; this was years ago. And the poems were so bad." He lowered his voice and glanced significantly from the photograph of Joyce on the wall to the slim green volumes of *Pomes Penyeach* displayed beside *Ulysses*. "Almost as bad as that fella's."

I had never read anything by James Joyce, but making fun of him made Sylvia seem a little more human to me. "That's blasphemy in here, isn't it?" I whispered back.

"Heresy," he said.

We shared a muffled laugh as a narrow-faced, fair-haired man let himself into the bookstore with a kiss on the cheek for Sylvia and a sausage-end for the terrier. "Any mail?"

"Speak of the devil," said Anson, as the taller man reached into the wall of pigeonholes behind the cash till. "Well, if it isn't Bobby Nightinghoul."

"Anson, you bum. Whatcha up to?" Bobby asked, knifing across the room to our back corner. He had thinly blue eyes and a turquoise earring in one ear. Looking me up and down, he gave Anson a punch in the ribs. "You lucky son of a gun."

"Show some respect, Bobby," Anson said, punching back.

"This place is a post office, too?" I asked, to get Bobby's eyes off my chest.

"Annie bought the pigeonholes for Sylvia. Aren't they handsome?" asked Bobby.

"Annie?" I asked.

"My loving wife."

"Marriage of convenience," Anson explained. "Annie lives in Switzerland with her girlfriend."

"Rich English parents. Nobility. *Very* conservative," said Bobby. "You would set off a fire alarm in their house, honey." The combination of his sissified gestures and his needling sexual attention confused me.

"Annie writes letters to her parents and sends them here," Anson explained. "And then Sylvia puts French postage on them so the parents don't know she's in Switzerland."

"They think we're two lovebirds," said Bobby, laughing. "Whatever keeps the money coming in." Hearing about yet another female couple, my breathing felt a little shallow. Anson was right; Paris was full of them. "Come on down to the Sélect, Handsome Hall, and bring your little *panna cotta* with you. Janet and Solita will be there. Let's all have some drinks on my in-laws."

"In an hour, Bobby."

"Don't you fail me, boy."

"Will you really go join him?" I asked, after Bobby chatted his way out of the bookshop.

"Not right away," said Anson, amused. "He's a drunk and a letch, but he's not a bad guy. He buys drinks for everybody. He publishes his friends." Anson gestured back at the framed list of names, which made me think of a question: I held on to it as he continued. "He even typed part of *Ulysses* for Joyce *and* lent him money. Adieu to *that*," he said, waving good-bye to Bobby's said money. "But the thing about Bobby is, he's a stranger to the concept of paid work. So you can't just drop by for a drink unless you're ready to knock off for the night."

I laughed, and asked my question. "Are you writing another book now?"

"You don't give up, do you? But no. Really, it's for the best. I used to think I was going to be the next Gabriele D'Annunzio. You didn't know how to pronounce that name either, did you?"

"What do you take me for?"

"Sorry. Well, to make a long story short, I lost all my work, and that's what brought me back to my senses."

"Oh, Lord. Was there a fire?"

"It was stolen. No, it's not like that," he said.

"What happened?"

"You really want to know?" Anson's expression was equal parts embarrassment and gratitude. He idly picked up a copy of *This Side of*

Paradise and reshelved it backward, spine facing in. "Well, my first winter here, I went to cover a story in Switzerland." Switzerland, I thought, getting distracted, where Bobby's wife lives with her girlfriend, writing deceptive letters to her rich parents. Imagine! "While I was in Lausanne, I met a man from a publishing company who said he wanted to read some of my work. Of course I was over the moon. So I told my wife in a letter, and she packed up all my stories into a suitcase and brought them to me on the train. Except the stories never made it to Switzerland. They never even left Paris. She loaded the suitcase on the train; she stepped out to buy a Perrier for the trip, and when she got back on the train, the suitcase was gone." I gasped. He laughed. "It was a cheap suitcase, too. The poor thief couldn't have gotten more than a few centimes for it."

"I think I'd be heartbroken," I said.

He forestalled my pity with more laughter. "It did put me off writing stories," he said.

"It put you off your wife a bit, too, I imagine?" I asked lightly, trying to match his tone.

Anson recoiled. "It's not like that," he said. Suddenly he wasn't laughing. I didn't understand. What I'd said *was* callous, but hadn't he started it? He was looking down, as if suddenly fascinated by the copies of *The Little Review* shelved at my feet. "I met somebody else," he said stiffly.

I chose my words with care, trying not to offend him again. "Is this the person your friend's wife mentioned? The night we met?"

"I should've known you'd weasel it out of me," he said, his momentary touchiness gone. "It's not a very original story. My wife and I were young; we were in love; we had a son. And then I met another girl. Polly and I fell in love, but I still loved my wife."

"Despite the suitcase."

"Of course despite the suitcase," he said, snappish. I couldn't read his face. "So I asked her for a divorce. She said if I could stay away from Polly for a year and a day and I still wanted that divorce, I could have it."

"A year and a day. Like in a fairy tale."

"And what a fairy tale it is, my friend. I'm here, and Polly's waiting out the year with her family in Missouri."

"Why did you agree to this?"

"That's personal."

"Sorry," I said, and this time I knew better than to push. "How long has it been?"

"Ten months."

"You're nearly there."

"Maybe so," he said, gazing at the titles behind me: *Canzoni*, *Personae*, *Umbra*. "But after ten months you start getting a little funny."

"You're still sure of you and Polly, though?"

He nodded.

"And you've never wanted to just go back to your wife?"

"'Course I have. But I never—" he began. "I just didn't want to confuse either of us."

"And there's been nobody else this whole time?"

"Well, there *have* been little things here and there," he said. He sounded *so* casual about it, I wondered if he was exaggerating. "But nothing serious. I'm full up with serious."

"Evidently."

He laughed.

"Do you ever get to see your son?"

"Now and then," he said. "We go to the zoo. He's four."

"Sweet."

"Well, now you know my whole sad story."

"You already know mine," I said.

"You do what you have to do," he said. I heard no judgment in his voice, only a benign, tacit complicity: there were things he wasn't telling me, and there was plenty I wasn't telling him.

"Well, what I have to do *now* is figure out how to tell Ginny what you just told me. Or not."

"I can't help you there, sweetheart."

Just then, the bookstore terrier burst into an ecstasy of barking: a moonfaced Frenchwoman entered the store. Sylvia clasped her briefly, without stooping, even though the woman was half a head shorter. "That's Adrienne Monnier," Anson explained, following my eyes. Adrienne wore a black waistcoat over a flowing shirtwaist and a billowy full-length skirt. Unlike her bobbed companion, the dumpling-shaped Frenchwoman wore her long hair in a chignon; she was fanning herself with her hat as she and Sylvia talked, their faces close.

"How long have they been together, then?"

"Ten years, I think," he said. "Love *does* work out for some of us mortals."

I knew I was staring again, and that I should stop. But it was a lot to take in, all at once.

The next morning, after Daniel left the flat, I bathed and dressed quickly, then brought a flask over to Café Lorette. "Oh, Rafaela, you shouldn't have," Gin said when I returned with coffee for her.

"Gin," I said seriously. As I opened my mouth to deliver my preamble—*You know I'd never say anything to hurt you*—I looked at her: she really *had* been transformed by love. There was a soulful, meditative look to her sharp features I'd never seen before. Her eyes shone so wetly, I lost my nerve, and said instead, "We've had so much fun in this flat."

"Oh please, don't use that tone of voice, Rafaela."

"What tone of voice?"

"Like I'm dead and buried in Meaux already. Please, please, please, please, please don't tell me you've found another girl for the flat?"

Gin's eyes weren't shining with love; she was just upset. "What is it?" I asked.

"He said September first!"

"You mean, instead of August first?"

Gin nodded. "So I went to Madame Florin and got my job back," she gulped, and then began crying in earnest. I was surprised such great honking gasps could come out of such a tiny person.

"Oh, Ginny. Oh, Gin."

When Tamara had cried over her husband a few days before, I hadn't known how to comfort her. A year of hangovers, achy shoes, and high-rolling men had eroded that sort of physical shyness between me and Gin. We had cried in front of each other before. Not only had we fooled around the one time, we had mopped up each other's vomit on more than one occasion. When I threw out my homemade granny rags, Gin was the one who took me to buy my first box of sanitary napkins. Now I drew circles on her back with the flat of my hand, like a mother with a sick child. Telling her at this point just seemed cruel. But what if not telling her made her suffer longer? "I have to ask you something."

"What?" she sniffled.

"What if you found out he wasn't divorcing his wife at all?"

Gin wiped her eyes. "Rafaela, I ask myself that all the time. Of course I want to believe him, that he'll leave her. But you know what I decided? These things happen. I wouldn't be the first married man's girlfriend in the world."

"So you'd still go to Meaux?"

"Whenever he wants," Gin said. Then she looked up hopelessly, speaking more to herself than to me. "But why did he say August first and then September first? It's not fair."

I didn't feel cruel when I said the next thing I knew: I felt mythic, implacable, possessed by something larger than myself. "What if you found out he had a mistress in Meaux as well as his wife, and that's why he didn't want you to come?"

"Oh, Rafaela, why are you so awful?"

"Well? What would you do, if you *knew* it was true? If you had proof?"

I had seen Gin onstage a few times at Le Casino, and had been arrested by the purity with which she could express emotions, even those she herself had never experienced. I was stunned all the more so now as she considered my question. She looked crushed. Then angry. And then I saw her dainty face transformed by a kind of savage possessiveness. It jarred me. I recognized the ferocity I had recently seen in Tamara's body, that I had echoed in my own when I had made fun of her. Gin's face shut down and a voice I had never heard her use tore its way out of her: "I would still go to him."

5

GIN AND I DRIFTED APART a little after that morning, perhaps because it pained me so much to see her suffer Daniel's lies, perhaps because I began spending so much time on rue de Varenne. Tamara called the monstrously sexual pose I'd struck to tease her *La Belle Rafaela*, or *Beautiful Rafaela*: I lay supine, torqued, with one hand behind my head, the other, it seemed, fingering my own breast. Looking longer, as Tamara planned it, the viewer would discover that my hand was actually lifting the barest scrap of red silk robe toward that breast, as if to mock the very idea of modesty. She cut a sleeve off the robe so that she could place it on the floor beside the couch—a zone of red—and she taught me how to drape the rest of the robe across my lower legs the exact same way each time I posed. It would not simply be a robe; it would govern the colors of the painting: red robe, ochre flesh, gray couch, black background wall. She bought me a lipstick the same red.

Tamara painted me in the *Belle Rafaela* pose daily, driven. September first became for me not Gin's moving day (especially since, soon enough, she announced it was October first instead), nor the day that Anson's girl was to set sail for France, but the date by which Tamara would have to submit two paintings to the jury of the Salon d'Automne, which would open November fourth. One of them, she decided, would be the painting of her daughter on the balcony, which had just won a medal in an exhibition in Bordeaux. The other would be me.

I could not hold the pose for long. It hurt. Tamara handled this by working on at least two paintings at a time, one with a difficult pose, the other with an easy one: half asleep beside a book, nude, or on my side, wearing the silk slip I'd reclaimed from Gin. When I had my period, which animated Seffa so much Tamara had to lock him in her bedroom, she posed me clothed—wearing a white shawl flocked with dots, holding flowers—for a painting she called *Full Summer*.

Every day I posed for *Beautiful Rafaela*, I experienced the same thing. First, the simple strangeness of being naked in a place not designed for nudity. Being naked in a room whose other inhabitant was clothed. Being naked in a room with windows, even if no one could see into the room from the outside. A separate shock: being naked in a room with windows open to every stir of summer air.

Then, as I moved into the pose, I felt two separate waves of lust: one as myself, just wanting the workday to be over so I could drag Tamara off to bed; the second, oddly, as the woman in the painting. The glow from the window fell plumb down my body from sternum to navel until the front slab of my ribcage became a hot slam of light to the eye. The more I arched my ass, the deeper that light fell across me, and the louder the voice of the painting purred in my throat: *Aren't I beautiful?*

Every time I took the pose that summer, it took *me*, the way an actress's role might dictate her feelings to her, the way Gin's songs made her their own. For a few seconds out of every day that I posed, the pose rode my body; she haunted me. *Have you ever seen anything like me?* she said. *I was made for this, for you to want.* They say, *Kneel, pray, and you will believe in God.* Arrange your limbs the way I did, and you will believe you *are* a god, a goddess made to subjugate the earth with a glimpse of your flesh alone.

Until your back begins to hurt. A few seconds in, the ecstasy would pass, and within five minutes, I would experience four separate unpleasant sensations, like four telephones ringing in the same room. Sweat that filled the instep of my right foot where I braced it on my left. A throb at exactly the spot that the trick of the painting, Tamara had told me, would announce as "closest" to the viewer: my right kneecap. A stabbing cramp exactly where Australia would fall on the right globe of my ass. And halfway between the wrist and elbow of the hand that tugged the red robe, a tendon pain like nothing I'd ever known, a pain remarkable for its precision and inevitability. Having the spot drilled with a dull pencil and electrocuted at the same time might have felt similar. After one especially long day when I collapsed out of the pose, Tamara groaned with disappointment and impatience. "*You* try doing this," I snapped.

"You try doing *this*!"

But there was nothing else I wanted that August, as my body burned like the linden leaves scorching in the sun outside, than to be looked at by Tamara. The only minutes that went slower than the ones I spent posing for *Beautiful Rafaela*, watching Tamara sink into the marks she made, were the ones I spent without her: during two of my hourly breaks each day, Tamara took Seffa on a short walk, alone, she said, so as not to waste time on my dressing and undressing. I waited all day for Tamara to come back from those walks, for her to climb up out of her work and touch me. We wracked the poor bed those summer afternoons. Sometimes Tamara would rub cocaine into her gums before we made love, and even after she came and came, she still glittered with hunger. The next morning she would have shadows under her eyes. "I could not sleep. The state you had me in." And we would wait all day again.

The last week she worked on *Beautiful Rafaela*, Tamara painted less and less, looked at me more and more. On the last day of August, after a week of applying tinier and tinier strokes of paint, Tamara stepped back, midday, and took off her apron. "Not bad."

"That so?"

"I am going to miss this painting so much. Look at it."

I felt a jab in my wrist—the one cramped from reaching for the red robe for six weeks—as I finally *did* tug the one-sleeved robe across my chest to go stand before the painting. "It's me." But it was me as I had never seen myself: lit from the inside, magnificent. I could not see a single brushstroke until I put my face up close to the painting, and then they appeared, like single strands on a head of hair, like the single interlocking fronds that compose a feather. Even half a step back, they disappeared, and I emerged again, radiant. "It's beautiful," I said.

"I know."

We stared at it quietly for a moment.

"Rafaela, there is only one way I can let this painting go, even for just a couple of months to the Salon."

"If you know you have a buyer?"

"No. If you let me paint it again."

"What?"

"I have never copied one of my own paintings before. I have never liked anything I did enough. Please, Rafaela—"

"You are. Never. Painting. My hand like that again."

Tamara blinked at me. "Well, what if I don't paint your hand?"

My mother and stepfather had sent me away to get married without asking me. My first boyfriend in Paris was a man I'd been passed to like a secondhand toy. I had made a grand stand just then, but I hadn't expected to be taken seriously. I stared at her. "Well," I said. "In that case."

6

"*WELL, WHAT IF I DON'T PAINT your hand?*" I repeated, as I walked down rue de Varenne. I was laughing to myself, a tight loud laugh, like a whole balloon of air forced out of a narrow tube one hiccup at a time. With Guillaume and Hervé, my choices had been as clear as they'd been with my mother and stepfather: go along with what they wanted, or just go. With Tamara, however, it occurred to me, maybe I could have something different. Could she teach me, I wondered vertiginously, how to have a lover who was also a friend? My neck felt rubbery and strange, the way it had when Guillaume first had my hair bobbed. I was in no state to get on the Métro and go home to the dress I was making. The day was brilliantly blue: I walked down the Boulevard Saint-Germain until the ringing tightness that I felt loosened. I went to sit in Sylvia's bookstore again, because it was nearby, and because, as with the prospect of telling Tamara what I wanted and did not want, what I would and would not do, the bookstore made me aware of just how much I didn't know.

As I approached the shop, I saw Adrienne Monnier walking toward me, dressed once again as if from another age, in a nipped-in black velvet waistcoat over a flowing gray skirt and shirtwaist. The chignon crowning her round face made me think of the distinctive knob on a brioche. She seemed agitated, and as I greeted the overeager shop terrier a moment later, I learned why. Sylvia stood mid-conversation with a harassed-looking French postman holding a large flat package in one hand and mopping his brow with the other. "You're Anson's friend, aren't you?" she asked fondly, and seemed about to tell me something when Adrienne burst in.

"*Et voilà,*" huffed Adrienne, counting out money for the postman, at whose departure the two women exchanged smiles—tinged with indulgence on Sylvia's part and with irritation on Adrienne's.

"Well, that was a madcap caper," said Sylvia, as if to me, to which Adrienne replied in French with something quick and pointed, though not, it seemed, aimed at Sylvia.

"What was?" I asked.

Sylvia pointed to the package. "Joyce is in Delft and sent himself a Vermeer print to the store, charging the postage to me, because he's running out of money again, the poor thing. And just as luck would have it, I didn't have enough in the till. So I had to send for Adrienne to lend me some."

Adrienne sighed. I was struck, despite her annoyance, by her high, sweet voice. "He may have no money of his own," I understood her to say, "but he has no trouble spending yours or mine. Or Bobby's, for that matter," she added, pointing out the window. Anson's friend Bobby Nightinghoul was approaching the store, turquoise earring and all, an arm across the shoulders of a slim young woman in a pale straw cloche. Because of the hat, I couldn't see her eyes at first, but I could tell from the shape of her beautifully made-up mouth that the woman was crying.

At first glance, I took the pair approaching the open door for lovers, unhappy ones, but when the woman's shipwrecked eyes came into view, it was clear that the cause of her misery lay elsewhere. "Thelma just can't help catting around, sweet pea," came Bobby's flat voice through the open doorway. "You gotta let her go." They paused briefly outside the store, as if about to enter. The woman saw the three of us watching, and turned away, embarrassed. Bobby gave a tiny, apologetic wave, and followed the woman up the street.

"What a shame," said Sylvia.

"She did go looking for trouble, but still . . ." Adrienne agreed, wincing on the girl's behalf.

Wasn't Bobby married, for money's sake, to a woman who lived in Switzerland with her girlfriend? Had the two women broken up? "Is she his wife?" I asked.

"June? No, she's one of his authors," Sylvia explained, gesturing toward a stack of woodcut prints on the mantel. "In progress, that is. He publishes a lot of our friends," she said, indicating someone I couldn't see on the far side of the room. I watched the pair walk up the street. I liked him better when he wasn't looking at me. "*We* published *him* too," Sylvia added. "We translated him into French for Adrienne's magazine."

"That man's *language*," Adrienne said, fanning herself in mock scandalized horror. In English, her voice lilted and fluted just as much as it did in French. "Just think, all the American men who want to learn the French they don't teach in school have two little women to thank," she said, with a minxy glance at Sylvia.

"I just about went blind on that translation," Sylvia said, pleased. "On New Year's, Joyce and I had matching eye patches!"

A protective look darkened Adrienne's face. "Bobby gives the man a hundred and fifty pounds a month," she said. "Why are we paying his postage?"

"And to top it off, Joyce wants us to have this framed for him at Vavin's," Sylvia added, brandishing the letter that had come with the package. She laughed. "With a thick black frame, like the ones Vermeer paints into his paintings."

"*Mon Dieu,*" said Adrienne, shaking her head. She leaned in for a quick kiss good-bye.

"What would he do if it weren't for us?" Sylvia asked as the shop door closed.

"I guess *she* won't be the one framing that picture," I joked.

"Oh, she's publishing the French edition of *Ulysses*," Sylvia rejoined. "I wouldn't worry about her."

I had overstepped myself. "She has a pretty voice," I said.

Sylvia smiled. "Doesn't she? Her people come from Savoy," she explained. "I like to imagine them yodeling to each other over the Alps."

I laughed. "What's Vermeer like?" I asked. I had heard Tamara mention his name in such a way I couldn't tell if he was a friend or an enemy.

Sylvia cocked her head at me quizzically. "You're younger than you look," she concluded. "But still, didn't Anson say you worked for a painter?" She looked across to the far side of the room again, perhaps to check on her other customers, and then pointed out a low half-shelf of art books by the register. "Here it is," she said, pulling out a tall thin volume. "Whoops, it's in Dutch, but the words aren't the point."

I curled up in a chair and flipped through the pictures. I felt foolish when I discovered that I had completely misunderstood the way Tamara talked about her fellow painter: he predated her by some three hundred years. Her paintings were slicker, bolder, and fleshier than his, but like him, she painted in the same room again and again, using the same furniture, draping her models in the same fabrics, asking them repeatedly to do painful things with their hands. In the cool Northern light of his paintings, a girl sat holding a quill pen, lost in her writing, while another girl, bored, stood looking out the window. A girl played out a spool of thread, bent over a sewing frame. A girl—most painful of all—held a pair of scales. My right hand burned with pins and needles just looking at her. *Well, what if I don't paint your hand?* I remembered, and smiled. I looked again at the girl at the sewing frame. Working for Tamara had taught me to notice something I wouldn't have seen before: the objects "closest" to the viewer, which ought to have declared themselves most, were a dark blur, while the more distant female figure sat in sharp focus. Though the painting seemed at first glance to offer a simple window into the sewing girl's room, it actually paid attention the way a person might, noticing some things, ignoring others.

"*The Lacemaker*," said Sylvia. "You like it?"

"Oh, I thought she was sewing," I blurted as I looked up, startled. Half an hour had passed in a moment. "Thank you for showing me this."

"Of course," she said, still amused by my ignorance. "You know, you *could* go see it in the Louvre sometime."

"When I went to the Louvre alone, men kept trying to talk to me. And then when I went to the Louvre with my friend Ginny, *she* kept trying to talk to me. I think I'll see more if I just sit here by myself."

Sylvia laughed. "Just wait until you're thirty," she said. But she looked at me gently and asked my name. "Well, come in anytime. Read anything you want." Something in her face—her choice not to judge me—reminded me of Anson the night we met. It made sense that they were friends. "And sometime, you should join the library and you can take books home."

I was carrying a new beaded purse full of modeling money. "I'll join today," I said. As I filled out the card she proffered, she gave me a thoughtful look and lent me a book called *A Few Figs from Thistles*. I wasn't sure I'd like it, considering the woodsy title, but I thanked her.

"'Rue Laffitte,'" she said, reading aloud the address on my subscription bunny. "Isn't that the street full of art galleries leading up toward Montmartre?"

"You can see the Sacré-Coeur from my front door," I said. I had wanted to tell Tamara about the optical illusion, particular to rue Laffitte, that fused the Sacré-Coeur with Notre-Dame-de-Lorette, but her contempt for the art dealers on my street had stopped me. I tried explaining it to Sylvia instead.

"Sacré Dame," she replied playfully. "Or Notre Coeur."

"Oooh."

"Or how about Lortre Courette?" she proposed.

"L'Ochre Courette?" I attempted.

"I like that," she said. "The little yellow-brown courtyard of the heart."

I grinned.

"I bet you'd like Apollinaire."

Was he another regular at the store? I could see why so many people came by. "Anson thinks the world of you, you know," I said.

Sylvia looked across the room once more and offered a wry, apologetic grimace. "Well, you'll never guess who's here. I keep hoping he'll wake up." She gestured with her chin toward a plush chair in a far corner where I found a man asleep behind an open newspaper. I turned down a corner of his *Herald Tribune*: it was Anson.

My friend smelled of liquor. He seemed at some point to have dipped his cuff into his dinner. I had never seen his face unshaven: his patchy, boyish facial hair reminded me of nothing so much as the thick Italian single brow I'd had as a child. I returned to Sylvia and made a face. "He's had a rough year," she said. "But he's got a heart of gold."

"Rough how?"

"Sylvia opened her mouth to tell me something, then seemed to rein herself in. He's more accident-prone than anything else. For example, he boxes, and so does our friend Jean Prévost. *He* works with Adrienne on her magazine. He's a hardheaded man; that's his claim to fame. If you ever meet a man in here who asks you to hit him on the head, don't do it. Anyway, they both box; they both write about sports. I thought they might like each other. I introduced them, and organized a match for them—and Anson broke his thumb on Prévost's head!"

"No!"

"Prévost didn't feel a thing, of course," she said, laughing.

Behind his newspaper, Anson stretched. I approached him again. His eyes, when he opened them, looked eggy and blood-streaked. "What a sight for sore eyes," he said.

"Literally, hmm?" I pulled out my compact. "Take a look at yourself."

He melodramatically turned away, hiding behind a raised arm. I laughed. "Any face but mine," he said.

"You're a mess."

"It's nice to see you, too."

"What happened?"

"Polly cabled me," he said.

"Your girl from Missouri?"

"That's right."

"She's not coming?"

Anson flung his head from side to side and slapped his cheeks a few times to wake up. Then he gave me a ghoulish smile. "She asked me to wait a little longer."

"Oh," I said. He did not elaborate. "If she really meant just a little longer, you wouldn't look like this."

"You are correct," he said, overenunciating like a wireless announcer.

"She met someone else, then."

"That would appear to be the case."

"After all this time!"

"I appreciate your sympathy, but I'm already quite aware of this fact."

I recoiled. "Are you relieved, a little?" I tried again. "I mean, you said you missed your wife. You could get back together now."

"Oh, that would solve everything." Anson's laughter was black and cold, as if he himself were the butt of the joke. What was the joke?

"Well, what are you going to *do*?" I ventured.

"Today?" Anson asked, fixing me with his eggy, bloody mien. "Drink."

I exchanged a shrug with Sylvia as I left the bookstore: there was nothing I could do for him. I was worried, though. I telephoned him the next day and was relieved to hear his voice back to its unflappable, smug self. "You caught me at a bad moment there. Can I get you dinner sometime, to apologize?"

"You've been trying to buy me dinner for months," I chided, relieved I could tease him again.

7

WHY WAS TAMARA PAINTING ME in the same pose again? I would have liked to think she did it in order to keep me around longer, but as hot September cooled toward fall, it became clear that she was doing it to calm her anxiety about the Salon jury's decision, which we would not learn until mid-October. She could have simply photographed her own painting if all she'd wanted was a copy, and the second *Belle Rafaela,* while similar, was in no way a copy of the first. The perspective was more distant, the canvas smaller. My right arm, as she'd promised, lifted out of the frame entirely. The red robe vanished from the couch, and on the floor beside it, Tamara spread a green one. The triangle of green she painted into the floor of the image lit my skin more coolly than the red robe had. It wasn't the *painting* she was copying, I realized: it was the feeling of painting it.

I understood how work could calm an anxious wait. Mid-September, Tamara went to London for a week to visit friends with a new baby. I missed her, but would she miss me? Would she bring home another model to replace me? The day she left, I decided to make a slip for her to wear against her skin, the way I wore the very thought of her against mine. Sewing for her would crumble the minutes into stitches. I could portion out the hours with the smooth push of my shears.

First I would need fabric from Le Sentier, a district whose narrow streets I had not discovered until after I broke up with Guillaume. My first winter in Paris, when I went back to Chanel to learn that they'd given up on my collecting the red satin dress, I did not bring Hervé with me, so I was alone to face the indignation of the *couturières* who thought I'd stiffed them. "We sold it as a sample, *bien sûr*," said the *directrice*, a black-clad picket of indignation. I searched the busy room behind her for a glimpse of the elegant seamstress who had fitted me, which only managed to annoy the *directrice* all the more. *"Pourquoi faire autrement?"* she asked, so icily that although I had Hervé's money in my purse, more than enough to order a new dress, I didn't even try. I walked down the mirrored staircase, stung. Outside, when I looked back at the Chanel entrance, I noticed the smiling stone girl carved over the door: she seemed to be laughing at me. I trudged away, remembering my neighbor Theresa in her slim rose frock. Why couldn't *I* have a dress that lovely? I stopped: Why *shouldn't* I have a dress that lovely? Could I copy it? Or something like it? I looked back at the stone girl, and inhaled. Why not? I would need fabric.

I asked the first person I saw—a man with a sample case, standing at a side entrance to the rue Cambon townhouse—where to find Le Sentier. The concierge in my building had once mentioned the fabric district to me when I had complimented her on her new apron. She had made it herself, she said; it was nothing.

I followed the tradesman's instructions west in the fading winter light. I crossed the Avenue de l'Opéra and looked away from the glistening sugary dome of the opera house, remembering my arrival in Paris. I lifted my chin as I walked away: *I won't have traded anything in vain*, I told myself. I walked down rue des Petits-Champs and passed the familiar arcades leading to the Palais Royal, with its aisles of manicured trees. Looking a few blocks to the left, I could see the columns of the Bourse, while before me loomed a statue of one of the Kings Louis on horseback, half naked in sandals, above a plaque showing him in what must have been his normal ruffly attire.

It wouldn't be my first time making a dress, I reflected. When I was small, my father and his brother, Elio, ran a small piecework shop out of the front of their long dark slit of a flat on Baxter Street. I can still remember the clack and shudder of sewing machines as my Zia Rina shooed me and my cousins out from underfoot, chasing us out to the kitchen where she pressed the finished garments, tying us to our chairs when despair—in the form of Lazzaro overturning a pot of *fagioli* or Beniamino soiling himself again—struck her. On Fridays at sunset when she lit the candles, adults and children faced each other warily, unknown to each other after a whole week spent at opposite ends of the apartment.

My father died when I was three, in one of the waves of tuberculosis that regularly winnowed the tenements where I grew up. I have one memory of him alive—him carrying me up the stairs, his heart under my ear—and one memory of him dead: in bed, on the far side of the flat. I'm peering around what must be my mother's leg at his gray deflated face, the dark hollows of his closed eyes. I can remember a funeral, my Zio Elio lifting me up to see a coffin that must have been my father's. I remember, with odd clarity, a phrase in Hebrew from the rabbi's eulogy, about the well in the desert that the exile found. Was America a desert for my father? I wish I could remember him with his eyes open.

After the funeral, my Catholic mother, living with her Jewish in-laws, continued going with them to Saturday services in the basement flat of New York City's only Genoese rabbi. On Sundays, however, she took me to church alone. My first clear memory of my mother is of her dressing me for Mass, my black frock belling out over layers of petticoats while the sewing machines storm in the front room.

"Black dresses are ugly!" I complain.

"Don't disrespect your father like that," she says, covering my mouth. She takes a handful of straight pins and cinches her own black dress tight across the chest. She is twenty-two; her wavy hair spreads in a thousand colors from dry wheat to wet sand. "If you're good, and you don't spoil your dress or cry in church, maybe one day we'll meet somebody, and he'll buy you all the dresses you want," she promises grimly.

When I was six, my mother married Sal Russo. My stepfather had immigrated to the States in 1890, and had spent twenty-odd years building up an import business with his brother back in Sicily: cheese and almonds, olive oil and wine. He was neither young nor handsome when he met my mother, but he was rich, and his wife was sick. When his quick remarriage after her death outraged the immigrant church ladies, he bought my mother the brownstone on West Tenth Street, where she bore him my four brothers in rapid succession. We traded Most Precious Blood for Saint Joseph's on Sixth Avenue.

I switched schools after the first grade. I liked English, and I was good at school, but although I was glad to get away from the snide girls of Precious Blood, I missed my aunt Rina. As often as not, I forged a note for my teacher and found my way back to Baxter Street, stopping first at my favorite candy shop off Prince Street for a chocolate star for each of us. I liked watching my aunt work. After each garment passed through the jaws of Zio Elio's loud machine, Zia Rina would take out the pins and hand them to me. Noting the galaxy I'd lovingly arrayed on the pincushion, she warned, "Don't stick them in all the way, like you're stuffing a goose. It takes me extra time, see, and it hurts my fingers more. Just the tips of the pins, *ragazza*."

If I had been a boy, I might have apprenticed with the Fanos; I might still be on Baxter Street today. The day I fixed a sewing machine, my uncle Elio made everyone stop work and applaud. When my Zia Rina told me I had learned enough to make a dress for myself, I felt like I'd won a prize. Puffed up from my visit to the old neighborhood, I went home and proposed to my mother that she give me a month off from making my brothers' breakfast if I could copy my school uniform so well that none of my teachers would notice. She agreed to my wager, and turned a blind eye when I cut one of my two uniforms apart stitch by stitch to trace it. A week later when I brandished my new navy pinafore for her—the same navy pinafore I was wearing when I met the ugly man on the ship—she stood by her word.

On the cold day when I first looked for Le Sentier, the winter before I met Tamara, I found that the neighborhood started to go downhill once I spoked away from the statue of King Louis on horseback, especially after I crossed rue du Louvre. I passed walled *hôtels* gone to ruin. The streets grayed, then narrowed. The buildings, which up until Place des Victoires had been fronted in *pierre de taille*, were whitewashed with calcimine in this quarter, and not often. With the butter-pale cut limestone, the fruity carved festoons vanished, too. Scruffy Place Caire was full of staring workmen. I knew I had reached the right neighborhood when I spotted a man wheeling a garment rack across the cobblestone street. That's when I realized the whirring hum that filled the air in bursts was the sound of dozens of sewing machines treadling in upstairs ateliers. I slid down an alley as narrow as a drain, quixotically named Street of the Moon. I passed the sullen little fortress of a columned church—Our Lady of Good Welcome—and found myself face-to-face with a massive arch featuring mythological naked men beneath suits of empty armor, weirdly fitting for the garment district. Mixed in with the armor, I saw a lionskin: representing the fur trade? The arch, one of the old gates to the city, dominated the Grands Boulevards, which had been built on the site of the old city walls. It seemed I had overshot Le Sentier.

One street over, I cut back into the neighborhood I'd left and walked quickly down a block of hard-faced girls wearing little under the coats they opened, cackling at the men who walked by: rue Saint-Denis. "Don't you like me?" a girl called after the man walking ahead of me. "Well, why not?" she screeched. *"Pédé!"* I pulled my own coat tighter and cut back toward the hum of the sewing machines. On the second pass, I found rue de Cléry.

My concierge had warned me not to bother with any of the

wholesale places, and although I lingered over many a lavish window display, I passed several shops before I found one that did not declare itself a merchant *en gros*. When I rang the bell of Tissus Léon, I noted the tilted metal case, no bigger than a matchbox, tacked on the doorframe: it was the first mezuzah I had spotted since my Zia Rina's. I gave the black box a superstitious tap and kissed my gloved fingertips before the shopkeeper could open the door. Blocking my way into the warm, silk-filled room, the big-bellied Parisian took in my good coat, my painted mouth, my kid gloves. "We only sell wholesale, miss," he concluded: I did not fit the profile of a buyer *en gros*.

"But you have no—" I broke off. At the sound of my accent, he drew back an inch or two. What was the word for "painted notice"?

"Aren't you Jewish, Mademoiselle?" he asked. Between the prayer box on the door and the little cloth cap he was wearing, I knew not to take offense. I nodded, trying to get on his good side. "Then surely you know no Frenchman in Le Sentier will sell retail," he sniffed politely.

I half laughed, flabbergasted. Obviously I wasn't from the neighborhood, let alone French, but were Jews so bound to the garment trade that I should just *know* what he was telling me?

"Go to the Russians, down the street," he said. "Go to the Poles." Back in the cold, I walked in the direction indicated by M. Tissus Léon's dismissive hand, until the quarter took an even shabbier turn. Garment racks crowded *this* part of the street, and the sewing machines jabbered overhead like cicadas, their sound blending with the smell of boiled cabbage and beets. If the Slavic voices jostling past me had been Italian ones, I could have been on

Baxter Street. The door of the first fabric store I saw at this end of
rue de Cléry featured, along with a black mezuzah of its own, the
sign I'd been looking for: *au détail*.

A quick look inside the brightly lit Tissus Léon had told me that
if I was looking for twenty shades of the same gauge of silk, I had
come to the right place. Two minutes in the dim aisles of Silovic et
Fils revealed that if I ever wanted to cover damp walls, patch an
awning, or make a mailman's bag, they had the sackcloth, oilcloth,
and canvas I was looking for, together with kitchen toweling,
cheesecloth, and table linen. I turned to go, disappointed and foot-
sore, but a vastly pregnant girl my age called after me in heavily
accented French. "Have you seen our other room, Madame? Ah,
Mademoiselle?"

"Anya!" called a man's voice from the back.

"My husband," she said apologetically, turning. "I'll be right
back."

At Anya's behest, I found an inner room full of wool, cotton,
and silk, the quality of which seemed just as good as Léon's, if the
range of colors more scattershot. I chose a white muslin, cheap but
serviceable, with which to make my pattern. I found the creamy
peau de soie—in the same shade of rose as Theresa's Chanel dress—
that would one day become Gin's tunic. And I discovered a sumptuous roll of silk, a jewel-blue shantung shot through with just
enough tussah to break up the sheen into dozens of glittering sur-
faces. My lucky dress.

Leaving, I realized I wasn't far from the Boulevard Haussmann
at all. I was only a ten-minute walk from the bank where Hervé
worked on rue Bergère, only a fifteen-minute walk from home. I
paused to memorize the address for Silovic et Fils. When I looked

back, I saw Anya Silovic lumbering out the door, a bundle of cut garments slung across her back. I looked at her and thought, I bet *she* would know where I could find a good pair of shears.

After botching several yards of muslin in the weeks that followed, I abandoned my idea of copying Theresa's dress from memory: it was a knit, not a weave; who was I fooling? I turned instead to a fashion magazine pattern for a similar cut—and soon I had a new dress. Gin was appalled when I returned so much of Hervé's money, but Hervé was charmed, and demanded we go out dancing the first night he saw me in my lucky dress.

Hervé was an excellent dancer, and thanks to him I became a good one. I did not enjoy the all-too-brief but all-too-frequent bouts of sex he preferred, nor did I enjoy performing the aria of gratitude he liked to hear every single time he got on top of me for a minute and a half. But I did like dancing with him. I liked his escutcheon-shaped face and his minky-thick hair. I liked how devoted he was to his children. I liked that he paid for more French classes, and I was touched by the simple cockiness with which he gave me pretty things. I didn't find out until I sold them, but the pearls he bought me were real. I wish I'd thanked him more.

I hadn't simply fallen in with Hervé, nor had I been handed to him like a bribe. It was on this wave of well-being that I labored over a letter in Italian to my Zia Rina, telling her I was alive and safe in Paris, and that I missed her. I was engaged to a nice man who took good care of me, and did she think I should contact my mother?

I guess I didn't lie so well about being engaged. No sooner had

I received a letter from my aunt saying that my mother wanted nothing to do with me than I also received one from my mother herself, saying the same. *You brought shame on our family, you little whore*, my mother's letter said. The day I got her letter, I took it to Notre-Dame-de-Lorette, lit a candle, and tried to pray. I loved the gloomy skylit domes of that little church, the milky-glass windows bordered in blue, forlorn above the baroque bric-a-brac. But when I looked up at the carved mild face of Mary, I knew she would have stayed on that Alia-bound boat like a good girl. *Fiat mihi secundum verbum tuum:* we'd sung that song in school. I knew she would have never run away with my father the way my mother once had. My mother and I were two of a kind, and our bitterness lay beyond the light of Mary's slim taper. I was too ashamed to write to my friends. I haven't been inside that church since.

My anger at my mother turned me against Hervé. I began to hate acting like I was having a good time when I wasn't. He had a wife and two children under the age of three, and he was stinting them for my sake. And for what? That March, when Gin was between boyfriends, I picked a fight with Hervé and she and I got the locks changed. From then until I met Tamara in July, I made do by selling Hervé's gifts, and each time I had to sell another, I'd delay it by finding a man in a hotel. My mother would have said I'd proved her right, but it felt more honest than pretending I was in love. All I wanted, after eight months of laughing and drinking with strangers whose language I spoke poorly, was to be left to myself for days on end.

Gin and I had eaten extravagantly when we'd had someone else to buy our dinners, and my French classes had made the cold days hurry by. The spring months after I broke with Hervé, however, trying not to leave home or spend money, passed slowly: I'll never forget shivering in the damp with Gin when the radiators went off. We'd slowly eat the tangerines I got by smiling at the fruit man, Gin peeling hers on the couch in the fur stole Yann had bought her, me eating mine section by section during one of my epic baths: the hot water, at least, was free. When the radiators clanked back on, they steamed us open like letters. We wafted around barefoot in our slips and fixed each other little summer cocktails. I made Gin her rose-colored tunic that season, and a sundress too. I was happier than I'd been since Baxter Street.

Tamara made me happier still, and made me anxious about losing my happiness. The day she told me she wouldn't need me for a week, I went home shaky. I looked at the book I'd borrowed from Sylvia's, and I couldn't concentrate. I had thought *Washington Square* would be about Washington Square, at least a little.

The next morning, Gin found me in the kitchen, bent over *Paris Vogue*. "Rafaela, it's a fashion magazine; it's not Greek. What are you doing?"

"There's this pattern for something I want to make for Tamara. I couldn't sleep last night." She leaned in to give me a *bisou* and I tongue-kissed her by mistake. We yelped simultaneously, recoiling. "I'm so sorry."

"Something on your mind?" she teased.

"I'm just distracted."

"Obviously. Don't you have to go to work?"

"She's away."

"Wait," she said, buttoning up her Belle Jardinière uniform.

"You want to spend the money *she* gave you to make something for her? Isn't that like not getting paid?"

"I have enough money," I protested. I had plenty, in fact. The modeling money was coming in so thick and fast, I had recently bought a Singer Electric with the wheezy old grandfather's five hundred francs.

"If you say so," Gin said. She squinted. "Are you in love with her?"

"What? No!" I snorted.

"You said you liked sleeping with her. 'I like it when she uses her fingers and her mouth at the same time,'" she mimicked.

"Shut up!" I said, mortified.

"And now look at you." Gin gestured toward the magazine. "How much proof do you need?"

"But I'm not in love with her," I insisted, crossing my arms. Something in her voice made me want to argue with her. "Because why? What would you say if I were?"

"Well, you're both girls," Gin said dubiously.

"So? I wouldn't be the only one." I sorted through the examples I had badgered Tamara and Anson to give me until I found the ones that would impress Gin the most. "Georgette Leblanc has a woman lover," I said, naming one of her favorite French singers. And before Gin could reply, I thought of two nightclubs where she'd been angling for gigs, and named the manager of each. "Suzy Solidor. Bricktop, too."

"Damn," said Gin. "So that's what I've been doing wrong." She looked at me as if thinking something over. "Well, that explains why you haven't had a boyfriend since Hervé. You like girls. How do you say that in Italian?"

"I don't like *girls*. I like Tamara."

"Suit yourself," Gin said. "I know you wouldn't try to kiss me on purpose, so I don't care." We both suddenly started laughing. "Yann," Gin burst out. "*Che pazzo*. Well, have fun with your dress, there," she said. "And try not to get arrested for kissing any lampposts out on the street."

After Gin left, I walked to Le Sentier and returned to Silovic et Fils, listening with my hands for the texture that seemed most Tamara's. I found a lustrous charmeuse in a pink so cool it almost shaded into purple: her skin would look all the more golden against it. I couldn't open a fashion magazine that season without reading about Madeleine Vionnet's new way of cutting fabric, *en biais*, and more often than not her sleek, clinging gowns were cut from silks like the one I fingered. In order to cut on the diagonal, I read, Vionnet ordered her fabrics two meters wider than all the other couturiers. I had never been tempted to try it myself: so much waste seemed crazy. But the extravagant, ridiculous way I felt about Tamara seemed crazy too. Maybe Gin was right. So, was this what she felt for Daniel? When I palmed the silk my body jumped inside with longing.

I leaned against the display table to right myself, and looked up to see Anya Silovic behind the counter, napping at a sewing machine with a baby tied to her back. She yawned, pawing back her heavy hair: I looked down, embarrassed. Here I was, languishing with desire, and there she was, with so many better reasons to complain. I felt confused, too. Only fourteen months earlier I had beaten at the ship's door to escape back to my Zia Rina's on Baxter

Street, back to a life very like the one that Anya had, and now here I stood in my fur-collared coat, pitying her. I remembered my mother's letter. I felt very far from home. I seized on the cool pink silk the way I had seized on Tamara herself. Slippery and fragile, it would require hand-sewing, which was just what I needed to steady me. I knew then that I would survive Tamara's week in London, that the hours bent over my thimble would become home for me, the way the hours I spent on her gray velvet couch, *seen*, had become home. I knew if I made something ambitious, the time would go by before I even finished sewing. Half a bolt remained of the charmeuse: I bought it all.

When Tamara opened her door a week later, she kissed me on the mouth. I wobbled in her arms, almost falling. "I missed you, darling," she said. "I brought you toffee. And scotch." Seffa jumped up to lick my face, and for once I let him. She'd missed me. I inhaled for what felt like the first time in days.

That morning, after we finished flouting her rule about no play before work, I noticed a sheet over the new *Rafaela*, carefully tented so as not to touch the oil colors. I asked about it. "I let my friend d'Afflitto stay in the apartment while I was gone," Tamara explained, pointing to a pair of gentleman's valises I hadn't noticed in the hallway. "But I did not want him to see the painting."

"D'Afflitto?" I asked uneasily.

"The Marquis d'Afflitto. He is from a fine old family in Amalfi, but his boyfriend is here in Paris. They are having a stupid quarrel, so I thought I would do him a favor."

His *boyfriend*, I thought, relaxing. "He has no place to stay?" It was funny to think of a marquis sleeping in a friend's apartment, like me sleeping in the coatroom of the Ritz.

"He likes to play the big spender, but the truth is, his father keeps him on a tight leash," Tamara said. "Not that the old man is any angel himself. I think he just wants to have some money left over for his new wife when he dies. When his first wife passed away, he married her twenty-year-old *nurse*," she added. Tamara flipped through the paintings that leaned against the wall until she found one to show me. "My friend," she explained, pointing at a pouting dandy in a rakishly tilted hat, his bow tie coming undone. He leaned against the railing of a staircase, feeling for cigarettes in his jacket pocket. He *did* look like the kind of *vitellone* who would spend his way through Papa's money unless he were kept in check. Once Tamara and I settled into work, I didn't give him a second thought, not even when I heard a key in the door: I assumed it was Jeanne, the housekeeper, popping in to drop off the morning's marketing. Because Jeanne tended to stay out of the salon when I posed, I did not rush to clothe myself, not until a stylish young man walked into the room, hat in hand, his lips as unctuously pink as those in the portrait I'd just seen, his expression as dissolute. *"Mon Dieu!"* he said, mock surprise only half concealing real embarrassment. *"Pardon, Mesdames."* With that, he took an enormous white peony of a handkerchief out of his breast pocket, lifted it like a sheet, and tossed it over his whole head. As I pulled on the green robe, amused, Tamara crossed the room, teasing her friend in English for my sake. "There is this thing, *chéri*, they call a *doorbell*? You *ring* it?"

"I'm sorry, Tamara," he said, pulling off his handkerchief, and as they made their *bisous*, I noticed that Tamara had quickly covered the new *Rafaela* back up again. When she introduced us, the marquis made an affected little bow. "I hear Tamara's pinned her hopes on you for the Salon," he said in English.

"I have my fingers crossed for her," I said. I braced myself for him to ask how Tamara and I had met, or what I did for a living.

He didn't ask. "If the portrait does you justice, her hopes are well founded," he said instead, kissing his fingertips before turning to Tamara to surrender her keys.

"Did you two patch things up?" she asked him.

"Not well," he said philosophically. "We'll see."

"How is your family? How is the nurse?"

"My brother, Aldo, came through town last week. He's well," he said. "But the nurse?" He offered a wicked smile. "Aldo told me Papà got a Steinach operation to please her."

Tamara giggled. "*La vasectomie*, does it really . . . ?"

"Everyone says so. My father even says so. But my brother heard them in the next room, and the verdict, *Mesdames*?" He made a wilting gesture. "Only in Papà's mind, poor thing. And the saddest thing is, that surgery was *not* cheap."

"You scandalize me!"

"I live to scandalize you, Tamara," he gloated. "Well, I have a friend in a little car outside," he said. "Jean Cocteau's invited me to a party tonight, if you'd like to go, *chérie*. There ought to be a whole smorgasbord of pretty young things there."

I willed Tamara to look up at me briefly, apologetically, as if to say she already had a pretty young thing of her own, thank you, but she did not. Instead she chuckled. "Surely you include yourself, no?"

"Darling, you flatter me. You just aren't taut and dewy at thirty the way you are at nineteen."

"At least your Steinach years are still a long way off," Tamara consoled him. They agreed to meet for dinner, and he vanished with his suitcases.

I liked d'Afflitto's combination of extravagance and extreme tact, I thought, listening to the car ferry him away. "You really didn't want him to see the painting," I noted, surprised. "Isn't he your friend?"

"You see, with the first *Belle*, I knew it was for all the world to see at the Salon. If, of course, I get in," she explained. "But this one? It is not a *secret*, exactly. Kizette has seen it, and Jeanne, of course. But it seems *private*, no?" she said. "Ours."

In that moment, I forgave Tamara for not turning to me when d'Afflitto mentioned the pretty young things. "Well, it's more fun than the last one was, with that hand business," I stammered. What she'd said had made me so shyly happy, I couldn't look at her. Maybe she was in love with me, too, a little. *Ours.*

While working on the private *Belle*, Tamara finished *The Pink Tunic* and began a new painting, *The Dream*, using the same gray velvet chaise, the same green silk robe. She sketched a few lines in charcoal on a sheet of newsprint and then transferred the image to a new canvas using a pizza-cutter-like tool I recognized from dressmaking: in English it's called a pouncing wheel. Even Seffa's ears went up at the delicate paper-punch sound the newsprint made as Tamara traced her lines with the spiky tool. She carefully tapped powdered charcoal over her perforated lines, working from bottom to top. She peeled away the newsprint, and *voilà!* The image lay on the canvas now, a pinpricked outline. I transferred pattern markings to fabric the same way myself sometimes, using powdered chalk. "Do you sew?" I asked eagerly, pointing to the lines dotted on the canvas.

"This is a fresco technique," Tamara sniffed. I still never knew when I might offend her, let alone why.

As with *The Pink Tunic*, Tamara planned *The Dream* using one of those first five-minute sketches she'd made in July, and, as with *The Pink Tunic*, *The Dream* called for a pose I could rest in, between sessions of *La Belle*: I sat propped on pillows, arms crossed over my chest, hand relaxed, looking directly at the viewer. The green silk robe hung behind me on the wall. "Do you want to see your eyes come alive?" she asked during a sitting for *The Dream*: I watched her add a cone-shaped dot of white to the iris of each eye. "It is an art-school trick, but it works. Cremnitz white. The purest of colors. There is no white more stable, and none more fateful."

"Fateful?"

"I mean fatal. It is made of lead." I had stopped hearing her way of speaking as Slavic or strange by then, but sometimes I noticed it afresh. "Relax your face," she said. I stared at her all the harder, my face suddenly strange to me. "Imagine we make love. You fall asleep. You wake up. That is all."

The Dream suited me. I wasn't trying to rush through autumn, the way Tamara was. I wanted to remain in her gaze, in her bed, forever; I wanted it to last, this floating, aqueous season, the trees queerly green into late September. The days were getting shorter, however, and Tamara shut the windows when the breeze began to nip.

8

I WASN'T SURPRISED TO LEARN that Gin's moving date had been pushed forward to November first. I *was* surprised, however, one night in early October, when she came home alone at nine at night. All this time, I had been holed up in my room three or four nights a week while Gin and Daniel pretended I wasn't there. I was startled to hear only one voice at the door, and that it was speaking to me. "Rafaela?" Gin called weakly.

I peered out, confused. "What is it?" Then I saw. One of Gin's slim plucked brows was distended by a lump the size of a duck egg. "Ginny," I breathed, and led her into my brightly lit room. The puffy bump was the blue of a new bruise. "What happened?"

"I went to Meaux. I had to speak to Daniel at his office. Well, first I had to *find* his office. And then the guard wouldn't let me in. Finally I threw myself at the door and the pig *hit* me. And then Daniel opened the door, to find out what all the fuss was about, and I was so ashamed I ran away before he could see me."

"Wait, wait. I don't understand. Let me get you something to eat."

I heated chocolate for Gin and spread her some jam on a baguette. "Thank you, Mummy," she said.

"I have scotch for the chocolate, if you'd like."

Gin nodded.

"So. Why did you go to Meaux?"

"I needed to talk to Daniel."

"But he's here all the time. Why not wait until he comes into the city?"

"Because I thought I could help. He keeps telling me there's one more form he needs to pick up at the courthouse there, so he can finalize his divorce, but he's always so busy. I thought I could go pick it up for him."

"You don't think he could send a messenger to get it, if it was so easy as that?"

"Well, he wouldn't want the messenger boys at the office knowing his personal business—" Gin said, then broke off. "The point is, I went to go try to help with the form, but really I wanted to show him how serious I am about this. Rafaela, I need him to marry me."

"I thought you said you didn't mind. I mean, I thought you said, *It won't be the first time a married man has a girlfriend*, or something."

"Well, that was then."

"What happened?"

Sitting on the edge of my bed, slim legs drawn up like a child's, the big bowl of hot chocolate in her two small hands, Gin fixed me with a look. I saw a spasm cross her face when she tried to raise an eyebrow through the bruise. "What do *you* think happened?"

"Oh, Ginny, no."

"Yes."

"Are you sure? I mean, when was the last time—"

"Six weeks ago. Middle of August."

"But you're so careful!"

"Maybe I stopped being quite so careful with Daniel, when I thought his divorce was coming through right away."

"Gin! I mean, he'd already put off your moving date *twice* by then!"

She put down her bowl. "You think he's a liar?"

I wavered. She looked so fragile; how could I disappoint her? But how could she be so stupid? "Well," I said.

"Some friend *you* are."

"Listen, Gin," I began seriously. If Tamara were a man, I stopped to think, who's to say I wouldn't be pregnant myself by now? God, I was lucky. I faced my friend, mentally gathering up Anson's facts and dates. "You probably don't want to hear this."

"You're right. I don't." She stood.

"But—"

"I'm going to bed."

"Gin, what are you going to *do*?" I said. But I was talking to her back.

At Tamara's the next day, I could barely stay awake. It didn't bother her at first—she worked on my open hand in *The Dream* all morning, and didn't care if I kept my eyes closed. At noon we heard the metal rasp and papery flutter of the postman's visit, and on our next break, Tamara excused herself. Within moments she lit back up the stairs with a thin torn envelope in hand. *"Acceptée! Acceptée!"*

"Really?"

"The jury of the Salon d'Automne has elected to exhibit both works submitted by Tamara de Lempicka," she read aloud in French, her voice swelling. "And—and—and—a member of the jury—represented by an Agence Binard—wants to buy *La Belle Rafaela* before the Salon even opens!"

"Brava, Tamara!"

We drank champagne, even though it was midday. Tamara gummed a pinch of cocaine and began to incandesce as she continued working. "This has never happened to me before. This has never happened to anyone I know. Rafaela, you are good luck. I knew I was doing something new. No one has ever treated the nude with this much frankness and finish. *The Origin of the World* is just a stuffy old Victorian pastel next to *La Belle Rafaela*."

Tamara's high was a bit much to take, in my state. As soon as she began talking about other painters and paintings, I felt fatigue and gloom seal up my face again. "That's right," I said heavily.

"Are you even listening?"

"Of course."

"You do not care about me as an artist."

"Sorry, I'm just sleepy."

"You just want to have fun and make money."

"This wonderful thing just happened for you, and I'm happy for you. What else do you want?"

"If you are so happy for me, why are you acting like this?"

"Like what?"

"Bored to tears."

"Things happen to me outside this room, all right? As it happens, I didn't sleep last night."

Tamara replied with a small, filthy, forgiving smile. How could she think that of me?

"Sorry to disappoint you, but it's not what you think," I said. I sat up from the pose entirely, pulled the green robe down from its hook on the wall, and wrapped myself in it. I started talking about Gin and Daniel, and by the time I wound up my story, Tamara's pupils had gone back to their regular size. "But the thing is, he's never going to marry her. His job is completely dependent on his father-in-law, so he'll never leave his wife. And even if something happened to *her*, he keeps *another* house in Meaux for *another* woman."

Tamara sat coiled at the foot of my chaise, arms crossed. "Your friend *told* you all this and she still thinks he plans to marry her?"

"No—" I began.

"Then how do you know?"

Would Anson want me to tell how I knew? "I just know."

"You just *know*. Based on evidence? Or jealousy?"

"What are you talking about?"

"I think you are jealous of this Daniel, and you make things up to paint him as a villain." Tamara gestured, rings sparkling. "You are probably driving the poor girl crazy, filling her head up with all these lies."

"They're not lies!"

"How do you know? Do you work with this man at Crédit Lyonnais? *Pardon*, were you just taking a little walk in the Bois de Boulogne on your lunch hour?"

"I *had* a job with a lunch hour, and I gave it up for you!"

"Oh, boohoo, that job selling gloves? The truth is, you hate seeing your friend get a good man so much you will even lie to her to keep her stuck where you are."

"I'm not lying!" I shouted, hurt. What was so bad about where I was? "I know these things because I researched him. Are you happy now? I have a friend who has access to all kinds of bank records, and I had him go find out what Daniel spends his money on."

Tamara backed down at once, startled. "Is that legal?"

I smiled.

"Oh."

What Tamara had said smarted, but I liked it that there was something about me she wanted to know. I milked it. "You might need to research someone yourself one day," I pointed out.

"He did this for you, just because you asked?"

"Well, I think he was trying to impress me a little."

"Could he research this Agence Binard? Could he find out who wants to buy my painting?"

"If you apologize for all the nasty things you just said, maybe he could."

"Fine." Tamara sighed. "I am sorry, Rafaela."

"What for?" I pushed.

"All the nasty things I said," she recited.

"Especially about the Bois de Boulogne."

Tamara's voice went tender. "I am sorry," she repeated. "It was not kind, what I said." She took my bare foot and held it.

"You thought I didn't care that you were accepted into the Salon, but I did," I insisted. "You said I don't care about you as an artist, but I do." You think I'm jealous of Daniel, but I think you're jealous of Gin, I didn't say. I didn't want to scare her. If I was careful, and didn't push too hard, one day she might just tell me that she loved me on her own.

"I am sorry I was bad-tempered," she said, releasing my foot. Sitting across from me, Tamara spoke as primly as she did to her daughter, but I could imagine her bare-shouldered in the slip I was making. I would finish soon. Couldn't she feel my attention, as extravagant and clinging as silk cut on the bias? Couldn't she see how much she'd changed me? There was something I wished I'd told her the first day we made love. I was afraid if I said it she'd think I wanted too much from her, but I wanted to say it so much. I gathered myself. "I don't want you to pay me for the time we spend in bed," I said finally.

"Oh," she said, surprise washing the starch out of her. She looked at me as if for the first time. I thought I saw something shy and gentle in the way she smiled, something that reached inside me. "Of course."

I told you in the first place, some people don't want to know the truth," Anson said. "They'd rather suffer." It was just barely warm enough to sit outside, as the two of us did, in the Arènes de Lutèce near the Jardin des Plantes zoo. I hadn't seen Anson in a few weeks, not since that day I'd found him at the bookstore, a mess behind his newspaper. He was happy I had called, and asked if we could meet near his home. We had the stone bleachers—and the broad round gravel stage below—to ourselves in the thin evening light. "Did you know this was even here?" he asked, pleased with himself. "Roman ruins. Not even ruins, really."

"How did they stay in such good shape all this time?"

"Buried completely underground. They only just dug them up in the past thirty, forty years." He tossed a few pebbles at an abandoned wine bottle, but stopped when I knocked it over on the second try. "Attagirl, Rafaela!"

"All those brothers," I explained, flattered.

"Have you ever shot a pistol?"

"When would I have shot a pistol? Back in my cowgirl days?"

"I could teach you," he said. "I think you'd have fun."

"You just don't quit," I said, patting him on the shoulder. "So, do you think they had sportswriters, back in Roman times?"

Anson replied with a dry *hmph* of a laugh.

"Taking notes in Latin on the hems of their togas? Lions four, Christians zero?"

"I'm sure they had bookies, at any rate," he said with a shrug. I was surprised he didn't want to take up my game.

"Anson, I hate to ask you another favor, but I was wondering— would it be too much trouble to ask your friend to research someone else?"

"Are you in trouble?"

"No. Why?"

"Everything's all right?"

"Of course. It's not for me, it's for the painter. One of the jurors of the Salon d'Automne wants to buy her painting—it's an anonymous jury—and I wondered if you could ask your friend to find out who he is? I can tell you the name of the agent he's using."

"Oh."

"Oh?"

"Well, that's not really an emergency."

"It has to be an emergency?"

"Well, obviously my definition of emergency is pretty loose, if it includes saving a flapper from bigamy. I did it because you were so upset."

"It was awfully good of you."

"It doesn't sound like it really helped much."

"Well, it meant a lot to me."

"I'm glad, then."

"So you wouldn't even ask your friend, unless it was an emergency?"

"All right. I'm going to tell you this because I trust you, and because I don't want to lie to you. It wasn't my friend. It was me."

"But how did you get the information? Did you break into a bank?"

"Rafaela, I'm not a sportswriter for the *Chicago Tribune*."

"No?"

"I work for Monsieur Bland."

"Wait. That business card you gave me, with Monsieur Boulind's information, and you said he was a friend of the family—but he's your boss?"

"That's right."

"So *that's* why you're always there when I call. You aren't just dropping by to pick up messages; you're there all day."

"Much of the day," Anson corrected.

"And *he* breaks into banks?"

"I've worked for him for five years and I don't know his real name, but I know it's not actually Yves Boulind. He's a very highly placed man in the French government. A fraud investigator. He has the power to request any bank records he wants. And when he's performing the will of the French government, he opens them himself. And when he's requesting documents for a client, he leaves opening them to his staff."

"You?"

"There are a handful of us. All foreigners. No rights. Paid under the table. Easy to blame, if he runs into trouble."

"Has he ever gotten into trouble?"

"No. Because he's very, *very* careful."

"Oh."

"He never even speaks to his own clients, he has 'Madame Bou-lind' do it. I don't know what her real name is either, but I know she's not his wife." Sitting beside Anson in the raw expanse of the Arènes, I tried to imagine his half-hidden work life. "The point is, if we want to request information, he'll do it, but every request is a risk. So just to slow us down, he makes us make it up to him in *devoirs*."

The word meant "duties," but it was also the word schoolchil-dren used for their homework. "Did you have to do *devoirs* when you looked up Daniel?"

"As many hours of work as would pay his rate, on top of the work we already do for him. And it's whatever drudgery he's been saving up for us. So when I looked up Daniel, let's see. I organized a dropped box of a thousand checks, by number. I typed up some documents that were in truly egregious handwriting. I converted a month's worth of receipts from pounds into francs based on each day's exchange rate. I waited around to talk to somebody who didn't want to pay his bills. Nothing difficult or dangerous, but that's what makes it so unpleasant. The tedium."

"And you did these *devoirs* in order to see Daniel's records, just because I asked?"

"Ten hours."

"Oh," I said, embarrassed. "And she wouldn't even listen."

"It wouldn't be the first time that happened. As a matter of fact, that's how Monsieur Bland started this business in the first place, researching his wife. Our bread-and-butter clients are rich ladies who want to know who their husbands are sleeping with. But I can't say it makes them happy to find out."

"Ten hours. Anson, thank you. I had no idea."

He shrugged. "So you see why I asked if it was an emergency."

"Tamara's curiosity about the man who's buying her painting is definitely not worth ten hours of your time. I would never have asked, if I'd known."

"It's really all right, Rafaela. I like you." And then quickly, before he could make me uncomfortable, he added, "If she wants to pay Monsieur Bland's fee, I'd be happy to put them in touch with each other."

"I don't want to make anything complicated for you."

"It's no trouble. I'll give you a telephone number, Tamara can call Madame Bland, and they can settle all the details between them."

"So whatever happened to his wife? *Was* she cheating?"

"He divorced her. But even after he knew the truth, it still took him years."

9

NOT LONG AFTER I MET ANSON in the Arènes, I gave his
card to Tamara. She accepted the telephone number eagerly, but
she must have decided her curiosity wasn't worth M. Bland's fee
either, because she decided to pursue her investigation on less
expensive lines. A survey of her friends turned up a particular
stripe of art world parasite: Agence Binard represented a professional collector with warehouses of cheaply gotten paintings by
new artists, some of which, if one played the odds, would one
day be worth a fortune. It was gratifying, I could see, for Tamara
to be included in such a pool, but the thought of *Beautiful
Rafaela* moldering in a warehouse took a bit of the shine off selling
it. Tamara *would*, she told me, retain the right to show the painting at any exposition she chose, so that was something. For my
part, I didn't care if the whole world saw the Salon *Rafaela* or
if it crumbled to dust unseen, as long as Tamara kept the new
one. *Ours*.

The day before the Salon opened, Tamara asked me to come in for a short session before she went down to the Petit Palais to hang her work. When I arrived, I looked at her twice, startled: her hair was dyed deep black.

"What happened?" I asked.

"The Salon," Tamara explained. "I am nervous every time I show."

Tamara moved restlessly that day: she took Seffa for a walk every hour, whether he wanted to go out or not. "I am not nervous about *Kizette au Balcon*," she said. "The Bordeaux judges loved it. But *Belle Rafaela*? I cannot change it anymore," Tamara fretted. "I cannot hide it. I cannot take it back."

"But maybe they'll love it, silly. And besides, you have a buyer."

"Well, when it is gone, at least I will still have this one."

"I thought it would feel funny to pose for the same painting twice, but it feels the same," I reflected. "Just longer."

"I am glad it has not been too dull for you."

"Do you want me to come in the day after tomorrow, then?"

"What is wrong with tomorrow?"

"Won't you be at the Salon?"

"I want to have a full day of painting before I let them crush me."

"That's the spirit."

That night I got my period, so the next day Tamara worked on *Full Summer* until it was time to go to the Salon. During our first break,

I brought out my small valise. "I have something here, to congratu-
late you."

"For me?"

"But you have to close your eyes."

"A surprise?"

"You have to close your eyes and take off your clothes."

"Cheeky! I like my surprise already."

"It's not what you think."

Tamara lay naked across the couch, eyes closed. "Will this do,
Miss Rafaela?"

It will more than do, you beauty, I thought. "Sit up and raise
your arms over your head."

"You never order me around like this."

"I can tell you're going to be so disappointed," I teased, and slid
the chemise I'd made over her head and shoulders.

"What is this?" she cooed.

"Keep them eyes closed, you!"

Everything was finished except the shoulder straps, which I had
sewn in back but not in front, wanting to get the fit right first. Pinning the first strap, I watched her sitting quietly, eyes closed.
Though her skin was taut and clear, her face at rest had a tragic
grace, with its down-tipped eyes and pale slender brows, the proud
prow of her nose. But it wasn't at rest for long. "If you wanted a
longer break, you could just ask."

"Be patient."

"I am only patient when working," Tamara chided. And then,
before I could do more than pin the second strap, her eyes flew open
and she leapt up from the couch. "I love it! Rafaela, this is gorgeous!"

"Let me finish."

"No, I love it just as it is," she said, looking for the mirror, yanking the skirt down over her legs. *"Ouille!"*

"If you'd let me finish, those pins wouldn't stick you."

"Fine, finish, finish. But do it during your next break, missy. Sitting still is *your* job."

With the practiced ease of a woman who had never bought clothes off the rack in her life, she shimmied out of the silk slip, pins and all, and changed back into her painting clothes.

Forty-five minutes later, when we broke again, I could only make five small stitches before she seized the chemise out of my hands. "Wait, there's only one strap."

"I do not care."

"How will it stay up, then?"

"A pin is fine. I love it. No one has made me anything to wear as a gift since I was a little girl. I want to wear it under my dress right now."

"Have it your way," I said, absurdly happy to see her in the shimmering little slip after spending so many hours on it alone. Her slender body seemed to curve opulently under the clinging silk: cutting on the bias was worth every inch of fabric I'd wasted. I grinned.

"I will wear it to the Salon this afternoon," she said. "For luck."

Tamara and I had never gone out together. I wanted to walk up the street with her. I wanted to parade her past Sylvia's shop, take her home to Gin and show her off. "Do you want me to come with you?" I asked shyly.

Tamara's eyes glittered as she nodded. "For more luck."

$\backsim\!\!@\!\!\backsim$

We left Seffa at home because there would be crowds. Tamara was too nervous about making a good impression at the Salon to notice that, despite my pleasure at going out with her in public, I was petrified to be at the Salon myself. I could tell myself that no one would recognize me, but there was still no way I would have gone alone, no matter how much I wanted to see the painting in its hour of glory. As much as I was glad to have Tamara by my side, I was glad, too, for the deep brim of my cloche. Luckily, many other women kept their outdoor things on in the unheated rooms: though she took off her gloves, Tamara still wore the jaunty red Paul Poiret cap that matched her red wool coat. Within moments of our arrival, a bubbly strawberry blonde emerged from the throng of art collectors and after-work types to kiss Tamara on both cheeks.

"Romana de la Salle! *Chérie!*"

"Tamara! Tamara! When is *Die Dame* going to print our painting?"

I recognized the pink champagne girl shrieking in French from Tamara's *Orange Scarf* image, and I did not like the way she said *our* painting. But Tamara kissed me on the lips in front of her, which both reassured me and caught the lively, pale-eyed attention of a man I thought I recognized on the other side of the room. As Tamara announced me to her friend as *La Belle Rafaela soi-même*, I saw a familiar turquoise earring come shuttling toward us through the crowd. "How's your mother, Romana?" Tamara asked in French. "Is she still with that tired old thing?"

"Mother's been with Bibi for nine years," Romana protested. "When are you going to remember her name?"

"The day that Bibi woman learns how to dress," Tamara said. They both laughed. "I love your mother, but she's such a puritan."

"She's only a puritan when it comes to Bibi," Romana said. She pantomimed sniffing cocaine, and they both laughed again. "You're just sore she turned you down."

"Madame de Lempicka, is that you?" said Anson's friend Bobby Nightinghoul, emerging from behind two ladies in beaded gowns. Tamara looked up at Bobby, but she did not smile. "Oh, I've seen *you* at parties, *ma belle Polonaise*," he said. "Have I! And isn't this Anson's little dish?"

"I'm not Anson's anything," I said, standing closer to Tamara.

"Look at that one, Robert," said his companion, a big American boy with a voice so low I felt instead of heard it. Bless him: he was pointing at a painting instead of a person.

"Oh, Clark. Romaine Brooks is so nineteenth century," Bobby complained. *"Peter, Une Jeune Fille Anglaise,"* he read aloud. "Whistler's mama in drag, more like."

Tamara was buttonholed by a friend, as were Bobby and Clark, leaving me alone for a moment with Romana de la Salle. I wasn't sure if I'd like her: she seemed soft and pretty and featherbrained. We looked together at *Peter, a Young English Girl*. "That makes me think of Tamara's portrait of your mother," I attempted in French.

"I see what you mean," Romana said in English. "The male dress. The single figure. The pensive stance. But this one has a cooler look, don't you think? Those grays. And the very thin paint, almost like watercolor. It's like a painting made of ice." I gawped at her. I was practically a native English speaker and I had never said the word "pensive" out loud.

"That's beautiful," I said. "Do you know her?"

"Not to talk to. I mean, she's a good twenty-five years older than we are."

"We?"

"Tamara and I."

I covered my mouth. "I guess I thought you were younger than Tamara."

"You dear thing! No, we're both twenty-nine."

"But she said she was twenty-seven. *Like the century.*"

"Oh-ho, did she? Well, don't tell her I spilled the beans."

We shared a laugh over having caught Tamara out, then turned again to the painting. "Was Romaine Brooks one of Tamara's teachers, do you know?"

"Not formally. But Tamara learned a lot from her, you can tell. The grays. The portraits. The foregrounded women. You should see Romaine's portrait of her lover Natalie. Those two have been together almost as long as Maman and Bibi."

"Natalie's a tramp," said Bobby, reëmerging from another conversation.

"Speak for yourself," said Bobby's friend Clark. "Romaine isn't."

"See the zeppelin and the scarecrow over there?" asked Bobby. "The big one's one of my authors; she collects Picassos. Your friend Tamara cut Picasso dead in a café once, and now those two don't speak. Mm-mm. The skinny gal's her wife. Anson used to run errands for them."

"Is there a woman left in Paris who sleeps with men?" Romana asked, imitating Bobby's bloodless Kansas vowels.

"Am I looking at her?" Bobby replied.

Bobby and Romana locked eyes for a moment, until Bobby's friend Clark interposed himself between them to admire my fur-collared coat. "Nice cut. Shall we go say hello to Gertrude and Alice, Robert?"

"I won't forget you, my little *tarte aux fraises*," Bobby told Romana, and the four of us laughed, though Clark's laughter came a little forced.

"I think I saw those two women on my street once," I realized aloud, "coming out of Galerie Vollard." I had noticed them because they were both carrying pastry boxes from Fouquet.

"That's Picasso's dealer," Romana explained quietly. "He handles a lot of Cézannes and Gauguins, too. This is Rue Laffitte?"

I nodded, surprised.

"Well, it's a shame Tamara turns her nose up at all that, but there are other ways of making a career. *Par exemple*," she said, gesturing again toward the Romaine Brooks painting. "Brooks painted Cocteau. Now he's one of Tamara's best friends. Brooks painted D'Annunzio. Tamara sought out D'Annunzio and he promoted her work. He gave her that topaz ring she wears. But she's the only woman who never slept with him," Romana added with a sly laugh. "Though it sounds like he tried." As Tamara glided toward us, Romana turned to her. "We were just talking about your influences," she said.

"My influences? The Quattrocento for color. The Dutch masters for light. And for perversity, the men I call the gilded mannerists. Pontormo. Bronzino. Greuze. Ingres. *Le Cinéma* said I reclaimed Ingres for 'Cubism'."

"Not a living painter on your list," teased Romana. "Don't forget Maurice Denis and André Lhote."

"Do not speak to me of my *teachers*." Tamara sniffed. "Those nobodies."

I looked back at Romana, uncertain. "Don't listen to her, Rafaela. We were in art school together. She's insufferable."

Would I ever speak French as well as these titled Europeans spoke English? Would I ever speak *English* as well? "Are you a painter, too?" I asked.

"It was just for fun." Romana giggled. "When I saw Tamara's work, I realized I didn't have half her talent, and I quit. Have you seen where they hung your painting, Tamara?"

"I was just going to show Rafaela, darling," Tamara said in French, kissing her friend good-bye when a handsome man approached the redhead. Romana gave Tamara an apologetic look. "You go have a good time," Tamara said. "Look for *Die Dame* next month if I don't see you before then."

When we were alone, Tamara leaned toward me. "I love my new slip," she whispered, and a single match flared under my ribs. "I have a surprise for you, too."

"I'm glad we're here together," I whispered back, grinning. "But Tamara?" I ventured. "I feel funny. You told your friend I was *La Belle Rafaela soi-même*," I said.

"Why is that a problem?"

"Now she knows what I look like naked. It's embarrassing."

"Beauty, my darling, is never embarrassing," counseled Tamara. "And do not think about Romana. What does she know?"

Tamara threaded us through the crowded halls. As we approached the main gallery, we passed Bobby and Clark again, standing in an antechamber with a woman in a severely tailored men's coat. Her eyes were two points of heat at the back of her cavernous hat. "But why do you let her treat you like this?" Bobby was asking.

An American woman's level voice replied, "I don't care what

she does when we're apart, because I know I'm the most important person in her life. Not that it's any of your business," the woman added, turning her back on him.

"Was that Romaine Brooks?" I whispered to Tamara as we hurried on.

"Was *who* Romaine Brooks?" she hissed. By then we had reached the main exhibition room, and she made me close my eyes. "Time for the surprise. Look where they hung it."

Floor to ceiling, paintings hung so close together their frames touched, but I found Tamara's right away: they had placed it at eye level, right in the very center of the wall.

"They gave you the best spot in the house," I murmured.

"They did," Tamara said, giving me a quick hard embrace. "Because *my* work," she explained, as we approached it, "is *finished*. Tight. Not one line out of place. Everything here is chaos and murk compared to my paintings."

We had reached the painting as she spoke, and when she did, a man turned to us. I noted his tiepin, a single gray pearl. "Is this yours?" he asked.

"It is," she said, extending her hand, which blazed with its massive topaz. "Tamara de Lempicka."

"Pierre Boucard," he replied. "I've seen so many paintings tonight, but this one? Perfection."

With his perfectly trimmed moustache and quietly lush double-breasted suit, Boucard had lively eyes and a smooth face that belied the shallow groove cut into his brow, the silver in his full head of slicked-back hair. More than young or old, however, Boucard himself seemed *finished*—not one line out of place—with a muted sheen as glossy as his gray pearl.

"Are you a painter yourself, sir?" asked Tamara. Boucard was too well dressed to be a painter, I thought, but he seemed like someone who might have been flattered by the question.

"I'm a doctor, Madame. A medical researcher. And an art lover. It's easy to get overwhelmed at these big exhibitions, but your painting—it glows. Is there a secret to your technique?"

Tamara thanked the doctor, pleased. A photographer and a newsman had begun to approach us, drawn by Tamara's beauty and her startling red hat and coat, and she waited until they were within earshot. "You ask about the unique luminosity of my paintings," she said for their benefit. She gestured toward *Beautiful Rafaela* for a flash-powder moment, then gave the reporter her card. "I will tell you. I use very thin coats of paint, and I work on several paintings at a time. This way, each coat of paint can dry completely before I lay down the next." I looked at her, as impressed as the doctor and the newsmen. And I had thought she worked on more than one painting at a time to give me a break between poses!

The doctor nodded appreciatively. "I have never seen a painting so commanding, so brilliantly colored, so polished, so simple, so sensual, so pure."

Tamara looked down, momentarily dumbfounded, and flashed me a look of childlike joy. Then she straightened, as if to hold the man at arm's length. "I'm flattered," she purred coolly. "You're very kind."

"I don't say it to be kind," he replied. "I say it because I'd like to buy your painting."

Tamara permitted herself a tiny smile. "Shall we go speak to Monsieur le Directeur, then?" she asked, without missing a beat. As we turned to go to the office, I looked up at her, with *What about your other buyer?* plain on my face. She gave me a warning squint, then took my hand, a gesture clearly chosen to catch the eye of both Boucard and the reporter: I saw the pleasure she took in the glitter of envy and interest she provoked as we left the newsmen behind. When she made to introduce me to Boucard, I gave her a warning of my own: a hard pinch to the palm in mine. "This is Ra—*chela* Dafano," she said. I turned to her in disbelief. Did I look like that much of a *Rachela*?

Boucard kissed my hand. "I see the blood of Zion here, mingled with the blood of Rome?"

I blinked at him. "Sorry, I don't speak French," I snapped in French.

In the office, a desiccated man bent over a ledger with a magnifying glass, searching for *La Belle Rafaela*. "Number 1377, are you sure?" he mumbled.

As the clerk ran his finger down the column of titles, the door jerked open behind us. "Madame de Lempicka?" asked the large man who burst in.

As Tamara responded with a tentative nod and smile, the clerk set down his loupe. "Baron Kuffner," he said.

"Raoul Kuffner de Dioszegh," the red-faced Teuton said with a bow. If Doctor Boucard was as smooth and compact as a pearl, this Baron Kuffner was a barnacle-encrusted shell: bewhiskered, balding, and bespectacled, with a sportsman's big-boned, stubbly-throated bulk.

"*Enchantée*," Tamara said, languidly extending an arm. In its slow movement I could see physical repulsion struggling with the mild interest stirred up by his title.

"You are the painter of *La Belle Rafaela*?"

"The selfsame."

"I have ten thousand francs here for your painting," he said bluntly. "I saw it this morning, I thought about it all day, and I've come back for it now."

"Pierre Boucard," the doctor said, shaking Kuffner's hand. "I was just here to purchase Madame de Lempicka's painting myself, actually."

"Messieurs," the clerk said, and there was something very French about the way he enjoyed his small exercise of power. "As you know, this is an exhibition, not an auction, so the painting does in fact go to the first comer, which would be you, Doctor," he said, bending down again over his loupe.

The Baron gave a dignified nod. "Fair enough," he said, while the doctor, clearly too well bred to gloat, looked smugly pleased with himself for *not* gloating.

The clerk looked up. "Gentlemen, my mistake." We all turned to him. "Number 1377, *La Belle Rafaela*, was purchased this morning by an Agence Binard. Very impressive for the first day of the Salon, Madame. Congratulations. *Messieurs, désolé.*"

The disappointed men turned to each other, then to Tamara. "I'm honored you liked the painting," she assured each of them. "It means the world to me. *Messieurs*, a month from now, the last night of the Salon, I'm having a studio party. Won't you both please come?"

"I'd be delighted to see more of your work," said Boucard. "Do you do portraits?"

"Will there be more paintings of that model, Rafaela?" Kuffner asked. "More nudes?"

"Yes, yes, and yes," Tamara said, exchanging cards with the

two men. "I'll send you a *pneu* with details first thing tomorrow." Tamara's eyes burned with pleasure as we turned away. She seemed unsteady on her feet, and dropped her Bakelite purse. As the two of us reached, simultaneously, to collect it, I felt the men's eyes on me and heard Kuffner ask Boucard, "Who's the girl?"

Of Boucard's answer, as we walked away, I only heard the word *Juive*.

"Why did you call me Rachela?" I asked Tamara. "That 'blood of Zion' stuff gave me the heebie-jeebies."

"I am sorry, *ma belle*. I was already slipping up, and it was the first name that came to mind."

"I don't like him," I said.

"Oh, darling. Some Frenchmen are just like that," Tamara said, brushing aside my unease. "Both Christians and Jews. They *live* to type each other." I remembered the wholesaler at M. Léon Tissus and took her point. "I think *Beautiful Rafaela* might just be his type."

"As long as *this* Rafaela's not his type," I said.

"Oh, no," she said protectively. "He may want you, but he cannot have you."

Tamara's overblown pronouncement made me giggle, reassured. "So why didn't you show them *Kizette au Balcon*?"

"Neither of those men want a painting like that. I can tell."

"Well, it's a good idea to show them your other work," I said, setting aside my distaste for Boucard. "They seem rich."

"*Seem?*"

We laughed. "How long have you been planning this party?" I asked.

"Oh, for about five minutes," Tamara said.

"That's what I thought."

"So," Tamara said. "We are going to sit down for a few minutes, to give those men time to walk away. And then we are going back for my ten thousand francs."

Tamara asked me to come home with her after the Salon, to sew up the strap of her slip that I'd pinned. "It *does* hurt. You were right. I was impatient," she said, contrite. As we climbed the stairs to her apartment, she flipped through her mail, announcing, "My friend Ira is back in Paris. Good."

"Who?"

"Kizette is at my mother's. She dropped off a note, see? Jeanne sent to say she is running late. Oh, no, do you hear that?"

"*Oh, no,* what?" I asked.

We had reached the top of the stairs, where we were greeted by a clamor of thuds and claws.

"Oh, no, somebody needs a walk," Tamara said, opening the door. Seffa whined with relief, setting both front paws on Tamara's shoulders. "*Bisou bisou,* yes, yes," Tamara said. "*Does* somebody need a walk?"

"Oh, no," I repeated, walking in behind them, shocked. The room was clotted with red. Red confetti. Red flecks of paper. Curds of wet red fluff. *What happened?*

I saw the overturned zinc *poubelle* poking out from behind the screen where I had changed, and understood. When I changed my sanitary napkin between poses that morning, I put it in a twist of paper in the *poubelle*. In our hurry to go to the Salon, I forgot to dump the garbage downstairs before we left, and Seffa had found it. "Mother of God," I said, horrified.

"Naughty Seffa!" said Tamara.

"We kept him locked in the bedroom this morning, and then we let him out before we left. I forgot to take down my things. I'm so embarrassed."

"It is nothing."

"All your beautiful gray velvet!" I protested, gesturing at the red-petalled walls and rugs.

"You naughty, naughty dog." Tamara clucked.

"I'm so sorry."

"It is human. You are a young girl. It is normal."

"Why don't you take your walk and I'll clean this up?"

"No, no, no," said Tamara. "We need to go. You can use the hall toilet if you need to. Jeanne will take care of this. I can tell her it was mine."

"But what about your slip?" I asked.

"Some other time," said Tamara. "I have a friend who just came back to town."

In the WC, I clipped a fresh napkin into my belt, still rattled. My brothers would have never let me forget this. *But Tamara's not upset*, I bullied myself. *Don't be embarrassed*. I washed my hands and then I dried them, and then I washed them again. Then I reapplied my lipstick for good measure.

When we went outside, Tamara walked me partway to the train, gossiping about people we had seen at the Salon. She really wasn't upset. I breathed deeper as we walked, happy again. "Thank you for coming with me today, *ma Belle Rafaela*," Tamara said. And then she kissed me on the sidewalk. I hadn't even realized, until that moment, that I had always harbored the nagging fear that she took Seffa for his daily walks alone because she didn't want anyone to see us together. "I was so proud to have you next to me," she said.

I could feel her words buzz inside my chest as she held me, and I curled into them, grateful. "Same here."

"My good-luck piece," Tamara said. "I liked watching them fight over *Rafaela* without knowing it was you."

I giggled. "I felt like a spy."

"You are our secret," Tamara whispered, her words hot in my ear.

10

OUR SECRET, TAMARA HAD CALLED ME. But when I walked into Shakespeare and Company the day after the Salon opened, I learned I was no secret to Anson's friend Bobby. He had seen Tamara kiss me and had seen *Beautiful Rafaela* on the wall. "That painting of you is gorgeous, Rafaela," Sylvia said when I walked in.

Anson, looking up from his newspaper, assented with a sigh of regret. "Now I know why you won't go out with me," he said.

"But you know that Neoclassical Cubism is a dead end, right?" Bobby piped up, poking through his mail.

"Excuse me?"

"I'm just saying that what your girlfriend does is *odd*. To say nothing," he added, in an insinuating coo, "about her *private* life."

Just the day before, Tamara had told me in so many ways that I had nothing to be ashamed of. Perhaps that's what made me speak up. My mind went white. My feet went clammy in my shoes. "Leave me alone, Bobby," I said.

Bobby stared at me, thrown. My heart was beating hard in my face, but I saw Anson's eyes widen with respect.

"You heard her," said Sylvia.

Anson nodded, and though he fluttered them sarcastically, Bobby lifted his hands, as if under arrest. "I hear and obey, Miss Beach. *Pardon.*"

In the weeks at work that followed, I was pleased, but not completely surprised, to see a new canvas emerge: Tamara was painting herself in my one-strapped pink chemise, against the same white dotted swiss she had me wear for *Full Summer.* Her use of white on white made the design on the backdrop look cut out, rather than embroidered. She used straight edges to define the sides of the buckled ribbon strap, as if creating a channel for the softer shading inside the lines to move through. In the painting, and in real life, I saw that the lace I had added to the bodice was beginning to fray. "You're sure you don't want me to stitch that up?"

"No. Now it is a painting. I do not want to change a thing."

"What's it like to paint yourself as a brunette?" I asked.

"I like it," she said. "In the painting, I am someone Tadeusz never knew."

My gift gave Tamara other ideas, too. A week after the Salon opened, once we had finished our sitting, she asked me to wait in her apartment while she stepped out for a moment with Seffa, whom I had already forgiven. He couldn't help being a dog, any more than my brothers could have helped being children. Tamara returned ten minutes later, accompanied by a beautiful green-eyed woman with dark red hair. She was carrying a baby, and Tamara followed behind her with a bassinette. "This lady wants to commission a dress," Tamara said.

A commission! I *did* spend all my spare time making dresses, true, but I had never really considered going into business. I'd never even traded anything for my sewing, not since the bet I'd made my mother over my school uniform. But this is how Tamara thinks, I reflected. She sells her work; why shouldn't I sell mine? I tried to stand a little taller in my lucky dress as Tamara introduced us. "Rafaela Fano, Ira Perrot," she announced. *Ira* rhymed with *mirror*.

"Enchantée," I said, unsure whether to shake the woman's hand or kiss her cheek.

"Ira is English," Tamara corrected. "She went home to have her baby and she stayed away a *whole year*," she said accusingly, then turned to Ira. "But now she's back, *n'est-ce pas?*"

Ira switched to English once Tamara did. "Tamara showed me that pretty chemise you made, and she said you were getting started as a dressmaker." I was? I realized this must have been how Tamara had gotten her own start as a portrait painter. She must have simply announced that she was one, just like that, before she ever sold a canvas. Could I be a *couturière* before I ever sold a dress? I watched Ira explain herself, gesturing airily toward Lulu, the baby in the bassinette. "I have a closet full of clothes I'm too fat for now, but I can't wear my maternity clothes anymore either." Her English was posh and crisp, her face fresh and open. "It *would* cheer me up to have something new."

"I could copy one of your favorite dresses a little bigger, if you want," I said, following Tamara's lead. "In a new fabric?"

"You're a darling," Ira said.

While we worked out a price, Tamara produced a roll of dress-maker's tape. "You left this behind," she told me. What was she talking about? Before I could contradict her, she held up a finger-and-thumbful of Ira's bobbed red hair. "What color do you think would flatter this?" she asked me.

"I think we should let the client decide," I said.

"I haven't had time to decide a thing, with Lulu," Ira protested. "But I do love *your* dress, Rafaela."

"Well . . ." I said, noting her measurements in Tamara's sketch-book.

"Don't tell me those numbers, Miss Fano," warned Ira.

"Do not talk nonsense. You have a newborn," said Tamara. "If you can trust me with the color, I could choose the fabric," she proposed.

"That would be the best gift of all," said Ira. "You choose it, I'll pay for it."

Later that month, before finishing our private *Rafaela*, Tamara asked me to try a new pose: seated, half rising, one hand in my lap, one raised to my face. "It surprises you," Tamara explained.

"What surprises me?"

"A dove."

"A duff?"

"The messenger of the Holy Spirit. The bird of Aphrodite."

I giggled. "Do you know, I'm such a city girl, I've never actu-ally seen a dove?"

Tamara's exaggerated sigh betrayed real tenderness. "You are so young," she said. She dug a small canvas out of a stack of austere little still lifes, from the days, she told me, just before we met. She drove a nail into the wall and hung a painting of two white pigeons and a birdhouse. "I will paint him here," she said, pointing to a spot on my forearm. "Your eyes will look here," she said, pointing at the birds. "Doves."

"They're cute," I said.

"This way you will not imagine a chicken or a cow," she said sternly, her voice freighted with mock disapproval. "It would spoil the painting."

"Well, we can't have that."

"I cannot believe you never saw a dove," she chided. For a moment, I envied Tamara's daughter. What wouldn't she have seen by the time she was my age?

Tamara wanted to try an Annunciation scene, she explained. She touched my face with her fingertips until she coaxed out the expression she was looking for: not startled, or fearful, but meditative. Listening.

"I couldn't stay this calm if you used a real dove," I cracked.

"If there were a real dove in this apartment, we would chase it out the window," Tamara said, with a shudder, to make me laugh. "This is what art is for."

After a few days of *Nude with Dove*, during which time Tamara's self-portrait in my chemise took shape as well, she presented me with one of Ira's old dresses and a length of silk crepe in a brilliant cobalt, a deeper blue than that of my lucky dress, with a finer sheen. "It's beautiful. Did you find it in the fabric district?"

"I made my housekeeper get it," she said. "I gave her the color to match." I was surprised that she deflected my praise, and surprised that a painter—and clotheshorse—as finicky as Tamara wouldn't do the task herself, but she offered no further explanation.

Once I got over the initial shock of making a dress, not as a gift, but for money, I liked to think this might be the start of something for me. Not life as a party girl, not life at Belle Jardinière. I could model for Tamara by day and make dresses by night. Tamara knew princes and duchesses and wives of rich men. I could make a name for myself, I began to daydream; I could build up a clientele of my own.

I did not see Tadeusz when he returned briefly a week or so later to visit with Kizette and claim Seffa for a few months, but I saw how his appearance—and the dog's absence—upset Tamara. She continued work on her self-portrait, and even finished it, but pronounced it no good: though it was no less polished than the other recent work, the effect was clownish rather than triumphal. Her breasts, emerging from the lace front of the slip, looked rubbery in their pertness, her short locks fussily twisted, her eyelashes cartoonishly long. She pointed out an anatomically impossible clavicle, and a spot where her mouth looked distorted, as if it were lightly touching a pane of glass. When I looked carefully, I saw the pattern on the lace had started to march up onto the couch: Had she painted it on one of her cocaine-sleepless nights? Or had she just been unhappy? But that wasn't the worst of it. "You can tell it was flawed from the start. If I hold my neck straight, my head does not fit in the frame."

"But you liked my chemise," I countered.

"I did," she said wryly.

"Well, I like your painting."

"Do not patronize me," she protested. "I am weak enough to give in to your flattery." I wasn't so sure: the next day she set to work on a second *Chemise Rose*.

As I worked on Ira's dress, Tamara completed our copy of *Beautiful Rafaela*. I finished basting the night she returned to *Nude with Dove*. The next morning, Tamara arranged a fitting: I had done faithful work, but Ira had already deflated a little at the waist in the time since I had first measured her. Lulu was loath to part with her mother, gumming Tamara's finger suspiciously before giving way to a pure howl. Finally Ira nursed her, and we all breathed easier.

"She's heavy," Ira said, breast in one hand, baby in the other.

"Very Quattrocento," Tamara pronounced. "You make a fine Virgin."

"Why thank you," Ira said demurely. The smile she exchanged with Tamara—complicit and charged with history—was anything but demure.

"How long have you known each other?" I asked.

"I moved to Paris just after the Armistice, and I met Tamara my first winter here, so that would be, what? Nine years!"

"Why Paris?"

"My husband's French. He was working in England during the war. We married when I was eighteen," she added, answering a question I hadn't asked, and I realized she was accustomed to being told she looked young.

"A child bride," said Tamara.

"Speak for yourself." Ira laughed.

"Your name sounds kind of Russian," I said. "Yra?"

"My godmother was Irish. My mother's best friend from school. So my parents gave me the middle name *Eire* to annoy their families. E-I-R-E; it means Ireland. I know, unspellable, unpronounceable. And my Christian name is so dreary: Winifred. Imagine! So Eire it was. But I spell it I-R-A. At least this way you can pronounce it, even if it *is* a Jew's name, and a man's name to boot."

I glanced uncomfortably over at Tamara, but her face was strangely opaque. Then she spoke in a light rush. "Ira took me to Italy not long after we met. I was very poor, but I wanted to paint, and Ira believed I needed to see the museums of Florence, Rome, Venice. And she was right. Botticelli. De Messina. I looked and I said, *They make it all so simple. Radiant. I could paint like that, too, no?* And that is what I have done with you, Rafaela. It took me years, but I did it."

I felt exposed as Ira turned to look full at me. *Beautiful Rafaela* was Tamara's triumph after all, but it was me, too.

"Ira paid for everything," Tamara bragged. "She is my"—here she groped for the English phrase—"*fairy godmother.*"

"Don't make me sound so old," Ira complained.

Tamara's second *Chemise Rose* filled the frame less awkwardly than the first. The neck seemed naturally tilted instead of torqued into place; the breasts sat modestly inside the pink satin. As with *Nude with Dove,* at first Tamara only outlined the face, leaving its features for later. "You're painting another brunette," I noted during my first break one morning. She had recently re-dyed herself a blonde.

"I want to compare the two paintings as closely as possible," she explained. What she loved about both, she told me, was my gift to her: "The lace across the top, it is exciting; it is difficult. I have never painted flesh through lace before. I like the challenge," she said, and smiled. "Look, you are sweating."

The radiators ran so hot in Tamara's apartment that we left the windows open. I was grateful, especially during the poses that made my muscles ache. Hours of arching for both versions of *Beautiful Rafaela* had been hard enough in warmer weather. In a chilly studio, holding the *Rafaela* pose—let alone the half-seated rise Tamara wanted for *Nude with Dove*—would have hurt even after my nightly bath. I looked again at her bare skin in the two self-portraits: I wasn't the only one who thrived on radiator heat. She had copied my chemise mercilessly in both paintings, down to the frayed lace.

"I *could* try to fix that for you," I offered again.

"No," she said, delighting me. "I love it just the way it is."

11

THE WEEK I FINISHED IRA'S DRESS, a month after meeting the two rich collectors at the Salon d'Automne, Tamara held a soirée to celebrate her Salon triumph, making sure to invite both the behemoth Teutonic baron, Kuffner, and the unctuous French doctor, Boucard. Three days before the party, as I lay in Tamara's bed at the end of the workday, she woke up, and turned to me. "Darling, I just had a dream. Would you do something for me?"

"Anything."

"Not so fast, *ma petite*. Listen first. This was my dream. I am at the party and everyone is here, a hundred people: princes and princesses, bank barons and movie stars, press people, everyone. And suddenly the lights go out. And then for one second, a bright light shines on you, Rafaela, like a singer on a stage. You are posing on the couch, just the way you posed for *La Belle*. You are stretching like a cat, but we only see you for one second, and then the lights go out again. Three times this happens, like three lightning flashes, and then the lights come back on, and you have disappeared, but everyone's eyes are stamped with you. Your image is floating in their eyes forever. They can see only you. They can think only of you. They can speak only about you."

I stared at Tamara, hypnotized.

"And then they go crazy and buy all my paintings."

"You want me to take my clothes off at your party?"

"Just for three seconds, Rafaela. One, two, three. We will have photographers, but I promise they will not photograph you."

"Hmm," I said, sitting, my arms wrapped around my legs.

"Please? If you do this, no one will ever forget my work. I would pay you anything."

What Tamara was asking for was less humiliating than some things I'd done for money, and even sounded kind of beautiful. It was nothing my bookstore friends hadn't already seen at the Salon, thanks to Bobby Nightinghoul's big mouth. I gathered the sheet to me, thinking. "What would you do for me?"

"Anything," she said firmly. "What do you want?"

I want you to tell me you love me, I thought. But I didn't want to ask. I wanted her to want to say it. "I want—" I said. I let the sheet fall away from me and gave her an eyeful. When she reached for me, I pulled away. "I want you to take me on a trip for Christmas. One week, just us, nobody else."

Tamara recoiled. "What about my daughter?"

"Her father's going to be lonely for her this Christmas. He'll be awfully grateful," I said, feeling cocky.

"Rafaela, you are a Jew. What do you care about Christmas?"

"I told you, I'm a Catholic," I said. "Not a religious one, but I care plenty." I didn't celebrate Christmas at home until my mother remarried, but ten in a row had left their mark. Gin and I had spent our first Christmas alone together on rue Laffitte while our boy-friends spent it with their wives and children. Homesick, we played records and ate tinned caviar with too much champagne. When Gin asked me to teach her an Italian Christmas song, I got sick to my stomach and went to bed. Of course I cared.

I watched Tamara's face cloud over. "I'm sure you can pay some other girl to do it," I said.

"No."

"No one will miss it if you *don't* have me at your party. It was just a dream."

"No."

I shrugged. "I knew you wouldn't want to go."

Tamara's face cleared. "Can we go *anywhere?*"

"Anywhere as long as it's just us," I repeated, like a child spin-ning out a story. "I want to sleep with you every night and wake up with you every morning."

"All right, then."

I grinned.

"I am taking you to Italy."

"Oh. Thanks."

"You *do* know your stepfather's little town is not even *on* the Italian mainland, darling?"

"I'm not *stupid*," I said, embarrassed.

"We can go as tourists, Rafaela. No one has to know you are Italian. You can tell them you are Spanish if they ask. We can go to museums and stay in hotels."

She did have a point. Maybe an Italian Christmas wouldn't make me feel so sick and sad if I spent it with her. And I *was* getting my way, after all. "Thank you, Tamara."

"Good girl," Tamara said. I didn't pull away this time. "You will be magnificent."

The morning of Tamara's party, she had me pose for just an hour, then enlisted my help moving furniture. We pointed three electric photographers' lamps at the familiar gray chaise, and set up the screen in front of it for me to change behind. "The wall lights go out," Tamara said, gesturing toward the electric sconces that lined the room. "My friend d'Afflitto moves the screen away. Then *these* lamps flash on, and there you are, just as you are in the painting. *Ravissante*. Flash, flash, flash. Then it is dark, and d'Afflitto returns the screen. When the wall lights come on again, you can dress with no one looking. All right?"

I nodded, remembering the Marquis d'Afflitto with his handkerchief thrown over his face. I liked him. "That's thoughtful. Thank you."

"You are comfortable?"

"Just make sure no one touches me."

"I will be standing right there."

"I'm not afraid then."

"Everyone wants the naked girl at the party," Tamara said, taking one of my earlobes between finger and thumb. I grinned. "But I am going to keep you for myself."

After the furniture, we moved the paintings. *Nude with Dove*, *Full Summer*, and the second *Chemise Rose* stood displayed on easels, while around them hung recent work that hadn't yet sold: the first

Chemise Rose, a couple of small abstracts, the spare little still lifes Tamara had been painting just before we met. Two large photographs sat side by side on a table crowded with flowers: one of *La Belle Rafaela*, and one of *Kizette au Balcon*.

Even so, Tamara's portrait of Tadeusz dominated the room, the way Tadeusz, even in his absence, cast so long a shadow on Tamara's days. Coolly monumental against a pewter cityscape, a handsome man in an overcoat and white muffler leaned into the frame of the painting, or rose out of it, an envelope tucked under his arm, top hat in hand. The largest shape in the painting was that of the man's lush black coat, a dense, form-fitting wool from the look of it, with wide—were those satin?—lapels. Above the bulwark of that coat, Tadeusz's eyes, wounded, wounding, met the viewer's directly, but without trust. His irises held no dot of white.

Also remarkable was that while Tamara's works-in-progress stood on easels, Tadeusz's portrait hung on the wall, even though it was not at all *finished* the way Tamara's other works were. There wasn't just *one* "line out of place": the man's whole left hand—braced on a ledge, holding the top hat—had been left conspicuously *un*finished. At first glance, the painting could have been of any good-looking society man out for a jazz night. On second glance, knowing Tamara, it was hard not to see the envelope and remember the divorce papers Tadeusz had brought. It was hard not to see the unpainted hand as Tamara's little revenge. It was a way to render her choice to render neither his wedding ring nor his bare finger.

I went home to bathe and change, and to avoid the embarrassment of being the first one at the party. By the time I came back, the salon was so crowded I could circle the room unnoticed. Trying to drop my coat off in the bedroom, I found myself caught behind Tamara's friend Romana de la Salle in a frothy pink dress, talking to a bulky crop-haired brunette in a suit. "You inspired Tamara's portrait of my mother," Romana piped in French, fingering the suited woman's collar. "Come, let me show you."

I let the two of them force their way through the crowd ahead of me to the bedroom. I recalled from the exhibition that Romana had had a flirty, girlish charm that she could turn on and off at will. She might have claimed at the Salon to be one of the only women left in Paris who slept with men, but that didn't stop her from sparkling at Tamara's party as she turned, often, to gaze up at her companion. "How long have you known Tamara?"

"We haven't met. I came with friends," the *donna-uomo* said tersely. Though she did not smile, her teeth appeared, sudden and white. When she and Romana stood together in front of Tamara's portrait of the mannish Duchesse de la Salle, I realized that the only trace I could see of Romana, the art school dropout who had startled me with her eloquence, was the stubborn jaw she shared with her mother. I realized, too, that the woman in the suit pretending not to enjoy Romana's attention must be the athlete Violette Morris.

Vi Morris, as the newspapers called her (Vi rhyming with *tree*, not *lie)*, thrust a hand in a pocket and rested her other arm on the heap of coats on Tamara's bed, mirroring the Duchesse de la Salle's pose in the painting. It was only then, by contrasting the two women, that I noticed the feminine details in Tamara's portrait: the marcelled hair, the rouged lips and cheeks, the white-collared neckline plunging far below that of any man outside of a costume drama involving pirates. When I looked at the duchess's pointing fingernail, life-size and painted exactly as I would have painted my own, I realized that Tamara had filed it to an oval point and given it a French manicure. In all these little respects, Violette looked much more the man, and yet the arrogance with which each figure claimed space was strikingly similar. From the offhand way Vi leaned against Tamara's bed, one would have thought she, not I, the little *grisette* despairing of a place to leave her coat, had spent more time in it. *"Mais non,"* she said, angling for a flattering reply. "Doesn't look a thing like me."

After the two women left the room, Romana with a dainty hand on Vi's shoulder, I took pleasure in hanging my coat, for the first time, in Tamara's closet, so that it wouldn't get lost among the others on the bed. Now I could leave whenever I liked. When I walked out of the bedroom, the first thing I noticed, through the crowded cigarette haze and the sultry gramophone music, was that Tamara, ablaze in beaded fringe, was posing for a photograph between the two rich art collectors from the Salon d'Automne. I recognized them, the suave French Dr. Boucard with the gray pearl tiepin, the shaggy Teutonic Baron Kuffner with his spectacles. Of their conversation, I could hear the titles *Full Summer* and *Nude with Dove*.

"Selling the work before it's even finished? Not bad," I overheard the Marquis d'Afflitto—elegant even in a purple bow tie—murmur to Romana.

"She's definitely trying," Romana agreed, impressed. While Violette signed an autograph, Romana greeted me, remembering our conversation at the Salon. "Romaine Brooks isn't here tonight, but her girlfriend, Natalie—" she said, gesturing toward a flash of blond hair on the other side of the room before the return of

Vi's attention sidetracked her. "Would you like to meet Tamara?" she asked Violette.

"No rush," said the athlete, narrowing her eyes at Tamara in a way that suggested she did not like what she saw. "She looks busy."

While the salon was crowded—in five minutes I spotted Nancy Cunard, bedecked in ivory, Tallulah Bankhead in a hundred ropes of pearls, Filippo Marinetti, and sere, sculptural Jean Cocteau—the dining room was even denser with people. In the arch between two feathered headbands, I saw why.

Everyone wants the naked girl at the party, Tamara had said. I hadn't realized she was speaking literally. I saw, draped across the dining room table, a girl my age wearing nothing but oysters. I blinked: no, she was wearing a massive silver tray, on which a dense mosaic of oysters on the half shell shone from a bed of ice. Only a small towel separated the tray from her bare belly. Seaweed lightly downed her hair, thighs, and outspread arms, while a white sheet caught her legs from knee to foot like a mermaid's tail. The silver tray covered the girl's midsection, though I could tell a few fellows down around her feet were able to see up her legs quite a bit—while her bare arms and chest rose from above the tray unhindered. Her mother-of-pearl eyelids never opened, her cornsilk-pale hair fanned out a yard around her, and though their oyster-laden hands passed within inches of her beautiful breasts, no guest dared touch her. I wanted the girl. I was afraid of her. I felt upstaged. I was so glad it wasn't me.

I was glad, too, that Tamara had promised to stay near me when I posed: when I saw her next, she was chatting with the lady editor of *Die Dame* as if the girl on the table were nothing more than a vase of flowers. It was clear from the editor's gestures that she was talking eagerly about *Full Summer*, and though I couldn't hear her above the hubbub, I could see her wheedle and plead—until Tamara pulled aside a gray velvet drape to reveal one of the stacks of paintings that leaned against the wall, their faces turned away. She flipped quickly until she came to one of two women in cloche hats, one with her back to the viewer, the other I recognized as Ira Perrot from her long nose and queerly lit eyes. I saw the *éditrice* nod with pleasure, and out of the corner of my eye I saw Kuffner and Boucard hungrily observe the exchange. Then Tamara noticed me and summoned d'Afflitto for help with the lights.

When I went behind the screen to undress, I found the one-sleeved red robe draped across the velvet chaise, just as Tamara would leave it for me when she worked on the first *Beautiful Rafaela*. The sight comforted me, and helped me settle into the routine of posing despite the clamor of the party on the other side of the screen. I let d'Afflitto know when I was ready, and saw him signal to Tamara, who rapped on a glass with an oyster fork.

"Ladies and gentlemen, I have brought you here tonight to celebrate a painting," she said. "In this, my sixth year of showing at the Salon d'Automne, I had two pieces accepted. The first, *Kizette au Balcon*, won a medal in the Exposition Internationale des Beaux-Arts in Bordeaux this past summer, while the second, *La Belle Rafaela*, resulted in my first ever Salon d'Automne sale."

"Before the Salon even opened!" called d'Afflitto.

"In any case," Tamara said modestly, "the paintings are enjoying one last night in the Petit Palais, and Kizette is enjoying a night sound asleep at her grandmother's, so I have for you here tonight a live painting, a live jewel. Ladies and gentlemen, I present *La Belle Rafaela*."

The wall lights, as planned, went out. I heard d'Afflitto move softly in the dark as he swept away the screen. And then the photographers' lamps blazed on like lightning, *flash, flash, flash,* just as Tamara had promised, while the gathered company gasped and squealed. My eyes slitted open a hairsbreadth to the sight of the room staring at me—Boucard and Kuffner, d'Afflitto, the *Die Dame éditrice,* Romana de la Salle quite suddenly in Vi Morris's lap—each mouth slack with wonder. I shut my eyes tight against the awe in their faces and heard the word *belle* whoosh through the crowd, like wind flattening grass.

As the party crowd stared at me, nude and spotlit, I felt gilded, splendid, radiant, afraid: I was a goddess, a statue, a blood sacrifice. The photographers' lamps went out again, and d'Afflitto—bless him—restored the screen. In the moment I reached for my clothes, Tamara joined me, more a wave of scent and warm satin than anything I could see. She must have abandoned her post by the wall lights. Her ringed hand found me in the dark and she whispered in my ear, "You were just like my dream." At that moment, as the crowd began to rumble for light, I felt as beautiful as she thought I was. "Your heart," she said, her hand on my breastbone. "It's beating so hard."

"It's because I'm happy," I said, kissing her.

Just then a murderous sound cut through the room. *"Sale fils de putain!"* screamed a woman. And that was the nicest thing she said.

The crowd erupted, Tamara with it, and rushed toward the source of the scream. "Someone touched the girl," I heard a man's voice explain. A light came on in the kitchen, making the dining room dimly visible, and the salon went from black to gray. "Some-one burned her with a cigar," said another voice. I heard a heavy, metallic cascade of smacks as the silver tray crashed to the floor.

I dressed quickly, rattled at the news, but when I began to circle the screen, I stopped. Tamara was gone. D'Afflitto was gone. Romana and Violette were just leaving, straightening their clothes on the way to the dining room, from which the voice of the oyster girl filled the apartment with blood and shit, with ice and nails, with clouds of rubble.

Two figures, however, remained in the salon, bending toward the paintings that rested on the floor. One, crouching, flipped open a cigarette lighter: I saw the two men were Baron Kuffner and Dr. Boucard. Red-whiskered, heavy on his feet, Baron Kuffner could have been an aging Norse god with a hammer and thunder-bolt. The smooth Dr. Boucard, flame in hand, would have been that god's younger and craftier ally.

Together, they moved quickly but thoroughly through the canvases propped against the wall like dominoes. Suddenly they stopped. "Look at this one," Baron Kuffner murmured in his accented French. I heard boyish laughter in his voice, as if sneaking around in the dark added to the pleasure he took in the paintings.

"Oh, let's," said Dr. Boucard, his voice calmly professional by contrast. Carefully, the two men lifted out a small painting, turned it around, and set it against the wall by itself. In the half-dark, the flaring cigarette lighter revealed the painting one splash at a time: *Rafaela in Green*.

"I think you should put that away," I said.

The two men looked up, alarmed by my voice in the darkness. Another light came on in the dining room, and then they looked from the painting to me and back again. "So *you're* the model," said Baron Kuffner, spectacles gleaming.

"Why, it's Tamara's little Jewish friend," oozed Dr. Boucard.

The long raw stare the two men gave me—followed by the short amused glance they gave each other—sent me scuttling into Tamara's bedroom, where claiming my coat gave me license to sink deep into my hat as well. If I could have exited out Tamara's window unscathed at that moment, I would have.

When I reëmerged, the two men were deep in conversation with Tamara over the painting. I waved good night, and she waved back, unseeing, as if the kiss behind the screen had never happened. She was doing her job, I consoled myself. I had done mine, after all: I could go. Just before I reached the door, I all but bumped into Anson Hall. I later learned that he and Natalie Barney knew each other from Sylvia's bookstore, but at the moment, I was simply stunned. "Oh, *you're* here," I said.

"Well, *you're* certainly here."

"I guess."

"Why not stay?"

"I'm embarrassed."

"You weren't having a good time up there? You looked like you were," said Anson. "I certainly was."

This is *exactly* why I want to leave, I thought, impatient. "I wasn't embarrassed up there, but I'm embarrassed to stay," I said, with an involuntary glance toward Tamara, Kuffner, and Boucard.

As if feeling my eyes, the three of them looked over at me just at that moment. Anson raised his glass to them in an awkward wave, and the French doctor's eyes lit in response, as if he were photographing the two of us, while the hulking baron gazed at me alone.

"You were the star of the show until that girl started carrying on," Anson said.

"You mean until some sick man got it into his head to *burn* her," I corrected. "That was disgusting."

Peripherally aware of Baron Kuffner looking up from Tamara to seek me out, I watched something complex and apologetic cross Anson's face, before Dr. Boucard appeared at his elbow. While the two men made their introductions—and before the Wagnerian Kuffner could thunder over to me—I slipped off, but not before promising to meet Anson for coffee the next day.

When I passed the taxi stand near Tamara's Métro stop, I was surprised to see someone familiar shimmy into a cab with an overdressed boyfriend. "Maggey?"

My friend from the Bois de Boulogne reached over to close the car door, a long twist of blond hair snaking out from under her hat. "That pervert bitch," she said in French. I stopped walking, brought short: Maggey had been the girl at Tamara's party. I hadn't recognized her naked, nor had I ever heard her scream like that before. She didn't hear me when I called her name again, but just before she pulled the door shut, I heard a deep, phlegmy cough. She sounded sick.

12

I WALKED ALL THE WAY HOME from Tamara's party, and when I got there, I paced my room, swooping between giddiness and nausea. At one extreme, I took off my clothes and looked at myself in the mirror, my familiar, fleshy body made strange and glittering to me, not just by Tamara's eccentric eye, but by the crowd's. At the other pole, I smoked half a cigarette and touched it to my skin, then flinched away, sickened, before locking the memory of Maggey's scream up in a box. Finally, unable to sleep, I worked on Ira's dress, the sky ebbing white as I tied off the last knot. Gin was out for the night, or I would have woken her. When I finished, I spread the little frock in my arms, alone, eager to show it off.

The next day I brought the dress with me when I went to pose. "It is almost as beautiful as you were last night," Tamara exclaimed. "I will go tell Ira on your first break. I cannot phone, because look," she said. The cord dangled from her telephone, unplugged.

"Doctor Boucard and Baron Kuffner's people have called me twice each in the past hour!"

"They want our *Rafaela*?"

"They do, but I will not sell her," Tamara said.

"What are you going to do?" I asked.

"Well, first, nothing. I will simply let them *want* her for a few days. Then I will decide what to do."

I knew Tamara had more in mind than she claimed, because she asked me to pose for the almost finished *Full Summer*, even though I didn't have my period. From my chair, paper flowers in hand, I could see Ira's blue dress glistening on the satin hanger I'd latched over one of the French doors to the bedroom. I hadn't liked the way the doctor and the baron looked at me, but the idea of Tamara turning them both down made me feel proud. I sat fizzing quietly over those four phone calls, the way the word *belle* had flattened last night's crowd, the shining blue lily of a gown I'd made with my own hands.

Tamara left during our first break, returning with chocolates and the news that Ira would come by with money that afternoon. I had promised to meet Anson at four, so when Ira hadn't appeared by quarter of, I reluctantly left the dress with Tamara and hurried out.

Tamara's apartment stood two long buildings down from the intersection of her quiet narrow street and the slightly wider rue Vaneau: it was impossible to enter or leave her apartment without being noticed by the patrons of Bistrot Varenne at the corner, or by its mild little waiter, who liked to post himself in the doorway with a cigarette in the afternoons, grunting appreciatively whenever I passed by. Though that afternoon, as always, I walked on the far side of the street to avoid him, I was still close enough to see a flicker of movement through the glass at my left, and catch a gust of warm sausage-laden air before a ruddy hirsute man lumbered out. Just as my eye registered that the big man had left his coat inside, I realized he was crossing the street to reach me. "Rafaela!"

It was Baron Kuffner. His small eyes through his spectacles shone yellow-green, and he was grinning.

I raised a hand to forestall him. "I know you want to talk to Tamara, but I can't help you," I said.

"But I want to talk to *you*," he said, gesturing toward the bistro door. "Won't you join me for a glass of wine?"

"I'm late to meet my friend," I said, taking advantage of an ambiguity in French to let him think he had a man to be afraid of.

"Some other time?"

I snorted and kept walking.

The shortcut I attempted to Shakespeare and Company added long minutes to my route. "Has Anson come and gone already?" I asked when I rushed into the bookstore.

When Sylvia looked up, with genuine politeness, from the letter she was reading, I felt like a lout: I hadn't even said hello. "Sorry, darling. He hasn't been in since the weekend."

"Thanks," I said, apologetic. "I'm sorry about the other day."

"You mean when you stood up to Bob?"

"I wish I hadn't lost my temper," I said.

"You didn't lose your temper. You were just being clear.

Sometimes he needs to be put in his place a little." I nodded shyly, thankful, and sat down by the warm stove. "To his credit," she said, "I think he was trying to be protective. It sounds like your painter friend turns up in some pretty louche places. But he can be obnoxious. I told him to mind his own business."

"That was really decent of you. I know he's an important customer," I said, gesturing toward the post-office wall of pigeonholes Bobby's wife had bought for the store. His name was painted below one of the largest mailboxes.

"I want *all* my subscribers to feel welcome here," Sylvia said. "Not just a few blowhards. You can get your mail sent here too, if you want."

"I never get any mail," I said. "But, thanks. For everything, I mean. Sorry. I interrupted you."

"Not at all," she said, shaking out her springy curls as she stretched. My pleasure at having finished Ira's dress made me notice clothing more than ever: Sylvia's little tweed jacket fitted her perfectly, but the cuffs were too short. "They're holding the next issue of *transition* until Joyce finishes 'Anna Livia Plurabelle,'" she explained with a smile. I had no idea what she was talking about, but that was part of why I liked her. Would an extra strip of brown velvet at those cuffs look elegant or fussy? She held up the letter she was reading, a barely legible list of names. "And then when it comes out, he says here he wants a copy sent to forty different addresses. But the thing is, forty copies plus postage means four hundred francs, and Adrienne put her foot down." She waved to someone walking by outside, and I saw it was, in fact, Adrienne, once again in her billowy costume and fitted black waistcoat. I remembered the Vermeer book Sylvia had shown me in September, and it occurred to me, first, that Adrienne Monnier was dressed like a Vermeer maid, second, that I had never seen her dressed otherwise, and third, that she had solved the problem of being a fat woman in an age of slim fashions by ignoring fashion altogether. In her chosen uniform, I realized, Adrienne looked iconic rather than dumpy. I waved to her, too, impressed, and she favored me with a dimpled smile. When I looked back at Sylvia again, she was knuckling the bridge of her nose. "So I say we compromise by holding a reading at the store as soon as he's finisheed," she decided. "And then what I can do is write all these people and invite them."

"That's a lot of letters."

"I *do* hate to disappoint him, but at least it's something."

"He's lucky to have you."

I heard no bitterness in Sylvia's laughter. "The luck is all mine," she said. "Now I've talked your ear off. Do you want to wait and see if Anson shows up?"

I nodded. "Do you have any new art books?"

"Not this week, but I did let someone trade me a big medical textbook full of plates for a copy of *Pomes Penyeach*."

I laughed. "You did?"

"I can't say no to a fan. And I have a fatal weakness for *les rossignols*."

"*Les* what?"

"Nightingales. That's what French booksellers call the books you can't *pay* someone to take. But it's handsome, in its way. Do you want to see?"

"Why not?" I said, and curled up with the book by the stove. At first the squishy viscera repelled me, but when I reached LE SYS-TÈME MUSCULAIRE, its intricate web of laces as pink as my long-ago

neighbor Theresa's Chanel dress, I felt a shudder of pleasure I only
half understood. *This* was what Tamara saw when she carefully
touched my limbs while working, staring with that flat-eyed painter's look. *This* was the distinct second rounding of thigh in *Beautiful
Rafaela*, the subtly separate rise under the arm. This new knowl-
edge took hold of me as I looked, but another thing did, too: I
wanted to copy even this. My head filled with stacks of interbraided
laces. I was seeing a dress in my mind, but what was it made of?
Satin? Leather? Tight fat coils of embroidery floss? The thousand
separate but parallel fibers split, fanned, re-fused in new combina-
tions, like the waters of a braided stream. A little dress shop, mine,
took shape in my mind, a place as warmly inviting as Sylvia's bookstore. In the window of my shop, I could see a mannequin wearing
the entire *système musculaire* itself—beautifully, impossibly—as a
dress. I didn't want to inflict this garment on anyone in particular,
I just wanted to see it, to make it, the dress itself, a confection as
elaborate as a matador's jacket, a vision as simple as a human body.
I stepped dizzily back from the textbook as if back from a long journey: it was suddenly five o'clock.

Anson clearly wasn't coming. I wished Sylvia a good night and
wandered outside, restless. My friend had stood me up and I would
have to wait a whole day to hear if Ira liked her dress. I'd never
even gotten to show Gin, I grumped, wondering if she'd spent the
night at a hotel. Then it occurred to me: surely Ira had been to
Tamara's by *now*. I could go back and find out right away. Delighted
with myself, I sailed down rue Saint-Sulpice back toward Tamara's
flat, refining my shortcut through the Sixth. Ira would look perfect

in the dress; she'd love it; she'd tell all her rich friends, and while I waited for the commissions to come rolling in, I'd have something to salt away. *It takes money to open a shop, after all*, I daydreamed, reaching rue de Varenne. No one rushed coatless out of the café to bother me this time, and the mild little waiter was too busy with his early-evening wine drinkers to grunt my way.

When I reached Tamara's building, I saw her electric lights on and her curtains down. One gray velvet curtain flapped at an open window, sucked in, then out, by alternating blasts of hot air from the radiator and cold air from the night. It was beautiful, the heaving curtain, the streetlight playing over the gray velvet two flights overhead. I stopped to look at it, to try to *see* it the way Tamara did, the way I'd just looked at LE SYSTÈME MUSCULAIRE—and then I heard a sound, two sounds. A baby's cry. And a woman's, scissoring its way up a private scale.

Unable to move, I stood gripping the railing in the long silence that followed, my little valise hanging from one arm. Through the gap in the curtains, I saw a shadow approach the window. Then a familiar pair of long-wristed, long-fingered hands reached between the curtains and closed it. I turned around and walked away fast, heels hard on the pavement.

Angry and lonely, I didn't want to go home. I took the Métro to Le Casino, where Gin danced and sometimes sang, and prevailed on the rat-faced manager to let me look for her backstage. We hadn't seen much of each other recently, not since she'd come home with that lump over her eye. I felt tentative, leaning into that dim room of mirrors, feathers, and dust: I had sided against Daniel, and she'd frozen me out. But it was empty. She hadn't arrived for work yet, so I settled onto the dressing-room daybed and fell into a thin black angry sleep. I wouldn't have even called it sleep, except that when I woke up, Gin was poking me. "Shove over, darling." Perching beside me in her half-slip and bandeau, she squirmed out of a pair of jeweled butterfly wings and pulled off a Cleopatra wig.

"Hi," I said, not sure if she was still sore at me.

"You missed my show," she said, not really angry. I felt relieved.

"Whoops." My lipstick felt crusty in the corners of my mouth from my nap. I fixed it with my thumb. "I didn't get much sleep last night. Sorry."

"Were you up all hours finishing that dress for the painter's friend?"

I was happy she'd been paying attention, but I winced nonetheless. "A lot of good that did me."

"Did you get paid, though?"

"Tomorrow, I think. Why?" Did I even need to ask? "I have modeling money if you need some."

"Nice work," she said. I was wrong; she'd just been making conversation. "Are you and the painter still together?"

"Well, today I wish we weren't," I said glumly, and told her about Tamara and Ira as she rubbed cold cream on her face.

"That's a rotten way to find out," she said. "But after everything you dug up about Daniel, surely *you* didn't think you were *her* only lover?"

Forgiven but not forgotten, I see. "But she's *my* only lover," I protested. "I don't want anybody else."

"*Do unto others,*" scoffed Gin, balling up her washcloth, and I realized I sounded as young as she had that bad night, with her bowl of hot chocolate and her black eye. "You'll notice Jesus Christ had no love life. I didn't want anybody but Daniel, and look where that got me."

"I guess you two haven't made up."

Gin shrugged and began wriggling into a black shift, a real pearl collar, and an opera-length rope of glass beads. "Not yet. I've got this lawyer I'm stringing along if things really don't work out. I'm drinking a lot so the baby will come out small—that way Remy will think it's his, just early."

"Is this Remy guy married?"

"Au contraire," sighed Gin, pulling on a pair of elbow-length black gloves from her own counter at La Belle Jardinière. "That is, in fact, his greatest charm."

"Does he look anything like Daniel?"

"Close enough."

"Nice work, yourself, then."

"But, Rafaela, he's *so* boring. Last night I kept thinking, I'm going to *die* of boredom. So, listen. I need to have some fun. *You* need to meet somebody new. I have an invitation to a student ball tonight; do you want to go?"

I was so upset over Tamara and Ira, dancing was the last thing I would have thought to do. "Sure," I said. "I'll pay for the taxi."

As the Seine lights swung past us, Gin and I took little sips of brandy from her silver flask. "You do know a student ball is a costume party, don't you?"

"Why didn't you tell me at Le Casino? We could have borrowed something from the dressing room."

Gin giggled. "I forgot. But all right. My costume is . . ." She
mused gravely, "I'm a girl who lives on rue Laffitte."

"Really?" I laughed with her. "Then that's my costume, too."

Half an hour later we were deep in a throng of bedsheet-clad
Roman senators and bare-chested Swiss dairymaids. An Eve with
an apple-printed bandeau wore a live snake on her shoulders. A
Sacco and a Vanzetti carried an electric chair between them, while
an Isadora Duncan, their comrade in poor taste, wore a noose made
out of a filmy scarf. The drums and the horn section blasted us
through the fast dance numbers, while the bass and piano lured
us through the smoky slow tunes. Gin smiled at me, her arms on
my shoulders, and drew in close to tease the boys who watched us.

I had to admit, her idea was a good one. I liked being out. I liked
being able to afford my own taxicab, my own admission ticket, my
own drinks. I could turn anybody down tonight, no matter how
rich he might be, or I could smile at that boy across the room with
ivy in his hair, even if he didn't have a *sou*. For once, dancing
felt like the first few seconds of posing for *La Belle*, or the way I'd
felt posing for Tamara's friends the night before. My body became
mine. It wasn't just something I carried around. Ever since my sixteenth birthday, my body had felt like a coin in an unfamiliar
currency: small, shiny, and heavy, obviously of value to somebody,
but not to me. I had never understood what Guillaume or Hervé
saw when they looked at me. I'd watch them greedily respond and
think, why this? Why me? My body felt coincidental to me—I
could just as easily be a tree, a stone, a gust of wind. For so long, I
still felt like the ten-year-old me, skinny as a last wafer of soap,
needling through Washington Square on her way to Baxter Street.
But my months with Tamara had worn away the lonely old questions

and replaced them with a greed of my own: my body was just a fact, this night, a kind of euphoria. I coincided with it, and with the dancing crowd. Throbbing with the horns and drums, we formed a waterfall passing over a light, each of us a drop, a spark, bright, gone. The music danced us, and I knew it wouldn't last, this body I'd learnt to love. I'd turn eighteen one day, and then twenty, thirty, as Sylvia promised, invisible. Gravity would have her pitiless way with me. My buoyant curves would sag into ordinary fat, and I'd have to dress as shrewdly as Adrienne. The weird fuckable radiance that clung to me would drift off to gild and baffle younger girls than I. So enjoy it now, I told myself, smiling back at Gin. *It gives a lovely light.*

Gin peeled away to dance with Sacco and Vanzetti, and I found myself in the lap of the curly-headed boy with ivy in his hair, an engineering student. He said he was twenty years old, so I said I was, too. He was wearing a cape made from a torn-open pillowcase over his regular clothes; he was shouting in French over the music; he was calling me *tu*. "Are you a student, too?"

The old question. My stomach sank, but I looked into his doe eyes and tried to summon, not my anger at Ira and Tamara, but the pleasure I'd felt that afternoon in Shakespeare and Company. "I'm a fashion designer," I shouted back, testing the word *couturière* in my mouth for the first time, trying to purr those two French *R*s out harsh and throaty.

"Ah, oui?" He believed me, simple as that, or he didn't care.

Exultant, I held up the *fine* he'd brought me. "If you can keep your hand still, then I'll drink," I bellowed in French, leaning in to reapply the lipstick I made him hold in his stubby-fingered hand. He grinned. I could feel him through his clothes and I knew, giddily, that he didn't give a goddamn if my lipstick went on straight or not. "But if you move, then *you* drink," I warned. *"D'accord?"* I wished Tamara could see us; I felt vengefully beautiful. But then I saw Gin across the room through the glaring music, the noisy lights, on her hands and knees. Was she sick? *"Ma copine,"* I said, pointing her out. The boy made a *moue* of distress on her behalf. I gave him a wistful kiss, quick but full, and tasted cognac and cigarettes, an eager, salty rasp. Then I reclaimed my lipstick and slid away to help my friend.

When I pulled Gin up she fell against me, sloppy, laughing. "Ring Daniel!" she shouted over the blaring horns. "Tell him I don't feel too good!"

I stood her up like a rag doll and walked her toward a chair. "We're going home, sweetie. Don't worry. You'll be fine." I was going to need money after all, I thought sadly, as she stumbled against me. A lot of it. Suddenly the dancers all looked so young. What was Gin going to do with a baby?

13

⁓

KISSING A STRANGER MAY HAVE EVENED up the score with
Tamara a bit, but it didn't make me any less angry with her. When
I arrived at work the morning after the student ball, she was on the
telephone: she tied her key in a handkerchief and tossed it out the
window instead of coming down to let me in. Our *Rafaela* stood
against the wall, facing out into the room. I did not change into my
model's robe. I waited for her in the salon, fully dressed, my mouth
a hard line. The second *Chemise Rose* stood on an easel in front of
me, so I stared at it. This morning it pained me to see my handi-
work so faithfully copied: the unraveled stitching, the single strap.
Tamara was as careless with me as she was with my gift. She was
only careful with her painting, only faithful to the tilt of the head,
to last month's brunette hair. Suddenly, I gasped. Tamara had
painted the face, and it was Ira's.

Tamara's own face, in the first version, had been highly stylized,
a seductive mask. This second face was far more human: lovely but
somber, perhaps convalescing, a face that had been hurt, but wanted

to trust. Not only had the hard-edged detail of the drapery behind her vanished, the very texture of the second painting was more porous than the first: it seemed more like *paint*, less like shining metal. I suddenly felt small on that couch, like a shell left behind by the tide. In a room full of monumental paintings of myself, confronted with this small, tender portrait, I felt cheap. The rage I'd honed all the hours of my second near-sleepless night began to dissolve into a poisonous sadness. When Tamara walked into the room, she blinked. "Why are you still dressed?"

I pointed at Ira's face: the large green eyes, the long nose, the warily hopeful mouth. "You slept with her, too," I said, choking.

"Rafaela. I am an artist. Do you think I cannot look at a beautiful woman and just paint?"

I closed my eyes in reply, hurt.

"Do you think I sleep with all my models? Or just the ones who sit on my couch and waste my time with silly accusations?"

"That's not fair," I said.

"Guess what? I have Ira's money for you here, and she loves the dress you made. She said she wants to wear it every day."

I smiled thinly, undeterred. "That's wonderful."

"She is going to tell all her friends about you."

I set my forehead in my hand. "It's just—I came back last night to see if she had come by." I looked up and swallowed hard. "I *heard* you two."

"Rafaela, what I do is my own affair. You know that."

"I thought—"

"Ira is an old, old friend. Do you understand?"

"Evidently."

"You are sulking," Tamara said, disgusted.

Who did she think she was? I stood. "Well, don't even think of painting another *Belle Rafaela* for those guys, because I'm not going to pose for it. And I'm not going to pose for *Nude with Dove* either," I said, pointing. "It's stupid. Doves are just pigeons, and pigeons are dirty. And you don't even want to go to Italy with me. You just said that to make me take my clothes off for your friends. Well, I'm not doing *that* again, so don't get any more ideas." I was panting, my hands on my hips like a fishwife. I felt ridiculous, but I enjoyed yelling at her, too.

Tamara stared at me. "Are you quite finished?"

I stood there, flushed, wishing I could think of more things to say, and then I saw her face had changed. "You darling," she said. "You beautiful, beautiful girl." She was crying.

I looked away from her, disarmed.

She sat down on the couch and reached for my hand. I sat down tentatively beside her. "Rafaela," she said. "I would never, *ever* paint *Belle Rafaela* again unless I had good reasons, my own reasons, from the heart, not because some people wanted to buy it. I made one to sell and one to treasure, and no more. I am not a factory. Painting one for every collector who came along would cheapen the painting. It would cheapen me as a painter. And would cheapen the way I feel for you."

"I'm glad to hear that."

"I think you are being childish about *Nude with Dove*, but if that is the way you feel, you do not have to sit for it anymore."

"Thank you." Even if I *was* being childish, I refused to take back what I'd said. I continued to look at her, expectant.

"I promise I will never ask you to pose nude again like that for other people."

"And?"

"And I cannot wait to go to Italy with you, my darling." I looked at her, still hurt, my arms crossed over my chest. Tamara looked from Ira's face around to the three canvases of me. Her eyes went flat and she reached for her topaz ring. When she looked up at me again her voice was sad and careful. "Rafaela, Ira and I are close, but I do not love her."

I held my breath. I wanted her to say more. I wanted to fight how much I wanted it. "You slept with her when you went to London, didn't you?" I pushed.

"But I did not love her," she repeated. "I love you."

I was seventeen. I had been waiting to hear those words since the day Tamara left for England. Tears filled my eyes. "Really?"

She reached for me, the back of her hand just barely touching the invisible down on my face. Despite the radiator, I was shaking. My teeth began to chatter. Tamara said, "Why not pose for me, and then let me show you?"

"I will if you put that painting in the other room."

When Tamara gave herself over to me at the end of the day, she told me that she loved me again. "This is all I want," she whispered, when I woke in her arms. "Nothing but this."

Before Kizette could come back, I roused myself to leave. When I glanced back at her, stockings in hand, I saw Tamara wasn't looking at me like a lover, or even like a painter. She was *gazing* at me. "I want to dress you up in peacock feathers from head to toe," she said dreamily.

"For real?"

An excited, planning look came over her. "I think I could," she mused. "I *bet* I could." She reached for the sketchpad by the table. "Rafaela, you know I promise, promise, promise I will never ask you to pose nude for anyone else, but if I *could* do it—there is this party at the end of the month—would you let me show you off again?"

"Dressed in peacock feathers from head to toe?" How crazy! She nodded. I laughed, feeling as indulged and indulgent as I'd felt hurt and cold before. "Show me our Italy tickets tomorrow, and I'll say yes."

Tamara *did* show me two train tickets to Italy the next day—for late Friday night, December 23rd—along with a bale of peacock-feather trim she said she'd sent the housekeeper to buy, which at first she set aside. After finishing *Full Summer* over the next few days, she began a new painting, a double nude of the two of us. First she had me photograph her lying behind me spoon-fashion, eyes closed, one arm draped over me as I squeezed the rubber bulb to take the shot. Then she roughed the two of us in with quick charcoal on newsprint, transferred the image to canvas, and began slowly painting me alone. She did not display Ira's portrait while I modeled. *Nude with Dove* disappeared before she finished painting in the face. I saw it in her bedroom once, when I went to borrow her hairbrush. I recognized Ira right away: the whites of her eyes took up more of her face than most people's did; her long nose turned up slightly in certain lights; her mouth looked as ready to cry as to kiss. When I saw Ira's face on my body, I seized Tamara's hairbrush and walked away fast.

Baron Kuffner waited for me at Bistrot Varenne often, and I firmly but politely rebuffed him. At the same time, his and Dr. Boucard's calls kept pouring in about the private *Rafaela*. The prices they offered were so high that Tamara hired Anson's boss Boulind to look into whether either man was as wealthy as he claimed. When a preliminary round of inquiries proved fruitful, Tamara dealt with each man coyly, hinting that if he proved his interest by purchasing one of her other *Rafaela*s, she'd be willing to consider his request. It worked. Baron Kuffner agreed to purchase *Nude with Dove* on its completion: Tamara didn't mention anything to him about the change in model. Dr. Boucard, for his part, purchased *Full Summer*, agreeing to license it to *Die Dame* for the cover of August 1928, with Tamara to receive a good portion of the fees. Meanwhile, the first of Tamara's magazine covers appeared: *The Orange Scarf*, featuring Ira, Romana, and the wisp of chiffon Tamara had given me on the day we met. On the December day it first appeared, I wore the scarf, simply for the pleasure of grinning when I passed it on a newsstand.

14

WHEN I ARRIVED AT HER APARTMENT in the orange chiffon scarf, an inky-fresh copy of *Die Dame* in hand, Tamara took one look at me and declared a short workday. I was lying asleep in her bed when Dr. Boucard came to claim his painting: I half awoke to Tamara dressing in a scramble, and when I wakened fully, he was standing in her salon. "I'm so sorry," Tamara said. "I thought you were coming at *deux heures,* not *douʒe heures.* I was just taking a nap when you rang my bell."

"Should I come back in at two, then?" he asked.

"No, no, this is fine." She didn't say *Come back at two,* and she didn't say *Don't mind my model, she's just leaving.* Boucard's persistence unsettled Tamara—both men's did—so I knew she was glad I was there, though I wasn't sure how useful I could be to her from the next room, naked under her sheets. One of the bedroom's curtained French doors stood closed, the other only partway open: through it I could see the mirror over the salon mantel. The bedroom looked like a dark fold in its glass, like the lair of an animal, inside of which glittered a single light: my reflected eye.

Below the mirror, a large sheet of brown paper sailed across the room. *"Full Summer,"* Tamara announced, unwrapping a painting. I heard Boucard murmur in admiration.

"Oh, and you had it framed at Vavin's?"

"Is there anyplace else?"

"Well done."

"Thank you for sharing your painting with *Die Dame*," Tamara said, over the rattle of wrapping paper.

"No thanks needed. Seeing thousands of copies on the news-stands next summer and knowing *I* have the original will be rather nice, Madame de Lempicka. This is a delight."

I hadn't really thought that far ahead. Imagine that, walking up the street with Tamara and passing, not just my orange scarf, but my own face on a magazine!

"I'm very happy with my choice," Boucard said. "But I was wondering, could I take a last look at *Nude with Dove*?"

"If you understand that it's still not finished?" Tamara asked.

"Of course, of course."

Tamara swung suddenly into the bedroom and I pulled the covers over my head. "Sorry," she whispered. When she returned with the painting to the salon, she left the door half open as before.

"Oh, Kuffner's going to wish he'd bought mine," Boucard said, chuckling as Tamara showed him *Nude with Dove*. "This one is larger and a nude, but it could be any woman. *Full Summer* is a real Rafaela. I'm honored to purchase it."

"I'm glad it's in the hands of such a discriminating collector."

"Which brings us to my proposition, Madame." What proposition?

"Have you thought it over?" At this, as quietly as possible, I sat up a little higher in bed.

"Doctor, I've read it over, and I'm ready to sign."

I heard Boucard's exclamations of pleasure, and then the unfolding of papers; briefly each person appeared in the doorway as they crossed over to Tamara's desk. "You're going to find I stand by my word," Boucard assured her.

I heard a flicker of sexual heat in Boucard's promise, but none in Tamara's reply. "You're going to find that your faith in me is well founded."

"And now, regarding *Belle Rafaela en Vert*," he said, calling the private *Rafaela* by its full title. "You don't want to sell it to me. You don't want to sell it to Kuffner. Well and good, you're an artist, and my respect for you is profound. This contract applies only to work you *sell*, after all. However. If you sell any of your work—especially the *Belle en Vert*—to anyone else, I'll know. I'm not going to get swept up in an auction here, and I'm not getting involved in a battle of wills. But I'll know. Your French is impeccable, but perhaps you were not brought up with our legal terms—you are familiar with *breach of contract?*" The phrase he used was *"rupture de contrat."*

"You forget my husband practiced law," Tamara said coolly.

"Then I'm glad we understand each other."

"Perfectly."

W hat was that?" I asked, after Boucard left.

"Now I have a patron," Tamara announced, unfurling on her chaise in a glittering arc. "I will not have to worry about money at all for the next two years. Watch this," she said, reaching over to her desk. On it, beside Boucard's contract, lay Tadeusz's large white envelope, untouched since July. She slit it open, signed its contents, and sealed them up in an envelope of her own. "Out it goes," she crowed. *"Et voilà!* I'm a *divorcée."*

"Just what kind of a patron *is* this Doctor Boucard?" I asked, shrinking.

"Oh, no. No no no no no. Some mistakes, a woman needs to make just once in her life, and that one, I have already made." I heard pride in her voice as she made this pronouncement.

"What happened?"

Tamara lit a cigarette, as if to suck in all the more pleasure from the story she was about to tell. "I once had a friend named Renata Treves, a baroness with a salon. She set me up with the Castelbarco gallery in Milan; they gave me a big show two years ago. So Renata's husband commissioned a portrait. I painted her portrait. It is a beautiful portrait. But then they introduced me to their friend Gabriele D'Annunzio. *Mon Dieu.* What a favor to me, the chance to paint such a famous man."

"When was this?"

"Just last winter. So I go to Il Vittoriale—D'Annunzio's villa— and I try every day to paint him, and all he wants is to sleep with me. He was a compelling man—*not* a beautiful man, but compelling—but he refused to sit for a portrait until he had sex with me. And *I* refused to do a thing with him until he sat for me. Day after day, chasing me around Il Vittoriale like a dog. The man sleeps in a coffin, Rafaela. Ridiculous. So I leave, very disappointed, no portrait, and I go to sleep in a hotel instead. And the next morning there is a man on a horse knocking on my shutters. How does he know which room is mine? And I open my shutters, very nervous, still in my nightgown," she said, pantomiming. "And there is a messenger from D'Annunzio, on a white horse, handing me a poem through the window. And the poem is rolled up like a scroll, inside"—she lifted one hand—"this ring."

When Tamara flourished her topaz at the end of this tale, she made me think of Gin posing with the diamond earrings Daniel had given her in Capri. Gin had a pearl collar, too, from Jacques. An ermine stole from Yann. Guillaume and Hervé had given me jewelry, too, but I had sold it all. "You never slept with him, and he gave you a ring anyway?"

"I never went to bed with that man. And everybody knew, because I left Il Vittoriale and I stayed at that hotel. I made him look like a fool. So then D'Annunzio is angry with his friend, Baron Treves, for introducing him to such a disagreeable woman. He tells his friend bad things. And Renata Treves? Never collects her painting. They commissioned the painting, I painted the painting. For one full month I painted that painting. But she never paid."

"But you didn't do anything wrong."

"I did. I agreed to stay at Il Vittoriale in the first place. You know the way married women think. *How dare that slut make a fuss?*"

I nodded, thinking of my mother's hard face that morning on West Tenth Street.

"So when Boucard talks to me about a contract, about a portrait of his wife, I think, Tamara, this wife? She can kill your contract. You must never be alone in a room with this man. If we had not been asleep when he came by? Rafaela, I would have begged you to stay. I was ready to shout for you if he tried to do anything."

"So I could rush in and defend your honor? Dressed in a sheet?" I laughed.

"So there would be two stories against one."

While I bathed, Tamara left to intercept the postman with Tadeusz's papers, returning with a batch of fresh mail. Setting the rest aside, she opened a thin letter from Anson's employer. Boulind's service had informed her by telephone that Dr. Boucard and Baron Kuffner were capable of paying the prices they had offered for her work, but here was the full report. Kuffner and Boucard, Tamara read aloud, shared a love of performers: Boucard maintained a flat in Passy for a young Jewish member of the Comédie-Française; Kuffner did the same on the Place des Vosges ("The Place des Vosges!") for a Spanish dancer named Nana de Herrera. Boucard, Tamara reported, had retired at forty after making a fortune on a digestive drug—a patent which still earned lavishly each quarter. He bought new cars and furs yearly for his wife, mistress, and nineteen-year-old daughter, and owned homes in Paris, Lausanne, and Biarritz.

"And guess what, Rafaela? He's the poor one."

"What about Baron Kuffner?" I asked, drying myself off.

"The man owns half of Central Europe."

"No!"

"Before the war, Baron Kuffner held *the largest privately owned parcel of land in the Austro-Hungarian empire*," she read aloud. She looked up at me in my towel. "Boucard has houses? Kuffner has castles. Boucard retired at forty? Kuffner never worked. The man pays for a room at the Ritz year round, and he's only here three days a week." Tamara's face was flushed and glowing from the idea of so much money.

"Not bad."

"And listen to this. For the past year he has also been paying for his wife to stay in the best cancer hospital in Switzerland. *Sara, age thirty-five,*" she read. "So young. Their poor children."

"Who's taking care of them?"

Tamara consulted the letter. "They are both in boarding school."

"Why is he *here?*" I asked, my lip curling.

"Oh," Tamara said, shrugging. "To remember the world is bigger than a hospital, I imagine. To visit his Spanish dancer." Tamara burned the report with a cigarette lighter. "Money well spent," she mused. She was weighing something in her mind. I watched her read over Boucard's contract as I dressed; I watched thought spider across her face. What did she want more money for? She had a flat in the Seventh, a motorcar, a housekeeper, and a daughter in private school. She had all the new clothing she wanted. She could afford to pay *me* two thousand francs a month. What else did she need?

15

I HAD BOUGHT *DIE DAME* FOR TAMARA, but not for myself. The morning after *The Orange Scarf* cover came out, Gin gave me a copy of my own, and I found a vase of roses on the kitchen table. "It's not my birthday or anything," I said, nibbling at a slice of *gâteau au miel*.

"They're mine. My lawyer waited for me backstage."

"Sweet."

"Boring." I glanced at her still-flat belly. I wouldn't broach the subject until I had the money in hand. Ugh, I'd just have to ask Tamara for a loan. "Look what came back *Retour à l'Expéditeur*." Gin pouted, holding up a letter she'd written to Daniel.

"I'm sorry." I told her about lying in Tamara's bed as she'd signed Boucard's contract the day before, and about her burning the report from Anson's boss.

"She should go after Kuffner," Gin said. "Think of all that money."

"But she's already rich. And he's so repulsive. He sits there waiting for me all day in that restaurant on the corner. Watching. I feel like ants are crawling all over me when I walk by."

"Wait, what?"

I told her about the day Kuffner ran outside to talk to me, and she rolled her eyes. "Rafaela, what's wrong with you?"

"What?"

Feeling superior made Gin lay her British accent on extra-thick. "The man who owns Central Europe wants to have a drink with *you*. Why are you turning your nose up at him?"

"Oh," I said.

"There's no future in modeling, unless you meet somebody who takes care of you."

Silly me. I'd been putting off the loan idea for days now, and here was another option staring me in the face. I watched Ginny fix herself a breakfast scotch and water. I could brave the mild little waiter at Bistrot Varenne, I thought, and I could walk by. And if Kuffner were waiting for me there, I could just go in. "I feel stupid," I said.

"Good. Now, get wise. If you don't have the brains to go after him for your own sake, just think about how sore I'll be at you if you let him go."

"*Sì, sì. Grazie, Mamma,*" I said, indulging her Italian fetish to get her off my back.

"*Capisci?* Think about it: maybe the sick young wife will die and *you'll* be the next Baroness Kuffner."

I recoiled. "That's not. Necessary," I spluttered.

Gin shrugged. "You can bring a horse to water," she said.

⌒⊙⌒

Kuffner was not at Bistrot Varenne that day, nor did he appear over the next two weeks. I did, however, notice a pattern to his persistent calls about our *Rafaela*: three days in a row, then nothing. Three days in a row, then nothing. If Boulind's report was right, it seemed he called during the part of each week he spent in Paris. Tamara spoke with Kuffner for a few minutes every time he called, promising, without committing to a thing, that she would keep in mind his interest in the artist's copy of *La Belle Rafaela*, and assuring him that his *Nude with Dove* would be ready by Christmas.

Tamara may have worked on *Nude with Dove*, but she also spent hours painting the two of us together. She would call the piece *Myrto*, she decided, for the *myrtille* ices I loved. From my vantage—lying on my side, facing the easel—I could see across the street to the lace curtains of the discreet rooming house that Tamara's neighbor Mme. Grissard, unbeknownst to her aristocratic employers, ran out of the carriage house of the Hôtel des Castries. Each day a cigarette, attached to a man's gloveless hand, extended its slim length out a second-story window, disappeared briefly, and reappeared with an exhaled cloud of smoke, as if its chilly owner couldn't bear to raise the window another inch. I watched dozens of cigarettes appear and burn down each time I posed, so many that I began to feel sorry for the smoker, sitting in that room all day. The cigarette—or cigarettes—became for me a permanently steaming vent between the indifferent sky of the outside world and that stranger's private, smoldering hell.

Halfway through December, Tamara began making me a peacock-feather dress. "You never told me you sewed," I said.

"I don't," she said. "So, listen. Romana de la Salle and her mother are having a party the same night we go to Italy and they've asked me to do a five-minute live drawing as part of the festivities."

"Why?"

"Because I am quick, and I am good, and I can draw in an evening gown."

"I meant, why a drawing at a party?"

"Because photographs are so tired?" Tamara shrugged. "Anything is interesting when you are drunk. The point is, Rafaela: Will you let me draw you in this?" Tamara was building the dress tier by tier out of dozens of rounds of feather trim, the glittering peacock eyes overlapping like scales. I found it rather camp, and yet—even in progress—astonishing, a blinding glove of color and light. "Our train does not leave until nearly midnight," she said, when I did not reply. "If I draw you at eight or nine, we will have plenty of time."

"You haven't told me where we're staying in Italy or *anything*. It's like we're not really going," I complained. But I was smiling in spite of myself, staring at that dress.

"I thought you would not mind."

That weekend, at the Clignancourt flea market, I began to get an idea of my own for a dress. I had seen my first zipper in '23, on my stepfather's new galoshes, but by '27, I saw them regularly on boots, tobacco pouches, and suitcases, such as the much-abused one the flea-market dealer tried to sell me that Sunday. Because he had sold me the steamer trunk I used as an armoire, I returned to him for a smaller suitcase, as a way to daydream about my trip with Tamara. I laughed at the slashed and battered piece he tried to unload on me.

"But she zips," he insisted, demonstrating. It *was* impressive, I conceded, that you could make a kind of fabric out of metal. As I looked more closely, the zipper became beautiful to me, its tab hanging like a pendant necklace from the Fritz Lang future, its steely teeth fusing like ribs do at the sternum, or like vertebrae locking together. Staring at it took me back to the afternoon at Shakespeare and Company that I'd spent poring over the French medical textbook. Sylvia would have called the wretched suitcase a nightingale, but what if there were a dress that zipped? I grinned to myself, imagining it as clean and startling as one of Tamara's paintings, as simple and memorable as Adrienne's Vermeer uniform: a conservative, charcoal-gray wool gabardine dress, lined in black satin, its only ornament a slender column of metal, itself a delicate tissue of interlocking steel bones, the zipper tab hanging like a jewel from the vee of its neckline. Maybe a paler gray rib of piping on either side of the zipper, where the zipper tape met the wool. I don't know if Elsa Schiaparelli later copied my zipper dress design, but I do know I never copied hers. I had never seen a zipper for sale on its own, or I would have walked away from that bashed-in suitcase, but I bargained the dealer down that day instead. I could carry my little old valise to Italy, after all. Wouldn't Tamara be impressed when I unpacked my new dress?

A week before the Duchesse de la Salle's party, on the way to buy shoes for my peacock-feather confection, Tamara took Kuffner's *Nude with Dove* to be framed at Vavin's, off the Boulevard Raspail. When we arrived, I wasn't surprised that she demanded to speak to the owner, a thick-faced older man, or by the care with which she chose the color and shape of the frame—a streamlined ebony—but

I was astonished by how many other details she demanded M. Vavin adhere to. To make the picture jump out at the viewer, she wanted the canvas to extend out from the wall so far that you could have fit a medicine cabinet inside the box of the frame. She had brought an extra stretcher bar with her to demonstrate the thickness of the lip she wanted in back. The third time she showed Vavin exactly what she wanted, I asked, "Does it really matter?"

"Of course it matters," she declared, gesturing dramatically in her red wool coat. "The front of the painting is the painting, yes, but the back of the painting is the painting, too."

"Why, the frame of the painting is the painting!" M. Vavin concluded, before he could stop himself. Thinning hair fell across his scalp in a limp white flap, and when he tossed it out of his eyes, the whole flap moved. "Of course, when I frame a Matisse, it's not at all the same as when I frame a Pascin, or again when I frame a Picasso."

What a name-dropper, I thought, watching Tamara's face cool in irritation. Wasn't it in poor taste for him to mention one living painter to another? Yet he had plenty of clients: Why did they flock to him when he made them feel bad? Pondering this question as we finally left, I almost walked right into someone—Anson Hall!— on my way out. "Rafaela!"

"Are you following me?" I teased.

"I'm just—" he said, abashed, "picking something up for a friend." We were only minutes from rue de Fleurus, so it wasn't hard for me to guess who.

"How's your little boyfriend?" Tamara asked as we walked away from the frame shop.

I stuck out my tongue sourly at the epithet, then confided in her. "I'm wondering if he lost his job. I get the feeling he might be so hard up for money he's letting Gertrude Stein pay him to run errands again. I mean, didn't Vavin mention Picasso?"

"Who did he not mention?"

"I bet you anything Gertrude Stein gets her Picassos framed there."

"Oh, Picasso. Oh, Gertrude Stein," Tamara said. "She just wants to be a man, and Anson just wants to be a woman."

"Why say that?" I asked.

"Have you gone to bed with him?"

"No."

"Well, there you go."

"What?"

"He obviously likes you. So why not sleep with you? It is unnatural."

"Because," I said, indignant.

"Because why?"

"If you don't know, it's humiliating for me to tell you," I said.

"Why?"

"That, or you're just jealous, which is unfair, considering."

"What is it?" Tamara asked, impatient.

I stopped walking, but couldn't face her. "Because I only want you, all right? I only want you."

"Oh." Tamara stopped walking, too. A hand flew to her neck in an unconscious, wounded gesture. "I *was* jealous. How tiresome of me."

I saw Anson a couple more times in the neighborhood that week, once on Boulevard Raspail and once on rue du Bac, both of them streets that ran between Tamara's neighborhood and Stein's. Both times he was carrying groceries, and though we chatted for long minutes on the sidewalk, his mesh bags and his evasiveness about his work—and the fact that for once he didn't badger me to go have a meal with him—reinforced my suspicion that things were not going his way.

The day M. Vavin telephoned to say that *Nude with Dove* was ready—after yet another call from Kuffner—Boucard dropped by again. This time, I had enough warning to put on my robe and go dress in Tamara's bedroom, and when I emerged, she and Boucard were talking in relaxed fashion about the American show—the painting was for exhibition only, she assured him, not for sale—that *The Dream* was bound for. Knowing Tamara would want me to, I stayed as they chatted on, over scotch, about Americans and Poles, about the second car Boucard wanted to buy for his daughter. I was impressed that he managed not to say anything offensive to me this time, though once or twice I caught him staring at my features the way most men stared at the rest of me. After an hour, just as he left, Boucard gave Tamara a sudden, careful look. "I just want to let you know," Boucard said, "that when I found out you took a painting to be framed without showing me, at first I was disappointed in you. But when I learned that it was *Nude with Dove*—I know your sale agreement with Kuffner predates our contract—I was ashamed of myself for ever doubting you." His voice was jovial, and he changed the subject before Tamara could reply.

Tamara chatted and laughed as gaily as before, but the moment Boucard left, she clouded over. "That whore Vavin. Boucard has him in his pocket. He came *specifically* to tell me that he knows I framed a painting."

"Why does it matter if you framed a painting?"

"Because I am selling it, and not to him. I am completely within my rights to make good on my commitment to Kuffner without notifying him. A contract is a contract, but who does Monsieur le Médecin think he is? My father?"

"You know this is about just one thing."

Tamara turned to me, puffed up with anger, then deflated as the thought occurred to her, too. "Of course. Our *Rafaela*."

"He just wants to make sure Kuffner doesn't get it."

"And he wants me to know he is watching. What am I supposed to do, find a new framer?"

"Do you *want* to sell our painting to anybody?"

"No!" Tamara's eyes went wide.

"Then you don't have anything to worry about. You found yourself a patron. Let him feel like a patron."

"I am very angry," Tamara said. "I am very upset."

"Do you want me to stay? Do you want to keep working on *Myrto*?"

"No," she said, exhaling grandly. "I think I—well—I promised the man who bought the Salon *Belle* that I would go to his warehouse and varnish the painting soon. I can do that today. So please come tomorrow," she concluded. "I will work better then."

"I should go? Are you sure?"

"Unless *you* can think of some way I can have Boucard's money without Boucard."

16

When I left on the heels of Boucard's surprise visit, Kuffner was waiting for me at the bistro. This time I didn't pretend not to see him as I walked by, so he didn't rush out coatless to intercept me. He merely stood and pointed to the chair opposite his. "Come in?" he mouthed in French, palms open. *This is for you, Gin,* I thought. I went in.

I had had this kind of drink with a handful of men, and I knew what to do with one kind: listen, smile, laugh at his jokes, let him touch me. Ask questions that allow him to brag. Some of the other kind—the ones who didn't talk—liked being drawn out; some liked being mocked or teased, and some just needed a hand on the knee, to know not talking was fine, too. Kuffner might be one of those.

"Well, hello, Baron."

"I could not bear the thought of you walking past me again," he said, in an unfamiliarly accented English, "so I stopped coming for a while."

"But here you are," I said.

"I'm so glad I came back."

When Kuffner poured me wine from a carafe, I realized that he had been keeping a second glass on the table waiting for me. "You're awfully persistent."

"Who could blame me?"

"Have you been here all day?"

"Most of it. What have you been doing all day?"

"I worked," I said, trying to conceal my surprise that his English was even better than Tamara's.

"You posed for *Nude with Dove*?"

"She didn't tell you it was ready? It was for a new painting."

"What do you do in the pose?"

"I lie on my side with my arm like this." I showed him.

"Is it another nude?"

I nodded.

"I would love to see you pose for it."

"Oh, would you?"

"What I would really love is to see you pose for it while Tamara paints you." A different sort of man, before spelling out his particular fantasies, might have tried to tell me about the book he was writing, according to Tamara's report, on agrarian reform, but not Kuffner.

I knew what to say next, and six months ago, I would have said it. *Well, aren't we direct? I like that.* Or even, *What's it worth to you?* With the weather turning colder, I had caught wind of the spicy, meaty cloud of heat that poured out of Bistrot Varenne a hundred times, and I had often told myself, *One day, I won't be put off by the mild little waiter. I'll go in and demand some thin-skinned Alsatian sausages and a good glass of Riesling.* Now here I was, inside, with a man whose ear and nostril hairs sprouted as plentifully as the ones on his throat, and the little waiter was never going to come ask what Mademoiselle was having, because Monsieur was taking care of everything. When I sipped the perfectly appropriate red that Kuffner had poured for me, I realized I didn't want to say the next thing. It had been six months since I'd gone to bed with anyone who repelled me, and I didn't know if I could do it anymore. I didn't worry about rent now. I could eat well if I avoided restaurants. I had new shoes, new silk stockings, all the fabric I wanted, my very own stainless-steel mechanical pencil. *Oh, Tamara*, I thought, chilled. *You've spoiled me for my old life, but you haven't taught me anything else*. I would just have to ask *her* for the money.

All these thoughts happened quickly, in just the time it took to bring that unwanted wine to my lips. Now I had to step out of the corner I'd talked my way into. "What interests you the most?" I teased. "The painter, the painting, or the model?"

When Kuffner's eyes widened in reply beneath his thick brows, he looked all the more like a hermit who'd strayed from his cave. "That's exactly it!"

"What?"

"Rafaela!"

I'd been trying to get out of the conversation with my question, not deeper into it, but suddenly Kuffner was holding my hand and squinting, pained. "Baron, do you need me to phone for a doctor?"

"Not at all. Your question. I don't know. I *don't know*. I sit here waiting for you and when you walk by, I am disappointed because you walk away, but I'm also disappointed you're not the painting. I sit here waiting for a glimpse of Tamara on her way home, and I'm disappointed *she* is not the painting. And if I even had the painting? I would be disappointed it was neither of you."

I set down my glass. This was not what I had expected at all. Who was this man, this stark Saint Francis, so naked in his perversity? "Well, I'm afraid I can't help you there," I said dryly.

"But Rafaela, you can," he said.

What now? I thought. He was still holding my hand.

"You can do two things for me. You can meet me for dinner tonight."

"I have plans."

"Of course you do. Saturday night?"

"I'm going out of town for Christmas."

"Tomorrow, then," he said. I raised a noncommittal eyebrow. "Eight o'clock, Lapérouse?"

"Maybe."

"If you don't come, I won't be offended," he said. "But think about it. Promise?"

"I'll think about it," I granted.

"And Rafaela, do you know, is Tamara going to the Duchesse de la Salle's party this Friday?"

"Of course. Are you?" I asked, surprised.

Kuffner opened his wallet. I felt sweaty and alarmed, my legs suddenly stuck to the seat of my chair. "This"—he set down a few coins—"is for the wine. This," he said, unfolding two banknotes, "I am just leaving here. You can take it or walk away from it. I won't be here. I won't know what you decide. And I'm not going to ask you to do anything. But if I went to Tamara's on the night of the party and the doors were unlocked, there is a good chance you would accidentally run across more of this," he said.

What lay in front of me on the table were two five-thousand-franc notes, enough to buy a new motorcar. Far more than enough to pay for Gin's doctor. Tamara had charged as much for the Salon *Belle*. I was surprised by the delicacy with which the rough-looking man skirted outright bribery.

"I think you dropped something," I said.

"Beg pardon?"

"On the table. I think you dropped some money."

Kuffner's face lit with understanding as I gathered my purse and gloves, and before I could walk away from the banknotes, he was halfway across the restaurant with his coat under his arm. "Tomorrow night," he called back over his shoulder. "Eight o'clock."

I looked down to avoid his eyes, feeling them on me as, peripherally, I saw him backing out of the café. At three, the place was all but deserted, the few other patrons too engrossed in their conversations or newspapers to watch Kuffner leave. The mild little waiter noticed, however, glancing from Kuffner to the money on my table as he approached it with a rag. Before he could take a step closer, I set my beaded purse down on the banknotes. Our eyes met for a moment: I weathered his stunned contempt with a smile that would have done Gin proud, and when his back was turned, I took the money.

Gin didn't come home that night. After I posed for Tamara the next day, after I made her recite once again the stops on our trip and each place where we'd stay—a sleeper car after the de la Salles' party, two nights each with friends of hers in Florence and Rome, two nights in a Venetian hotel—I asked, "Tamara?"

"What is it?"

"I'm worried about our *Rafaela* while we're gone," I said, gently palming her back. "Boucard's using your framer to spy on you.

Kuffner's phoning all the time. Last night, he even offered me money to help him steal it. I don't think you should leave it alone."

Tamara turned over in bed and looked at me. "He did what?"

I told her about Kuffner's request, but the thought of Gin's sharp little face kept me from mentioning the banknotes in my purse. "I think you should hide the painting while we're gone," I said. "That, or take it with us to Italy. We could leave it at one of your friends' houses, for safekeeping."

I watched Tamara silently consider and reject a series of possible hiding places before arriving at a new problem: "Won't Boucard know if we take a painting to Italy?"

"Only if you frame it first, right?"

Tamara's eyes went gray, slid away from me like minnows. "Truuue," she mused, her voice gliding down a scale.

"So we can just stop home after the party and pick it up when we collect our suitcases."

"Let me think about that. The painting will be safer if I take it to Italy, but do I want to leave it there?"

"We could bring it back with us."

"That's a lot of travel for one painting," Tamara murmured to herself uneasily. "Let me just think over how to do this."

I caressed her, feeling less guilty about Kuffner's money. I'd taken it, sure, but I hadn't helped him. "Can you believe we're leaving on Friday?"

"Can you believe I have to finish your dress in three days?"

"Oh, no!"

"You should go. I need to work on your dress, and I also need to get to the framer's before they close; Monsieur le Baron is coming for *Nude with Dove* tomorrow."

⤳◦⤴

I never even considered going to Lapérouse that night. I bought a bottle of Riesling for myself, just because I could, and drank a glass at home with a pâté sandwich. One of my rare cigarettes for dessert. While working on my new zipper dress-in-progress I realized, proudly, that for the first time I wasn't making a template from a dress I already owned. I wasn't using a pattern from a magazine. I was working from imagination and experience alone, and so far, the dress fit beautifully. I carefully sewed Kuffner's banknotes into the hem. Gin came home from work at midnight, and we played records on her gramophone and drank the rest of the wine together. *"Baby won't you please,"* she purred along with Bessie Smith. *"Baby won't you please come home?"* I could hear Colma breaking through Mayfair. Her face was wet with tears.

"Do you know what you want to do, Gin?" I asked.

"No."

"Because I can give you the money if you want."

"I said I don't know."

"You'd never have to pay me back."

"Mind your own beeswax."

"I just want you to be happy."

"That's what *I* want, Rafaela. I just want to be happy."

"I have to leave early," I told Tamara the next day. I did not want to see Kuffner when he came to pick up his painting that afternoon. "I have to go with a friend to a doctor's appointment," I lied, changing quickly for *Myrto*.

"I wish you did not have to leave early," Tamara said on our first hour's break, as we lingered over Jeanne's *chocolat chaud*. The housekeeper was working mornings that week; she had family visiting for the holidays. "Vavin botched the frame and I have to wait two more days. I am afraid Kuffner will be a monster when he finds out I have no painting for him."

"Oh, no."

I dreaded seeing Kuffner, especially since I'd stood him up the night before, but Tamara sounded so upset, I considered staying for her sake. When we confronted the baron, if it came out that I had kept his money, I could just as well return it, at the rate Gin was going. What did she think was going to happen? Just as I came to this conclusion, Tamara said, "I am not going to tell him about the bribe."

"Pardon?" I said, blushing. What did she know?

"I am not going to tell him I know he tried to bribe you." Oh, she *didn't* know I'd taken the money. Good.

"Why?"

"I think the English is *I want to string him along*," Tamara said. I didn't notice her accent much anymore, but the sound of one of Gin's phrases passing through its dolorous sieve amused me. It also made me think of Gin the week before, telling me how angry she'd be if I let Kuffner go. What if she was right? Even if I had lost the stomach for it, wouldn't it be smarter to *string Kuffner along* than reject him outright? And Gin might yet come to her senses, and ask for the money. "All the same," Tamara added, "today's meeting will not be pretty."

I couldn't agree more, I thought. I had yet to work out my own string-Kuffner-along plan, but I knew that Tamara's framing troubles weren't part of it. "Well, Jeanne will protect you."

Tamara smiled. "She will beat him with a wooden spoon."

"Can't you ring him up and tell him not to come today?"

"I kept telephoning him before you came, but he must already be on his way."

"Oh," I said, alarmed. I thought about making an excuse, but decided instead to tell the truth, at least in part. "Do you mind if I go get a cup of coffee down the street?" I said. "Baron Kuffner makes me uncomfortable."

"You are not the only one." Tamara sighed. "But do as you like." At that moment, proving her guess correct, the doorbell rang. "Ah, just what I think of when I look at you," Tamara razzed, watching me dress. "A shrinking violet."

I had my coat on by the time Kuffner reached the top of the stairs. I squeezed past him in the doorway, but not quickly enough to miss the disappointment and desire in his face. "Good morning," he said stiffly, leaning in for a pair of air-kisses that served as cover for a whispered plea. "Friday? The door?"

"We'll see," I murmured, as his cheese-grater stubble scraped against my face.

When I came back from the café near the Métro stop an hour later, Tamara looked drained. "Was Kuffner angry about the painting?"

"An absolute beast."

"I'm sorry I left like that."

"You could not have helped," Tamara said. After a second restorative cup of chocolate, she worked for two more hours on *Myrto*, then had me try on the peacock dress. The shining unfinished gown fit tightly, with just enough room for me to sit and walk. "I think you should not come tomorrow," she said. "I need to spend the rest of today on this dress, *hélas*." With her accent, French *alas* sounded like English *loss*. "Tomorrow, too. But I will miss you terribly. Come early on Friday morning?"

"Gladly."

"And Friday night we will run away together," she declared. "Come here." She kissed me. "I have been thinking about your idea, Rafaela," she said. "It is a good one. I felt afraid at the frame store yesterday. Monsieur Vavin gave me a look, like *this*," she said, squinting. "And my heart went *ton ton ton*. Doctor Boucard knows everything I say to Monsieur Vavin. He has eyes everywhere. And Kuffner? *Pouah!*"

"I'm sorry."

"So you are right. I do not want to leave the *Belle* behind. What we can do Friday night is this: *I* can go straight from the party to the station, and *you* can stop home and bring the painting. That way if Boucard comes to the party to keep an eye on me, he will follow me, not you."

"Why all the sneaking? You're not breaking your contract to move the painting, just to sell it."

"If Boucard thinks I might want to sell it in Italy, he could be within his rights to keep it from leaving France," she said.

"If you say so," I said. Fear both sharpened and complicated her thinking, I mused, but that did not make it her ally. "If it'll make you happy, I'll bring the painting to the station, sure."

"Thank you, *ma belle*."

"Thank *you* for taking this trip with me," I said, my sudden happiness making me queerly formal.

"You did not want to go to Italy at first."

"But it's with *you*," I said.

17

Apart from Tamara for two whole days before our trip, I finished my zipper dress over too much coffee, shaky with desire, shaky at the thought of so many days and nights together. Sometimes, alone, I'd cross my arms around my chest and squeeze myself hard: the happiness crashing around inside me was almost too much. Going to her two mornings later, my new dress packed in my valise, I all but floated up the stairs. "Tonight," I breathed, as we made our double *bisous*. A canvas wrapped in paper and twine dominated the salon, and beside it sat a small traveling bag.

"We are alone," Tamara whispered in my ear, touching me. "Jeanne is *au marché*."

I chuckled. "Don't you have a rule?"

"Today is special."

After we made love and napped, I woke to Tamara sitting very close, watching me. "How about a bath, and then some work?"

"What were you doing?"

Tamara showed me a little sheet of pasteboard covered in gold leaf. On it, she had painted a quick sketch of my face, eyes closed, lips parted.

"Is that what I look like when I'm sleeping?" I asked.

"That is what you looked like an hour ago," she said, smiling.

"It looks like *Belle Rafaela*." It resembled the face in the paintings, but much softer: blurry and rushed, the mouth a little smeared.

"It looks like *you*," she said. I rolled my eyes at her, too happy to reply.

At the end of our painting day, Tamara slipped into a pleated column of gold-white Fortuny silk, and then helped me put on the peacock gown. "We will go straight from the photographer's to get a bite to eat, and then to the de la Salles'," she said. "I cannot wait to show you off." She hooked a last hook. "Again, remember, *you* made it, not me."

"I still don't understand why. It's so beautiful." It was. Tamara's three mirrors reflected a woman in a sheath of feathers, a slinky, shimmering, unearthly creature.

"It is hard enough to be a woman painter," she said tightly. "But a woman painter who *sews*?"

"Oh." My mouth went faintly sour: *I* sewed. "You said you sent Jeanne to get the peacock feathers, but you got them yourself, didn't you?" I said. "And the blue silk for Ira's dress?"

"That *would* be telling, no?" Tamara said, raising a hand to my mouth, and one to hers. "Now let me take care of the back."

Tamara had designed the train of the dress both to attach at my waist and to suspend from my shoulders by a pair of braided silk straps. When I wore the straps, the train—dozens more feathers, each three or four feet long—pressed tight to my back like a quiver; when I let the straps hang down around my waist, the train fell behind me like a peacock's tail. "And you will need this," she said, handing me a matching mesh bag on a long silver chain. "Taxi money. Your lipstick. Keys for when you stop back to get the painting tonight." I grinned, and hung the silver chain across my chest like a pageant sash. "Perfect. You can pick up our suitcases then, too. Make the driver carry them downstairs for you, *comprends? Et voilà.*" Tamara sighed, taking a step back to admire me. "I should paint you like *this*."

At Studio Lorelle an hour later, as the photographer scrabbled around an inner room with electric lamps and cords, Kizette trotted up the stairs to bid her mother good-bye for the holidays. The girl took me in with a hard look and then stood together with Tamara, talking softly: Kizette sulky, Tamara half bullying, half coaxing. I had been so stubborn, demanding a Christmas vacation like a child. Of course Kizette would be angry. Next time, I thought, we should all go together.

The photographer crossed over to them, charmed at the sight of Kizette in her school uniform and Tamara in her evening gown. "How about a picture?" he interrupted. "Mother and daughter?"

Both looked up, startled: they had the same set mouth, the same flat gray eyes. They replied to him at the same time—"No!"—as the camera snapped. Kizette broke away in a run. *"Bonnes vacances, chérie,"* she called brusquely up the stairs behind her.

"Is anything wrong?" I asked, out of earshot from the photographer.

"Kizette is just being Kizette," she said. *"Why can't I come to Italy too?"*

"I feel bad," I said.

Tamara waved an admonishing finger. *"This is a grown-ups' trip,"* she said, solemn and wide-eyed. I laughed with pleasure. "Think of that while Philippe is shooting," she said, swatting me.

I wish I had one of those photographs: slender brows, cupid mouth, Tamara's ridiculous, campy, magnificent gown. The face of a girl who knows she'll sleep and wake with her lover for days on end. At one point, waiting between shots in my sweep of feathers, I suddenly thought of Kuffner's ten thousand francs. *That man has more money than sense*, I thought. If he wanted to throw around his fool's francs and run his fool's errand, let him. I only wished I could be there to laugh at him when he tried getting into Tamara's flat.

Before heading off to the party, Tamara and I paused for a bistro dinner. At our table by the window, I tried not to smirk into my *moules*. I had never gone out with her to a restaurant before. I had never tried salty little cheese *gougères* with champagne. "To *La Belle Rafaela*," she toasted, kissing me.

"To *you*, Tamara," I insisted.

Tamara took out our train tickets and tucked one into my mesh bag, one into her Bakelite purse. "So tonight at the party, you will leave at ten and I will leave at eleven. That way Boucard will follow *me*, not you."

"What if he follows you all the way to the station?"

"Then I will wait until the last possible moment to get on the train, so he will not know which one to buy a ticket for. And then we will leave him behind," she said, smiling.

"You thought of everything," I said.

"Oh, I did." She leaned in and whispered, "Remember when we made love this morning?"

At her words, I liquefied like hot wax. I remembered when I sat up after I came, the way she'd pressed the heel of her hand into my sternum, lowering me to the bed for more. I exhaled a soft, involuntary sound, and pulled myself together. "It's only a few more hours," I whispered back.

Tamara looked up to meet the eyes of a woman outside who had stopped to wave. "Ira!" she called. "Monsieur Perrot!" As Ira and her husband ducked into the bistro, my stomach went cold, sinking down to that night outside Tamara's open window. I could hear them again, a woman's climbing sobs. And I could see a pair of arms, Tamara's, reach around the blowing curtain from either side.

"Are you going to the de la Salles' later? Have you dined?" Tamara asked.

I refused to look up as Tamara commandeered a pair of extra chairs for Ira and her husband—a beaming, thickset, older man. "Rafaela, you're a vision," Ira cooed.

"Stand up," said Tamara. "Let them see!"

Uncomfortably, I accepted their tributes—Ira's effusive, M. Perrot's hearty—before sitting again quickly.

"Did she—" Ira began eagerly.

Tamara nodded, beaming. "She made this one, too."

"Guess what, Rafaela?" said Ira, reaching to unbutton her coat. "I'm wearing your dress!"

"*Tiens!*" said Tamara as Ira emerged, a cool slender vision in blue *crêpe de Chine*.

"I haven't seen you since the fitting, darling. I wear it almost every day, don't I, Gilles? Tamara?"

"She does."

"She does."

"So I have to thank thank thank thank *thank* you. Isn't it divine? Listen, after dinner, I have a friend who asked for your card."

As I nodded, smiling numbly, Tamara leaned in to tell Ira about Kizette's sulk that afternoon, and M. Perrot tried to interest me in a conversation about his Rolls-Royce. As I learned how hard it was to trust young mechanics these days, especially veterans, Tamara and Ira talked quietly together, Tamara's hands fluttering around Ira's shoulders and face. When Tamara came to the high point of her story, Ira's gasp—so scissor-like, so uniquely memorable— made me bury my forehead, briefly, in my hand.

"Headache?" M. Perrot asked. "Do you need some fresh air?"

"I want to ask you something," said Tamara, summoning me to her side of the table.

"Isn't Rafaela a genius?" Ira murmured, fingering my dress, letting the feather-fringe at my hem trace her palm.

"What is it?"

"We have a little problem. I cannot believe it. I had my char-coals and sketchpad all ready for the de la Salles' party, and I set them carefully by the door in their own little bag. And then I for-got them. I am so sorry, but could you go back to the flat for them? And then meet us at the party? You can take a taxi both ways," she said, pressing a banknote into my hand. "Please?"

Snug in a taxi bound for rue de Varenne, I exhaled deeply, allowed myself a little cry. Ira had no idea I'd heard her and Tamara. That, or maybe she didn't care. Maybe she went through life being

friendly to her lovers' lovers, the way her husband kissed Tamara
on both cheeks and told her, heartily, how beautiful she looked.
Didn't he mind when his wife went to Italy alone with her lovely
neighbor, a woman who caressed her in front of him? Earnest,
bland M. Perrot seemed only beneficent toward the two women.
Tamara was having a grand time. The Perrots were having a grand
time. Only *I* had a problem, only *I* had ground glass in my throat
when I saw Tamara touch Ira. If I had tried to confront Ira, she
would have asked me to wait until she could find her friend's card,
her friend—here I had to laugh, bitterly—who wanted to pay me
to do what I loved best. *I'll be so glad when this night is over,* I whispered to myself.

It wasn't until I let myself into Tamara's building that I felt
angry. How *dare* Tamara? She *knew* Ira upset me. She knew enough
to put away Ira's portraits when I came to pose. Ira might be blind
to my feelings, but Tamara wasn't. Halfway up Tamara's stairs, I
went black and spiny inside; I was an ocean, a windy night. How
could she so unapologetically, so matter-of-factly, choose to hurt
me? It was so easy for her. As easy as—I suddenly realized what I
had in my purse: Tamara's keys. As easy as a man walking into a
room and walking out with a painting. As easy as a woman closing
a door, and neglecting to lock it.

18

❧

I HAD NOT KNOWN I WOULD BE ONSTAGE. It was a small stage two steps up from the de la Salles' salon, but it was marked off nonetheless by an honest-to-god red velvet curtain. Behind that curtain, while talking almost constantly to Romana de la Salle and the Marquis d'Afflitto, Tamara posed me on an enormous pouf. She seated me with my legs tucked to the side, leaning on one arm, while the three of them fanned my train around me, pinning it to the ottoman in dozens of places so that I seemed to swirl up from a sweep of feathers like an upside-down tornado. My anger had taken me to a new, numb state, as if I were not a person, but a camera, being affixed, not to a hassock, but a tripod.

I had not been told that the de la Salles' party would have a name: The Nine Amusements. Red-blonde Romana, wearing brooches shaped like stars at her shoulders, would represent Urania, the Muse of Astronomy, and at the end of the programmed entertainments would lead the guests up to the roof to gaze at the murky Parisian night while smoking opium. "Who's Dance?" I asked.

"Mother was *trying* to get Josephine Baker," Romana said, "but no luck there. And then for a minute we thought we could get the Spanish dancer Nana de Herrera"—at the mention of Baron Kuffner's mistress, Tamara and I glanced at each other—"so I even bought some records." She gestured toward the far end of the room, from which the gramophone smoldered with a tango I recognized from a Valentino movie. (So young to die!) "But Miss de Herrera wasn't sure when she'd have to leave. So I saved the day, and got Vi Morris to agree to shadowbox. She should get here any time."

"*Vi* as in Violette Morris, the athlete?" Tamara asked, and as they switched to French, I remembered the princely young woman at her party, posing face-to-face with the Duchesse de la Salle portrait in the bedroom.

"Exactly the one," said d'Afflitto.

"How did you manage that?" Tamara demanded, stretching out on a chaise.

Romana drew her arms girlishly behind her back. "She gave me her telephone number," she simpered.

"Romana, shall we say, *spent a lot of time* with Vi Morris at your party," d'Afflitto said. "But I guess you were too busy with your admirers to notice."

When Tamara smiled I realized just how much she *enjoyed* Kuffner and Boucard's pursuit, despite her protests to the contrary.

"Does your mama know you were sitting in the lap of that *apache*?" d'Afflitto teased.

"She does *not*," Romana said, with a sugary grin. "And I plan to keep it that way, thank you very much."

"I wonder if she'd pose for me sometime," Tamara murmured.

"I can't imagine her posing for you," said d'Afflitto. "Like an elephant in a china shop."

"I don't know," Romana teased. "Tamara might like that sort of thing."

"André Gide? Why, yes. Jean Cocteau? Of course. But Vi Morris? The lady boxer?"

"I'm sure if the painter put her mind to it, Mademoiselle Morris would find posing for Tamara irresistible," came Baron Kuffner's voice before he circled the curtain to join us. Hearing them all through the filter of my imperfect French compounded the detached, glassy nature of my anger, so much so that I could look up at Kuffner unmoved.

"We're not ready!" protested Tamara.

"How can we open the curtain in a burst of revelation if people keep barging in?" d'Afflitto groused. A foot shorter, and in his usual bow tie to boot, he appeared particularly slight beside the older man.

"You're always a revelation, Rafaela," Kuffner said.

I did not squirm. "So, where's Mademoiselle de Herrera?"

"She'll arrive on her own time," he said, following my unblinking lead. "For you, Madame de Lempicka?" he offered, extending an opalescent cocktail.

"My god, is that real absinthe?" asked d'Afflitto.

Romana nodded. "Mother had some brought over from Spain."

"No, thank you," said Tamara. "Not before I draw."

"But I insist."

"I'll relieve you, Baron," said d'Afflitto, extending a manicured hand.

Kuffner pulled his extra glass up out of the way, forcing the smaller man to reach high, like a boy. "I'm not interested in the kind of relief you can offer, Marquis," Kuffner replied, his smiling teeth thick and square.

Seeing a flash of hatred pass over d'Afflitto's face, Tamara stepped in to distract the two men. "I *would* like a drink, Baron." In the sudden tension, with the four of us watching, Tamara claimed Kuffner's glass and raised it. "To Art," she said brightly, and drained it at one go, provoking a glance of alarm between Romana and d'Afflitto. "What do *you* know about lady boxers?" she asked, returning to her chaise.

"I know that boxing with one can only end in humiliation," Kuffner said, amusement creeping up behind his moustache.

"Afraid of being beaten by a girl?" teased Romana.

"An old farmer does not fight a national champion, especially when he is a guest of that nation," Kuffner said, with a chilling smile. "He might win."

Romana laughed, impressed.

"When I said *humiliation*," Kuffner explained, "I did not specify for whom."

"You *are* a brute," said Tamara.

"Well, *I'm* going to be a brute if you don't get off our stage," Romana said. "We're about to start."

"Don't make her call her mama on you," d'Afflitto sneered.

"Pardon me, ladies. Marquis," Kuffner said, backing away to greet someone beyond the curtain.

"Romana, I've never seen you brutish," said Tamara.

"D'Afflitto's right, though. I *would* just call my mother if he didn't leave."

"The national boxing champion doesn't scare him, but the mention of Marika de la Salle sends him running." D'Afflitto chuckled.

Perhaps Kuffner had spotted Mlle. de Herrera, or perhaps he *had* actually changed his mind about Violette Morris, because just then Romana gave a sudden "Ooh!" as a pair of blunt-nailed hands appeared over her eyes. Our little party stared as the athlete, resplendent in a gangster's suit, a cigarette tucked behind one ear, leaned in to trade *bisous* with Romana. "Am I late?"

"Not at all," Romana gushed, pulling aside the curtain and beckoning. "*Maman!*"

Even in my frozen state, I gasped when the Duchesse de la Salle emerged backstage. I had been staring for months at that marcelled hair, those long riding boots, the beauty mark above the lip that lent the plain face its sinister humor. The portrait that hung above Tamara's bed was faithful: it was hard to imagine anyone, least of all giddy Romana de la Salle, calling this woman Mother. No wonder Kuffner had vanished when d'Afflitto threatened to summon her!

Now that they faced each other, I could see that Romana's mother, Greek and in her late forties, bore very little resemblance to the French boxer in her twenties, but their mannish clothes were similar, as were the possessive glances they shot at Romana. "So good of you to come," said the duchess. "What can we arrange for you? Some special kind of lighting? A punching bag?"

Noting the businesslike and slightly offensive haste with which the duchess leapt to the subject of the evening's entertainment, I realized I had never seen two *donne-uomini* face off before. The expression in the duchess's eyes said that Vi Morris might be a celebrity, but she was not from the right sort of family, and was, like me, only welcome in her home if on display. The expression in Vi's eyes said the duchess might have brought her in as some sort of dancing bear, but she planned to make her pay for the privilege. "I just use a mirror," she said icily, never letting go of Romana's pretty hands. Through the half-open curtain, I could see more than a handful of feathered and tuxedoed onlookers leaning in curiously.

"That can be arranged," said the duchess. "We're so grateful you could make the time. How ever did my daughter persuade you?" The question itself, though friendly—flirtatious, even—was delivered in a slightly menacing fashion, as if to say *Keep your hands off her, you lowlife.*

"She said she might make it worth my while," Vi Morris said, to the laughter—disapproving and hopeful, respectively—of mother and daughter.

"Not in so many words." Romana giggled.

The duchess raised an eyebrow at her daughter. "Well," she said, her face smoothly recomposing itself, "can we get you a drink while we set up for you?"

Vi Morris seemed to take the duchess's failure to be provoked as provocation itself. Riffing off the tango on the gramophone, she spread a hand across Romana's back and dipped her in a deep swoop. "I've never been asked to play the Muse of Dance before." She chuckled as Romana emitted a soft thrilled shriek. It might have been nothing, a little horseplay among friends, but Romana and Vi Morris were not friends.

"We'll have Tamara draw while we get your mirror," said the duchess. "Romana, come with me."

As the duchess marched her daughter away, leaving d'Afflitto to finish pinning me alone, Tamara told Vi Morris, "I'm sending *my* daughter to boarding school, you wicked thing." Kuffner's absinthe had clearly hit: Tamara's voice was rich and throaty. I remembered the narrow-eyed look with which the boxer had sized up Tamara at the end-of-Salon party, because I saw her repeat it now. Recognizing—or pretending to recognize—someone across the room, Vi peeled off, and Tamara drew the velvet curtain closed.

"You never know where the duchess will draw the line with her daughter," said d'Afflitto, shrugging. "Opium, yes, *les hommasses*, no."

"She's just upset because Vi's a bigger *hommasse* than she is."

"Did I miss anything?" asked Romana, reëmerging. She looked a bit rattled.

"Not at all. Are you in trouble, darling?" asked Tamara.

In an effort not to sound upset, Romana spoke in an accent and sprinkled her sentence with English words. "I'm a little *cross* with *Miss Morris* for making *Mother* look bad like that."

D'Afflitto looked uneasy at Romana's discomfort. Tamara looked disappointed with Romana, and I could tell both that she had already calculated what she would charge *Miss Morris* for her portrait, and that she was bidding that money good-bye. "So which Muse are we, *chérie*?" d'Afflitto asked.

"Polyhymnia, the Muse of Religious Poetry," Tamara intoned with faux gravitas. "Which makes Rafaela my goddess. Wear this." Tamara handed me a feathered eye-mask with a single plume rising from the back strap to dangle, absurdly, over my head. I looked at it coldly, thinking, if I were really your goddess, would you *trompe* me with Ira like that? If I were really your goddess, would I have to wear this dumb mask?

"Are you sure we're not meant to be Comedy?" I said aloud. "Doesn't this feather make you think of"—I pointed to my throat and made a dangly gesture before I remembered the French word from Sylvia Beach's medical textbook—"an epiglottis?"

"Don't be silly," d'Afflitto chided. "You look divine."

"Suzy Solidor's doing Comedy," Romana said, perking up somewhat.

"You know that's not her real name," whispered d'Afflitto.

"Suzy Solid Gold?" asked Romana. "I guess not."

"It's Suzanne Rocher," he explained, to a round of laughter. "But you should paint *her*, Tamara," he said, as if to console her for losing Vi Morris.

"Wouldn't I like that?" Tamara said. "You can tell she has beautiful breasts."

I knew Tamara was just saying it to make herself feel better, but her frank sexual praise of this woman I'd never seen made me feel even more grotesque than I already did. "Maybe she's beautiful," I said, sounding brittle. "But is she funny enough to be the Muse of Comedy?"

"Absolutely," d'Afflitto assured me. Something in my voice made him give me a second look. "I heard her practicing a dirty song about being a pirate," he said. His voice was playful, but he glanced from me to Tamara and back, offering me a quick, pitying look.

That look alone cracked the cool lens through which I'd been watching the others. "As long as it's not a dirty song about being a peacock," I said. I hated my chin for wobbling.

"Rafaela," Tamara coaxed, switching to English. "Is it the mask that bothers you?"

"It makes me look stupid."

"You do not look stupid. You look like you came all the way from a sultan's paradise to let me draw you. Some kind of pomegranate heaven of peris and houris and peacocks."

"Isn't there a Muse of Love Poetry?" asked d'Afflitto.

"Natalie Barney snapped up that one," said Romana. "Are you surprised?"

"I'm happy with my lot," Tamara insisted in French. "Painting is my religion. Besides, Rafaela," she added in English, taking my hand, "in that mask, you will be able to look into the eyes of all those people, but they will not be able to look into yours."

I squeezed Tamara's hand, still too hurt over Ira to thank her out loud. With eyes shiny from her quickly drunk absinthe, Tamara gave my train a last tug, pulled my shoulders back a hair too sharply, and perched behind her easel, charcoal in hand. "Ready?"

"I'll let Mother know," said Romana.

Moments later, I heard a female voice address the room in stentorian French. "Ladies and gentlemen, I present the painter Tamara de Lempicka as the Muse of Religious Art, Polyhymnia. Like all of us," she said with a good deal of irony, "Polyhymnia is a Vestal at the altar of Love. Ladies and gentlemen, I also present to you the divine Rafaela Fano as the Cyprian goddess herself, Aphrodite."

The Duchesse de la Salle parted the curtain. Pressed together in the low light, the crowd looked like a slab of black-and-white rock, their jewels like flashes of mica. Bespectacled Kuffner and suave Boucard stood in the front row. Boucard's elegant graying wife had claimed a stool in front of him while a slim woman with handsome black eyes and impeccable posture stood by Kuffner: Nana de Herrera, no doubt.

The crowd watched in reverent silence as Tamara fought to neutralize the effects of the strong spirits, first stepping out of her high heels, then bracing herself against the base of the easel with the fingertips of both hands. This was the second time I had faced a roomful of people, but this time my eyes were open, so it was worse. I could not summon back the cool glaze that had left me. When Tamara's eyes met mine, I realized she had never drawn in front of a crowd like this: she had accepted Kuffner's absinthe because she, too, was afraid. But then, with a long look at me and a bold sweep of charcoal, Tamara plunged into the familiar ritual of looking and drawing, and even despite my anger, watching her made me relax, too.

After a long silent minute, whispered words and phrases began to twinkle up into the room: *Aphrodite. La Belle Rafaela. Salon d'Automne. Agence Binard. Dix milles francs. Belle. Belle.* As I listened, I discovered Tamara was right: I could see into their eyes, but they couldn't see into mine. Their eyes were a wave and I did not let it flatten me: I began to ride it like a little ship. They did not want to drown me; they wanted to float me; they wanted feathers and glitter and dazzle. They wanted me to be their dream. I forced myself to breathe and I gazed back through my mask, inhaling steadiness, even if I exhaled fear.

"Comme c'est beau," said the Duchesse de la Salle at full voice, looking over Tamara's shoulder.

"Merci," replied Tamara, and kept drawing.

After this, the crowd eased, as if deciding they'd been silly to whisper. The twinkling explanations rose to a gossipy murmur,

while below it I could hear the rustle of certain less public information: *Elles sont amantes. Deux copies. En Rouge et en Vert. Boucard.
Kuffner.* Similarly, the exchange between Tamara and the Duchesse
de la Salle seemed to lift the ban—implied by the red velvet curtain, the stagey setting—on speaking directly to the performer.
"Another drink, Madame de Lempicka?" Baron Kuffner offered.

"Not while I'm working," Tamara said, in what I thought of as
her painting voice: the quiet one she used to keep herself from fully
registering an interruption.

"Oh, please, let me get it." Boucard jumped in, not hearing her.
The way he spoke was controlled and smooth, but I could tell Kuffner's offer of *another* drink irked him, as if Kuffner were claiming
what was rightfully his. "I have something special for us to toast,"
he said, raising two flutes from the bar beside him.

Tamara, still in a charcoal trance, set the champagne on the
floor by the easel without bringing it to her lips. Boucard, unaware,
faced the crowd, but his eyes addressed Kuffner alone. "For my
beautiful wife, Hélène, on her birthday," he said, champagne aloft.
Mme. Boucard smiled at her husband indulgently, embarrassed by
the attention. "I am commissioning a portrait by the esteemed artist you see before you, Tamara de Lempicka."

A polite murmur suffused the crowd and a scattering of friendly
glasses rose in the air. A few necks craned around for a better
look at Hélène Boucard, modestly grand in her long gown, her
marcelled hair shot with bands of steel. She would look noble in
Tamara's portrait, statuesque. Given Dr. Boucard's predilections, I
was interested to note that his wife was one of the least Jewish-
looking Frenchwomen I had ever seen. I wondered which birthday
it was for her. Though she carried a little heaviness under her eyes

and chin, her long body was enviably firm for its age, her skin as smooth as fondant. "Happy twenty-ninth," called Kuffner, so jovially that I was for a moment surprised he didn't know she had a nineteen-year-old daughter, then stung on her behalf.

Nana de Herrera was among those who stared at the older woman hardest. Though I knew a crowd that planned to end the night smoking opium on the roof was not a prudish lot, Nana was unusual in pressing her head to Kuffner's chest so early in the evening. She laid a large expressive hand on the baron's shoulder and sighed dramatically. "She does portraits, too?"

"She certainly does, *Mademoiselle*," said Tamara. Her hand had stopped moving, but she didn't take her eyes off me.

"Would you like her to do *your* portrait?" Kuffner offered, loudly enough for Boucard to hear.

"*Would* you, *mi amor*?" Nana cooed.

"Would *she*?" Tamara corrected through gritted teeth, so quietly that only I could hear.

Kuffner's arm tightened around Nana's waist. "I give you my word."

"Immortality on the side of a Gitanes packet isn't enough for you, *Señorita*?" d'Afflitto asked, sidling in to join them. As the men spoke, half the crowd seemed to lose focus, wandering off to other rooms or talking among themselves. The other half—including the Duchesse de la Salle—leaned in closer, enjoying the spectacle brewing between the baron and the scientist as much as they had enjoyed the live drawing and the feathered girl.

"I didn't know she made portraits," Nana continued, oblivious to the tightening faces on either side of her. "I thought she only made, you know, *Rafaela*s."

"The *Rafaela*s are only the most famous of her paintings, my dear," Boucard said, annoying both his wife and Kuffner by addressing Nana directly.

"De Lempicka excels in portraits of lovely young girls," Kuffner volleyed back. "Now, any painter who is paid for a portrait tries to show his subject off to best advantage," he said with a cutting glance at Mme. Boucard, "but painting *you*, Nana, would be as much a pleasure as it would be a commission."

At this, Tamara ducked behind her champagne, charcoal clenched between two fingers like a cigarette. She drank the whole glass. Boucard, watching, offered Kuffner a thin-lipped smile and raised his flute again. "Indeed. You do love de Lempicka's work, Baron. Let's toast your new painting now. To *Nude with Dove*. A gift for your wife, perhaps?"

As Kuffner's wife, Sara, was known to be bedridden with cancer in a Swiss hospital, Boucard's comment was, in its way, as insulting as Kuffner's.

"Doctor Boucard, how gracious of you," Kuffner replied. "I'd like to toast *your* acquisition of *Full Summer*."

"Ah, yes, now we each have, as Miss de Herrera put it so charmingly, a *Rafaela*. Too bad yours doesn't look like Rafaela."

"Too bad yours is wearing clothes."

At this, d'Afflitto gasped. Romana *tsk*ed. Tamara turned away from me to look at both men. I held the pose, mortified. Was *that* why Tamara had given me a mask? Would she, like Kuffner, rather look at my body than my face?

"Actually," Boucard said, brushing Kuffner off, "according to the terms of my contract with the artist, not only have I commissioned *four* portraits over the next year—"

At this, Nana looked up at Kuffner, as if planning to ask for another three portraits. Tamara, feeling the crowd watching her, turned back to the easel, stony.

Boucard continued. "I furthermore have first rights to purchase any other work de Lempicka cares to sell in the next two years. So if she chooses to sell the drawing she's making right now, Baron, I'll have *two Rafaela*s, and where will you be? And maybe Tamara will come to her senses and then I'll have three, won't I?"

The hand in which Tamara held her charcoal hung limply at her side. Kuffner's face was red and curdled. "Well, it's too bad Madame de Lempicka has no interest in selling her copy of *La Belle Rafaela* to anyone, isn't it?" he said. At this, though I knew all he could see of my eyes through the mask was an infrequent wet flash, Kuffner looked over at me, and winked.

I had made a terrible mistake. If I weren't, literally, pinned in place, I would have stood up right there onstage and run all the way back to Tamara's, to lock both doors. I didn't care about Ira Perrot. All I cared about was the look on Tamara's face, as fierce and vulnerable as a wild bird in a trap. She hadn't seen Kuffner's wink. She hadn't seen my throat tighten with horror at myself, at how badly I'd betrayed her. She only saw me. *"Just two more hours,"* she mouthed. All she wanted was to survive and leave and get on that train with me. And all I wanted was to be worthy of her.

"You both have to stop," I said quietly, still holding the pose. "You're distracting her."

The look Tamara gave me in response was so grateful, so trusting, I almost cried. The two men didn't hear me, but Romana did. "That's right!" the redhead snapped. "Mother, get these gentlemen out of here so the artist can work in peace."

The Duchesse de la Salle, until that moment as rapt as a specta-
tor at a cockfight, lurched into action and together with her daughter smoothly led the two men out of the room, each in a different
direction.

Tamara looked down from me to her easel then. She drew quickly
and badly, and the red curtain fell to unfocused applause. D'Afflitto
and Tamara wheeled the pouf—with me on it—backstage. Through
the half-open curtain, I could see a clutch of the Duchesse de la
Salle's friends at the bar, crushing hash pellets into their sloe-gin
fizzes. Kuffner stood among them, obviously uncomfortable, while
Nana swanned around the room saying her good-byes, off to work at
the Paradis. As Romana joined us to help d'Afflitto unpin my train
from the pouf, whispering with him over the scene that had just
exploded, Tamara collapsed onto the backstage chaise. Once again
Kuffner moved aside the curtain and entered, glass in hand. "Beautiful work, Madame de Lempicka," said Kuffner. "We were all so
impressed."

"You and Boucard really stole the show, with your nonsense."

"Let me give you a drink, to try to make it up to you."

Tamara turned to him, large-eyed. I couldn't tell if she was
going to slap him or cry. Romana reappeared, noting the tension
between Kuffner and Tamara with a glance. We watched Tamara
take the proffered glass.

"It's a shame Nana has to go before Violette's performance," I
said to Kuffner in angry French. Romana looked down, abashed,
and it occurred to me, as a raucous purr that could only have been
Suzy Solidor's filled the room, that after taking liberties with her
hostess's daughter, Violette might not be invited onstage at all.

"Oh, I think she's seen plenty of sparring tonight," said

d'Afflitto. "Maybe she'll even work it into her act, *mi amor*," he said
with a meow, and tapped at an imaginary punching bag.

"Oh, you are a card," snapped Kuffner. "An absolute cutup."

Tamara drank deeply, never taking her eyes off Kuffner.
"You're both so awful," she sighed. Her eyes went heavy. She
sprawled on the chaise, feet extended, one pump dangling off a
big toe. Kuffner sat on a chair beside her, pitying attentiveness and
impatience crossing his face by turns. Then I realized: on top of the
absinthe and champagne Tamara had already consumed, he had
given her one of the doctored sloe-gin fizzes—without drinking a
drop of his own.

The moment my train was unpinned, I hiked it up by its straps and
ran with my coat under my arm, dodging guests and caterers, side-
stepping a woman in a man's suit so narrowly that her monocle fell
out. Rushing down the hall, I suddenly found myself eye-to-pearl-
tiepin with Boucard. "Kuffner's in the music room," I told him.

"Oh?" he asked, his expression as mild and featureless as that
single gray pearl.

"And he just called your daughter a name," I said, rushing
away. *That ought to buy me some time.*

I lost my grip on the train on a long marble staircase and felt the
peacock tail sweep behind me. I ran, the center of a pool of feathers
and rage. *You think you can drug her, leave her passed out at a
party, and go help yourself to the painting, Baron?* Hurtling pell-
mell toward the taxi stand, I didn't feel small and hurt anymore. My
stupid jealousy over Ira was gone. All I wanted was to run, to protect the woman I loved.

19

I FELT LIKE A GHOST, letting myself in for the second time that evening. I slid into the building, up the stairs, and into Tamara's apartment, locking the unlocked doors behind me. I wanted to turn on an electric light, but resisted. *Kuffner could turn up any moment,* I thought, reaching forward in the dark. When my hand met the hard edge of the painting, wrapped in paper and twine, my heart thudded in my temples: I had beaten him to it. I did not want to run into him by accident, so all I had to do was wait in the dark for him to arrive, find the doors locked, and leave. Then I could take the painting to the station.

Presently I heard a motorcar grumble up the street, and I stood by the balcony window so that I could see the lamplit street but not be seen. I was not surprised when the driver opened the door for Kuffner, though I did allow myself a quiet snort of laughter at his expense. He was a baron, not a professional thief: approaching the apartment quietly on foot clearly hadn't occurred to him.

I was surprised, however, when a second figure unfolded from the cab, a flash of gold. More than surprised, too surprised to breathe: *Tamara*.

I only had time for one thought: *I'm not supposed to be here*. Tamara was already at the door below me, out of sight, while Kuffner stood a little away from the building, staring at her—and, no doubt, at the building door. I heard Tamara's key in the lock below me; Kuffner's streetlit face relaxed, then went suspicious: he looked quickly up and down the block, no doubt for me. "Come." I heard Tamara's voice, low and commanding, and then he stepped forward out of sight.

Then I acted without thinking: I let myself out through the window, onto the balcony. With the sound of high heels rising up the stairs, I tugged the window as shut as I could by its mullion bars and retreated behind a column on the balcony, visible neither to Kuffner's driver outside nor to anyone—I hoped—inside.

A light went on and I saw Tamara with her back turned, pouring them each a neat finger of scotch. Because I had not been able to pull the last inch of window closed behind me, I could make out Kuffner's French clearly: "Is your daughter asleep?"

"She's at my mother's," Tamara said.

Standing close, Kuffner gazed at her from behind. "You didn't say a word to me in the car, you know."

Briefly, Tamara leaned back, decanter in hand, resting her body against his. "I don't know why you agreed to that duel with Boucard."

"It would have been insulting not to," Kuffner murmured into her hair.

"Your wife is in a *cancer* hospital. He would accept an apology."

"I wanted to impress you," he said, sliding an arm around her waist. "I admit it."

"That's not why I invited you here," Tamara said trimly, setting down the decanter as she pulled away.

"I beg pardon—"

"I can see why you'd assume," she said. She turned to face him with a glass in each hand, and smiled. "And if I were a handsome man, and used to getting what I wanted—"

"It's not—"

"—And I wanted a painting by a woman who was known to have a weakness for handsome men, I might try to persuade her by every means I could."

Kuffner backed away. "I did mistake your invitation, Madame de Lempicka," he said stiffly. "I made an assumption based on experience."

"Understandable," Tamara said.

"I hope my assumption doesn't mean you'll sell the painting to Boucard," Kuffner said.

"I don't want to sell it to Boucard."

"I know. And you don't want to sell it to me."

"Listen. I've put the good doctor off for so long, he's got someone watching my house."

"Has he?"

"If you look across the street, you'll see a man smoking at the window. The one with the lace curtains." Kuffner, indulging her, stood at the window to look. Flattening myself against the wall, I looked as well: I found a tiny point of orange across the street, and used it to make out a hand, an arm, perhaps a head-shaped shadow.

"Do you remember? He was there when we came inside," Tamara said. "No cigarette lasts that long."

"I didn't know what I was up against," Kuffner said, less archly than before.

"He's been there ever since the Salon party. At first I thought he didn't sleep. Now I think there are two of them."

There *was* always a smoker at the window, but I had pictured a brokenhearted man, not a professional spy. Why hadn't Tamara told me? Why had she told me she was afraid of being followed by Boucard, who was nowhere to be seen? Why hadn't she mentioned *this* man, right across the street?

"Now that you've seen him," Tamara said, finally passing Kuffner his scotch, "I will tell you why I invited you here, since you're clearly too proud to ask."

"Please do," said Kuffner. He raised his glass.

"Chin-chin," Tamara replied. "I don't want to *sell* you the painting, Rollie. And this is why, as far as I'm concerned, you and Boucard really, really, *really* don't need to shoot each other."

Why Rollie? I thought. And then I remembered his Christian name: Raoul. Kuffner looked at her, waiting.

"I want to give it to you."

"I—"

"But Boucard can't know, because of our contract. Promise you won't display it until my contract with Boucard is up? If you do, I'm ruined. Do you understand?"

Kuffner said nothing for a long moment, then cleared his throat. "You're *giving* it to me?"

"Promise you'll drop the duel? Promise you won't display the painting for the next two years?"

"I—I promise," said Kuffner, stunned. "I'll keep it in a vault."

"But I thought you liked looking at it."

"I'll build it a secret room, then," he extemporized.

"I'm not joking."

"Neither am I." Kuffner shook his head, as if to clear it, then downed his drink at one go.

"If I've done everything right, Boucard will think Rafaela stole the painting and took it to Italy on tonight's last train."

His head jerked up. "Rafaela?"

"If that fellow with the cigarette doesn't see Rafaela get on that train with the painting, Boucard will never leave me alone."

"But why would Rafaela steal the painting?"

"I told her we were going to go hide it together in Italy, to keep it away from both of you." Tamara's voice as she said this was teasing, intimate. She pointed to the canvas-shaped package that dominated the room. "She should get here in twenty minutes to take the painting, so we can't waste any time."

"So you're only *saying* that you're giving me the painting," Kuffner countered, confused. "Rafaela's hiding the painting in Italy until your contract is up with Boucard?"

"No," Tamara said. "I'm giving you the painting tonight." She turned to the packed canvas. "Rafaela's taking *this* to Italy. They're not the same thing." I recoiled. How long had she been planning this? With that, she flipped through a set of canvases leaning against the wall and drew one out from the back. "See?"

Kuffner sighed, visibly shaken. It was the private *Belle Rafaela*. It was me.

"Now hold this," Tamara commanded, handing him a tack hammer. "We have to work quickly."

"What are you doing?"

"Mounting a canvas," Tamara said briskly. "I do it every day."

She didn't mount the canvas. She tapped out the struts from the back of *Nude with Dove*, placed our *Rafaela* so that it fit into the back of the other painting, and replaced the struts. "These will need to be varnished in six months, of course," Tamara said. "But for now, don't worry. There's a lip of wood inside the frame so that the two canvases don't touch."

I suddenly, sickeningly, understood why she'd had *Nude with Dove* reframed to such exact specifications. "You're damned clever," Kuffner murmured.

Tamara rested her hands on her hips, pleased. "Now we can walk right out the front door. Boucard's man will see us leave with the *Dove*, and then he'll see Rafaela leave with a wrapped painting. Who do you think he'll follow?"

"This is why I want you, Tamara. You're an extraordinary woman."

"And you're an extraordinary man. With a wife and a Spanish dancer," Tamara admonished.

Kuffner looked sheepish, but persisted. "I just have one question."

Tamara leaned against the back of her chaise, arching her back like a movie star. "Oh?"

"When did you decide this? Tonight? At the party?"

What a dumb cluck. How could she have decided tonight when there was this packed-up painting, this lie, waiting for me in her apartment? I pressed closer to the window to hear her reply, nauseated. "Not tonight . . ." Tamara said vaguely, relishing her power.

"I mean, why me? Instead of Boucard?"

It hurt to hear Kuffner ask Tamara the very question I had once asked Guillaume and Hervé, and to watch Tamara consider her reply so seriously. She tilted her face up toward him. Her voice wobbled and dropped—I recognized it—the way it had when she realized how rich he was. "Because I love you," she said. My mouth fell open. Black floating spots crawled across my eyes.

"Tamara," Kuffner said, moving toward her.

Tamara extended a long white arm and rested her flat hand on his chest. A sharp pain stabbed into my belly. "You're not ready for me yet," she whispered. She half turned away to look at the painting. Even modesty and regret were tools of seduction in her hands, I marveled, beginning at the same time to realize just how much she had betrayed me. "This gift is my prayer that you will be—ready—one day."

Kuffner covered her hand on his chest with both of his. She was a column of white gold. He was shaking like a boy.

"We should go," she said.

"What if I were ready for you now?"

Tamara lowered her arm and Kuffner did not let go of her hand. "Prove it," she said.

"I would drop Nana for you in no time. I can drop her tonight. If you come with me, we'll stop at the Paradis first and you can watch me leave her."

Tamara said nothing.

"You're afraid someone's going to follow us?"

"That's not it," she said. "It isn't me Boucard wants. It's the painting. He's not watching me; he's watching my house." I swallowed. So, she had never been afraid Boucard would follow her home from the party. I understood: she wanted the smoking man to follow me *and* the painting to the station, and she had told me whatever would make me do it.

Kuffner gave Tamara a look of helpless confusion. "You *don't* want me to drop Nana?"

"Of course I do," Tamara snapped. She inhaled sharply, then steadied herself. "I don't want to be a mistress, Rollie."

Kuffner nodded. We both watched him take the gold band off his ring finger and set it in her hand. "My wife is dying," he said simply. "She and I—we're both waiting for her to die."

Tamara stared, fingers refusing to close around the ring. "Don't say such things."

"I mean it," he said. "Go ahead, put it on."

Tamara's hand was flat and taut. "I can't wear this."

"Then just take it. Keep it. See?" Casting about, Kuffner opened the nearest drawer to hand, in her escritoire. I heard the slap of gold on wood. "There."

"I'm impressed," Tamara said.

"Come with me, then? We'll stop at the Paradis first, take care of a little business? I can write Boucard something flowery, too, if you want to watch."

"You know I can't make you any promises," Tamara said. I watched his face lean in and cover hers. "Not right now," she breathed, her grin as wet and dizzy as a girl's.

Kuffner held her face in his hands a moment longer. "You don't have to promise me anything," he said. I heard joy in his voice. My eyes squeezed shut for a long pained moment. When I opened them, he had stepped away from her. "Well," he said, with a nod at the painting, "may I?"

"You may."

Kuffner set both hands on *Nude with Dove*, lifted it, and set it down, turning to her. "I'll confess, Tamara," he said, buoyed up by happy confidence, "I wanted this painting so much, I was prepared to hold it hostage to make you sell it to me."

"How were you going to do that?" Tamara asked, pleased.

"Rafaela," he explained. "You don't know how much money I gave her to leave your door open tonight."

"You bad man," Tamara whispered, half teasing.

"The little whore took my money, but I see she's loyal. Your door was locked."

"Rafaela kept your money, did she?" Tamara laughed. "Oh, poor you." She planted her hands on her hips. "Pass me a cigarette, you awful man. That's the least you deserve."

"You aren't angry?"

"Of course I'm angry. But I'm flattered."

"I love this painting."

Tamara's eyes glittered with satisfaction. "I know. I wanted to see what you would do for it," she said. She smiled, took a long slit-eyed pull on her cigarette. "Is that what you were doing at the party? Making sure I was drunk so you could go let yourself into my apartment?"

Kuffner flinched. "I'm sorry." When Tamara exhaled, she tipped her head back, watching Kuffner's eyes widen at her exposed white throat. *"Little whore?"* she repeated, haughty. "You really thought my door would be unlocked?"

"I believed I had reason to hope."

"Stupid man. She told me all about you. That's *my* little whore."

I brought my hand to my mouth and bit it hard as Kuffner laughed. "I've learned my lesson, then."

"Let's go."

Kuffner's driver started the car. The smoking man stirred in the window. Kuffner opened the door for Tamara, then circled the car. He carried the painting face out; even I could see it: my own heavy thighs, Ira's long nose, that sentimental dove. As the car gunned away, the orange point of light disappeared briefly, then reappeared.

When you're standing on a balcony on a December night dressed in nothing but peacock feathers, it's a little hard to break into a lover's flat inconspicuously, harder if she has just broken your heart. My hands shook as I silently edged open the balcony door and flattened myself into the apartment, just out of the smoking man's line of vision. Then I lay down on Tamara's floor and cried.

It hurt to cry as much as I did, but I couldn't stop. Each gulping sob tore slowly out of me. I choked out one on top of the next, and when I came to the end of each stack, I started all over again.

And then I sat up on the floor in my ridiculous dress, resting my chin on my knees. I didn't know what to do next, but I had to blow my nose. Knowing that the smoking man would see the lamps through the sheer curtains, I turned on the electric lights—*Let him wonder how I got in*—and went to Tamara's bedroom for a handkerchief. I climbed into her bed for the second time that day and crushed a pillow against my face.

I could have lain there all night, crying myself to sleep. I could have gone to Boucard and told him what Tamara had done. I could have piled up Tamara's paintings and burned them all. But Tamara had given me the one thing I thought I would never

feel: the ability to love someone I went to bed with, to feel desire
without calculation. That feeling of choosing her, of running back
to lock her door, of wanting to protect her, was the best thing that
had ever happened to me, and I didn't want to let go of it, even if I
was terribly, terribly mistaken. I put on my coat and shouldered the
painting she had left for me. I found a cab at the stand by the Métro
entrance and told the driver, "Gare de Lyon."

We eased through the blue winter night and the empty streets. I
saw another taxicab not far behind, and knew Boucard's man had
seen me, was watching me, would see me enter the station, find the
platform, mount the train. I had a ticket and he didn't, which meant
if my timing was right, he would see me and not reach me; he would
see the painting leave Paris without being able to stop it. Boucard
would think the painting was out of both his reach and Kuffner's.
And Tamara would think I was a fool. At first. Then she would
discover Kuffner's wedding ring was missing, and that's when she
would know I knew. That's when she would know—here we sat
waiting for the light on the Boulevard Saint-Germain—that someone in this world had loved her better than she could love anyone.

The other, sadder reason I took that taxi to the station was this:
she had told me to. We had a plan. How could she meet me on the
train if I wasn't there? How could I disappoint her? How could I
fail to bring the—here, as we pulled away from the light, the painting swung back, striking my head—*Wait*, I gasped—*what painting?* The streetlight flashed on the split my forehead had dented into
the brown paper that covered—*what?* I fingered open the split
paper and pulled, looked at the back of the canvas, kept tearing

paper until I reached the front, looked again. We swung past another light overhead, a still-lit room on a second story.

Tamara had packed up a blank canvas for me to bring to Italy.

That was when I began to cry again, when I looked up at that empty, electric-lit room, those diamond-paned windows. My head was full of tears, and had been waiting for this movement: chin up, eyes down, bare mute throat. Lifting my face to look up tipped it back like a glass and everything in me spilled out: I loved her.

Tamara was not at the party. Tamara was not drinking one last champagne, was not touching a beautiful boy or girl under the chin with a long gloved finger, was not calling *goodbye-my-love* to the hostess or descending the stairs in furs. She was not telling any other departing guest that her car was in the shop, so she was taking a taxi. Tamara was not looking at the black lit waters of the Seine and thinking of me right now, nor was she paying the driver, nor finding her platform or train car or seat. She was not waiting for me on that train. She was not waiting on that car nor would she burst in late, breathless and golden, tipping the porter and chiding the conductor for his impatience.

We were crossing the Pont Sully. Suddenly I didn't care about doing what Tamara wanted. I looked across the inky water at which she was not looking while thinking of me, and I said, "Stop."

"Eh?"

"I'll get out here."

When I paid the driver, he got out of the cab, tugged the canvas free, and set it in my hands before I could stop him. His expression when he handed it to me was so polite, so offhandedly kind, that I started crying again. I turned my back to avoid his pity, to let him drive away.

I was standing at the center of the bridge facing the river with a broken heart wrapped in paper and twine. I chucked it into the river. And then, before the canvas could hit the Seine, before my brain could even form the word *drown*, I clambered up the railing and pitched myself over, too.

20

THE MOMENT THE COLD OF THE WATER shocked through me, my body took over: it did not want to die. My heavy coat filled with water and my body, wrestling free, refused to sink with it. The river sucked the train right off my dress.

Half naked, I reached for the nearest floating thing to hand. The canvas had landed facedown: I clung to it like a lifebuoy. As the muscled current pulled us downstream, I tucked the frame under my body, inch by inch, until, briefly, I could crouch on the canvas that was filling with black water; I could let go and use both arms to reach for the stone wall that bounded the river, to scrabble for purchase as the icy maw of the river sucked the canvas out from under me. There were iron rungs driven into the river wall; I seized hold of one just as I spotted the edge of the canvas nosing out from the water. It was caught on the stone foot of the next bridge: a stretcher bar strained against the current, then cracked. The canvas racked, collapsing like a kite in a storm, and vanished silently underwater.

I clung to the iron rungs in the stone wall, and then I scaled them.

My shoes had gone the way of the canvas; the narrow bars stabbed into my feet as I hauled myself up, up, and onto the quai. I was dressed in nothing but wet feathers and gooseflesh. My heart was broken and I couldn't even drown myself. I threw up once, then huddled, frozen, on the paving-stones and began to rock so slowly, so numbly, so *comfortably*, even, that I think to this day my blue body might have been beginning to close up shop. I meant to get up, but I couldn't. I would get up soon. I heard footsteps rushing down stairs and heavy breath huff toward me: I didn't even care. My eyes were iced shut and I could only concentrate on not biting my numb tongue. I was shivering so violently that at first I didn't feel the thick coat thrown over me, didn't hear the voice shouting my name.

It was Anson. Of course. I had known it without knowing it: Anson was Boucard's smoking man. The slight heat that clung to his coat made me shake all the more as I staggered up against him. I dug my lowered head into his ribs. "Doesn't he want you to rescue the *painting*, not me?" I asked numbly.

"Are you crazy?" he said. "I mean, sure. But are you *crazy*?"

In the streetlight I could see the dark weal on his white cotton shirt where it was soaking up the water from my hair. "Take back your coat," I mumbled. "You'll freeze, too."

"Don't be ridiculous." His heart was loud in his chest and his breath steamed into the dark. "God, you're barefoot. And it's starting to rain. Come on, get up on my back. Let's find you a cab."

I saved myself from drowning that night, but Anson saved me, I think, from dying of cold. In the taxi, I curled up in a ball inside his coat. "She told me she loved me," I said, looking up at him briefly.

Anson didn't know what had happened between me and Tamara, but he gave me the kind smile of a doctor on a lunatic ward. "Sorry."

"I know I sound as dumb as Gin," I said. "I guess I just thought, because we were both girls—"

"That you'd be like Sylvia and Adrienne?" His pity made me dig my face back into my knees. We took a hard right and my balled-up body swung toward the window. "Rafaela, some of these women are like Gertrude and Alice, and some of them sleep around with other girls, like Natalie Barney. Some of them sleep around with men, too, like Djuna Barnes's girlfriend. And I hate to say it, but according to Bobby, there are some who like to get coked up and fool around with two sailors at a time."

I was almost sick again, remembering the dirt-floored shack by the Seine that Gin had once told me about. It was uncannily easy to picture Tamara in that crowd, especially when I recalled those summer mornings when she told me she hadn't slept the night before. "Oh, God," I said.

"I think you maybe drew the short straw, there."

The cab turned even more steeply, and my cold forehead touched the colder window glass: I shrank away from it. I had once wondered, when I told Gin what I knew about Daniel, why, though she couldn't bear to hear me, she wouldn't contradict me, either. Now I understood: she knew it was true the moment she heard it. I kept my eyes shut as my question lifted into the quiet car: "Why didn't you tell me before?"

"Because you didn't want to know," he said softly. "Sylvia told me she tried." I remembered, suddenly, the "louche places" that Sylvia had mentioned. I remembered, too, that beautiful woman in the pale straw cloche outside the bookstore, June—no, Djuna—weeping in the street. I remembered Bobby asking Romaine Brooks why she put up with Natalie's lovers. There were a lot of things I had chosen not to notice. "I really would have told you sooner," Anson said, "if I'd thought that you could take it in."

By the time we reached the Place de la Contrescarpe, the rain was coming down hard. Anson insisted I wear his shoes and crossed the wet cobbles in his sockfeet. Inside, he turned on the gas lights, lit a fire in the Prussian stove, and ran a tub behind a screen for me, drying his shirt on a chair. He didn't say much as I shivered and wept in the bath, even when I vomited, again, over the side of the tub. He just pattered through his small neat flat, passing over tea and cognac, a wet washcloth for the floor, and, later, as I huddled under a quilt in the union suit he'd lent me, a reefer. I felt warm and safe and grateful on the couch beside him, listening to the rain, gazing at his bare scarred feet. I wanted to float in his world of liquor and smoke forever. "Can I stay here tonight?"

"Of course. You'd die of cold out there."

I knew what I was setting myself up for by asking to stay, but I didn't want to be alone. Gin was out for the night with her lawyer, no doubt cutting the same stunted deal. Anson won't care how unhappy I am, I thought. Either he'll ask for it or he'll just take it. Either way I'll like him less. It was a shame. I could think of only one way to weather the next few minutes with my good opinion of him intact. Oh, well. I *did* like him: it might even distract me. "I'm about to fall asleep, but—" I offered.

He pushed my hand away. "Don't."

"Oh, sorry—"

"It's me," he said. "The war."

"Oh."

He looked away from me.

"That's a raw deal," I said.

"At the Italian hospital, they said, *You have given more than your life, Americano.*"

"I'm so sorry."

"Please don't say you're sorry."

"I'm—" I stopped myself. "All right, I won't."

"Why did you try that?" he asked.

"I *said* I was sorry."

"It's all right," he insisted. "I just want to know."

"I guess I should go."

"Oh, Rafaela," he said, his voice thick with loss. "But it would have been a bad idea. You're a mess tonight."

I *was* a mess. I shrugged. "It's fine. I was only—"

"Oh," he said, disappointed. I felt terrible. "Oh." He looked at me again and said quietly, "You don't have to pay me to stay here."

I hadn't known that's what I was waiting for. "Thank you," I said, and I let go, leaned into him, my cheek finding his shoulder. I felt him sigh, as if he'd been holding his breath for a long time. He took my arm and lay it across his waist. I could feel the pulse in his throat through my forehead.

I remembered something. "But. You have a son."

His breathing changed. "He's not mine."

"Oh."

"I never begrudged her. I couldn't."

"But still."

"No, it's not like that. And now they have each other."

"That's true," I agreed.

Poor guy, I thought. What had he hoped to accomplish by chasing me all those months? Funny, I'd heard him use the courtyard WC and hadn't noticed anything remarkable. Maybe he was better off than he made it sound: before modeling for Tamara, I had once encountered, in addition to the wheezy grandfather, another old man in a hotel—drained, gasping, briefly beatific—who actually came without ever getting it up. But then again, he'd never been *shot*. He'd tasted like bleach, I recalled. I had hated him for that, and for his self-pity, but I had not been in a position to like any of them. It must be lonesome, I thought, my grip tightening around Anson. "Well, that's not the only game in town," I said aloud.

I felt his jaw harden, his pulse go fast. I said nothing, suddenly careful. He inhaled, thinking. I burrowed my cheek deeper into his shoulder and his pulse slowed.

"You would know about that," he said, finally.

"I would."

The outstretched arm resting on the back of the couch settled then, across my back, like snow.

21

I SAT UP, HUNGRY, MY HEAD POUNDING, and after a moment remembered where I was. The moon through the windows made the whole flat glow silver. I didn't want to wake up Anson by snooping around for food, so I reached for my little mesh bag. The long chain that had hung across my chest was still wet from the Seine. Maybe, just maybe, my silver cigarette case had proved airtight as well as decorative, and a smoke could stave off hunger. Yes! Sitting up made my head spin, so by touch I found Anson's lighter on the coffee table, right there by the ashtray. The brief flash lit up the contents of my silver case. Four more cigarettes, a five-franc note. Last night's train ticket, *ouch*, and the slim stamped book of my passport. Idly, I flicked Anson's heavy lighter again, opened the passport, and caught a glimpse of my sixteen-year-old face. I was a year and a half older now, I thought. Only that much? My mother's name, briefly spotted, burned inside my eyelids. *Little whore* was what she'd called me, too.

Could things have happened differently for me in the first place?

Could my mother have ignored her husband's widened eyes when I ran into the kitchen on my sixteenth birthday, my dress soaked through? Could she have trusted me?

For once I could see her as an immigrant girl like me, a girl who had sacrificed everything she'd known—parents, friends, a life in her native language—for a man now dead. A girl who might have liked to go home. If she had returned to her parents, flat-bellied and virginal, without a half-Jewish daughter in her arms, would they have taken her in? Perhaps. Perhaps. But she had stayed, and cared for me. For my sake, she had traded her beauty and youth for the things Sal Russo could buy her, and she'd be damned if I was going to take him away from her. I could picture it. I could understand. I had trusted my future to Tamara the way my mother had trusted hers to my father, and we had both been disappointed. We were both so far from home.

I fumbled with Anson's lighter again: something had caught my attention, there, below the photograph, my *luogo di nascita*. I had known the name of the ship on which my parents had come to America—the *Maroni*—but my passport also included the name of the shipping company: the Compagnie Générale Transatlantique. Anson's Autolex had heated up with repeated use, but I wrapped a bit of quilt around my scorching fingers, thumbed the lighter one last time, and stared at those three French words. I thought about that immigrant ship, looked at my unused train ticket, and grimaced.

I had wanted to have with Tamara what my own parents had with each other. In 1910 they defied both families and eloped together to

New York, where my uncle Elio and aunt Rina had immigrated years before. I was born en route. My very first memory is of my father carrying me up a flight of stairs. When he reaches the top, he kisses my mother without setting me down. My first memory is of being held between their two embracing bodies.

My own journey to a new life—with the ugly man from the ship—was nothing like my parents'. We had made a trade, and I paid my end on the night train from Marseille. I paid in his room at the Grand Hotel when we arrived that morning. And I paid at the matinee that afternoon, in the red plush depths of his employer's opera box, its stage-side partition up, its porthole curtain closed. I had expected it might be painful or frightening, but perhaps because of the crude experiments I'd been conducting on myself alone at night that year, I was more disgusted by his heavy, deliquescing body itself than by what he did with it. I climbed a ladder inside myself and watched, feeling repulsion, curiosity, and a kind of brittle daring. In the black mirror of the night window, I saw the pair struggling on the narrow train bunk and thought, *Don't you both look shabby.*

The morning after the opera, I woke up to the sound of the ugly man on the phone. He was speaking in English. "It's a shame. I wish I could afford to . . . Really? I *did* hear he'd been an absolute beast since the dancer left. How long has it been? Well, of course I can bring her, but she doesn't speak a word of French." At his interlocutor's reply, he gave a long belt of laughter. "Too true!"

"There's someone I want you to meet tonight," he told me later. "You'll have to thank him for the opera." That night I joined him and a group of his friends in a private salon in the hotel. Many bottles and cigars later, they left me alone with the fattest one, named

Guillaume, who took me up to the ugly man's room. All my things were there, neatly arranged, but every trace of the ugly man's presence had vanished. The fat man sat on the bed in his butter-colored suit and watched me scan the room, confused and alarmed, until I figured out for myself what had happened. I was one man's gift to another, and a thriftily rewrapped gift at that.

I had wanted to go to Paris, but I hadn't given a thought to what I'd do once I got there. I had no money. I had a small valise full of unstylish dresses, an Italian passport, five words of French, and a sixteen-year-old girl's body. If I left the room, chances were I would have to do exactly what I'd have to do if I stayed. The fat man sat on the neatly made bed with his hands at his sides, patient and engaged, as if watching a concert staged for his benefit. When he saw me reach the end of my short list of options and turn to him, what he did made me feel all the more trapped. He smiled.

And now the coat he'd given me was in the Seine. I remembered the old man in the opera box, remembered the Spanish grandfather ruining my new uniform. I remembered the day Seffa tore up my sanitary napkin: Tamara's salon sequined with blood, my own blood staring back at me like the live eyes of birds. And suddenly I remembered that day in the Bois, the dog grinding into the torn-open rabbit, four legs in the air, flanks slick and red, lost in a wriggling orgy of blood and scent, lost as carnally, as impersonally, I realized in that moment, as Tamara liked to lose herself in my body. I understood. Any sailor could have done as much for her. *So this is how you loved me*, I thought. "I loved you—" I said aloud, choking, "differently."

Without sitting up, I set my little train ticket on fire and held it over Anson's ashtray, watching its small flare light the room and die. My throat felt sore, and when I coughed, I sounded as bad as Maggey had earlier that month, getting into her taxi after Tamara's soirée. Of course, I realized. Tamara had picked up Maggey exactly where she'd found me. I pictured Tamara driving through the Bois to find another girl for her party, and I felt sick. And then I imagined Maggey working all winter in the cold, and I felt afraid. There but for the grace of God, and so forth. I began to wonder if I had survived my first year and a half in Paris not due to any cleverness on my part, but just to dumb, dumb luck. I lay for long minutes before I slept again, my closed eyes filling with tears. I had imagined Tamara and I would be together right now, rewriting the story of how I came to Paris, hurtling through the night on a train, this time for love. But Tamara and I hadn't had what my mother had had with my father. I saw it now. We'd had what I'd had with all the others.

22

"YOUR FLAT IS VERY STRANGE," I said, late the next morning. My voice was unusually loud and my mouth tasted sour. "Why is it so bright over there?"

Through a glass door, I could see a second room, brilliantly lit by a skylight, under which stood a bare desk and a small bed. "It *is* strange," Anson agreed. He was already dressed and shaved, and a fresh slab of baguette lay on the table by a pot of jam. "It used to be a plant shop. We're in the storefront. That's part of the courtyard they glassed over for a greenhouse. Look, cobblestones."

I tried to look, but that would have involved raising my head. I was sore all over, and blinking felt difficult. "It must be freezing in there."

"I'm from the Midwest. I like it."

"Why are you shouting?" I asked.

"Was that more cognac than you're used to?"

"Mmm."

"I'm sorry. There's coffee when you're upright."

"Thanks."

"After you fell asleep, I went to the de la Salles' party."

"Why?" I asked, my brain moving slowly.

"I wanted to talk to Boucard."

"He was still there?"

"Tight as tight could be. Strutting around like the cock of the walk because Kuffner sent him some sort of apology."

I sat up slowly and took the cup Anson handed me. "You told Boucard you followed me?"

"He asked if he could talk to you, but I told him I had followed the painting, not you. I said I ran along the quai and followed the painting until I saw it go under, and I told him I didn't know where you were."

I blinked at him, surprised: he'd lied for me.

"I mean, I don't know why you did what you did, but I think it was private," he said, as if inviting me to say more about Tamara.

I couldn't. "Thank you," I choked out.

"After all, it's *her* painting, not his. No doubt you already have hell to pay."

I swallowed. I wasn't ready to tell him where the painting was. Not yet.

"Of course he's heartbroken that it's gone, but he's glad, too, now that Kuffner can't get at it either."

"I should go," I said.

"Are you sure? You don't want to try standing first, and then decide?"

I stood with extreme care, and then sat down again. "Oh. Do you mind if I stay here a little longer?"

Anson laughed out loud.

"You told me you were a researcher," I said. "I didn't know you spied on people, too."

"I was there to watch the painting," he insisted. "I wasn't spying on you. Per se. But still, I'm sorry. I really tried to get out of the job, because you're a friend."

"Thanks," I said, not hiding my distrust.

"I'm sorry," he repeated. "Bland was doing that thing I hate: once your painter had him research Boucard and Kuffner, Bland went to each of them to drum up business. Boucard had us look up you and Tamara, both, but he really just wanted the painting followed. Kuffner declined his services entirely, but for all I know, that's where he got the idea to wait around for you all day the way he did. In any case, again, I'm sorry. I felt like a creep watching you come and go like that. But it was my job."

"You were watching me pose?"

"Your window was higher up than mine, Rafaela. I was watching the front door of the building and dying of boredom. Again, I'm sorry. Believe me, I'd rather read bank statements than sit around smoking for twelve hours a day."

"What happened the other twelve?"

"One of his other guys."

"What did you find out about me?"

"That you, my dear, not surprisingly, have no records at all, because you're a foreigner operating in an all-cash economy. According to our friends in Immigration, you disembarked at Marseille on an Italian passport in 1926, and then you disappeared."

"Well, I could have told you that. But can I ask you something? I know if you have an Italian father, you're Italian. That's how I got my passport. But if you're born on a French shipping line, are you French?"

Anson looked up at the ceiling for a moment, as if consulting something he'd read once long ago, and concluded, "Yes. Technically. You are. Or—that's it—you qualify for French citizenship, if you haven't already forsworn it in order to be a citizen of any other country."

I nodded my thanks, albeit gingerly. "Bravo."

Anson grinned at his own powers of recall. "Why?"

"I think I could be French," I said, and explained.

"You should look into this. We can throw you a party if it all pans out," he said. "France's prettiest new *citoyenne*."

"France's most hungover new *citoyenne* is more like it," I said. "What did you find out about Tamara?"

"Well," he reflected. "Not surprisingly, I found out that she has income from her paintings that she gets in dribs and drabs and quickly spends. One thing *did* surprise me, however. How long has it been since she and her husband divorced?"

"She only signed the papers recently," I said. "But he left her this past spring."

"That's what I thought. From what you said, it was so bitter, I was surprised he still gives her money every month."

"He does?"

"For the past year at least, every month, there's a transfer of funds from an account at the Banque de Commerce"—where Tadeusz had worked, I recalled— "to Tamara's. Ten thousand francs."

"Oh," I said. I was sitting upright on Anson's couch, but at this, I sank down flat on my back again.

"Why are you crying?"

"I don't know."

Anson patted his pockets for a handkerchief, and gave me a napkin from the table instead. "Here. Sorry."

"Thanks. I'm so embarrassed," I said. I rubbed my salty face with my wrist. "I mean, do *you* have anyone who gives *you* money every month?"

"Uh, Monsieur Bland?"

"No, I meant—"

"My imaginary rich parents? I know, that's what I told you when we first met. I wish."

"Really?"

"Rafaela," he said gently. "When I saw you coming out of the lift that night we first met, you looked so sad and angry that I felt for you. I really did. But at the same time, I got a little sore at you, too. I thought, oh, so *you* think *you're* so special because *you* hate *your* job? Bland owns me as much as Boucard owns your painter."

"I hadn't thought of it that way," I said, smarting at the memory of that night in the Ritz, but even more so at the memory of Tamara's grand speeches about supporting her daughter on her own.

"My wife had some money from her family," he said. "But *that's* over. Maybe that's why those bank transfers from de Lempicka's husband struck me. Now that it's over, I can't imagine taking money from my wife every month."

"Maybe it's for his child," I said, my mouth like cotton. "Well, now she wants to marry Kuffner for *his* money."

"Rafaela, I saw Bland's report. If I could, I'd try to marry Kuffner, too."

I realized, just then as I groaned in reply, that I had completely forgotten the suitcases. The little valise I had packed for Italy was still sitting in Tamara's apartment. And my coat was lost in the Seine. I stumbled as I stood. "I'll just take this behind the screen," I said, reaching for my bedraggled dress.

"It's *December*. You're not going out in wet feathers. Can't I lend you something to wear?"

"You're a pal, Anson."

"And then I should probably drift into work sometime. Tie up some loose ends before the holiday."

"I'm sorry to hold you up. If I can borrow this," I said, gesturing toward the gray union suit I was wearing, "and you lend me the biggest coat you can spare, I can scuttle home and change."

"I have just the thing for you," he said, digging into his wardrobe. "*Voilà!*" He produced a thick Italian military cape. "But someone will check you into the Salpêtrière if you go around with those woolly underwear legs poking out. Let me at least give you *something*. All the girls are in trousers these days."

"All the rich American girls who think it's fun to break the law," I said, but I accepted what he gave me and changed behind the screen, pausing to note a medal tacked to the wall beside a clipping in a frame. *Al Valore Militare*, the medal said. The *Sun* article, yellowing under glass, ran under a photograph of Anson: it said that he had been distributing cigarettes for the Red Cross *in the Piave district in the front line trenches when a shell from a trench mortar burst over his head. The surgical chart of his battered person*, it also said, *shows 227 marks, indicating where bits of a peculiar kind of Austrian shrapnel, about as thick as a .22 caliber bullet and an inch long, like small cuts from a length of wire, smote him.*

Anson had cut his own name out of the article. Why? Had he since changed his name? Or was it out of shame at what the war had done to him? I would ask him one day, I decided. It was weird that Anson kept so many relics of a war that had cheated him so badly. It was weird not to see his book anywhere in his flat, or even a clipping from his sportswriting days. He had excised his life as a writer as much as he had enshrined his life at war. I saw a photograph of him on the wall, holding the hand of a stocky little boy outside the Jardin des Plantes zoo. Through a gap in the screen, I saw him opening the passport I'd left on the coffee table: the happy, potato-faced boy looked exactly like him. But how could that be, given what Anson had told me the night before? The war had ended eight years back, and Anson's son was only four. Had he made up that story about what they said in the Italian hospital? Why would you lie about a thing like *that*? I looked from son to father again, and my fogged but clearing brain suddenly climbed a dense braid of intuition and logic. Perhaps it was the loss of his writing, and not the war, that had crippled Anson. I would ask him that someday, too. Who might he have become if he hadn't lost his work, I wondered, or if losing it hadn't broken him? What might he have written? What might he still write yet? Just as I opened my mouth to ask about his book, Anson coughed in horror. "Rafaela," he spluttered. "You're seventeen years old."

"So?"

"I have a sixteen-year-old sister in the tenth grade. Shouldn't you be in school?"

"Oh, for crying out loud. I think it's a little late for that," I said, my voice dropping uncontrollably. *Not again with the tears*, I thought, glad he couldn't see me.

"It's not too late," he countered. "I mean, isn't there anything you want to learn?"

Just then, a metallic whine sheared the air: we both jumped. "What's that?"

"Don't worry, it's only the sawmill," he said, as the groan of wood, motor, and steel rattled the glass in the windows.

"Ohhh," I said, gently pressing my skull into my hands. "The sawmill?"

"Ten to five except on Sundays."

"Oh, that's very bad."

"It's not so bad when you haven't drunk too much."

"God help you."

"It keeps my rent down," he said, as I emerged to face him. "Well, look what the cat dragged in."

"It's a good thing all you have is that shaving mirror," I said, looking down at my ensemble: a pair of putty-colored trousers from a sacque suit that had seen better days, held up with braces over a union suit, mercifully hidden from sight by Anson's military cape.

He didn't try very hard not to laugh. "You really make quite the officer."

"Spare me the hat that goes with this," I said, laughing at myself. "No, I want it, in case *les flics* are awake at this hour."

"As you wish, Mademoiselle. I do have the boots, unless you want to wear my shoes from last night again."

"Oh, Lord."

"And the pistol, too. Want it? I'm still going to teach you how to shoot one day."

"Well. I have to think about today."

"Let me send you home in a taxi."

"I—appreciate it," I said, brought short by how much I meant it. "And then I can go *pay hell* in my own clothes."

"I don't envy you."

"Thank you—" I said, "for all of this."

"Thank *you*," he said, with a smile so sudden it embarrassed us both. "You know you're welcome here anytime."

Tamara did not say a word to me until she closed and locked the door. I was wearing a too-tight coat I had borrowed from Gin's closet: I did not take it off, nor my hat. "You are not in Italy," Tamara said.

"Neither are you."

"I am sorry about last night. I tried to find you, at the party, to say we could not go, but you left early. Why?"

I didn't answer her question. "You spent the night with Kuffner."

"Well, he invited me," she said huffily.

I blinked.

"I have to invest in my future, Rafaela."

In the furnace of her enormous betrayal, the only sentences I could form felt like tiny flakes of snow. "But I thought you didn't want him."

"I would be a fool not to take him," she said. "You would do the same, surely?"

My throat began to close. "No," I choked. "No. I wouldn't." I handed her a paper sack. "Sorry your dress got rained on," I sneered.

Tamara opened the sack. "Completely ruined, I see," she said lightly. "It is a good thing we took those photographs, no?" I looked away. "But where is the rest of it? Where is your peacock tail?"

"It's in the Seine," I snapped. "Along with the *painting* you gave me."

Tamara started, then gave me a calculating look. "Did Boucard's man see you?"

"Yes," I said savagely.

"You know who I am talking about? The man at the window with the cigarettes?"

"Yes, I know who you're talking about. What do you think Anson was doing in the neighborhood all this time?"

Tamara gasped. "Was Boucard paying *you*, too?" At the look on my face, she laughed. "No, I see. Your friend was just spying on you and you were too dumb to know. Some friend. Maybe you should choose better ones."

"Maybe I should," I said. "Look at yourself."

She was not looking at me. She was stroking her collarbone, thinking. "If Boucard thinks you threw the painting in the Seine, we can never display it now," she murmured.

"You lied to me," I said. "You used me." Tamara continued to look away. I took the gold ring from my coat pocket and flung it at her. "You *gave* our painting to Kuffner!"

A chilly sound hung in the air after the ring snapped to the floor. Tamara did not look down for it. "Rafaela," she said patiently. "When I marry him the painting will be mine again."

"But I thought—"

"What?" Tamara laughed.

I didn't know what I'd thought until I'd begun to say it, but I swallowed it fast.

"You thought I would marry *you*? Rafaela, can you make me a baroness? Can you make me a rich woman? Can you give me a *child*?"

Despite everything I had learned about Tamara in the past fourteen hours, I began to shake. I thought my face would crack open. I turned my back to her and faced the bed carved with those nymphs in each other's arms, the portrait of Romana's mother in her suit. I was crying as hard as I had on Anson's couch that morning.

I felt a hand on my shoulder. Tamara's voice was solid honey: golden, gritty, particulate. "Rafaela, come here, you beautiful thing," she said. My whole body blushed. I shrugged the hand away.

23

"YOU POOR THING," said Sylvia an hour later, passing me a handkerchief. I had sought her out in the bookstore, where she and Adrienne were sharing a late breakfast alone in the fat morning light. I hadn't thought I'd wanted to *marry* Tamara, not in so many words, but now that she'd mocked me for it, I felt humiliated, exposed: she was right. And was it so strange, to want what I'd wanted? What Sylvia and Adrienne had, was it so impossible as all that? I was crying all over again as Sylvia said, "But just think, most people get their hearts broken and have nothing to show for it. At least you can point to those gorgeous paintings out in the world. She's kind of a genius, no?"

At Sylvia's soothing words, I began to suck in little gusts of air that threatened to burst into sobs at any second. Adrienne looked impatient. "Ah, genius," she said wryly. I looked up at her and held my breath. "There's no excuse for treating your friends badly," she said in French, more to Sylvia than to me, and glanced toward the copies of *Ulysses* by the till. She patted my back and pointed at a basket of croissants atop a neat stack of books. "You should sit down and eat something."

As I reached, gratefully, to take off my borrowed coat, my eyes fell on the little suitcase I'd lugged all the way from Tamara's. "I even made a dress to wear on our trip, and she'll never see it," I said, sniffling.

Sylvia looked over at Adrienne, half pitying, half amused. I would become better friends with them in time, so close that I would one day vacation with them to Adrienne's family cabin in the Savoy Alps, which is where I'm perching now. But I *was* imposing on them that morning, on their goodwill and on their breakfast, too. I wiped my eyes again and tried to look a little less morose. I realized the basket of croissants was sitting on Sylvia's unsold medical text, and remembered, dimly, the pleasure I'd felt when I first looked at LE SYSTÈME MUSCULAIRE. "You inspired me, Adrienne," I said, opening my valise to show them my zipper dress.

"Well, will you look at that," said Sylvia, almost touching, unawares, Kuffner's money still sewn into the hem. *Enough money to change my life*, I realized. *But how?*

Adrienne was looking from the dress to me, puzzled.

"I mean, you inspired the feeling of it," I explained. "You don't dress like anybody else, but you dress so much like *yourself.*"

"You *do,*" Sylvia told her. "Look at this. It's beautiful."

"I've never inspired a dress before," Adrienne said, pleased in spite of herself. "You should keep at it, Rafaela. You have a gift."

Part Two

24

WHAT DOES IT MEAN, that the devil has cloven hooves? That there's nothing firm to stand on. I was raised in comfort. I married a count. When the Reds took my husband away, they took away the ground on which I stood; no, they took away my very means to stand. They cleft my feet in twain. When I circled from prison to prison, when I painted in a frenzy, I did it with broken feet. My painting had a cloven-footed mountain goat's confidence until I married Rollie, became a baroness, resumed the life I was bred for: it had the confidence borne of balancing eight points on broken rock, the devil's confidence, bent on reclaiming heaven. That's what I was painting for. Not for gallery owners. Not for critics. Not for my teachers. Least of all for other painters: painters were poor, and I wanted to be rich. I was painting to recover a lost world and to claim a place in it. I was painting for the people who would buy my work and make me rich again. I was painting as a way to stand apart from all the penniless White Russian ballerina girls desperate to sell themselves back into nobility. There weren't enough aristocrats to marry us all, and I wasn't young or thin enough to go it on looks alone.

And this is the devil's part, the genius part: I just happened to be painting for anyone else who had lost a world, too, and because of the war, that was everyone. I was making our heaven myself, stroke by stroke, with the materials to hand. Prince Gabriel with his borrowed uniform. Suzy Solidor with her phony name. I took the chips and splinters of a broken world and I burnished them whole again. I recovered paradise, and from its depths called forth exactly what I needed: Baron Kuffner. My shaggy Galatea, my little homunculus. Indulgent daddy. Cock-at-dawn. Once I had him, the devil's work was done. You would think, then, that I would have turned into a baroness wife, the kind of woman who paints as a hobby, who could just as easily throw parties or breed dogs. And maybe I could have once become her, when I was still young and unformed. If the two men hadn't taken away my first husband. If we had emigrated together before they came, if we had joined my family wintering in Copenhagen, already fled, maybe that's how I would have turned out.

But they took him, the two men. Until then, we could have left any time. *He's* the one who needed to stay and be a hero for the Czar.

It happened at night, when we were in bed together. They pounded at the door: the Cheka, the Bolshevik police. They didn't even wait for Thade to go to the door; they just kicked it open. Then they came upstairs. *We're taking you in for questioning, Lempitzky,* they said. *Get dressed.*

Could you give us a little privacy? my husband asked. And they laughed. I couldn't get dressed because they were standing in our bedroom. I was naked in the bed with the sheets wrapped around me and they were standing in their leather jackets, staring at me. Black and white: those jackets, my own pale skin.

I could not find the prison where they kept him. I asked everyone I knew for help. I went to the Swedish consulate and the official told me what he wanted. "But how do I know you'll help me?" I asked.

"You don't," he said.

Afterward, I went outside and vomited in the snow: I slid and fell, and landed—yes, I landed—on a dead horse. They took my husband away and they threw me onto the body of a dead horse. A cloud of flies leapt at the wet thump. I screamed. And when I looked down, I saw that parts of the horse had been chopped away with knives, for meat.

So I left Russia. I had my own passport. I couldn't save my husband. All I could save was myself.

And in Paris I became a painter. No dirt. No mess. Not one line out of place. And even though I stopped needing to summon the devil, once I started, I never stopped needing to trace runes on the floor and chant. Now that I have what was cut from me, you would think money and a title would have closed the wound. But I lost myself to Rafaela along the way, to painting her: I'll always leak a wire of blood here, at the corner of the mouth.

25

Now Rollie is dead, so I can live anywhere. I just heard Hector's pretty cousin Ana call Cuernavaca a *rich expatriate bubble* under her breath, to which I replied, full voice, "And why is that a problem?" The fact is, I chose to live here for the volcano. The gardener has somehow managed to spend all morning hanging a new lamp, but look there, past the ladder he left out: El Popo, through the bougainvillea, smoldering whitely in the distance. I told Hector that when I die I want my ashes scattered over El Popo, and he said, *Okay, querida.* Everyone here from the good old days finds it exotic that my best friend is a Mexican boy, but Hector Oliveras is a sculptor. Artists understand one another. He is a homosexual—all the good-looking ones are—but I like to think I'll change his mind one day.

Inside, at my white Saarinen table, Kizette brings the mail as we sit to eat. Romana and her husband are bringing that handsome nephew they've talked about, so we'll be seven for dinner, but we're four for lunch now: my daughter and myself plus Hector and his young cousin Ana, returning to Mexico from New York City. "What's in it, Hector?" I ask.

Kizette surrenders the mail, wounded. Her expression annoys me: she's sixty-odd years old; surely she has more to live for.

Hector gives Ana an apologetic glance before sorting through the cards and letters. Not yet forty, Hector is boyish, but Ana at twenty-two might as well be a child. "You're all creamy and golden, aren't you?" I can't help noting. "Like a little pot of flan."

Ana looks uncomfortable and Kizette pouts. Kizette was pretty once too; I don't see what she has to complain about. "Invitations to parties," Hector reports.

"We can go over those with my schedule later."

"Oh, oops, the Osaka gallery's listing your birthplace as Moscow."

"Warsaw," I say more sharply than I care for Ana to hear. "Make them correct it."

Ana gives me a shrewd, alert look. "Why did they say Moscow, then?"

Hector glances from her to me and, like me, he pretends he didn't hear her. "The Zurich people want to show *Rafaela*, too," he says, holding up another note.

"Did you send Osaka my letter about that?"

My daughter jumps in. "I thought we agreed to hold off on that, *chérie*."

"Excuse me? Kizette. I asked you to send my letter and you didn't send it?"

I can't see the look Kizette and Hector give each other, but he surprises me by taking her side. "Tamara, remember? The three of us talked about it and you decided to send the Osaka people *The*

Dream for now, and then offer your new *Rafaela* once everything's firmed up."

"Osaka? Zurich? Rafaela?" Ana looks from face to face. If I were younger, I simply wouldn't talk business in front of a girl that pretty, but these days I never know how much pep I'll have.

"Mother has a solo show in Japan coming up, and she has work in a big Art Deco show in Zurich, too."

"La Belle Rafaela," I say, pointing.

I follow Ana's eyes to the photograph over the doorway. "Oh!" she says, startled. Fifty-three years later, it still shocks: I'm pleased.

"It's her most famous nude," says Kizette dryly.

"I feel like I've seen it before," Ana muses. "Yes! When I was a kid." God help me. For her, eight years ago is *when I was a kid*? "Hector sent me a poster from your big rediscovery show."

"I was not *rediscovered*."

I know the child is not trying to provoke me, so I *am* controlling myself, but Kizette hears the ice in my voice and breaks in quickly, anxious. *"The Sunday Times* called *Beautiful Rafaela* 'perhaps the most important nude of the twentieth century.'"

"And they reproduced it in *The New York Times* last year," Hector chimes in. I know what they're doing, buttering me up, and I resent it, but I'm grateful, too.

"Wow," says Ana.

It's gratifying when the youth stop condescending, isn't it? "I made a million dollars by my brush before I was thirty, *guapa,* and don't you forget it." The girl looks from Kizette to Hector to see if I'm joking, and back to me, impressed. "Arsène Alexandre called me *a perverse Ingres.* I think the Osaka people should be flattered by my offer."

"A copy—" says Kizette.

"It's a de Lempicka. It's a contemporary interpretation. It's not a copy."

"What happened to the original painting?" asks Ana.

"After the big '72 show, *La Belle Rafaela* was bought by a private collector. And he won't lend it out anywhere."

"That's the problem? They only want the one painting?"

"They'll take other work. Tamara's too important for them not to."

"And there *is* another option, an obvious one—"

"There's the one I proposed, Kizette. I don't see why you and Hector are being so difficult about this. I can paint a *Rafaela* for Zurich, too."

Ana looks back at the painting, and asks, "Where is she now?"

Hector looks grateful to Ana for changing the subject, but clips a glance my way. Am I so difficult to lunch with as all that? "Who?" I ask the girl.

"Beautiful Rafaela. The model in the painting. What happened to her?"

"She went to *couture* school and opened a dress shop with some friends. Then she married a part-time journalist who got himself killed in Spain."

"Where is she now?"

Is she trying to provoke me? I shrug. "Wherever she wants to be, I suppose."

"She was just a model," Hector explains quickly. "That was fifty years ago."

"Oh. But, I mean, you're copying her now, so I figured you'd know . . ."

"It's the *image* she's copying, not the person," he says.

"I'm sorry. I didn't understand."

"You don't have to be sorry, child," I say, touching her cheek. "Just be your beautiful self." It's easy. She smiles. Bless Hector for saying the right thing at the right time.

She is bright as well as pretty, it seems. She has won a scholarship to graduate school, she tells us over lunch, but her Pinochet dissertation bores me.

"All the men I talk to know something, but they aren't telling," she says, some minutes into her explanation. "All the women *could* know something, and maybe some of them aren't telling, but many of them—I feel it—aren't *asking* their husbands and fathers. And I'm interested in this business of not-asking. What I, a privileged North American, see from the outside as an unforgivable lapse of curiosity? It might just be a survival strategy."

She *is* sharp. But she can't cut me. *An unforgivable lapse of curiosity:* Was that for me? "I showed her a good deal more than *curiosity* in 1939 and look at how she repaid me."

They're staring. All three of them. "I'm sorry?" asks Ana.

She's just like my daughter. Think you can fool me, all wide-eyed? "I saved Rafaela Fano from the Nazis, and she never spoke to me again."

Ana looks at Hector, alarmed. Kizette, who is not clumsy, knocks over her wine and calls for the maid.

Ana says something soothing in Spanish to Luz as she swabs, excluding me, so I turn to Hector. "While you and your cousin are in town—there's money in my purse—would you pick me up a tube of vermillion?"

"Of course, *querida*."

"The good Belgian stuff."

"I know what you like."

"Don't let them sell you anything else. None of those cadmium reds, *écoutes?*"

"Yes, Tamara."

Luz asks if I need anything else and I wave her away. "China red, darling. Real ground cinnabar."

"That's right," Hector assures me.

With Luz gone, Ana looks at all three of us and decides, it seems, to humor the old woman. "Is it for the painting you're doing now?" she asks.

"That's right. Nothing makes me feel so alive as painting for a show."

Kizette's jaw stirs. Hector says nothing. One of them is hiding something from me, but not well.

"May I see?"

"No, child. I'll unveil it when I finish."

"Oh. Sorry."

"I've always been private about my work in progress," I say, giving Kizette and Hector a sharp look. I was not private about my work in progress until a specific incident last week, as they well know. I wonder which one of them will dare to contradict me.

26

HECTOR AND ANA HAVE LEFT for town in a flurry of *bisous*; Kizette is reading one of her Bibles (*must* she own three?) in the bedroom that we share. I'm on the chaise in my studio, sipping alternately from my cigarette and my oxygen tube. I can't see the painting from my couch anymore because last week, after someone tampered with my work, I turned the easel away.

Last weekend, I gathered together a first round of canvases for my Osaka show. They're borrowing most of the pieces from collectors in Europe, but a few of them I own. *The Dream. Tamara in the Green Bugatti. The Orange Scarf.* A dozen others, including my latest: a new version of my 1936 *Saint Anthony.* The owners of the 1936 painting are touchy about showing it, and it's too good to go unseen: those hands. I'll send the new *Rafaela,* too, when it's ready.

So last weekend, I invited Hector over and I put the whole house to work—Kizette, the staff—until all the paintings were leaning against the studio wall, waiting for the art handlers to pack and collect them on Monday. I needed to sleep the whole morning, but Kizette and Hector kept an eye out for me, and the art movers came and went without incident.

Or so I thought. Monday evening in my studio, unable to sleep, I saw something out of place: a small painting, leaning against the wall with its back to me. My new *Saint Anthony*.

I confronted both of them when Hector came for lunch the next day. "How did one piece get left behind?"

I watched them: so surprised, so apologetic. They didn't know how it possibly could have happened. They counted fourteen paintings against the wall and fourteen paintings in the truck, so the art handlers must have moved it before they started work that morning. Maybe they missed a painting at the end of the row. They'd make sure it went into the second shipment, absolutely.

But when we had set the paintings out over the weekend, *Saint Anthony* hadn't been off to the side. I remember, it was standing in the middle of the row, with the *Orange Scarf* on the left and my painting of Ira with the mandolin on the right. (I think of Ira, her hair the red-black of cherries, and grimace.) My *Saint Anthony* was right there among its neighbors, and it was left behind. One of them left it behind. One of them, Hector or Kizette, set it aside, thinking I wouldn't notice. Of course I noticed. Ever since my exhibition in '72—what Ana blithely called my *rediscovery show*— museums and galleries have been asking for work from the Twenties and Thirties: I send it, they show it, and the world thinks all the more that I stopped painting in '33. A nobody named Larry Rivers copied that painting of Ira with the mandolin and had the temerity to think I'd be pleased. My friend Romana says it would behoove me to cultivate some young New York painters, but the gall! I stopped doing those portraits fifty years ago! But I never stopped painting. Still lifes. Geometric experiments. Landscapes composed of the tendons of the hand. In the Sixties, I spread loose dreams with palette knives: *Une Semaine de Paris* called them "beautiful frescoes, inspired by Pompeii." The thing is, I dared to make new work, and this is a world that rewards artists for rolling the same little scarab's ball of dung up the same little hill all their lives.

They want to dig my grave, those museums, mausoleums. Which one of them left my painting out, Kizette or Hector? Which one of them agrees with the gravediggers? Daughter or friend, which one?

27

~~~~~~~~~~

Nosy Ana. *Where is she now?* What kind of a question is that? I was upset that Rafaela left the way she did in '27, but I had so much to do. I found another girl to pose for *Myrto* and then I didn't think about Rafaela much, not until a spring day years later. Or rather, I thought about her with an occasional, impersonal pang. Have you ever had a favorite café close? It was like that.

I should have been on top of the world, that spring of '31. I had finally pried Nana de Herrera off Rollie for good by painting a portrait that showed her in her worst light. His wife, Sara, had entered her final decline. Only then, my title all but assured, had I shucked off Boucard's contract and secured one commission after another, despite the crash. I had bought a new home in Montparnasse. I was working at the rate of more than one painting a month, thanks to judicious doses of cocaine. It was never a problem for me. I may have painted the occasional six-fingered girl, but my daughter never noticed a thing.

Sweetest of all, my on-again off-again fling with Ira Perrot was on again. The stock market crash meant that she and her husband couldn't take the trips they'd planned, so I had her to myself to paint: a winter *Die Dame* cover in a red sweater. Larger than life in Rafaela's blue dress, holding a mandolin. Seated in oyster-white satin with crimson drapery, bearing an armful of arums.

All morning with Ira, painting. All afternoon in bed. It was like having Rafaela back, but better, because Ira never had Rafaela's American absolutism. When Ira and I first went to Italy, just ourselves, we ate, we made love, we looked at paintings, and then we went home to our husbands, cheerful. When Rafaela and I planned our trip to Italy, I could tell: she wanted to run away with me and never come back.

I could see the difference when I painted them. While Rafaela brought a stupefied Ingres odalisque to every canvas—with her solemn, carnal tenderness, her honest surprise at her own pleasure—there was a coolness to Ira that made her into a grave Fra Angelico figure, a mathematically plotted angel, no matter how we dressed her. Going to bed with Ira was a small decadent miracle, like wearing orange blossoms in the snow. But Rafaela? During those months she modeled for me, I spent my nights in rough bars by the Seine just to keep it from weakening me: her need, her earnest love.

One day in the spring of '31, after spending the afternoon with Ira, I suddenly remembered that I had an appointment with a collector. I threw on a dress and left Ira, naked, to go home at her leisure. En route to the collector's, I realized I hadn't brought his address. I turned around, cursing, and when I pulled up to my studio, there was Ira, just leaving. I was halfway out of my car, smiling and waving, when I saw that she held a canvas in either hand.

I stopped. My hand died mid-wave. "Darling!" she exclaimed, her voice high and breathy.

I had one cool thought before the anger hit: I could call the collector and apologize when I got in. I had all the time in the world. I slammed the car door behind me. "What's this?" I asked.

"Oh, Tamara, I had no idea you'd come back," she said, talking too quickly. "You've just been so good to me, and I wanted to surprise you."

I couldn't speak.

"I was just taking these to the framing store, to surprise you," she repeated.

"I am surprised," I said. The fury was cold metal in my veins. "I am very surprised." Slowly and deliberately as I spoke, I gestured, and Ira surrendered two crudely wrapped paintings.

"I just wanted to surprise you," she said a third time, her voice weak. I tore open just enough brown wrapping paper to see that she had taken two portraits of herself: the recent one in the brilliant blue dress, and a smaller one, from '27, in the chemise Rafaela had made for me.

"But Ira," I said slowly, carefully, the steely wires of anger turning me into a marionette. "I haven't even varnished this one yet. And that one is already framed."

I knew Ira's husband had lost a great deal, including his banking job, in the crash. I knew they had sold their second house. I knew the rents on our street were among the highest in the city, and that they were buying a small building in the Butte aux Cailles where they could take the landlord's flat and rent out the rest to live on. But it had not occurred to me that the price of a pair of paintings could make a difference to the woman who had once brought me to

Italy on her own largesse, let alone warrant the loss of a thirteen-year friendship. "They were of *me*, Tamara. All those years you painted me, and I never asked you for a thing."

"I thought we were friends," I said. "I thought painting was the way we spent our time together."

"You were young and pretty and ambitious, so I let you paint me. But you took advantage," she said.

I looked at her, this woman whose scent was still on my hands. I opened my mouth to speak, and shut it. I tried again. "If you want a model's wage for the past ten years, let's go inside and calculate your hours."

"You have so many paintings up there. You have stacks and stacks. You'd never even miss these two."

"Of course I would miss them. I'd never think *you* would be the one to take them."

"I can't keep giving and giving to you, Tamara. Let me sell these and we'll share the profit," she said, but her voice shook with guilt.

"I'll mail you a check for your services," I snapped. I carried in the paintings with my head unbent, knowing she was watching. I burned my way up the stairs, and when I got into my apartment, I wept. It occurred to me that this might be how Rafaela had felt when she saw me give our painting to Rollie. At that, I washed my face. I would never speak to Ira again, I decided. And Rafaela? I would never think about *her*. And I didn't. Not for three years.

28

You can't trust anyone. One of them is in league with the mausoleums, Kizette or Hector. One of them wants me to stop painting. I defy you, gravedigger. I've got a show coming up; what have you got?

Painting *Beautiful Rafaela*, it's like making love to her was: you just want to do it again. I painted two in '27, one for the Salon, against red, and one for me, against green. This one, today, is against red. I don't think of them as copies. I once *copied* a painting, *Kizette en Rose* (was it Kizette?) but that was only because my model had aged, and I missed the little girl. What could be more different than nine and eleven? (Or, as I told the world, than seven and nine? I'd had to shave two years off her age to make her French instead of Russian, but I never lost track.) With the second *Kizette en Rose*, I was painting from a painting. But Rafaela *Red* and *Green*? Neither was a sketch. Neither was a copy. Both were from the girl in the room.

I think it was Kizette who moved my new *Saint Anthony*. When my daughter was nine, I painted *Kizette en Rose*. When she was ten, I painted *Kizette au Balcon*. At ten, she had a trace—as faint as the trace of rose in *Kizette en Rose*—of the sour, sagging woman she is at sixty-three. A hint of thunder at the corners of the mouth and eyes. When she wasn't simply flouncing on the couch or slamming doors. And just when my husband had left me. And then there was the time I met that Texan. Inviting me to his home for Christmas like that, with no intention of sleeping with me! Did he really think I'd sailed all that way just to meet his wife and children? When I came home to Paris, Kizette had cut my hats to shreds.

I always thought boarding school put an end to all that. When my daughter joined me in California, she was a sunny, placid girl of twenty-three, almost her child self again. My sister was safe, thank God, I told everyone. (How could I have a grown-up daughter, at my age?) I'd fished her up from the war like a bright coin from a dark well. But here she is, with her husband gone, clomping and gloomy, burying me before I'm dead. She *did* move my *Saint Anthony*. But why would she sabotage me now, when I've rewritten my will for her? Maybe she wants to punish me for outliving her husband. But she's timid. She knows I could change it back anytime.

I'm not painting from a painting right now, but from the memory of painting. My eyes and my hand remember that sweating summer. A girl like ripe strawberries, hot with light. A girl like ripe *myrtilles*. A summer girl who never ceased to be summer. Those lips. Those liquid eyes.

Let ochre-gray and blue be plush. Let gray-ochre and pink be flesh. How close can they get and still differ? Let a greenish halo lead the way from lit to shadowed flesh. I never liked painting skinny women. This knee radiates two bones like spokes: shin and thigh. Hard of bone makes flesh look full. Hang of flesh makes bone look hard. Shadow under bone. Darker darker darker darker. Brighter brighter brighter brighter. Fine defined foreground shadow: calf. Spongy darker background shadow, so softly applied, so edgeless: thigh. Short thigh. Not if you're face to knee. Make a sharper knee. I can feel my heart beat in my wrists.

The knee is a globe. The knee is a world. The knee has mass. The knee is any joint of meat. The knee is a moon. The knee is a round wheel of cheese. No. The knee is a knee. The knee is paint. The knee is rimmed in light below—slim crescent—and shadow above—slim eclipse. Three bright lobes form hills of bone, split and joined by a vee of tendon. The lobes of the knee blush the faintest red. Same red as the lifted fold of cloth but light, light, as pale a red as Kizette's *Rose* was rose.

That lifted fold of cloth. The thin distinct line of the drapery's crest, and the fat curve of its deep trough. China red. Vermillion. Cinnabar. So was it Hector? Was it because of the will? Red, red. Paste. Pulp. Make it like the lip. But he begged me. He insisted. Blood is thicker than water, he said. Red. He said, you already gave me your house. Sold, not gave, I said. For nothing, Tamara! Do right by your daughter, he said. But now he's angry, is that it? He moved my saint out of spite. He changed his mind. He wants the money after all. He wants me to think Kizette did it, so I'll change the will back for him.

I stop. I need another cigarette, and then more oxygen. I should only take it when I smoke. Sometimes I want it more, but I hate to give in like that. I'd hate to be an old lady strapped to a tank. I let

Kizette and Hector fit the prongs of the tube in my nose at night, to humor them, but some nights I take it out after Hector goes home (was it Hector?), after Kizette falls asleep in the other bed (was it Kizette?), just to prove I can.

But once or twice a day, when I'm painting, I feel tight behind the eyes. A door in my throat begins to close. There it is. My cigarette burns down to an ash worm, unsmoked, gone. I'll light another; let me just breathe with the tube a bit first. Oh. But this hasn't happened before. This odor, like tar and pennies. Is this a new tank? Did they send me a bad one? No. That smell. It's the same tank, new yesterday. And it's the same smell, with or without my tube in. Tight eyes and closing throat. Tar and pennies, and something else. Is it the smell of the hospital when I swam up from the ether? They were cutting out the side of my tongue—cancer, smoking—a small price to pay for all those years of pleasure; I can still talk, still eat. So is it that, a surgery smell?

No. I know it now. I'm lighting another cigarette. My long holder keeps it that much farther from the flammable tank. I'll want it as soon as my throat opens up a little. The tobacco will burn that smell away in one blue breath. But there it is again, a gust of it. I know I know it.

Oh.

It's the dead horse.

I shut off the oxygen and smoke. When I'm done, I soak a cotton rag in linseed oil: pale amber, sharp and clean. I breathe until my throat loosens, until the smell drifts away. Tobacco and linseed are incense, a prayer. They disperse rot.

I've painted the white skin and black leather a hundred times, but I've never painted the horse.

I'm almost finished, but I'm often almost finished. I'm often almost finished for a long time. And then finishing comes to me all at once, and leaves me feeling empty, shaken, private. At first I don't want anyone to know. I clean my brushes like it's any other day.

I just need to clarify the knee. I just need that hint of red—my last gasp of red before Hector comes back—to marry knee to lip, marry both to that red drapery. There. Is it finished? This empty sudden rush. This stillness in the room. Rafaela has been floating in my mouth like a spoonful of *myrtille* jam, and now she's ebbing away. She's been splayed at my feet, all summer sweat and poppies, and now she dresses, stands in the doorway with her back to me. Is it finished?

I'm happy with the eyelids, closed in erotic concentration. Two soft sand dunes. Two shadows for lashes. Two rounded, fleshy triangles, plastic rhyme to breasts and nostrils. Gold, like her skin, but violet, shadowed, all those fine capillaries. Bruise-colored: a girl who stays out late. But should they be a tint of red instead? What red I have is no good. By this point it's almost white. I could poach a little from the painting, but I've worked that surface so fine, I could lose hours to fixing what's already good. I can take my knee-blush red, my almost red, and dull it down, but then I'll have more gray than red. I could do knee-red with skin-gold, but no. Too muddled. Leave it. Wait for Hector. The eyelids are right the way they are. I am finished. I feel so alone.

29

THE ONLY SMELL NOW IS THE JASMINE in the garden. The windows are open to the softening air. Late afternoon. There's the judder of a car pulling up; Hector's back. "Kizette!" I call, and she emerges from the bedroom, sleepy-eyed, to walk me down the hall, unsteady on my pins. We pass Luz, bound for the living room with a platter of little pancakes—my mother's recipe, adapted for the tortilla griddle—and a tray of ice that floats dishes of minced onion, *crema fresca*, and flying-fish caviar: tiny crunching grits of orange light. By the time I reach the foyer, my chauffeur is parking Hector's car and Hector himself is tripping up the three steps to greet me. Ana is trailing behind, one cheek lumped and red. "Look who got stung by a bee!" Hector announces.

"Are you allergic?" asks Kizette.

"No, just embarrassed," murmurs Ana. I hate to see anything spoil that face, ripe as *myrtilles*, round and taut as a brown pear. My throat closes at the sight of her marred, and I catch just a breath of it again, the odor of tar and pennies. "Too sweet to resist," I joke, gesturing with my cigarette holder.

"Let me see," says Kizette, clearly grateful for something to fix, some simpler foe than what age has made me. "Let me make you a baking soda poultice."

The crisp, capable Kizette—the one who rowed crew at Oxford and raised two daughters—always surprises me when she appears, as she does, for strangers and stray cats. Why can't I have her instead of the moody, bovine one, the Bible-cud ruminant? As Kizette inspects Ana's cheek for the stinger and Luz wheels out the champagne bucket, my old friend Romana and her new husband, Paul, pull up with the young nephew—handsome as promised—and emerge with a slapping flutter of car doors, Romana in lemon silk, Paul gauntly elegant in gray linen. Cuernavaca is too small a town to fool with a friend's husband, but there's no harm in looking. Hector leans in, his hand in mine, to kiss each cheek in turn. "I'm sorry, *querida*, I couldn't get the paint today. We were getting ice for Ana's face, and it was later than we thought. I promise I'll bring you some tomorrow."

So that's how it is, I think, and the wire door of a trap clips shut inside me. "Don't worry, darling," I purr, cigarette holder to lips. "You're a dear boy to even think of it."

Unfair! say Kizette's eyes beside me, as she watches me laugh off Hector's slight apology.

But she doesn't understand: I don't want him to know I know. Hector is the one who moved my painting. Now I know.

30

SUDDENLY, I CAN HEAR, but I can't move. My eyes are closed. Then the scent of jasmine cuts through to me and I'm home on the living room couch, buoyed up by bubbles of warm chatter which suddenly pop, flat. Paul Wilson's U.S. Open story breaks off mid-McEnroe. My nostrils, propped open with plastic tubing, are damp with cool oxygen. So they have me in my Space Age necklace, do they? My cannula. "Should we leave her alone?" Ana's voice whispers.

"No," Kizette says. "As long as she has the oxygen, she's fine; she just falls asleep like this sometimes. It would hurt her feelings if we left her."

"Tamara loves a party more than anything," Hector agrees.

"In that hat, she looks like a sunflower drooping on its stem," a young man's voice says softly. Whose? Oh, yes, I forgot about the Wilsons' fine-looking nephew. Martin, yes. I can't open my eyes.

"Are you sure you're not a poet?" asks Hector, and I know he's leaning in with his shy-boy smile.

My eyes fly open: *Traitor!* "Me? Drooping?" I interrupt, to spite him, to break the hold of his gaze on that dark-eyed, thoroughbred boy.

"I was just wishing I could catnap as gracefully as you, Tamara," says Romana. I don't like to date myself, but suffice to say I met Romana de la Salle just after I arrived in Paris, when we were little art students at the Académie Ransom. She was prettier than any of the models, with her strong jaw and her red-blond hair, and one day when I sketched her instead, she caught me looking. She smiled: she was drawing me, too. It was the third or fourth time we had been subjected to Maurice Denis's sycophantic tale of the time he presented his *Hommage à Cézanne* to the master *soi-même*—that cluttered, muddy excuse for a painting! At the end of that class, I dropped out to find a new teacher, and Romana dropped out, too, never to paint again. But we traded sketches that day, and here we are together, decades later. "Dear Romana Wilson," I reply. "You're so cunningly made. Don't you just want to pick her up like a lizard and walk around with her on your shoulder?"

Romana smiles her cool dry lizard smile, basking, and Paul laughs. "No, I can't say that I ever have. We were just raving about these blinis," he says.

I wave my cigarette holder at him. "They're not blinis, darling. They're Polish. Look how they're so thin you can see through them."

"We hate the Russians for how they treated Poland," Kizette explains to Ana and Martin.

"No politics, no politics, please," I insist.

"Crêpes it is," Ana assents, her syllables glopping their way around her swollen cheek. "No Russian tonight. We promise."

I wonder if she has the presence of mind to be happy that beautiful Martin is sitting on her good side. *"Nyet!"* He laughs, catching her eye.

Laugh at me if you must, children, but those men killed my husband in the end. Thade enjoyed himself too much, living it up as a diplomat in Toulouse when everyone back home in Poland was a good self-sacrificing Communist. In 1950, Stalin's puppets summoned him to Warsaw for a short trip, and when he arrived, they hospitalized him. Within days he was dead. He was only sixty-two.

Only Kizette and I know this story. I haven't even told it to Hector, so I'm not surprised he joins the young people in their nonsense. *"Nyet-nyet!"* he choruses, smiling at Martin. Usually I would pity him for throwing himself at yet another unattainable boy, but tonight, knowing that he moved my painting, I'm glad to see him look the fool.

31

THE NIGHT IS A BOSOM OF STARS over the bougainvillea. We've left our lobster shells and gazpacho cups inside on the Saarinen table, and now our cigarette smoke climbs up toward the new garden lamp, an intricate Moroccan confection of iron and blue glass. It's the hour of liqueurs in chocolate thimbles, drunk in quick gusts before the cups melt away.

All evening Paul, as he often does, has been trying to interest the others in a doubles match tomorrow, but for the wrong reasons. Since Kizette came to live with me after her husband's death in November, she has been most herself at tennis, and she and Paul, despite the difference in age, are perfectly matched: strong players with an easy rapport. This, however, makes Paul feel disloyal to his wife. "You can team up with Martin, Romana. Everyone else will be jealous."

"Oh, Martin doesn't want to play with me. I'll just drag him down," Romana says, chuckling gently.

"How about Hector, then? He plays just for fun."

"And that way Martin can play with Ana," I add. "Don't you just want to eat her up?"

"But *I* just want to eat up Martin," Hector protests, camping up the raw truth.

"Oh, Paul," Romana sighs, a little fiercely. "Just play with Kizette. That's all you really want to do anyway."

The spring my husband left me, I tried to win him back with a trip to Lake Como, just the two of us and the child we'd made. Though we were passing her off as eight, she was ten then, and no longer sweet, but she was all we had. On the morning of the night that marked the end for us, we sat together, all three on the terrace, looking at the lake because we could not look at one another. "Aren't you having a good time, Thade?"

"You're not making it easy," he said.

"But isn't this nice?" I asked brightly. "Isn't this more fun than running out on your family?"

"I don't know," he said. "Are you sure you wouldn't rather be sharing a hotel room with Ira Perrot?"

"Oh, come on."

"Or Gabriele D'Annunzio?"

"Darling."

"Or crashing from cocaine on the bathroom floor? Or sucking off one of the waiters?"

"Oh, look at yourself, Taddi. Passed out drunk every night." I spoke in a low growl, but then Kizette began to cry.

This was hours before our worst fight, our loudest fight, when we circled each other with stumps of broken wineglass and the hotel men came to the door, hours before Tadeusz left for good to marry his little mouse. This was hours before the sight of his eyes in Kizette's face—as she crawled out from under the desk where she'd been hiding—made me see black and fall down. This was when hope was still possible, when Kizette's tears could still move us.

And when we turned, simultaneously, to tell her to behave herself in a restaurant, we froze, because we could both see the swans. They wafted in like gods seated on clouds. They stopped us both mid-breath. "Look, Kizette, darling," said Tadeusz—it pains me still that he could summon so much tenderness when he wanted to—"swans." And Kizette stopped crying and looked.

That's how Rafaela came to me in the Bois later that summer, cutting through the bitterness of Thade's departure like a swan through water. That's the way I cut now, through the sudden hard silence of my guests. "I have something to show you," I offer.

"Ooh, show us something," says Hector gratefully.

"New work?" Paul and Romana each ask, almost in chorus, and the taut thing between them loosens.

"Hector, darling? Could you bring out the painting that's on the easel in the studio?"

"Of course, *querida.*"

"Don't lose it on the way," I say, watching if he'll flinch. What a good actor he is.

Overhead, the new Moroccan lamp spits light in jerks until it rights itself. As we watch, Kizette murmurs, "We might need Paco to bring out the ladder again."

"Is this the Rafaela painting you were working on?" asks Ana. "The girl you saved from the Nazis?"

"You saved a girl from the Nazis?" asks young Martin, turning to look—really look—at me for the first time all night.

"I wish you'd stop with that, Mother," sighs Kizette. "It's grandiose."

"I just arranged some papers for her to get out, that's all," I say, giving my daughter a glare. "Really, she saved *me* from the Nazis, in a manner of speaking, so it's the least I could do." Kizette may have heard this story before, but she doesn't have to look so aggrieved about it. Doesn't age count for something?

"How did she do that?" asks Martin.

"*You* needed saving?" asks Ana.

"My husband was half Jewish," I explain. "My second husband, the baron. We never discussed it, but there it is."

"You never discussed it?" Ana repeats, seizing on this fact.

"It was nobody's business. Until Hitler made it everybody's business. So one morning in 1935, I was on my way back from visiting family in Poland, and my train home to Paris stopped in Berlin. I have friends staying in Berlin, I thought. I'll visit with them and go home tonight. So I take a taxi to their hotel, and everywhere in the streets, I see Nazi uniforms. I meet my friends, we have a nice lunch, and then they ask me, Tamara, how did you ever get the papers to come here? *What papers?* I ask. I was sure they were just being dramatic, but they were afraid I wouldn't be allowed home on the train.

"So we go to get my silly permit, and the police are very rude. They keep my passport for two hours. They make us sit in a hot room. And then they split my friends up and take them in separately for questioning. That's when I start to get scared. And that's when they send me in to see the chief of police. His office is large and dark. His desk is a mile of shiny black wood. The only color in the room is the bright red Nazi armband he's wearing. I haven't seen my passport in two hours, but now it's in his hands, and he's inspecting it *very* carefully.

"'Madame,' he says, 'what is your citizenship?'

"'French,' I say.

"'And where do you reside?'

"'Paris,' I say.

"'So why do you come to Berlin without a *Reisegenehmigung*?'

"I did not know what this word meant when I came into the station. I thought it was a sneeze. Now I know what it means. And I am not laughing. *I did not know*, I say. I am sweating and I start to shake.

"And then he looks at my papers one more time and he asks, 'Are you any relation to the Lempicka who painted covers for *Die Dame*?'

"'I am that Lempicka,' I say.

"'My wife has all those covers,' he tells me. 'She saved them. A few years ago, I saw one of your paintings in a magazine, and I cut it out for her. It was called *Rafaela*,' he says. 'Very beautiful.' And he shakes my hand, and I see he is actually quite young, and now I'm not afraid. 'I wish I had the magazine here so you could sign it.'"

"And he let you go?" asks Martin.

I know Romana has heard all this before. What a good sport. I know she could bore us all now with stories of how her sainted mother and that Bibi woman smuggled Jews into Geneva, but she doesn't, bless her. Kizette, on the other hand, glowers.

"He says, 'Madame de Lempicka, I'm only going to fine you

this time. But we know about your family, and there is no way you can ever come to Germany again.'"

"So Rafaela *did* save you," Ana says.

"Now I'm dying to see this painting," says Martin.

At that moment the garden light crackles out. In no time, Ana is up on the picnic table, her body as supple as her bee-stung face is clogged. "We have the same problem with the light at home," she explains, stretching toward the bulb. She can't reach. "You just have to give it a little tap." Though tall Martin, joining her, could simply adjust the bulb himself, instead he spreads his hands around her waist and, on a count of three, lifts her higher. They both look awfully pleased with themselves when the light blinks on.

"Come on in, everybody," calls Hector. "I thought I would set the painting up in the living room."

"Are you sure it's the right painting?" I ask, as he approaches me. "Are you sure you didn't replace it with something from the Twenties? Are you sure you didn't just set it against the wall and forget about it?"

"*Ay, querida*. You know that was the art handlers, the other day. We promise *Saint Anthony* will go into the next shipment."

"You wanted me to think Kizette did it, don't you? You could afford to be generous when you thought you had it all coming to you, didn't you? Now you're having second thoughts?"

"If I did anything to hurt your feelings, Tamara, I'm sorry, but I have no idea what you're talking about," says Hector gently. As I search his flat features for what he's hiding, the garden light shivers out yet again. His moon face, half lit from the lamps indoors, doesn't change, but without the blue outdoor light, the blankness of calculation could be the blankness of innocence.

I can't let him think I'm a fool. "You don't care if I paint any-more, you just want my house," I say, trying to make him confess.

"Tamara, I'm sorry about the paint. We just had to take care of Ana's cheek."

"What happened?" Martin asks Ana sotto voce.

"I have no idea."

Kizette sighs. "Just show us the painting, so everyone can go home."

"I think it's very beautiful," says Hector staunchly, but I can tell he's hurt. If he weren't being so immature, I would wonder if I'd made a mistake. Maybe he isn't siding with the mausoleums. Maybe he doesn't want my money. If he were to turn, I wonder if I would simply see the friend who visits almost every day, the friend who promised to scatter my ashes over the volcano. I wonder if I would see the Mexican boy I met in '57, over lunch at the Ritz with d'Afflitto. Jean Cocteau was with us, nearly seventy then, but rejuvenated as ever by the presence of a beautiful boy. "Tell her what you told me when we first met," he begged Hector, his voice breaking.

Hector gave his friend an indulgent smile. He was just an art student in a turtleneck then, not even twenty, with ambition far in excess of his slender portfolio. But he had a face like a Mayan angel, and he kissed my hand like a courtier. *"Encantado,"* he said: he was an enchanted thing. As he leads us from the dark garden into the bright room, I wish he would turn back and look at me. But he does not turn.

32

THE SIX OF THEM STARE at my new *Rafaela*. "I can't believe I'm seeing new work by a famous painter," Ana says.

"I know," Martin agrees. "Pinch me. Am I dreaming?"

"Oh, it takes me back," sighs Romana in her smoker's burr. "I wouldn't have the stamina to keep working the way you do."

"You just don't quit, Tamara," Paul chirps aggressively, the edge in his voice meant for his wife, not for me. Perhaps it is too much to ask of a painting that it mend more than one quarrel at a time. Romana and her husband haven't spoken to each other since she snapped at him over his tennis plans, and Hector won't look at me now. As soon as they've seen my *Rafaela*, Paul and Hector stand to go claim their cars, and within moments, all my guests fold away into their small machines.

As the two cars lurch their awkward way around each other in the driveway, I stand at the veranda in my Alix Grès gown. I raise my cigarette holder in farewell. I hope Hector remembers this night the next time he tries to manipulate me. I didn't like calling him out in front of our friends, but he has to know I'm serious. Just two weeks ago I gave in to him and willed the money to Kizette; he can't keep changing his mind like this. He soured things for all of us tonight.

But I know my painting set a better seal on the evening. Turning back to the lit house, I sit down before my *Rafaela*. (I knew it was Hector when he came back with no paint. *Should* those eyelids be more red than violet?) I'm glad they can leave with an image in their minds, not a fight: Rafaela, floating as fresh as the day I first painted her. No, the eyelids are right. They're the same violet as the shadowed thigh, a violet absence of color. And they're true to the girl: the violet hint of weariness that belied her youth. How she stood at my door in yesterday's tight dress, as if she'd never gone home to bed. How tight she closed her eyes with me inside of her. How violet brown those eyes were when she opened them.

The year my husband left—the year I feared poverty most—was the freest year of my life, and the day I met Rafaela was the freest day. A man could find what he wanted in the Bois as a matter of course, but I was a woman, and I got her into my car anyway. When she agreed to model for me, Rafaela seemed, however lovely, like an ordinary girl hard up for cash, but then she took so much pleasure in my borrowed green car. I felt her eyes on my pale gloves and hood, and when I reapplied my lipstick at a stoplight, I realized I was doing it to make her watch me. And she did. Suddenly I had a girl like plump blackberries, glossy and eager, watching my mouth. She looked out at the trees of the park as we drove, and up at the sun. The top was down: she turned her face from side to side in the wind. "These seats are nice," she said, looking over at me, the bare sensitive palm of her hand pushing at the gray leather. I watched her stroke it for long seconds, unaware of herself. Her eyes were closed. Her mouth fell open. I looked at her thighs through the tight silk of her dress. She looked up at me then, as if I were a dream she was having, and that's when I thought it: *I can do whatever I want to her.*

33

I LOOK UP AT *RAFAELA*. My daughter blocks her briefly, bustling across the room. The oxygen prongs feed coolly into my nostrils; Kizette must have seen to that. What is she doing with that tray? "Kizette. Stop fussing. Luz can clear that away."

"It's just a couple of things."

"You know I can't stand it when you talk with your back to me."

She leaves the room with the tray, and suddenly the air in my tube tastes wrong. It has an odor. The taste of copper and a fresh-tarred road. How I fell in the snow. The two men who took my husband: they're looking for me.

"Kizette!" I call, afraid.

"Mother?"

"Darling, there's something wrong with my oxygen."

Kizette looks from me to the tank. It's three-quarters full, she reports, but she sets me up with a new tank just in case. Within moments, I'm breathing again.

"I guess Rafaela just took my breath away for a moment there," I joke.

"You pushed yourself too hard today, finishing that painting," she says.

"I needed it for Osaka. And now Zurich wants one too."

"Mother. Stop wearing yourself out. You know we can just send them the other *Rafaela* from '27. The private copy."

"No. We can't."

Kizette looks away, irritated, and together we look up at my painting. "I wish you'd stop with that story," she says.

"What story?"

"The whole thing. I Saved Rafaela from the Nazis. Rafaela Saved Me."

"What about it?"

"What about saving *me*? You made me wait so long, I barely got out." It's true. Kizette slipped out of Poland the day before the Germans captured Warsaw. We couldn't get her out of France until just two days before the border to Spain was sealed.

"Haven't we been through this before?" If we hadn't played our cards right, America would have turned us away. Cuba, however, had no quota restrictions against Jews, so the plan was to come in through Havana—with Rollie as an "expert agronomist," of course, not a refugee. Only then could we get papers for Kizette. She knows this.

"I'm just saying. If it was so easy to get false papers for that tart, why couldn't you get them for me?"

"Darling, she was a nobody. You were a somebody. Your Papali and I, we had our names in the paper all the time. If she came with me to New York under a false name, so what? But if you'd had bad papers, we all could have gotten in trouble."

"You go around like you're a big hero because you saved Rafaela's life. But you never sound proud you saved mine. You never talk about it at all. I used to think you got her out first because you loved her more," she says. She looks down at her Bible. Have I driven the little darling to *prayer*?

Fine. You want to see some Christian self-restraint? "Kizette," I spit. "You're my *daughter*."

"But now I think it's because you couldn't admit you were afraid for me. You couldn't admit you were afraid for yourself. You still are. You still can't admit that I was born in Saint Petersburg. You still can't admit that *you* were born in Moscow. Gurwik isn't even a Polish name, it's—"

"We were never Russian. Those people killed your father, Kizette."

"He died in *Poland*, Mother. He had *cancer*."

"So *they* said. Don't ever let me hear you use my maiden name again, do you understand?"

"Your father—"

"Shut up, Kizette. Would you please shut up?" That's it. That's enough. Kizette does not know all my secrets, but she knows enough to hurt me, and now I see how long she has been waiting to do just that. What I took for passivity was patience. It was Kizette who moved my *Saint Anthony*. She left it where I'd be sure to find it, because she knew that's what would hurt me most. And here I am, helpless, alone in the house with her. If I don't watch her, she could send anything to Osaka she pleases. She will not care about the promise I made to Rafaela when I called the painting *ours*. Nothing would please her more, in fact, than to break that promise.

"Kizette, call Arlo Mendez."

"Mother, not again."

"Call the Wilsons."

"You do this every other week."

"I'm an artist. Don't tell me what I can and cannot do."

"It's eleven at night. Your lawyer is in bed. The Wilsons are asleep. You can't keep waking everyone up like this."

"Call them. I could die before morning."

"Don't say that!"

Though I fix Kizette with the look I use to force her hand, I reach for the coffee table surreptitiously, suddenly afraid. They could come tonight, the two men. I pretend to grope for my cigarettes. I touch wood.

Suddenly I miss Hector desperately. I miss his easy kindness, his humor, his radiant face watching me paint. He would come, if it were an emergency, if I were dying. I touch wood again.

"Call Hector, too."

"*Chérie*. No. He's probably showing Ana a night on the town."

"Oh, Ana. She's in bed with Martin right now."

"Not everyone's like you, Mother."

"You want it on your conscience that you wouldn't let an old woman change her will?"

Kizette sighs, and turns to the telephone.

34

AROUND THE WHITE MARBLE TABLE AGAIN, without gazpacho, without lobsters, without candles, the Wilsons look older
than they did at dinner: Romana without a lick of lipstick, Paul in
his fraying robe. They are my neighbors, my witnesses. They've
come all the nights I've been afraid. Arlo Mendez, plugging in his
portable typewriter, looks as crisp as he does at the office, and why
shouldn't he, billing by the hour? Cuernavaca is home to many
retirees, and he has been summoned late before. The three of them
glance warily from Kizette to me and back again. "Well, you haven't
invited us back for a nightcap," says Paul. Arlo and Romana
acknowledge his joke with smiles that are thin—his from professional restraint; hers from fatigue. Kizette doesn't smile at all. I hope
I'm scaring her.

I'm disappointed Hector isn't here yet, but Kizette did wake his
mother for me, asking that he come as soon as he can. He is not a
witness, because more than once he has been my sole heir, but he
should be here, too. To allow extra time, in case he's coming late,

I ask Kizette to set up another painting next to today's *Rafaela*. I know she knows exactly where it is.

"Would you like it up on another easel, Tamara?" Romana offers.

Paul gives her a look—*Don't encourage her*—but I'm grateful. "You're so thoughtful, Romana. Kizette would never think of a thing like that," I say. Kizette is returning down the hall, arms spread into wings by the painting. I hope she hears me. "Kizette, hold on to it until Paul comes back with an easel."

She holds the painting facing her. Are your arms getting tired, darling? Good. If anything, her expression is even duller than it was before she lashed out at me. Is she steeling herself to lose the money again?

"As you know, I've gathered you here tonight because my health is not good, and I need to make a change in certain instructions. What are you taking notes on, Arlo? How can I trust you if you insist on using such poor-quality paper?"

"I use a legal pad like this every time I come to your house, Baroness."

I'm stalling. Paul sets up the second easel, but Hector does not come. Kizette sets the painting on the easel, and Romana gives a quiet whimper of pleasure.

There she is, Rafaela, against gray and green, 1927. The hand that fingers the silk in the Salon *Belle en Rouge* reaches beyond the frame of the private *Belle en Vert*. The undercolor of her flesh— though gold in *Belle en Rouge*—is blue. I'm prouder of the *Belle en Vert*'s left thigh, but I was prouder of the *Rouge*'s right knee. Just as I'm noting how the painting I finished today borrows from the best of each, Paul speaks up: "God, what a knockout."

"A triumph," Romana agrees. "I remember the year you painted it; you used to show that girl off at parties. She was beautiful. But this is *more* beautiful." It is gratifying to show them work twice in one night.

"I don't understand why we can't just send this one to Osaka," says Kizette.

"No," I agree. "You don't. But you don't have to." So, Hector isn't coming, then? Fine. I look from face to sleepy face. "I want it added to my will that this painting, *La Belle Rafaela en Vert*, belongs to Rafaela Fano."

"Do you have an address?" asks Arlo Mendez.

"No," I say, impatient. If I had her address, why would I have her painting?

My daughter rolls her head back to give her most epic of sighs. "Then how will we find her?" she asks, thirteen again.

I catch Paul and Romana's eyes: *Aren't children awful?* "That's not my problem," I say. I turn to her. "I know you want to send this to the Japan show the moment my back is turned, and I forbid you. During my lifetime, even if I am unconscious, the painting is not to leave this house for any reason. And after my death, it cannot leave this house except to go to Rafaela. If Rafaela does not claim the painting within ten years of my date of death, it reverts to Hector Oliveras."

Now Kizette appeals to Paul and Romana with a glance. I smile coldly. Let's see you hide my new *Rafaela*, the way you hid *Saint Anthony*! As Kizette looks back at me, as if protesting her innocence, the icy rage that has fueled me ever since she began spouting all her nonsense ebbs just long enough for me to ponder, now that I've dealt with *Rafaela*, what shall I do with you?

In her sixties, Kizette is even more mine than she was as a child, when she could have grown away from me. She could have become anyone then, but she's become no one. All these years, she has lived off her husband or me. I married money, a title, and I made my own money, too. She married a little geologist, and she has nothing to show for it but that house in Houston, eating itself up in taxes. She wouldn't last a year without me. And yet, I thought she was too weak to be disloyal, but I was wrong.

So: I could defer her inheritance for a few years, just to make her pay. Or I could cut her out entirely. Hector slinks into the room, like a student late to a lecture, and it occurs to me that I could make her have to ask *him* for every little check. I haul myself up, looking down at her, bring my cigarette holder to my lips, and smile.

That's when I look up at *Rafaela in Green*. I gasp. That summer never ended. That summer is now. Rafaela shimmers, alive, as if she were about to open up her eyes, sit up, speak. What would she say? I grip the table, suddenly afraid. Her eyes would be pits of fire. Her voice would be the voice of lions, her breath hot tar and wet copper. She would say, *Yes, Tamara, you can punish her for reminding you how it really ended, between us.* She would say, *But you can't change what happened.*

I sink into my chair, afraid, glancing from face to face to see who heard.

In the silence that follows, Paul and Romana look from me to Kizette, then at each other, baffled. Arlo Mendez looks up from his yellow tablet. "Was there anything else?"

I stare him down. "Why would there be?"

My daughter blinks up at me, gray, surprised.

"We thought you were going to disinherit Kizette again," Romana says baldly.

I permit myself a smirk. If I *did* scare them all a little, I'm not sad. "I promised Hector I wouldn't do that anymore," I say flirtatiously, willing Hector to look up. And he does for a moment, betraying himself with the flicker of a smile. "You were all there, remember?"

"So you got us up in the middle of the night over one painting?"

For a moment I can see what they see: a crazy old woman. But I'm not crazy; I'm desperate. I almost turn earnest on them. I almost say, *If you were haunted like this, you'd wake me up, too.* I almost say, *She was my one chance to do good that mattered.* I inhale again. Command, Tamara. "Come on. Admit it. I'm the most fun you've had in years."

At that, Paul shakes his head at Romana, and even the cool eyes of Arlo Mendez crinkle at the corners.

I look back at *Rafaela in Green.* She is inert, a painting, but the odor that flooded me a moment ago still clings to my mouth: rot and copper, oozing asphalt. I suddenly feel too small to carry it all off. "It won't happen again," I say, chastened. "I promise."

They close on me. I feel their thin-lipped condescension. They're all thinking, *Until the next time!* They don't know how well I keep the promises that matter.

"It was important," I say weakly, as Arlo Mendez begins typing up what I've said into legal language. "And I'm grateful."

When I gesture for the oxygen and Hector goes to bring it, Paul watches, half awestruck, half annoyed. "What a diva. I gotta hand it to you, Tamara."

Once Hector loops the tube over my ears, Romana gives me an awkward seated hug. I can feel her, loose in her skin but warm, alive. It's a shame we were never lovers in Paris. "Please don't wake us up like this again, Tamara," she says.

"I won't," I say. I feel afraid as I hear the words aloud.

The Wilsons sign Arlo Mendez's paper, and he promises to bring copies around again in the next few days.

"We're old friends by now, Arlo," says Paul. "We'd be lonely if you didn't visit."

"This really is the last time," I say. Is it something in my voice that makes Paul exchange a glance with his wife?

The shaken pity in Romana's face when she turns to me then is what scares me most of all. "No, but really," she says. "Call anytime."

35

At the doorway, when the others leave, I ask Hector in for a drink. "I think we could all use some sleep," he demurs.

"Please? Just for five minutes? There's something I need to tell you."

"Oh, Tamara," he sighs, and comes in, perching on the very edge of the couch. "Okay, shoot."

"I'm sorry about those things I said earlier."

Kizette, pouring Hector's drink, glances up at us, frankly jealous. Hector looks startled, and worried about me—I suppose I don't apologize often—but he's still hurt, too. "Then why did you say them?"

"I thought you moved my *Saint Anthony*, but now I know it was Kizette."

Hector and Kizette exchange glances. There's a long silence, until the weariness in Kizette's face finally congeals into words. "Fine. You win. It wasn't an accident."

Before I can even savor the fact that I've worn her down, Hector speaks. "Kizette and I decided together not to send the painting."

The two of them! Kizette looks to Hector for support, and I grip the arms of my chair. "*Chérie*, look at these two paintings," she says. "One of them, you painted in your twenties. One of them you painted in your eighties."

"Seventies."

"You were born in 1898."

"Don't tell me when I was born."

"Mother. Look at them."

I look at today's *Rafaela*. The eyelids are different in this light. I wish Hector *had* brought the red so I could try it, to be sure.

Kizette is still speaking. "See? Your hands didn't shake then the way they do now."

"My *hands*?"

"When you showed everyone your new painting, they couldn't think of anything to say. Remember? They all left in a hurry because they were embarrassed for you."

She's wrong. "They all left because of what I said to Hector."

"No," Hector says gently. "I was the only one who heard you, *querida*."

"Thank you for coming back," I say, taking his hand. He squeezes mine. I look up at today's *Rafaela* again and reach for another packet of Viceroys from the dish on the coffee table. I hate the thin plastic wrappers they've all started using on cigarettes. I began opening them by anchoring the plastic tab between my teeth as a joke years ago, but now I wonder, just briefly, if I can still do it with my fingers. I pluck at the tab. I look up. Kizette and Hector are watching my hands. Ashamed, I lift the package to my face and coyly bare my teeth. "You really think that's why they left so fast?"

"Well, it's why I didn't want to send your *Saint Anthony*."

"Excuse me?"

"I thought it was embarrassing, because of your hands, and then Hector thought we *should* send it for that very reason, but that didn't seem right to me."

"I thought it documented your struggle with aging in a very moving way, *querida*, but then Kizette pointed out—"

"My *struggle*? With *aging*?"

"See?" says Kizette. "I thought that was a terrible reason to send it. I thought that would offend you even more."

"Because Kizette pointed out that your work has always been about total mastery of the surface, so it wouldn't be right to send anything less."

"You made magic, time after time, and you never let anyone see you sweat," Kizette says.

"Not even when the times changed and people paid for sweat. You hated that," Hector agrees.

"You had Papali, so you didn't need to please anyone but yourself. It didn't matter what the galleries wanted," says Kizette. I can hear what she's not saying: the galleries stopped wanting my work. It occurs to me that she is better than I deserve, and this is a very hard fact.

I straighten my back. "You don't have to coddle me," I tell them. I take a long drag on my Viceroy, caressing the tip of my holder with the scar on the side of my tongue. So there it is: I paid not to care about the world, the same way I paid for all my other pleasures. I could afford to. "Hector's right. We could all use some sleep. Ana's probably wondering where you are."

A wicked smile crosses Hector's face and I turn to Kizette, vindicated. "See?"

They have walked me to the bedroom that I share with Kizette. They have strapped my tube on for the night, and Hector has returned my paintings to the studio and gone home. Asleep in the other bed, Kizette breathes the long even breaths of her childhood. At first, in my living room chair, I couldn't even stand up to come to bed. I had to take a long drag of oxygen, then reach for Hector's two hands. Upright at last, I had to walk the way I do when I'm at my most tired, resting my hands on the shoulders of the person ahead of me. I walked behind Kizette. I leaned on her, one step at a time.

36

I REMEMBER WHEN I FIRST SAW Rollie's apartment on Mythen-Quai, in early '34. It reminded me of my aunt and uncle's vanished flat in Petersburg, all that dark and shining wood. Over coffee and hot rolls on the morning after my second wedding, Rollie told me to go look in the room at the end of the hall. "I have a surprise for you, *chérie*." The first thing I saw when I opened the door was the large window, the view of his toy city dusted with snow. On the far side of Lake Zurich, I could see the bridges crossing the Limmat. I could make out Saint Peter's clock and snowy steeple. The Fraumünster spire. Then I saw the easel, the ready-made canvas panels, the fresh new wooden box of paints: the kind of kit a rich man might give his restless daughter. And then I turned and saw her on the wall behind me, beside the mahogany door, bathed in the wintry light of the lake. *La Belle Rafaela en Vert*. My painting, there in the stately flat for which I'd traded it, mine again, just as I'd told Rafaela it would be. I'd never meant for Rollie to keep it. Well played, Tamara, I told myself. But why did I feel so tired?

I could not paint in Switzerland. I could not go back to Paris, at first, because of the riot, so we honeymooned in Egypt. And then I went back to my studio on rue Méchain, and I could not paint there, either. I had not married my husband for his body, so I tried a weekend in Milan with an old flame. I went to the Seine and found a sailor. I went to the Bois and found a girl. I knew Rollie would deny me nothing. I sat alone in my Montparnasse studio, and I could not work.

I did not miss Rafaela. I had heard about her wedding and her dress shop from Adrienne, but after the time Ira betrayed me, I did not even like to think about her. Nevertheless, because my trouble painting dated from the morning I saw my nude of her by that snowy Swiss lake, I dug out my sketchbooks from the months she had modeled for me.

It seemed I had given away, sold, or tossed out all my *Rafaela*s. I did discover that I had more than once drawn the hands of her little friend—Boucard's snoop—during those weeks he smoked at the window across the street from me. I had watched those hands for hours, I remembered. I set the drawings aside.

Suddenly I recalled one *Rafaela*: a nude called *The Dream*. Almost as soon as I had painted it, the piece had gone to an American exhibition, and then I had lost track. After a Byzantine round of telephone calls, I discovered that the painting had never sold, and I had it sent to me at rue Méchain. When I unwrapped *The Dream*, I looked at the clumsy slab of a body I had given Rafaela. Who painted that nightmare? I had made dozens of paintings since then, and so many of them better. But then I looked at Rafaela's face, and I remembered how it felt when she would come to pose. A gratitude, a joy that translates badly into words. *I know how to mix these colors. I know what to do with these lines.* Had I ever been that happy since? I looked at that painting, and then I locked up my workroom. I telephoned Rollie, barely able to speak. I said, *Get me out of here.*

I had been working at the rate of one painting a month up until my second marriage, but then for a year and a half, I did not paint. I traveled. I went to parties. I played house with my ugly husband, and then I moved to Hôtel Baur au Lac. I spent months at a time in bed. Finally, Rollie took me to a sanatorium, and that's where I met my Saint Anthony, my patron of lost things.

My Zurich psychiatrist is the only person I have ever told what happened when I looked at those two paintings of Rafaela. How the *Belle en Vert* shone like water on the wall of my husband's house. How she lifted off that wall. I had painted her in a blinding state of hunger to be the woman I had become, Baroness Kuffner on the morning after her wedding. The life I had been forced to leave in Russia lay before me as if it had never been torn away. I had, at last, what I had hungered for. And now I was a husk without that hunger.

My Saint Anthony listened and made notes. I told him about looking at *The Dream*. The points of white in Rafaela's eyes. Lead white, pure and toxic—resist it—like a young girl's love. Like the dream I would have been a fool to dream, those years between husbands. That I could live on my art alone, and she could live on hers. That I could paint and she could run her little dress shop; that she could support us both if things went bad, the way Matisse's wife— Matisse, ptff!—had made hats. That I could live without a baron's bankroll. That I could do without travel, without parties, without jewels, without cocaine. Oh, Doctor, who would I have been fooling? And why bother? I was not put here on this earth to be simple and earnest and sing Bolshevik songs about tilling the fields of the Motherland. Spare me.

And then I told my Saint Anthony the secret I have never told anyone since. *She was the model for my best painting*, I whispered. *And what if I can't do better?*

To soothe myself, I painted Saint Anthony with my doctor's face. And to torment myself, I gave him the long smoking hands of the man Rafaela married. At least I was painting again. That was something. How like her, to leave me for that nobody. What could Anson Hall give her, with that errand-boy job of his? Think of that dumpy houseboat!

Last month, painting Saint Anthony again, when I traced the hands of a man now dead forty years, it occurred to me what a shame it was that Rafaela was with him all that time and never had children. She was forbearing, loyal, trusting, good at repetitive tasks, didn't mind boredom, and had no ambition. What else was she going to do with her life, the poor thing? Work in that little dress shop?

When I completed my *Saint Anthony*, I sought out Rafaela, but Adrienne wouldn't give me her address. "You'll have to ask someone else," she trilled, and because all those years with that curly-headed Pollyanna had Americanized her, she added, "She is a married woman now."

"That's no way to run a business," I said. But she had become a bit of a loose cannon by then, even cutting ties with that Irish author she had championed. So I waited, and I began, groping, to paint again.

Some three years later, in September of '38, Adrienne gave in. She was worried for the girl: Rafaela's husband had gone to cover the war in Spain for his friend Janet's magazine, Adrienne said, and had gone missing before he could file a single story. I had my hands full at the time: no sooner had Hitler annexed Austria than I began convincing Rollie to sell off his ancestral lands. My husband had never discussed his father's Jewish family with me, but anyone opening up the *Zidovsky Kalendar* could read all about it. Staying had been a mistake in 1917, and I was not one to make the same mistake twice.

But then the land was sold and Rafaela's husband dead for certain, by his own hand, she nonsensically claimed. When I invited her to my new studio, she padded down the halls with her arms crossed over her chest, watchful. She tallied with her eyes how few paintings I'd made since my marriage, and looked at me with the face of a doctor who'd seen cases like mine before. I looked back at her grave and lovely face and wondered, what made her so sure her husband had killed himself? She said she'd sit for me again, but not nude, and not for pay. Eleven years before, when she had meant nothing to me, she'd been irresistible. How could I do without her now? She was the years when I had hungered most. She was the city where I had become a painter. She was a Jew, and I could save her.

At the end of '38, in a winter as cold and brilliant as their misplaced hope, Parisians were drinking and dancing like the Munich

Peace would last forever. Rafaela and her friends were even expanding out of their Contrescarpe workshop into a tiny showroom on Place Vendôme. What were they thinking? I finally got her back into my bed, and I convinced her to come to New York with me. Only for three months, I said at first, because she seemed so attached to that dress shop. To her dead husband's leaky houseboat by the Pont Sully. To her friend Virginia with the bastard son. I had to work to win her over. I even told her how I got out of Russia—the Swedish consul—to show her how easy she had it. See? I never looked down on you, I assured her. All the same, it was hard enough to persuade her to come with me for three months, let alone indefinitely. When I finally told her she should stay out of Europe until the storm broke and blew over, I even offered to set her up in her own shop in New York. Let me save you, I insisted. You are my chance to do one good thing. Why can't I remember her reply?

This evening when Romana showed Martin some photographs of my paintings, she paused over the portrait of her mother, Marika de la Salle. "I'm glad you stopped telling everyone you were painting her *à la* Violette Morris," she said.

"Well, of course I did," I said, "ever since that night she made your mother look bad. Not that you helped, Mademoiselle."

Romana laughed, a dark, throaty echo of her girlhood giggle. "Did I tell you, some biographer telephoned me all the way from France to ask about Vi Morris, based on one little thing you told the papers in '25?"

"Well, how could we have known how she'd turn out?" I demanded, feeling both apologetic and hostile.

"Wait, who was Violette Morris?" Ana asked.

I explained by pointing to my portrait of the Duchesse de la Salle. "See how she's dressed? See how she's standing?" I asked, before telling them about the champion boxer of 1923. "At one point Miss Morris took a little shine to our Romana here."

"We never did more than fool around once or twice at a party," Romana said with a shrug, shocking the children, but not her husband, who simply looked amused. "I'm glad now, that Maman interfered, but at the time I was furious. *Incensed*. My mother really put her foot down about Vi."

"It's because they were two of a kind," I said. I remembered the night Rollie first proposed, in '27, the night of the de la Salles' party. I'd been so angry at Romana for playing the tramp with Vi like that in front of her mother. Getting the athlete ejected from that party was a sure way to scotch any chance I might have had at painting her portrait. I remembered how those two women swaggered, facing off in their suits.

"Touched a sore spot, I think," agreed Romana. "But *really*," she said with a shudder, "it's just as well. In her later years, Violette Morris became a Nazi collaborator," she told the children. "She went to the '36 Olympics in Berlin as Hitler's personal guest. Before the invasion, she gave Germany the plans to the Maginot Line, and she taught them how to destroy French tanks. During the Occupation, she spied on the Résistance, and she turned in Jews." I shook my head, remembering how like a romantic hero Vi Morris had seemed, showing up Romana's mother at that party. How foolish, how impotent Marika de la Salle had appeared by contrast. And now who looked bad? "When the war was over," Romana continued, "the Résistance shot her in the head."

"Oof!" cried Martin. "Just like that!"

"I had no idea," I said. "It's awful to think we used to see her at parties all the time during the Twenties, and then think about how she turned out."

"Well, we judge the Twenties by one set of standards, and we judge the Thirties and Forties by another," Ana reflected. "So it's not so strange that the same person could be a hero in one era and a villain in another. That one could make the right choice for one era, but—"

"Oh, Ana, are you an existentialist on top of everything else?" I teased. But I was not alone in staring at her, this strange, cold girl, so sure of her own pronouncements, so oblivious to her own beauty.

"Wait, what standards?" asked Martin.

"Well, look at Auntie Mame," said Ana. "Fun. Extravagant. Daring, for a woman. Nobody asks whose side she took in the Spanish Civil War."

"Interesting . . ." Martin murmured, still staring.

"Well, whose side *did* she take?" Hector butted in, clearly unable to stand another moment of Martin's inattention.

"Who knows?" Romana said testily. "She was imaginary."

"Who *cares*?" Ana corrected her. "That's my point."

Sick of politics, I turned away from Ana. "It sounds like you didn't have any news for that biographer who telephoned, Romana. Did he have any news for you? Anything about people we know?"

"Not especially," she said. "He did tell me what happened to Vi Morris after Mother and Bibi and I left Paris. Before she started working for the Germans, she ran a garage and built racecars."

I yawned. "I think I heard about that from somebody."

"And she lived on a houseboat in the Seine."

"Oh," I said sharply. The blood suddenly pounded in my ears. "Did he say where?"

"I think near the Île Saint-Louis," she said. "Do you remember that quai full of houseboats near Pont Sully?"

I felt a black sick wave push through my throat. "No, not so well," I choked out.

I knocked and knocked at your houseboat door that morning, but you were gone. I prayed you had taken a taxi to the station—I *had* arrived five minutes late—and I took the train to Le Havre with my husband, barely able to breathe. I looked for you in the Cunard waiting room and you weren't there. I didn't want my husband to know just how upset I was, so I left your passport with the purser for you, and I waited in my room. I took a sleeping pill and lay down for a nap to make the time go faster. When I woke, the ship was moving. I went to your door, as we had planned, and I began to knock. You did not answer. You said you would come with me, and you didn't come. I knocked and knocked, Rafaela. I pounded on that door until I sobbed.

All month I have been painting you, and I cannot remember a word you said. And now, tonight, with Romana's words—and Kizette's—fresh in my mind, I almost hear your voice. No one has called me by my father's last name in decades. This is all I can remember of him, before he left my mother: he held me in his lap when I was small. He called me Tomchek. He fed me tidbits off his plate. I remember bites of hot new bread and sweet butter, his patient hands. Your memories of your own father were just as scant: he carried you up the stairs. And you remembered his funeral, a phrase from the rabbi's eulogy: *vayifkach Elohim et eineiha*. That one thing I remember in your voice, those Jewish words. I felt exposed to ask, but I asked it: "What does it mean?"

You told me what the words meant, Rafaela, but I have forgotten what you said. It was something like *God opened my eyes*. Why is this all I can remember of your voice? *God opened my eyes?* Or was it *our eyes? God opened the man's eyes?*

I can't sleep. I feel for my slippers, test my feet against the floor. I've rested; now can I stand? Good. I wheel the oxygen down the hall. I made Kizette leave one of her Bibles and a concordance in my studio the other week: I consulted them when I painted my new *Saint Anthony*. They're still there, the English ones she gave me; they're right by the couch when I settle in, finding the light with my fingertips.

Eyes, eyes. I search, passing my finger down the column of words and phrases, and the whisper of the paper stirs something— what? I can feel my heart beating in my wrists again, and I wonder, was Kizette right? Is my hand shaking? I watch it, feeling the beat of my pulse: no. My whole body is shaking.

I look up. Hector has placed my new *Belle Rafaela* and its easel so that she faces me, not the wall. I can see today's *Belle* the way Kizette does now: she is a thousand separate kisses of paint. But I can see you too, Rafaela. Why didn't you open *your* eyes? Why didn't you come with me when you could? Were you deported, in the end? Are you alive or dead?

There, I found it. *Eyes.* When I try a first, wrong, entry, I slap the Bible shut, alarmed. Because the line ran, *I will smite every horse with astonishment, and his rider with madness: I will open mine eyes upon the house of Judah, and I will smite every horse of the people with blindness.*

No. No. I can taste it now, the tar and pennies. I thought those two men who came for my husband were coming for me, but now I see it: they don't need to come for me. The rotting horse will come instead. Is coming. The stench of it is a black flood that pours in. It rises higher every time, and it will drown me. I am so afraid. *Ma belle*, you are the last thing I will ever paint.

I can't hunt down a Hebrew phrase in an English Bible. I will have to make my own translation, my own heaven, the way I always have. And yet I hear the words so clearly in your voice. Surely there is a sensible explanation. Did I actually hear you say them? Or did I once—suddenly my memory spares me one more glimpse of my father—hear them read aloud to me and translated, my eyes following a small silver pointer that made the paper whisper, a wafer of silver pressed under his finger, a talisman shaped like a pointing hand?

I was never careful to remember what you said, Rafaela. You were my chance to do good, and—I see it, finally—I had already hurt you so much that you refused to let me.

I never told you I was afraid for myself, only that I was afraid for you. I told you what I thought you wanted to hear, anything to make you come with me. Anything except the one truth that might have made a difference. I never saved Thade, and I never saved you.

You have given me no hope that you are living, but I have paid good money to search the records of the Paris dead for your name, and yours is not there. Adrienne or her American might have known, but I was too proud to ask, and then they died. Maybe you survived in hiding. Maybe you joined the Résistance. Maybe you lived outside Paris after the war. Maybe you opened another shop. Maybe you married again and had children late, or maybe you found a new muse for your dresses, someone whose igneous devotion matched your own. You know where you are, Rafaela, and I don't.

I stand carefully, and turn to the brushes I cleaned this afternoon, to the palette still wet with today's colors. I work steadily for an hour and I set the brushes down, this last one tipped in Cremnitz white. I am finished. I did not need red.

These are good brushes. I will clean them again. The palette they can throw away. I will wheel the oxygen to bed, so as not to alarm Kizette. Her husband died so recently; she should get as much rest as she can. I will get into bed, I will take out my tube, and I will sleep.

I do not think Vi Morris turned you in. I do not think you were killed, Rafaela, but I do not know. You know. Come to my show next year, if you can, and see: this time, I have painted your eyes open.

Many thanks to the Corporation of Yaddo, the University of Pittsburgh English Department, and the Virginia Center for the Creative Arts, in particular the Elizabeth Ireland Graves Columbus School for Girls Endowment, for their support of this book in its early stages.

Thanks also to Alain Blondel of Galerie Alain Blondel, Zina Fergani of Gaumont Pathé archives, Matthieu Goffard of the Paris Ritz, Rabbi Barbara Aiello, Jill Anderson, Lisa Cohen, Julie Crawford, David Henkin, Lynn Jeffress, Edward Mendelson, and Carol Ockman, for their generous assistance with the research for this book.

Thank you to Megan Lynch, Sarah Bowlin, Ali Cardia, and everyone at Riverhead Books; thank you to Jean Naggar, Jennifer Weltz, Tara Hart, and everyone at the Jean V. Naggar Literary Agency.

Thanks, too, to the many people who cheered me on in the writing of this book, and especially to those who worked with it in draft form, including Amanda Atwood, Emily Barton, Adam Biles, Alexander Chee, Deborah Cohen, Emma Donoghue, Jennifer Epstein, Denis Flannery, Geoff Gilbert, Aaron Hamburger, Sara M. Ingram, Tina Isaac, Cassandra Neyenesch, Lisa Pasold, Alison Smith, and Caroline Wampole.

Greatest thanks go to the artists and authors who inspired this novel, and to their biographers and cataloguers. To Katrin Burlin, a professor of mine from twenty years ago, who began a course on women artists with the cheerfully tendentious idea that whatever women make is art. To my grandmother, in memory. To my mother, in memory. And to Sharon Marcus, without whom the book you are holding would not exist.

FURTHER READING

For readers interested in learning more about the world of this novel and the people whose lives inspired it, I recommend the following memoirs and works of nonfiction:

Beach, Sylvia. *Shakespeare and Company*. New York: Harcourt, Brace, 1959.

Benstock, Shari. *Women of the Left Bank: Paris, 1900–1940*. Austin: University of Texas Press, 1986.

Blondel, Alain. *Tamara de Lempicka: Catalogue Raisonné 1921–1979*.

———, Ingried Brugger, and Tad Gronberg. *Tamara de Lempicka: Art Deco Icon*. London: Royal Academy of Arts, 2004.

Claridge, Laura. *Tamara de Lempicka: A Life of Deco and Decadence*. London: Bloomsbury, 2000.

Fitch, Noel Riley. *Hemingway in Paris*. Wellingborough: Equation, 1989.

———, *Sylvia Beach and the Lost Generation: A History of Literary Paris in the Twenties and Thirties*. New York: Norton, 1983.

Flanner, Janet. *Paris Was Yesterday: 1925–1939*. New York: Viking, 1972.

Garland, Madge. *Fashion*. Harmondsworth: Penguin, 1962.

Green, Nancy L. *Ready-to-Wear and Ready-to-Work: A Century of Industry and Immigrants in Paris and New York*. Durham: Duke University Press, 1997.

Hemingway, Ernest. *A Moveable Feast*. Great Britain: Jonathan Cape, 1964.

Kert, Bernice. *The Hemingway Women*. New York: Norton, 1983.

de Lempicka-Foxhall, Kizette. *Passion by Design: The Art and Times of Tamara de Lempicka*. New York: Abbeville, 1987.

McAlmon, Robert, and Kay Boyle. *Being Geniuses Together: 1920–1930*. San Francisco: North Point Press, 1984.

———. *The Nightinghouls of Paris*. Urbana and Chicago: University of Illinois, 2007.

Monnier, Adrienne. *The Very Rich Hours of Adrienne Monnier*. New York: Charles Scribner's Sons, 1976.

Reynolds, Michael. *Hemingway: The Paris Years*. Oxford, UK; Cambridge, MA: Blackwell, 1989.

———. *The Young Hemingway*. New York: B. Blackwell, 1986.

Ruffin, Raymond. *La Diablesse: La Véritable Histoire de Violette Morris*. Paris: Éditions Pygmalion/Gérard Watelet, 1989.

Souhami, Diana. *Wild Girls: Paris, Sappho and Art: The Lives and Loves of Natalie Barney and Romaine Brooks*. New York: Saint Martin's, 2004.

Stein, Gertrude. *The Autobiography of Alice B. Toklas*. New York: Harcourt, Brace, and Company, 1933.

Weiss, Andrea. *Paris Was a Woman: Portraits from the Left Bank*. San Francisco: Harper San Francisco, 1995.

Wiser, William. *The Crazy Years: Paris in the Twenties*. New York: Atheneum, 1983.

Ellis Avery's first novel, *The Teahouse Fire*, set in the tea ceremony world of nineteenth-century Japan, has been translated into five languages and has won three awards, including the American Library Association Stonewall Award. Avery is also the author of *The Smoke Week*, an award-winning 9/11 memoir. She teaches fiction writing at Columbia University and lives in New York City.

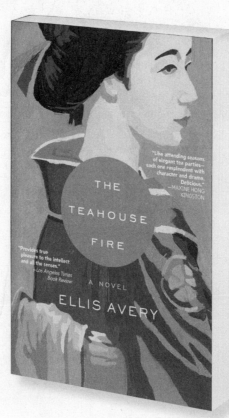